# Siren's Cove

Sara Judson Brown

# DEDICATION

To all my early readers, friends and family, who supported me through this journey. Without your encouragement, these characters would never have found life on these pages.

## ACKNOWLEDGMENTS

The line of poetry in chapter 16 that Ann remembers is from "The Jabberwocky" by Lewis Carroll. The poem first appeared in the novel "Through the Looking Glass, and What Alice Found there" (1871)

# ACKNOWLEDGEMENTS

# ONE

## *THE KAIROS*

*"Well done, Lieutenant."* The voice from Command Control squawked through the ship's comm. *"How does she feel?"*

"Solid. Not a wobble." Lieutenant Anaya Chapman beamed under her flight helmet. The test flight had gone smoothly. She'd taken the *Kairos* through its paces as planned, the ship's new engines rumbling underneath her like a beast through every maneuver. Anaya triggered the comm again. "Command Control, did you want to see anything else? I could run that last sequence again." The *Kairos* had performed so well she almost didn't want to head back yet.

*"That's all for today."* The voice squawked again. *"Stand by for approach coordinates and we'll bring you home."*

Anaya let out a contented sigh. *Oh, well. It was fun while it lasted.* She checked the ship's onboard clock. Her brother, Sean, had suggested getting a celebratory drink after her flight. She smiled to herself. Now they could have more than one.

A sudden change in the pitch of the engine's steady rumble caught Anaya's ear. Her eyes flicked to the gauges. And then… The hair prickled on the back of her neck. *What was that?* She triggered the comm link.

"Wait a minute…I'm picking up a vibration."

Anaya pressed a palm to the control panel, head bowed in concentration, as she listened to the deep bass throbs coming from behind the cockpit. *There it was again.*

The engine's steady rumble had changed—perhaps only a slide of a half step sharp—but it was there...and growing worse. The *Kairos* was in the early stages of a cascade engine failure. Anaya's mouth twisted into a frown. It was the vibration underneath the sound of the engines she couldn't explain.

She reached across the engine controls and tapped the time coil indicator lights. The glass bubbles remained dark. The ship shuddered again in protest—the vibration stronger. Anaya looked up from the control panel. Her eyes widened in surprise. This time her senses had pricked to the flutter of an electrical impulse hidden underneath the engines' persistent rumble.

Anaya squeezed her eyes shut and focused her senses. With an effort of will, she pushed the deep throb of the engines from her mind, peeled back the layers of musical notes of the *Kairos'* electrical impulses, and searched for the cause of the vibration. Through the use of her electro-perception, the *Kairos* sounded in her mind like a great orchestra, rhythms and melodies of ship's systems playing in harmony, curling and sliding around and through each other, as a multitude of energy sources swelled to a crescendo then fell away as other ship functions cycled and took up the chorus. All of the *Kairos'* components sang together yet never quite singing the same song. The complexity of the music made it difficult to focus on a single... Anaya's breath hitched in her throat. Adrenaline slammed through her veins and sent her pulse racing. A trail of thin breathy notes came from the time coil in the starboard engine.

Anaya unbuckled the jump seat harness and turned to look out the cockpit's rear window. Her breath fogged the glass for an instant and she wiped the condensation away with a gloved hand. The long sweep of the *Kairos'* metal hull spread out behind the cockpit. The ship's twin engines glowed red against a backdrop of stars. Ripples of space glistened in the area surrounding the starboard engine. Space time had already begun to warp.

Anaya twisted back around to face the control panel. The time coil indicator lights remained stubbornly unlit. *Impossible.* Time coils didn't just switch on by themselves. They weren't even part of today's test flight. The only way that could happen was if the mech techs had completely lost their minds when they did their final inspection or... A jolt ran through her. *My God... What if...?* Anaya re-buckled the harness. Security around test flights was always tight. *Sabotage?* She'd have to survive the next few minutes if she ever wanted to find out. She opened the comm link.

"Command Control, this is Lieutenant Chapman. The Kairos is in a level one cascade engine failure, and the starboard time coil has engaged." Anaya flipped the control switch back and forth to try and deactivate the time coil. Cold dread squeezed her heart. She triggered the comm link again. "Time coil is unresponsive. Attempting manual override."

Anaya's hands raced across the control panel, rerouting power away from the time coil to force a shutdown. Her mind listed options while her fingers worked. With only one coil engaged, the vibration would increase until the ship tore itself apart. She could sense the electrical notes of the time coil growing stronger as its power cells charged to full strength. The ship shuddered again as if to underscore the point. The engines were in a level one cascade failure. Anaya's eyes flicked to the power gauges. The red line crept across the display panel as she registered the slide of another half step in pitch. *Correction—level two cascade failure.* She would need to perform a cold shut down of the engines before they burned out. *But killing the engines with the time coil engaged was suicidal.*

Anaya finished rerouting power and tried to deactivate the time coil a second time. The trill of notes played on, mocking her attempt. A cold sweat broke across the back of her neck and under her black flight suit. She couldn't shut down the time coil. Anaya gripped the yoke to steady her nerves, head bowed. She was out of options. The ship would tear apart with only one time coil engaged. *But I still have two time coils.*

Anaya snapped her head up, eyes darting to the power gauges. The red line pushed across the screen, slowly overtaking the white. A quick calculation told her she only had a few minutes before the red filled the entire screen and the engines seized. Anaya routed the power back along its original path, her finger resting a moment on the last switch as she blew out a breath and activated the port engine's time coil. Anaya triggered the comm link and talked fast.

"Command Control, this is the Kairos. I can't shut the coil down. I'm going to attempt a time jump. I'm relaying coordinates now." Anaya punched numbers into the nav computer and ignored the voice in her head that screamed a time jump during an engine cascade failure was impossible. "If the engines can hold out through the jump, the time coils might disengage on their own, then I'll hit the kill switch to prevent any further damage to the engines. Kairos out!"

Anaya didn't wait for a response. She didn't have time to ask for permission. *Time...* She smirked at the absurdity. The *Kairos* was the most sophisticated time ship Andarria had ever built, capable of traveling to any *where* and any *when*, and yet she was most likely going to die for the want of a few minutes. Anaya gripped the throttle. Her thoughts turned for an instant to her brother...and then to Vincent. She'd left his engagement ring in her locker when she changed into her flight suit. Anaya swallowed the lump in her throat that threatened to break her. She gritted her teeth, pushed the throttle forward, and felt like she'd pulled the rope for her own execution.

The *Kairos* leapt forward, streaking deeper into Andarrian space. Stars lengthened and rushed past the cockpit windows. Anaya watched the power gauges and listened to the time coils' flute song. The harmonics between the two coils needed to be pitch perfect before she could attempt the time jump. The notes slid over and under each other, refusing to lock. The ship bucked in protest and buffeted Anaya in the pilot seat. She grimaced and tightened her grip on the yoke. *Level 3.*

The time coils refused to sync, growing in volume, but not locking in tune. The discordant notes made Anaya's teeth ache.

*"Come on! Come on!"*

The sudden lock and ring of notes swelled the cockpit. *That's it!* Anaya triggered the jump.

An explosion ripped through the back of the ship, breaking one side of the cockpit harness and throwing Anaya hard against the controls. She pushed back into the jump seat and clenched her teeth against the scream of metal as the starboard engine ripped from the hull. The *Kairos* slipped and rolled right. Anaya braced her feet against the control panel. She clutched the yoke with both hands and fought to regain control of the ship.

The port time coil shrugged off the loss of its twin and twisted open the blackness of space. Anaya could see through the cockpit window that the portal wasn't large enough, but it was too late. The *Kairos* broke through the spacetime barrier with a roar. Orange flames pressed around the ship. Sparks shot across the control panel. Cockpit windows cracked under the pressure as the *Kairos* twisted, forcing its way through the portal.

Anaya yelled, her scream joining the chaos around her, and tried to break the ship free of the jump. The ship bucked. Her helmet slammed into the control panel. The cockpit blurred as black feathered her vision. Her face pressed hard against the controls, switches digging into her cheek.

*A monstrous roaring filled her ears. Her body stretched and pulled apart—joints separated, sinew snapped, muscles tore, bones cracked. Ripping, searing pain exploded through her then . . . darkness.*

# TWO

## *SIREN'S COVE*

A fork of lightning split open the sky above the tavern. The rain, which had poured down for an hour, finally began to slack, but the thunder and lightning still made a good show of it. Low rumbles rolled over the countryside.

Inside Siren's Cove, Captain John Galeas relaxed in the tavern's sitting room. His tall stocky frame filled the leather chair while his legs stretched out in front of him, boots rested on the footstool. He finished tallying the daily receipts and checked the shipping report on his data link pad.

*No new freighter pirate sightings in this sector.*

John breathed out a sigh of relief. Bands of pirate raiders were making their rounds again, but so far, they'd steered clear of the galactic trade routes closest to the Colonies. He switched to the weather report. The data pad's digital screen protested, flickering as it competed feebly with the flashes of lightning behind the curtains covering the bay window.

Frowning, John laid the temperamental device on his lap and stretched. He brushed black hair from his forehead with one hand and fingered the small pigtail at the back of his head.

"Looks like the worst of the storm is over, but I'd give it a little longer," John called to his cook in the tavern's kitchen. "Are you sure you don't want me to give you a ride home?"

Mrs. Beaumont appeared in the kitchen doorway, wiping her hands on a dishrag just as another low rumble rolled outside. Her white hair, cropped short, was as neat and crisp as the white baking apron that covered her blouse and hung down the front of her long skirt.

"I hate to put you out, Captain," she said. "Let's give it a few more minutes."

John picked up the data link pad again and grunted as he flicked through the screens as fast as the reception would allow.

Mrs. Beaumont stepped back into the kitchen and returned carrying a silver teapot. She refilled John's cup and topped off her own before resting the pot on the silver trivet on the table. Finished, she took a seat on the red velvet settee across from the captain's chair.

John glanced to the teacup on the side table as if surprised to see it refilled. He muttered a quick "thanks…" and reached for his cup.

BOOM!

An explosion shook the building to its foundation. John felt the shock wave hit as if he'd been struck across the chest with a bat. He doubled over, clutching the back of his head. The lights frizzled and dimmed, threatening to go out completely. Somewhere in the kitchen, something crashed to the floor.

"Good heavens! What was that?" Mrs. Beaumont gripped the trembling saucer, her other hand pressed to her heart. The teacup lay broken on the floor.

John gulped air and willed his heart to start beating again. *That wasn't thunder.* He yanked the small drawer from the side table and dumped its contents. He grabbed the black and steel laser pistol from the mess on the floor and bolted for the door.

John burst onto the stoop. The cool air chilled his senses. The butt of the pistol felt slick in his hand. He wiped a trickle of sweat from the side of his face with a sleeve and tried to slow his breathing and the pounding of his heart.

A rectangle of light from the open doorway illuminated the steps and the puddles in the rutted drive along the side of the house. Flashes of light silhouetted the clouds over the ocean as the storm continued to roll inland. Except for the smell of burned ozone, everything seemed as it should. The shed across the drive was intact. The large trees behind the back fence stood untouched except for the breeze that blew through their leaves and sent shivering rain droplets to the ground. The pile of scrap metal by the shed had been knocked over, but that was the worst of it.

John blew out a sigh of relief. It was just a lightning strike after all. He felt foolish for having brought the pistol with him. He would tidy up in the morning. John turned to go back inside when he thought he saw something move near the junk pile. He froze on the stoop.

"Who's there? Show yourself!"

Mrs. Beaumont called from inside. "What is it?"

"I don't know…" John said, his jaw tight.

John flicked off the laser pistol's safety and tightened his grip. The weapon chirped then emitted a soft, high-pitched whine as it charged to full strength. John stared at the junk pile, searching for any sign of movement in the shadows. A rusty can toppled off the pile with a clatter, making him jump, and rolled into the drive.

*Probably just an animal.* John took a few hesitant steps. As he edged closer, he saw a curled and blackened hand and then an arm. The outline of a body lay stretched on the ground half hidden among the junk pile's scattered debris.

John raced to the figure. He flipped the safety on the pistol and crammed the weapon into his belt. He lifted the stranger and carried the crumpled form back into the house.

Mrs. Beaumont gave a fresh shriek when he entered the sitting room. "What in heaven's name?"

"Get Dr. Brainard on the comm!"

The figure moaned and stirred in John's arms. He moved to lay the stranger on the settee, but Mrs. Beaumont stopped him.

"No! Not there! The guest room!"

*Please not the guest room. Any room but that.* John opened his mouth to argue but the older woman had already dashed ahead of him up the wooden staircase and opened the door at the top of the stairs.

John had no choice but to follow. The figure was deathly still and no longer made any sound. He regretted his decision to follow Mrs. Beaumont as soon as he passed over the threshold. The room's dark memories pressed on John's thoughts as his cook threw back the bed's flowered comforter and swept the ruffled pillow shams from their place by the wooden headboard. John laid the stranger down on the clean sheets and stepped back to get a better look at who he'd brought into his house.

John flinched—a sudden intake of breath. The stranger was a young woman. His heart gave a painful, familiar ache. Blackened from head to toe in what John thought was soot from a fireplace, she reeked of the same burning ozone smell as from outside. The woman's pants and shirt were scorched and torn. Her hands and feet were burned and painfully blistered. Blood clotted in her hair from a large gash just inside her hairline.

Mrs. Beaumont leaned over the stranger and checked for a pulse. "I'll call Dr. Brainard."

"No! I'll do it," John said.

When John returned, he found Mrs. Beaumont tending to the woman with a large washbasin and pitcher of fresh water. A pile of clean towels sat within reach on the writing desk. John stood in the doorway and watched as Mrs. Beaumont cleaned the stranger's wounds and wiped the grime from her face. The woman moaned every time the washrag touched the gash on her head but otherwise did not move.

"Dr. Brainard is on his way."

Mrs. Beaumont dipped the washrag in the basin and wiped the cloth across the woman's head, neck, and arms. A knot tightened in John's chest. The sound of dripping water as the washrag returned to the basin made him shiver.

Mrs. Beaumont, absorbed in her work, did not look at the captain. "What could have happened to her? Do you think she was hit by lightning?"

John did not answer. He dropped his eyes to the floor and stared at his boots, but he could still hear the rag and the dripping water. He could not stand to be there anymore. Not here. Not in this room. Grief won again. John turned and headed back downstairs to wait for the doctor.

# THREE

## *AWAKENING*

*She sped faster. Deep, bass throbs chased her through the darkness until…*

She woke with a jolt. She squinted her eyes against the light and blinked.

*Flowers?*

Tiny pink flowers covered the white comforter and stretched across the bed as far as she could see. Beyond the bed, the room slipped and lurched sideways in the haze. Her stomach rolled. She squeezed her eyes shut and swallowed hard. When she opened them again, the room blurred around the edges but didn't pitch and roll like before. Her mouth twisted into a frown as she looked around the room.

Bright sunlight peeked from behind a curtain. A wooden writing desk and chair sat next to the bed. Her frown deepened. *This room.* She had been *somewhere else.* She was sure of it. The pounding rhythm from her nightmare played in her memory and made her head throb.

She lifted a hand to her cheek. Brown sterile epidermal wraps covered her palms and smelled faintly of fresh mint. She felt the same wrapped around her feet and on the top of her head. The bandages explained the headache, she thought, but she could not remember what caused her injuries.

Footsteps in the hallway followed by a soft knock on the bedroom door sent her pulse racing. The door opened and an older woman with a grandmother's face and short, white cropped hair entered carrying a tray followed by a man with thinning brown hair. The man wore wire-rimmed glasses and a dark suit coat and carried a black leather bag. She eyed the strangers as they approached the bed.

"Hello! You gave us quite a scare," the man said with a warm smile. "I'm Dr. Brainard and this is Mrs. Beaumont."

She looked up at the strangers and gave a dim smile, too lightheaded to speak.

"Let's see how you're doing today."

Dr. Brainard pulled a digital notepad from his bag and made a few entries. The pad chirped each time his fingers touched the screen. Satisfied, he then unclipped a handsome jade and gold pen from the breast pocket of his coat. She watched the doctor with apprehension as he waved the pen over her from head to toe.

"Beautiful, isn't it? It was my father's," Dr. Brainard said with a smile. "I had the pen fitted with a scanner, so it reads all of your vital signs and sends the information to my notepad." He watched the screen. "Best of all, it really is a most wonderful writing instrument." He finished the scan and seemed pleased with what he saw.

"You've had quite an ordeal, but I'm confident you will make a full recovery." The doctor pulled the chair from underneath the desk and sat facing the bed. "How are you feeling?"

She opened her mouth to respond, but her tongue wouldn't loosen itself for her to speak.

"Maybe some water, Mrs. Beaumont?"

The older woman held a glass to her lips. She swallowed eagerly, took several gulps and came up gasping for air.

"Gura mie ayd!"

*Wait...What did I say?* She tried to say *thank you.*

The older woman mirrored her confusion for a moment

then smiled and set the glass on the nightstand.

The doctor cleaned his glasses with a small cloth. "Well, that should help." He returned the glasses to his nose. "Are you in much pain?"

She shook her head. "Tha mo cheann goirt." She snapped her mouth shut. Her eyes grew round as confusion swept over her. *That's not what I wanted to say!*

Dr. Brainard and Mrs. Beaumont traded confused looks.

"Sorry?" The doctor raised an eyebrow and leaned forward as if to hear her better. "I'm afraid I'm not familiar with that language." He looked to Mrs. Beaumont. "I don't have an e-polyglot with me. I'll bring one with me next time."

Nothing made sense. She wanted to say. *I have a headache.* She swallowed and tried again, but the words tumbled nonsensically out of her mouth. She looked frantically from one to the other. *What's wrong with me? Why can't I talk?*

Dr. Brainard picked up the notepad, his face tense. The pad chirped madly as his fingers flew over the screen.

Mrs. Beaumont leaned across the bed. "What's wrong?"

"I don't think she's speaking a different language."

Dr. Brainard held the pen directly over her head for several seconds while he watched the pad's screen. "Everything looks fine. I thought maybe the blow to your head, but everything is normal." He put the pen and notepad away and looked grim. "Can you tell me your name?"

She opened her mouth. *My name is…* Panic twisted her insides. She tried again. *My name…* Her memory was an empty vessel. Nothing – not her name or where she was from – came to mind. She pressed her bandaged hands to her temples.

"You can't remember?"

She shook her head and drew in a few deep breaths to slow her pulse. *Fear is the enemy. Don't let it win.* She flinched at the touch of the doctor's hand on her shoulder.

"It's all right. You've had a terrible shock. I'm sure you just need time and rest." The warmth and sincerity in the doctor's face helped push down the last of her panic. "I'll be back soon to check on you later."

She watched the doctor as he stood and left the bedroom. *Just breathe...* She clasped her hands in front of her mouth and tried to think clearly. *I'm injured... I don't remember who I am... I'm with people I don't know... I need...* Her head swam with the effort. *I need to...* She rested for a moment against the pillow.

Mrs. Beaumont picked up the tray from the stand by the door and brought it toward the bed with an encouraging smile. "I brought you something to eat." She placed the tray on the nightstand. "Everything will seem a little brighter once you get some food in you." The tray carried a plate covered by a metal dome. Mrs. Beaumont tapped the top of the dome, and the lid retracted with a whooshing sound.

The smell of chicken soup and warm rosemary bread filled the air. Her stomach growled in appreciation. She looked up at Mrs. Beaumont and pantomimed as best she could.

The older woman looked puzzled for a moment and then smiled. "I'll tell you anything you want to know," handing her a spoon. "Just eat."

She nodded, taking the tray onto her lap, and eagerly spooned broth and noodles into her mouth.

As she ate, Mrs. Beaumont explained how Captain Galeas – the owner of Siren's Cove, the tavern where she currently resided – found her covered in soot and lying in a junk pile.

"And that's all there really is to tell about that." The older woman eyed her curiously. "You *have* heard of Siren's Cove before, haven't you?"

She shook her head as she smeared a thick trail of butter on a piece of bread.

"What about the town Llewelyn? Or the Colonies?" Mrs. Beaumont prompted with a hopeful smile. "We're in the top ten for tourist destinations among the three closest star systems."

Anxiety fluttered her insides again. The Colonies sounded familiar, but only in the most general sense. There was no awareness that she'd ever traveled to the Colonies before.

"Hmm..." The older woman's expression turned thoughtful. "All right then," she said and stood brushing her skirt into place. Mrs. Beaumont excused herself and when she returned a few minutes later, she dropped an armload of books on the desk. "We'll start from scratch."

For the next hour, she flipped through travel guides, while Mrs. Beaumont quizzed her on the names of colony towns. When she exhausted every local option, Mrs. Beaumont moved on to the intergalactic guides of nearby star systems, using an old star chart as a reference. She could find no spark to light her memory. She tried to read the words on the pages, but the letters made no sense and set her head to pounding. She contented herself with looking at the pictures and listening to Mrs. Beaumont's explanations.

She turned a page in one of the history books and it stunned her to see a picture of a group of Colonists dismantling what looked like a shining spacecraft. She pointed to the picture and looked at Mrs. Beaumont.

"Ah, yes. That would be confusing for you," the older woman said, leaning forward in her chair. "You see the original Colonists were war refugees from our home world, Andarria. They couldn't bring much with them, so they ended up stripping their ships for parts."

She reached across the bed, pulling the star chart forward, and pointed to a planet Mrs. Beaumont had previously identified as the Colonies then to the other planets in the system. Mrs. Beaumont shook her head.

"No, dear. Andarria isn't in our star system. It's much farther away than that."

Mrs. Beaumont opened a hidden flap in an empty quadrant in the far corner of the map. The flap unfolded to show a new star system with four planets.

"This is Andarria," Mrs. Beaumont said, pointing to a blue-green planet, the largest of the four. "It's not easy to get to. That's why the Colonists couldn't bring much with them. When the war was over, Andarria sent supply ships, but by then the Colonists had discovered they could get along just fine on their own. They took only what they couldn't make for themselves and continued to live as they always had.

"So here we are, one-hundred and fifty years later and not much has changed except for our success with the tourists. Oh, we're not completely without creature comforts. It's all a ruse, you see?" Mrs. Beaumont flashed a cunning smile. "We have technology, but we try to use it sparingly or disguise it for the tourists' sake. We wouldn't want to disappoint them."

She arched a skeptical brow at the older woman. She didn't see why the lack of technology would be a tourist attraction. Mrs. Beaumont lifted a shoulder in a half shrug and sighed.

"The tourists come because they can't believe anyone would want or even could live this way," she said. "I was born in Llewelyn so I can't say I understand it, but I guess the Colonies give the tourists a bit of magic that all their technology on their home worlds can't."

She looked at the picture of the Colonists with their spacecraft. The plucky Colonists were clearly resourceful.

The slam of a door downstairs rattled the bedroom window.

"That will be Captain Galeas," Mrs. Beaumont said and stood, taking the tray with her. "I better get back to the kitchen. I'll come back later."

She nodded to Mrs. Beaumont, watching her leave, then returned to the book. The next picture showed a group of tourists gathered on a dock, watching colonists offloading a fishing boat. The sun beat down on the shirtless men. The fish glistened in wheelbarrows full of ice. *Hardly an enchanting scene unless you find smelly fish magical,* she thought.

Later that evening, she leaned against her pillows after dinner and listened to the faint sound of music and laughter coming from the tavern at the other end of the house. The dinner tray Mrs. Beaumont had brought still rested on the bed.

Her ears pricked to the sound of footsteps on the stairs—heavier than Mrs. Beaumont's—it must be the captain. Throughout the day, she had heard the sound of a third person in the house, but the captain had not yet come to see her.

The footsteps came closer, pausing outside the door. A soft

knock. Startled, she lifted her head, but before she could answer the door creaked open.

Her muscles tensed. Her eyes darted to the bed tray but only a spoon lay next to her bowl of stew from dinner. The door pushed wide as a tall stocky man with black hair stepped into the room. He wore a maroon waistcoat over his broad chest. White shirt cuffs were rolled to his elbows, exposing muscled forearms. The tops of brown boots came to his knees. His hair was tied back. Loose bangs hung low on his forehead, making his eyes appear dark.

The man stared at her without speaking. She stared back, eyes never wavering. After a beat, his mouth slipped into an easy grin. "You're a lot cleaner than the last time I saw you."

She raised an eyebrow at the remark but gave him a small smile in return.

"I'm Captain John Galeas. I'm sorry I haven't stopped by before, but I've been busy with other things," he said as he approached the foot of the bed. His gruff voice held no trace of warmth or welcome. "Have Mrs. Beaumont and the doctor been taking care of you okay? Is there anything I can get you?" Captain Galeas bent over to pick up the bed tray. The sweet, earthy scent of whiskey and smoke drifted from his clothes.

She relaxed back against her pillows. Maybe if she tried a different approach? She gave him a broader, more genuine smile and tried to thank him for letting her stay. Her mouth mangled the words, but she kept her tone soft, her eyes sincere. She hoped he would understand.

Captain Galeas returned her smile. His blue eyes crinkled in the corners. Then just as quickly his face clouded and he looked away.

"Siren's Cove is a tavern, not an inn," he growled. "I hope you feel better soon."

Her stomach knotted around the captain's words. He'd made his opinion clear enough. He would not welcome her to stay at Siren's Cove for long.

The captain left with the tray, shutting the door behind him.

# FOUR

## *SAINT ANN'S DAY*

The young woman peered at her reflection in the mirror. Having no memory, she'd worried if she would recognize herself. She was relieved when she saw a familiar face looking back. Seeing her hazel eyes and playful smile was like spotting an old friend. The only feature out of place was the ugly, black and purple bruise that covered her forehead and right eye. The splotchy purple, now yellowing around the edges, extended from the hairline to the top of her right cheekbone.

Mrs. Beaumont stood behind and brushed out her dark auburn hair, careful to avoid the strips of epidermal wrap on the top of her head. At first, she had refused the older woman's help, but after several frustrating attempts to dress herself with bandaged hands she grudgingly accepted.

Mrs. Beaumont gave the brush one final pass through the young woman's hair. "What do you think? Your hair has such lovely waves you could wear it down."

Now as she considered Mrs. Beaumont's question, something about the weight of her hair on her shoulders felt odd. She gathered her hair up with both hands and pulled it up in the back. She turned her head from side to side to see the result.

"It's been awhile since I've done an up-do," Mrs. Beaumont said, chuckling and running fingers through her own neatly cropped white hair. "But I think I can manage a braid." The older woman's fingers went to work crafting a tight plait.

The young woman's thoughts returned to her situation as she patiently waited for Mrs. Beaumont to finish. Captain Galeas' brusque manner told her she would not be welcomed to stay for very long, but her injuries left her few options. Her head still ached, and occasional bouts of vertigo meant she needed to rest frequently to keep the room from slipping out from under her. And then there was her memory loss. Whatever had happened had been horrible. She could feel it even if she could not remember the accident. As distasteful as it was, she would still need to rely on these strangers at least until she could manage on her own and get back to… She bit back her frustration. The holes in her memory kept her from seeing the bigger picture and left only the nagging sense that she was not where she was supposed to be.

"Oh, I like that much better," Mrs. Beaumont said, as she admired her work and held up a hand mirror so the young woman could see the back. "And much more practical for around the house."

The young woman studied her reflection. Her hair, now pulled into a tight braid, ran down between her shoulder blades. She couldn't explain why, but the braid seemed more like her, and she liked the feel of it as it swung back and forth when she turned her head.

"Oh, I almost forgot." Mrs. Beaumont reached into an apron pocket, pulled out a jar of cream, and set it on the dresser. "It's a local remedy for cuts and bruises. Helps the skin heal faster. Our local sailors swear by it."

She picked up the jar and chattered a quick word of thanks.

Mrs. Beaumont beamed in return. "I need to get back to the kitchen. Join us downstairs for breakfast when you're ready." She left the bedroom in a swirl of efficiency.

She studied the ugly purple bruise again. It would take a miracle cream for sure to heal that wreck, but it was a thoughtful gesture all the same. *If only the captain was as kindhearted as his cook, she thought with a smirk.*

After applying the cream, she stood and took one last look in the mirror. The clothes Mrs. Beaumont had found for her, a plum-colored blouse and a long brown skirt, had the well-worn look of a secondhand shop. The skirt fared better but was too large. Mrs. Beaumont solved the problem by adding a wide leather belt. Not a perfect solution, but at least the belt kept the skirt around her waist instead of sliding down her hips.

She followed the sound of voices and the clang of pots and pans as she made her way down the stairs, through a small sitting room, and stepped cautiously into the tavern's kitchen. The kitchen had all the hallmarks of a professional galley. White cupboards and drawers lined the walls. Odd gadgets and appliances blinked and chuffed on the green counter tops or from where they were tucked between cabinets. Mrs. Beaumont flipped pancakes on an oversized griddle, her back to the kitchen table.

Dr. Brainard and Captain Galeas sat at the wooden table. The captain glanced up when she entered the kitchen, watching her from behind his coffee mug for an instant, before going back to his data link pad.

"There you are." Mrs. Beaumont said, turning from the griddle. She looked at the young woman, suddenly concerned. "You look a little peaked. Come sit down. Let the doctor have a look at you."

The trip down the stairs and through the sitting room had left her a little out of breath, so she gratefully took a seat at the table across from the captain. Dr. Brainard took a quick scan of her vital signs and checked the readings on his medical pad.

Mrs. Beaumont turned her attention back to the griddle. "How many pancakes for you?"

The young woman held up two fingers.

"And for you, Doctor?"

"Just coffee for me, thanks," the doctor said watching the data on the screen. He looked at the young woman. "Your readings look just fine. How are your headaches?"

The young woman frowned and waggled one hand.

The doctor nodded and tapped the pad's screen. "Rest. Drink lots of water. I'll give you some pain tablets before I leave." The doctor closed his medical pad and turned back to Mrs. Beaumont and Captain Galeas. "I'm going out on house calls this morning. I'm still hoping to find someone who might have heard or knows something about our patient," he said, nodding to the young woman.

She felt Captain Galeas watching so she collected herself and turned to him to say good morning. She slurred through the greeting in what she hoped was a cheerful voice.

The captain put the data link pad down and rubbed a thumb on the edge of his coffee mug. He gave a dim smile, which did nothing to lift the sternness from his face and nodded in return.

*So much for trying to be nice,* the young woman thought, but was careful not to let her irritation show.

"So you haven't had any luck yet," the captain said, turning to the doctor. "No reports of missing persons? No idea where she came from?"

"Well...er...no...I'm afraid not." Dr. Brainard pushed his glasses up more firmly on his nose as he turned to the young woman. "Your scans show you are Andarrian so that narrows things down a bit, but that still doesn't tell us exactly where you came from. Of course, the simplest explanation is you're a misplaced Colonist."

She nodded. But if she wasn't a Colonist then what? *I'm Andarrian...It's a start at least.*

"I filed a report with the local authorities," the doctor continued. "Constable Webley said they'll make the usual inquiries. He'll let us know if he turns anything up."

"It's been three days. Llewellyn isn't that big," Captain Galeas said. "If anyone knew anything about her, wouldn't we know by now?"

The young woman stirred her coffee to hide the anxiety building in her chest. If the captain didn't allow her to stay until her injuries healed, she would need to come up with another plan...fast. She could travel to Andarria, but from what Mrs. Beaumont told her the population there was so much bigger than the Colonies it would be a hopeless task to find someone who knew her there.

"The pancakes are ready." Mrs. Beaumont placed a large platter of cakes in the middle of the table. "I made plenty. Help yourselves to butter and syrup. Are you sure you don't want any, Doctor?"

Dr. Brainard eyed the stack of cakes. "Well, maybe just one."

The captain continued to look at the doctor.

The doctor took a bite, swallowed then turned back to Captain Galeas.

"That's true, Captain," he said, dabbing at the corners of his mouth with a napkin. "But I've been thinking we need to expand our search. Webley told me there are lots of cases of people wandering off—runaway teenagers, eloping couples, missing tourists—but they're all usually found in short order. I'm driving to Widdershins today. I thought maybe someone in one of the neighboring towns might have heard something. I also posted a query on the data network for any leads off-world."

"But that could take weeks," the captain said.

*So that's it then,* the young woman thought. *He's going to tell me he wants me to leave. Where would I go?* Her mind blurred. The more she tried to think of a plan, the more her head throbbed.

"Captain, these things take time," Mrs. Beaumont said. "She's barely out of bed. I helped her dress this morning. You can't possibly—"

Captain Galeas held up a hand. "We need to think long term." He picked up his coffee mug and leaned back in the chair with a creak. "If she's going to stay here for a while, she needs a name—at least until her memory comes back. We'll also need to get her more than one change of clothes."

22

The young woman snapped her head up from the table and looked at Captain Galeas. Did he just say she could stay? He said, 'for a while.' It wasn't anything definite, but he also wasn't chucking her out yet. She felt like she'd just been pardoned. The captain looked at her again. This time she thought maybe his eyes showed a flicker of compassion. Maybe she had misjudged him?

"Well, yes. Of course!" Mrs. Beaumont let out a flustered sigh of relief. "I should have thought of that myself."

"The clothes are easy," the doctor said. "But a name might prove more difficult."

Mrs. Beaumont eyed the young woman, index finger lightly tapping her mouth. "Hmm, you look like a Katarina. Something exotic maybe."

The young woman frowned, but before she could object Dr. Brainard sighed wistfully.

"I was once madly in love with a dancer named Katarina. Beautiful creature. She had the most lovely—" He broke off mid-sentence when he saw everyone staring at him. "Er...perhaps a good traditional name. You can never go wrong with the classics," he said, digging into a pancake.

Captain Galeas chuckled. "Let's steer clear of exotic."

"What about Maeve?" Mrs. Beaumont looked to the woman.

"Or Elsie?" the doctor piped up.

She banged her fist on the table, startling all three of them, and waved at them to stop. She blew out an aggravated breath. They may have had good intentions, but this name game was getting out of hand. She wasn't a pet.

The captain blinked, considered her for a moment, then looked at the other two. "I would take that as a definite 'no.'"

Mrs. Beaumont and Dr. Brainard seemed to shrink under her glare and exchanged nervous glances.

Captain Galeas broke the awkward silence.

"What day did we find her?"

Mrs. Beaumont thought for a moment. "It was the twelfth, I believe. Why?"

The captain grabbed his data link pad and scrolled through the screens. "According to my calendar the twelfth was the day of the Feast of Saint Ann." He looked across the table and met her eye. "What about Ann?"

Her heart fluttered. *Ann.* There was something… *Was it the 'A?' Did my real name begin with an 'A?'* She couldn't contain her joy as she nodded and beamed back at the captain.

This time the captain broke into a genuine smile before hiding it behind his coffee mug.

Dr. Brainard stood up. "I guess that settles it." He turned and took her hand. "It's a pleasure to make your acquaintance, Ann."

# FIVE

## *CLUES*

"What about how she talks?" John asked, examining the circuit board in front of him. "Shouldn't that tell us something?"

Captain Galeas and Dr. Brainard sat across from each other at the kitchen table. The commotion caused by Ann's unexpected arrival had settled and routine had returned to Siren's Cove, but she was often the topic of conversation whenever the doctor visited. The doctor's flora augmenter lay scattered in pieces between them. A toolbox and an open tin of cookies sat on the table in arm's reach, while a wilted potted plant waited at the other end of the table.

The doctor toyed with one of the augmenter's loose pieces, rolling it between his fingers while John worked.

"I've tried to translate Miss Ann's speech using an e-polyglot," the doctor said. "But I haven't found any similarities to any known languages. She repeats a word or phrase here and there, but there isn't any distinguishable pattern. There's nothing to indicate that what she is speaking is a language at all."

"Could it be some kind of brain injury? She had a pretty bad knock on the head." John jerked his chin in the direction of the toolbox. "Hand me the XL probe, would you?"

Dr. Brainard looked in the toolbox and rummaged around for a few seconds. John drummed his fingers on the table with impatience. The doctor handed over the probe, and John bent over the circuit board again.

"I thought of that, but all of her scans are normal," the doctor said, taking another cookie from the tin. "I suppose it could be simply an unusual dialect, or even a severe speech impediment the e-polyglot isn't able to decipher but that seems a bit farfetched." He took a bite of cookie.

John grunted. He hoped they would be able to sort out the problem with Ann's identity soon. He didn't necessarily mind her being there—she was quiet and didn't cause trouble—he just didn't want to be responsible for her safekeeping. Still, he couldn't help but feel a little sorry for her. John saw how quickly she tired and her frequent headaches and dizzy spells were still a concern. With any luck, it wouldn't be long before Ann was on her way and she wouldn't be his problem anymore.

John munched a cookie while he tested circuits with the metal probe. Each time the end of the probe touched the board, a small spark flared. Then on the last circuit he tried, no spark.

"Now we're getting somewhere. Atomizer." John held out a hand expectantly to the doctor.

Dr. Brainard searched in the toolbox again. John rolled his eyes, reached into the box and pulled out the probe. The gentleman doctor was one of his oldest and dearest friends, but he could be frustrating to have around when it came to basic household repairs.

"You're a lousy assistant," John said and bent over the circuit board.

"Humph," the doctor said with a shrug. "I went to medical school. I fix people, not gadgets."

John grinned. Dr. Brainard could be a bit fussy, but John

enjoyed his company all the same. And he knew he could always count on him if he ever needed a helping hand—just not with the toolbox.

Mrs. Beaumont hurried past on her way to the pantry. "Couldn't you do that somewhere else? My kitchen is not a repair shop."

John shrugged and looked up from under his fringe of black hair. "We needed a large table to spread out on, and what do you mean *your* kitchen?" Mrs. Beaumont grumbled at them from the pantry.

John whispered to the doctor. "Besides, this is where the cookies are." The doctor returned his grin.

"I heard that!" Mrs. Beaumont stormed back to the table and closed the tin with a snap. "You're not going to mow through all the cookies in one day." She opened a cabinet and put the tin back in its place on the shelf then headed back to the pantry.

The men watched her leave, craning their necks. When they were sure she was out of sight, John stood, opened the cabinet, and grabbed the cookie tin again—this time hiding it inside the lid of the toolbox. They worked in silence for a couple minutes, polishing off a few more cookies.

"My scans did show one thing I thought was odd," the doctor said, continuing his train of thought. "She's had a lot of bio gel reconstruction."

John glanced up from the circuit board. "What do you mean?"

"Anytime bio gel is used to replicate tissue or bone it leaves a signature imprinted on the cloned cells," Dr. Brainard said. "So even if a scar isn't visible you can usually detect it with a medical scanner." He gave John a sly grin. "You always light up my scanner like the Dao Luk Kai star cluster." John chuckled. "Anyway, she has a lot of old injuries. Some were rather severe. Her right knee and ankle were completely reconstructed."

"Rough childhood?"

The doctor shook his head. "Most of the injuries I saw

occurred as an adult over the last five years. The signature fades over time until the cloned cells are no different from the original tissue. The more extensive the injury the stronger the initial signature and the longer it takes to fade. The signature from Miss Ann's right leg is faint but my scanner can still detect it."

"Maybe she's just accident-prone," John said with a shrug.

"I suppose that's possible, but they weren't the kind of injuries I see every day." Dr. Brainard brushed crumbs from the front of his vest. "What about her clothes?"

"She didn't have any identification on her. I told you that."

"I know, but was there anything unusual about them? The fabric or design?"

"The only thing I noticed was she smelled like an ion fire," John said. "Like she was on the losing end of a phaser fight."

"Yes, I remember. Very strange." The doctor munched a cookie, deep in thought.

"If you want to know about Ann's clothes, you'll have to ask Mrs. Beaumont."

"Ask me what?" The cook reappeared carrying a large pot.

Ann slipped into the kitchen from the sitting room carrying an empty teacup. She put the cup on the counter and sat on the stool in the corner to watch the repair work going on at the kitchen table.

Dr. Brainard turned to Mrs. Beaumont. "When you found Miss Ann, was there anything unusual about the style of her clothes?"

Ann perked up at the question.

"Nothing I can recall," Mrs. Beaumont said with a nod to Ann. "They were beyond washing so I put them in the rag pile."

"I think I got it." John sat back from the circuit board. "Just one more tweak. Initializer." He held out his hand to the doctor.

"Oh…er…right. Initializer." Dr. Brainard fumbled in the toolbox.

Ann hopped down from her perch on the stool and moved

closer to the table.

"Sometime today would be nice," John said.

"You could give me a hint."

"It has a blue handle."

Ann peeked over the doctor's shoulder. She reached into the toolbox, pulled out the blue-handled initializer, and handed it across the table to the captain.

Impressed, John eyed her curiously. "I should have asked you to be my assistant."

"Lucky guess," the doctor said with a sniff. "She looked for the blue handle."

"You think?" John glanced up from the circuit board. He put the initializer on the table next to him. "All right. Let's try this. Ann, would you please hand me the fuse pullers?"

Ann poked around in the box. She pulled out the fuse pullers in a matter of seconds with an exclamation of surprise.

Mrs. Beaumont turned from the sink. "Well look at that! Maybe Ann can fix a few things around here when *someone* I know is too busy?" She punctuated her statement with a glance in the captain's direction.

John ignored the cook's remark and looked to the doctor triumphant as he put the fuse pullers back in the toolbox and picked up the initializer again. "Now we know two things about her. One—she knows her way around a toolbox."

"What's the other?" The doctor eyed the captain with suspicion.

"She didn't go to medical school."

Mrs. Beaumont snorted at the sink. Ann chuckled then cast an apologetic look to the doctor.

"Cheeky!" The doctor smiled at Ann good-naturedly then turned back to the captain. "Fine. I'll make you a deal. Don't ask me to assist you with your next repair and I won't ask you to assist me with my next surgery."

John grinned as he snapped the pieces of the augmenter back together.

Ann moved back toward the stool in the corner and reached for the autosweeper. Her shoulders suddenly sagged, and she pressed her fingertips to her temples, eyes squeezed tight.

Mrs. Beaumont looked up from loading glassware onto the handcart. "Headache again?"

Ann nodded. She pulled a bottle of pills from a skirt pocket and drew a glass of water from the sink.

"Why don't you lie down for a while," Mrs. Beaumont said, adding more pint glasses to the cart. Ann left the kitchen without another word, one hand pressed to the side of her face.

John watched her leave. He hoped for Ann's sake the doctor was right and her headaches stopped soon.

"She's all right, Captain," Mrs. Beaumont said, reading his mind. "She just needs to rest for a bit." She looked over a shoulder as she wheeled the handcart toward the tavern. "Miss Ann's a lot tougher than you think." She followed the jingle of glassware as she disappeared through the tavern door.

Once the cook was out of sight, Dr. Brainard looked at John and muttered in a confidential tone, "Did you happen to read the shipping report today?"

John grunted and continued snapping the outer cover back onto the flora augmenter. "I didn't know you followed the fishing fleet." He let a smile curl one corner of his mouth. "Do you have a wager on who hauls in the biggest catch?"

The doctor scowled. "I meant the attack on the *Jalisco*. The authorities say she was set upon by freighter pirates just as she entered our star system." Dr. Brainard arched a brow. "I take it you are not concerned?"

The muscles in John's jaw clenched. He *had* read about the *Jalisco*. He'd poured over the official account and even looked up additional reports, searching for any detail that might be a clue as to which band of raiders led the attack. He breathed a sigh of relief when he found a quote from a surviving crewmember that described the pirates as having the long, lanky build and bluish-green coloring of the Leukotheans. But now here the doctor was stirring up his anxieties again.

"Galactic trade routes get hit all the time," John said,

wiping his brow. "There will be freighter pirates as long as transports are slow and whores are cheap. There's no use getting worked up about it."

"This attack was close."

"I would hardly call four point six billion miles away *close*."

"It's three days at high-warp," Dr. Brainard said, face flushed with frustration. "If they have access to a space-time beacon they could slip past any patrols and be here in a matter of hours." The doctor darted a cautious look toward the tavern. The ring of glassware suggested Mrs. Beaumont was still stowing glasses under the bar. Dr. Brainard leaned across the table to John. "It's just one more reason why you need to contact Andarria and put all this trouble behind you once and for all. Have you heard anything from them?"

John narrowed his eyes. "No, and you should know better than to ask."

The doctor looked back at him with equal measures of rebuke and resignation, mouth tight. A look John knew all too well.

"If you won't contact Andarria, then maybe you should get off-world for a few days," Dr. Brainard said. "At least until you're sure the raiders aren't headed toward the Colonies. There could be more of them."

John looked at the augmenter in his hands and felt the familiar ache in his chest. The dispute with the doctor was nothing new. The argument had continued off and on for ten years, ever since Bonnie died. Maybe someday he could leave Siren's Cove. He'd told himself he would when the pain stopped. The longer he lived with the pain the harder it was to let go.

"The Colonies are small pickings compared to space freighters," John said. "There's nothing here that would interest them."

He heard the doctor sigh and settle back in his chair. John snapped the last few pieces in place and cleaned the outside of the augmenter with a work rag. He flipped the switch and the lights on its control panel blinked.

"Let's give this a try."

Dr. Brainard pulled the potted plant toward the center of the table. A heavy bud the size of a baby's head hung low over the edge of the pot. John pointed the augmenter and pushed a button. A wide silver beam fell on the plant. Immediately, wilted leaves unfurled and the stem straightened, lifting the enormous bud into the air. The bud opened into a spectacular golden bloom. A perfume of ginger and lavender wafted through the kitchen.

"Wonderful! You've saved me again from buying a new one."

Mrs. Beaumont pushed the empty handcart back into the kitchen. "Oh, doctor! That is beautiful." She moved to the table for a closer look then saw the empty cookie tin inside the toolbox. Her face crumpled in irritation as she glared at the captain. "You didn't! How many cookies can a grown man eat?" She snatched the tin and marched it back to the counter. "Keep it up and I'll be letting your trousers out next!"

Dr. Brainard and John grinned at each other like two naughty schoolboys. Mrs. Beaumont reached over and smacked the back of John's head.

"Ow! Why didn't you smack the doc? He ate just as many!"

"He is a *guest!*" Mrs. Beaumont stormed back to the pile of washed vegetables on the counter and dumped them into the food processor.

Dr. Brainard's medical instincts were right as usual and Ann's headaches began to slack. Mrs. Beaumont saw how she moved restlessly about the house and put her to work in the kitchen as her assistant.

John didn't even notice the change until one morning he sat down at the kitchen table and was surprised when Ann put a mug of coffee in front of him. He didn't like the idea of her working in the kitchen and told Mrs. Beaumont when Ann was out of earshot.

"You're getting overly attached," John said. "She's going to get her memory back, then she'll be gone. She's not some stray pup we can keep."

"I know that," Mrs. Beaumont snapped. "But she's here now and she needs a reason to get out of bed in the morning. Besides, it might help her remember who she is, just like with the toolbox. And haven't you noticed she seems happier?"

John scowled, but then reluctantly agreed. *That* he *had* noticed. Ann smiled more when she was busy. He also knew he would lose any argument with Mrs. Beaumont regarding kitchen operation.

\*\*\*

Ann hopped out of bed and shivered in her nightgown. She drew back the curtains and looked out the window. Sunlight had not yet warmed the courtyard and garden behind Siren's Cove. The blooms winding on the trellis outside the window were closed tight against the crisp, still morning air, and the sky shone like a blue china plate.

Not much had changed in the two weeks since her arrival at Siren's Cove. Physically, she'd made a full recovery. The bandages were off and the bruise on her face was almost completely gone, but her memory remained as empty as a broken vow and she still hadn't uttered a single intelligible word.

Worse yet, no leads of any kind of a missing person matching her description had come. Surely, someone somewhere missed her. Why hadn't anyone come looking for her? Every day she hoped Dr. Brainard would bring good news and every day she was disappointed. "Maybe tomorrow," he told her.

Ann felt untethered without any memories. Everything she called her own, the bed she slept in and the clothes she wore, had been given to her by strangers. She longed for a connection to her past, to someone who knew her before the accident, but the past hadn't come for her yet and she didn't know where to look for it. Maybe they had stopped looking already?

*Maybe they never looked for you at all.*

She shook off that last depressing thought. She heard the

doctor's voice inside her head, *"Maybe tomorrow..."*

Ann dressed quickly in her long skirt and blouse. Most days, Mrs. Beaumont arrived early and stayed until late, but morning errands on the other side of town would keep her busy until almost noon, so it would be up to Ann to take care of things until she arrived. She remembered Mrs. Beaumont's instructions about Captain Galeas. "Just keep him fed and watered and he'll go about his business. There's coffee and eggs—that will make him happy."

The task had seemed simple enough, so Ann had agreed, partly as a way to thank Mrs. Beaumont for everything she'd done, but also as a way to hopefully extend her welcome at Siren's Cove. Surely, the captain would let her stay longer if she proved herself useful. Not to mention that working at the tavern was the perfect camouflage until she could figure out who she was and where she came from.

Ann's thoughts skidded to a stop. *Camouflage? Camouflage from what? Who am I hiding from?* The question lay unanswered. Her memory as yielding as stone.

Ann frowned in frustration and finished buckling her wide leather belt. It wasn't the first time her thoughts had taken a dark turn since arriving at Siren's Cove. Was she a fugitive on the run? Could she be in danger? Until she knew for sure, *camouflage* seemed to be her best option.

Ann hurried down the stairs and turned the baluster. A sharp pain struck her temple and she stopped dead, her hand on the newel post. *Please, not now.* A roaring sound in her ears hunted on the edge of her hearing, but then faded and the pain lifted as quickly as it had started. Her headaches had improved, but they usually came in the evenings. *Maybe I just ran down the steps too fast?* She blew out a slow breath and headed to the kitchen.

Early morning light shone through the window above the sink. Kitchen appliances twittered and glowed from their corners. Ann pulled a white apron over her head and went to work.

She heard the captain's heavy boots a few minutes later as

he came into the kitchen. He took his usual seat at the table and slumped in a chair. He wore a faded work shirt and trousers. Exhaustion darkened his eyes.

The captain didn't intimidate her, but Ann still kept a sensible distance. She saw how his eyes could be sullen one minute then flash in anger. He seemed happiest behind the bar entertaining patrons or gossiping with the doctor about the latest news. But even during those happier moments the laughter never reached his blue eyes. On the best days, his face reminded Ann of a cloudy sky.

Mrs. Beaumont seemed unaffected by the captain's sometimes gloomy weather. She prodded or scolded him when she thought he'd become too sullen. Now and then the captain's mood would lift and he would riposte with a good-natured jab of his own. Mrs. Beaumont's nerve surprised Ann at first, but then she saw it was how they were with each other, familiarity honed over many years.

Captain Galeas looked up as Ann slid his mug of coffee across the table. "Mrs. Beaumont coming late today?" Ann nodded. "I forgot." He turned to his coffee.

The captain sat in silent contemplation. His solitary air filled the kitchen, while Ann whisked and cooked their eggs. Ann knew from Mrs. Beaumont the captain was a widower, and it was best to let him nurse his sorrows when in one of his moods.

They ate in silence. Ann heard the thundering in her ears and felt the sting of a headache. She winced and it was gone. The coffee and eggs woke the captain from his reverie, and she could feel him looking at her while they ate. Unable to make casual conversation, Ann waited for him to say something to her. The captain finished eating and took his plate and mug to the counter.

"You're easy company," he said. "Most people would feel the need to chatter over a meal."

Ann smiled quizzically at the strange compliment. Was that sarcasm? She replied in her nonsensical language, *Thank you...I think?*

Captain Galeas chuckled at her expression and gave a lopsided grin. "I'll be in the wine cellar." And with that he left the kitchen, leaving Ann bewildered.

Ann's headache continued to stalk her throughout the morning, and she was relieved when Mrs. Beaumont finally arrived. The afternoon dragged and Ann's headache worsened. She took the pain tablets Dr. Brainard had given her. Nothing helped. Ann tried to hide her discomfort, but Mrs. Beaumont could not be fooled.

"You have some time before dinner," Mrs. Beaumont said, glancing at the kitchen clock. "Why don't you lie down for a short rest. I'll come get you in a bit."

Ann reluctantly agreed. She left the kitchen and walked through the sitting room.

The low rumbling sound began without warning, heavy in Ann's ears. Closer. She winced and gripped the railing at the bottom of the stairs to keep the room from spinning. She tried to breathe through the pain, but it wouldn't release her. Icy fingers twisted behind her eyes and grayed her vision. Ann stumbled up the stairs and raced down the hall to the bathroom. She slammed the door shut behind her, dropped to her knees in front of the toilet, and vomited. She sat shaking on the floor, gasping for breath. She sensed the pain circling again then as suddenly as it began, the thundering stopped.

Ann grabbed the edge of the sink and pulled herself to her feet. She washed her face and looked at the reflection in the mirror. Her face, haggard and pale, looked back.

Pain like an electric shock jolted her spine. Her back arched. Ann fell and hit the tile floor with a crack. Waves of pain pounded as if to break her. She tried to cry out, but her jaw clenched, and the cry became a groan then a whimper. Breath came quick and ragged through her bared teeth. Panic gripped her as the fingers of her right hand twisted back until Ann thought the knuckles would crack. Her left arm and legs thrashed. The heel of her shoe kicked the bathroom door.

BANG! BANG! BANG!

"Ann, are you all right? Ann! Open the door!"

The floor split open with a loud crack. Ann fell into the blackness. The square of light from the bathroom above receded as she tumbled—then nothing.

*Whiskey and smoke...*

A low buzzing floated above her. Ann opened her eyes. Dr. Brainard leaned over the bed with his pen and medical pad, his face somber. Her head hurt, but it was only an echo of the headache. The rumbling sound had gone. Her entire body ached like someone had thrown her down a flight of stairs and she'd landed on a pile of rocks.

Mrs. Beaumont stood on the opposite side of the bed. Her eyes were red, and she clutched a handkerchief to her mouth. Captain Galeas stood at the foot of the bed and gripped the footboard.

"What were you thinking?" Mrs. Beaumont's voice shook as she choked back a sob. "You never lock the bathroom door when you feel sick. The captain had to break down the door!"

"It's all right, Claire. I can fix the door." The captain's tone growled, but his face was full of worry.

Ann tried to swallow the lump in her throat, touched by their concern. She didn't remember locking the door. Ann raised a hand to her head. *What happened?* She remembered running to the bathroom and falling to the floor, but the rest was a blur.

"You're all right, but I think you should stay in bed," Dr. Brainard said. "You're going to be fine. I just want you to rest." He packed up his bag and turned to Captain Galeas. "John, I think Mrs. Beaumont could use a whiskey."

Ann's headache continued to pound. She desperately wished someone would give her something for the pain.

"Headache."

The trio halted at the door. The doctor looked back at Ann, his face incredulous.

"What did you say?" He moved toward the side of the bed.

"Headache," Ann said, louder. Her eyes grew wide with comprehension. *Did I say that?*

"Can you say anything else?" Dr. Brainard lifted her chin and examined her eyes. Mrs. Beaumont moved to the other side of the bed. Captain Galeas watched from the door.

Ann felt a little flutter of hope in her chest. She tried to form the words, but they fell from her mouth broken and garbled. Her heart filled with disappointment. The doctor gave a warm smile and patted her hand.

"I'll give you a pain tablet. It's a start. Maybe tomorrow."

# SIX

## *THE CAPTAIN'S TALE*

Dr. Brainard couldn't offer any medical explanation for Ann's seizure (that much he had diagnosed), or for why she could suddenly say the word 'headache' when the rest of her speech remained garbled. He gave Ann the all-clear to return to her duties in the kitchen after a day of bed rest. John was incensed. He could not understand how the doctor could allow her to go back to work when he couldn't explain what caused her to collapse.

"All we can do is keep an eye on it," the doctor told Ann that night at dinner. "If you have another seizure—"

"Another seizure?" John dropped his spoon to his bowl. "You mean this could happen again?"

"IF she has another seizure, I'll run more tests but as of this moment there is nothing medically wrong with her."

John grumbled and shoveled stew into his mouth, but not before he caught Ann watching him. She met his eye, scrutinizing, then dropped her gaze. John frowned and took another bite. This woman he'd allowed under his roof and watched him silently... *Who are you?*

\*\*\*

Ann's speech continued to improve and after a few days she could say a handful of small words. Ann celebrated the unexpected development with Mrs. Beaumont and the doctor while John grew more irritable, growling out instructions or snapping impatiently when chores were not done to his satisfaction. Even Mrs. Beaumont could not lift his mood and she gave him a wide berth.

"He'll eventually work through whatever he's chewing on," she told Ann one day with a shrug. "He always does."

\*\*\*

*John sat in a chair in the hall by the guest bedroom and counted the diamonds in the pattern of the rug between his boots. He could hear the ticking of the clock downstairs. Siren's Cove had been closed for a week, so he did not even have customers to distract him from his grief.*

*The clock chimed, but it didn't matter how many bells. John rubbed his face in his hands, exhausted. He did not measure time by hours anymore, but by doctor visits. Over the past several days, he had felt anguish like the sharp snap of a violin string breaking in his chest, each one worse than the previous. How many more strings were left? What would happen when the last string broke? He felt so helpless. He could do nothing but wait and pray.*

*The bedroom door opened, and John stood as Dr. Brainard stepped into the hallway. John didn't need to ask. The doctor's eyes told him everything he needed to know.*

*"She's asking for you." John nodded. The doctor placed a hand on his shoulder. "John, I'm so sorry."*

*"Thank you." John's mouth felt tight. "I know you tried."*

*John closed the guest bedroom door behind him. The early morning light from the window brightened the sparsely furnished room. Bonnie slept under the blue coverlet, one hand tucked under her chin. Her head turned to the window so the washrag on her forehead slipped to one side—her breathing raspy. The infection had robbed Bonnie of her health in only a week.*

*John sat in the chair by the bed. Bonnie stirred when he picked up the washrag from her forehead and dipped it into the basin on the writing desk. He wrung out the water and placed it back on her head. Bonnie* opened her eyes and gave a faint smile when the cool rag touched her skin.

"No more washrags," she whispered. "I'm tired of having wet hair."

"Okay," he chuckled. "No more washrags." John returned the rag to the basin.

"I'm sorry."

"You have nothing to be sorry for," John said. He took Bonnie's hand and kissed her fingers.

"Your meeting. You were supposed to go to Andarria this week."

"It's all right. I rescheduled already," he lied. "I'll go next week when you're feeling better." John caressed her palm with his thumb. "You can go with me. We'll eat at that café you like."

"John."

He looked up. Bonnie's eyes were as blue as a cornflower and deeper than any mystery he'd encountered through all his travels. She knew there would be no next week for her. John felt another string break. He swallowed hard and looked away. Bonnie took a sighing breath.

"The café...by the reflecting pool?"

He turned back to her relieved. Bonnie looked at him, sadness in her eyes.

"Yes, the one with the red umbrellas."

John carefully climbed into bed and pulled her close. Bonnie rested her head on his shoulder. He held her hand to his chest, her body curved around his.

"Then...we could go to the National Museum..." Her voice barely a whisper, breathing ragged.

John stroked his fingers through Bonnie's long black hair. "You always wanted to see the Montressador exhibit..." He could feel her breath shorten. Her heartbeat struggled against his side.

"We could look...for a house..."

"Yes." A lump caught in his throat. His eyes filled with tears. John kissed the top of Bonnie's head, taking in her scent. She drew a shuddering breath.

"Stay with me," he whispered.

"I'm here."

"I love you."

"I...love you. John?"

"Don't leave me."

*"I…won't…"*

*"Bonnie." he stroked her cheek. "Bonnie? Oh, God! Please…no!"*

*John felt the final string break inside his chest, and a week's worth of grief poured out of him. He buried his face in Bonnie's hair and rocked her until Dr. Brainard returned and led him from the room.*

John sat on the floor of the upstairs hallway. The diamond pattern in the rug blurred. He rubbed his eyes to clear his vision. Ten years had passed and in his quiet moments he could still feel the curve of her body against his, hear her voice, smell her hair. Bonnie's ghost did not haunt Siren's Cove—her ghost lived in him.

John scowled and turned his attention to the bathroom lock in his hands. He dug into the toolbox. The simple repair job was taking longer than he expected. His exhaustion didn't help. Caught in the grip of another bout of insomnia, some nights he wondered why he even bothered getting into bed. He busted a knuckle on the doorframe and swore under his breath.

Out of the corner of an eye, he saw Ann carrying a basket of laundry to the guest bedroom. The basket rocked on her hip. Her braid swung gently past her shoulders. Irritation prickled the back of John's head. Almost three weeks had passed, and they were no closer to figuring out her identity or where she came from. His good deed of allowing Ann to stay at Siren's Cove was taking entirely too long.

John saw Ann emerge from the guest bedroom. She carried the empty basket down the hall. She put it down and watched him as he struggled to fit the doorknob.

"Bloody hell." John jerked the knob from the door again and turned it over. The lock kept jamming. He would have to open up the metal housing.

Ann mumbled something in her nonsensical language. Regret shaded her eyes.

John brushed his bangs from his forehead with an aggravated swipe.

"It's all right. I can fix it."

Ann knelt, reached into the toolbox, and pulled out a

screwdriver. She held it out to him with a hopeful smile. "Help?"

John turned to look at her. It was strange to hear her speaking recognizable words. He reached for the screwdriver, but as she leaned forward his eyes flicked to the drawstring bow at the base of her neckline and beyond that... His jaw clenched. John yanked the screwdriver out of her hand and slammed the toolbox lid shut.

"I don't need any help!" His face burned and he went back to work, refusing to look at her.

Ann watched him in silence for a few seconds then picked up the laundry basket and went downstairs. She returned several minutes later carrying a tray with a cup of tea and a plate of cookies. She bent down to put the tray on the floor next to the toolbox. John looked up exasperated.

"I didn't ask for tea! I don't want anything!"

John reached for the toolbox and bumped the edge of the tray. The plate and cup slid and tumbled onto the carpet. Ann set the tray down and reached for the teacup.

"Just leave it! I'll clean it up!" He lunged forward.

"NO!"

Ann pushed his hand away and shouted, each word a slap in the face. They burst incoherently from her mouth, but their meaning was of no importance. John could see the fury on her face.

Ann slammed the teacup back onto the tray and mopped up the spill with her apron. She picked up the tray and stomped back down the stairs. Seething with rage and frustration, John snatched a cookie left on the floor and threw it at his bedroom door.

***

Ann shoved the tray onto the kitchen counter, sending the teacup spinning on its side. At that moment, there was only one word she wished she could say to the captain. *Bastard.* Her actions of late had become more than simply camouflage, a mask to keep herself hidden from unknown dangers. She had truly wanted to repay the captain and show him gratitude for everything he'd done for her, but now she wished she didn't owe him this life debt. Captain Galeas was miserable and brooding. Maybe being a widower explained his behavior and maybe it was cause for some sympathy, but it didn't give him the right to be an ass.

Mrs. Beaumont pushed an empty handcart into the kitchen from the tavern.

"What was all that shouting about?"

Ann muttered curses she knew the cook wouldn't understand as she put the tray back in its cabinet.

Mrs. Beaumont looked up at the ceiling and shook her head. She put Ann to work at the back counter to knead bread dough.

Several minutes passed and Ann heard boots tromping through the sitting room as the captain headed for the kitchen. She felt another rush of anger and her back stiffened. He was coming to yell at her for yelling at him she supposed. She kept her back to the doorway and focused all of her energy on kneading the large ball of dough. Ann could feel the captain's eyes on the back of her head as he walked into the kitchen.

"The bathroom lock is fixed."

"Good. Bathroom locks can be very useful," Mrs. Beaumont said and hurried past him to the pantry. The captain's mood had been so foul the last few days, Mrs. Beaumont spoke to him only when absolutely necessary.

The captain continued to stand in the middle of the kitchen. Ann could feel him staring in her direction, but she refused to turn around. Her heart pounded. She picked up the ball of dough and dropped it hard on the counter with a satisfying slap. After another agonizing minute, Captain Galeas left to go into the tavern.

"I'll start setting up," he muttered.

Mrs. Beaumont watched the captain leave then moved to the counter.

"My goodness!" She chuckled as she watched the young woman manhandle the dough. "That's quite enough, dear. It's called kneading, not wrestling."

Ann helped to transfer the dough to a bowl. Mrs. Beaumont covered the bowl with a towel while Ann washed up. As the minutes ticked by, her anger grew. How dare he stomp around when she was only trying to show her appreciation. Ann started after the captain when she felt Mrs. Beaumont's hand on her shoulder, stopping her.

"A good cook always knows when to knead and when to let the dough rest," the older woman said with a wink. "That way you'll get a proper rise out of it."

# SEVEN

## *FORWARD AND BACK*

The fields outside of town browned to golden hues and the air turned crisp. Dry leaves fell in the garden, skittered across the courtyard, and chased each other in circles. The wind shifted. It wouldn't be long before the winter gales came to pound Llewelyn's harbor.

Evening settled faster and darker, but Siren's Cove stayed bright and warm. The kitchen buzzed and chuffed as Mrs. Beaumont and Ann made gallons of stew, platters of roasts, and rows of thick apple pies, filling the tavern with scents so edible you could practically scoop up the air and eat it with a spoon.

Ann avoided Captain Galeas for a few days after their argument while her anger cooled. The captain continued to growl but kept mostly to himself. In time, his mood lifted and as Mrs. Beaumont forecasted his storm clouds rolled on and were replaced with a more typical cloudy day. Nothing more had come of their quarrel, so Ann and the captain fell into an unspoken truce.

Ann tipped red apples from a basket into the food

processor. The appliance hummed as it peeled and chopped the fruit into tender bite-sized pieces. On the other side, the chopped pieces thudded down a metal chute into a bowl on the counter.

She listened for the door over the noise of the processor. Dr. Brainard said he might stop by sometime that evening on his way home. He had been gone for over a week at a medical conference in Idlewild. So far, no one had replied to the query the doctor posted on the data network, and the conference was the best opportunity to meet face-to-face with doctors from outside of town. Medical personnel from all over the Colonies would be attending the conference and as Dr. Brainard had put it, "Who better to talk to than a bunch of gossipy small-town doctors?" Ann hoped he would return with good news. In the weeks since the accident, she had not regained a single memory and had become increasingly discouraged by her situation.

The processor let out a growl as it powered through a stubborn apple. Ann winced at the sound and pressed a fingertip to her temple. She turned off the appliance and dislodged a large apple wedged between the blades. Ann turned the machine back on. The blades whirred and continued slicing apples. Her temples throbbed twice more before the pain left. While the debilitating headaches had stopped shortly after her seizure, the electrical hum and whir of the kitchen appliances sometimes caused discomfort. The pain was mild by comparison, so she never bothered Dr. Brainard about it.

Ann tapped and turned the bowl to distribute the fruit more evenly as it flowed down the chute. Mrs. Beaumont wandered over and eyed the basket still brimming with apples.

"How many pies are you making?"

"Six," Ann said, pointing to the stack of pie pans. Ann's vocabulary continued to grow, but at most she could only string together two or three recognizable words.

"Save enough apples to make applesauce," Mrs. Beaumont said. "I'll send some over to Mr. McTaggert to thank him for all the apples." She turned to check on the meat slow cooking in the large ovens.

Ann adjusted the setting on the control panel, swapped out bowls, and loaded more apples into the top of the processor.

Captain Galeas walked into the kitchen from the tavern carrying a wine crate. The bottles bumped together and jingled as he continued through to the pantry. He reappeared a second later and stood near the counter where Ann worked.

The captain helped himself to an apple from the basket and looked to Mrs. Beaumont. "What's on the menu tonight?"

"Ham and brandied peaches or chowder and bread, salad on the side, and apple pie," The cook said as she ticked off her fingers. "We also have a few beef bridies left if anyone asks."

The captain nodded. He took a bite of apple and watched the food processor churn out diced fruit.

His eyes flicked to Ann as he chewed a large bite. "Applesauce for McTaggert?"

Ann stiffened and nodded. "Missus said."

Captain Galeas muttered around the apple in his mouth. "Good. Poor man doesn't have the chops for much else."

Ann watched the captain amble toward the sitting room. His changes in moods perplexed her. Several weeks had passed without any outbursts, but she was still suspicious of this latest turn and wondered how long it would last.

Ann set the applesauce to simmer and prepped the pies for baking. Mrs. Beaumont gave the chowder on the stove a good stir then banged the spoon on the edge of the pot.

"There. I think we're ready," she said.

Ann finished tying on a clean apron. The captain returned wearing the maroon waistcoat, white shirt, and dark trousers he always wore when tending bar.

"Since it's your first night serving, I made menu cards for you," Mrs. Beaumont said to Ann. "All you have to do is write the table number on the top and a hash mark next to what they order. When the customers are finished, give the card to the captain and he will give you their bill. It's all very simple. What do you think?"

Ann looked at the cards. The letters twisted under her eyes, but she could make out just enough to read ham, chowder and apple. An uneasiness shifted inside her. Working in the tavern had been Mrs. Beaumont's idea. Ann had agreed knowing that someone from her past might recognize her, but it also made her more vulnerable. Her missing memory meant she might not recognize a threat until it was too late. Serving customers made her even more visible than simply bussing tables. Ann chewed the inside of her cheek. If she ever wanted to discover her true identity, it was a risk she would have to take.

"I will try," she said with a tight smile.

"Are you sure?" Captain Galeas frowned as he rolled up the sleeves of his shirt. "You don't have to. You can stick to bussing tables if you want."

"I think…" Ann started to reply but as she met the captain's gaze she hesitated. She thought she'd seen a flicker of concern pass over his features and just as quickly pull behind his stern mask. Ann drew herself up and said with a more confident tone, "Yes. I'm sure."

"See? She'll do fine," Mrs. Beaumont said. "Most of the regulars are used to seeing her, and I'm sure they will be more than understanding of her speech." She turned back to Ann. "You practiced writing your numbers?"

Ann nodded. Dr. Brainard had given her some writing exercises. Sheets of paper full of frenetic scribbling covered the writing desk in the guest bedroom. Writing letters still eluded her, but she could write numbers without too much difficulty.

"What if she gets into trouble?" The captain's scowl deepened. "You know how busy it can get out there."

"I'll be around to help her out if she needs it," said Mrs. Beaumont, her irritation beginning to show. "Look, we've been all through this. You can't keep serving. You're needed behind the bar." She turned to Ann. "We used to have a serving girl, but she quit suddenly." Mrs. Beaumont glared at the captain. "They all quit suddenly."

Captain Galeas narrowed his eyes. "It's not my fault if they couldn't do the job."

"Be that as it may," Mrs. Beaumont said. "You need to keep your charming, affable self behind the bar where you belong."

Ann chuckled before she could stop herself. She glanced to the captain. He glared back but instead of being angry she thought she saw for an instant a hint of a smile. Captain Galeas snorted in annoyance and paced the kitchen.

"Well, who am I to argue," he said. "It's a good thing you're here, Mrs. Beaumont. Maybe, if I'm lucky, I'll have my own tavern someday."

The cook rolled her eyes and silently mocked him behind his back. She knew the speech well. Ann was beside herself with suppressed laughter. Captain Galeas continued to rant.

"I can only hope I will have learned enough from you to some day run my tavern as well as you run yours!" He finished and turned to see Ann shaking with silent laughter.

"Are you finished?" Mrs. Beaumont returned his stare, arms crossed. She stopped the imitation a half-second before he turned around.

Captain Galeas eyed them both for a moment. His mouth twitched.

"Can we get on with it? May I let the customers in now?"

"Of course," Mrs. Beaumont said. "You're the boss."

He snorted again and stomped out of the kitchen to the tavern. Ann gave Mrs. Beaumont a pained look.

"Don't worry about him." The cook smiled and pressed the menu cards into her hands. "You'll do just fine!"

The tavern filled quickly and was soon bursting with color and laughter. Ann jumped right in serving the first table and didn't come up for air until last call.

The well-to-do and working men and women of Llewellyn rubbed elbows as equals in Siren's Cove. Everywhere Ann looked, she saw bar flies and housewives, gentlemen and ladies, dowagers and farmers and occasionally weary travelers from another town or tourists from off the Colonies.

She easily spotted the off-world tourists among the Colonists. The more experienced ones tried to blend in by wearing local fashions, but a pewter e-polyglot clipped to an ear always gave them away. The Colonists good-naturedly called them 'Off Tourists' or 'Offers.' The term was a bit of a local joke because it could be said there was usually something 'off' about them.

Captain Galeas worked the length of the bar as if it were the deck of a ship. He laughed and swapped stories with the customers. Sometimes he offered a listening ear or a warning look. Other times he gave a roguish grin before breaking into booming laughter. He rang a large brass ship's bell above the bar whenever someone contributed to the tip jar to the delight of his patrons and adding to the general din.

Ann watched the captain whenever she took him a table's ticket. She saw how his face brightened and the clouds chased away while he worked. Here he forgot his sorrows if only for a few hours every night. She couldn't help but smile to see him this way. The captain caught her watching him and gave a bemused look as he handed back the bill for a table. She blushed and turned to lose herself in the crowd.

The dinner service ended, and the band arrived. A cheer went up from the tavern as the fiddler struck up a few opening chords accompanied by a wooden flute and drum. The locals didn't need any invitation to dance. The tourists watched for a while, but then were swept up onto the dance floor, clumsily imitating the more practiced steps of the Colonists. Boots stomped, skirts swirled, and hands clapped in time.

\*\*\*

"Last call!" Captain Galeas rang three bells.

Most of the tavern had already emptied for the night, but a few stragglers remained. Couples lingered in corner tables nursing drinks before grabbing their coats and venturing out into the chill night. The captain waited for the last couple to leave and locked the front door. Ann restocked glasses behind the bar.

"Just leave it," he said wearily, brushing bangs back from his eyes. "That will keep till morning."

Ann stepped from behind the bar and started straightening chairs. Captain Galeas picked up his data link pad.

"Nice job tonight," he said. "Those menu cards work out

for you okay?"

Ann looked up in surprise. "Yes…thank you." He had never complimented her work before.

The captain put the data link pad in a vest pocket and reached behind the bar.

"Here." He tossed Ann a coin pouch.

The pouch landed heavily in her hands. "What's this?"

"It's your tip money."

"No. I can't," she said and tried to hand it back to the captain. How could she accept money from him after all his generosity? He waved her off, impatient.

"It's yours. You earned it," Captain Galeas said, but this time a smile lifted his tired face before he headed for the kitchen. Ann didn't know what to say.

She slipped the pouch in a skirt pocket. "Thank you," she stammered as she followed.

Mrs. Beaumont looked up from the tea tray.

"Well done!" She beamed at Ann. "Didn't she do well, Captain?"

"She did okay," Captain Galeas muttered as he passed through the kitchen to the sitting room. Mrs. Beaumont rolled her eyes and shook her head before turning back to Ann.

"Don't pay any attention to him. You did wonderfully." Mrs. Beaumont placed the teapot on the trivet next to the cups. She twisted a knob on top of the teapot with a click. The appliance whistled as the bottom glowed bright neon blue.

Ann felt her headache flair in perfect unison with the glow of the teapot then fade as steam drifted from its spout. Ann frowned in thought. *Why would the teapot trigger my headache?* She vowed to make note of when her headaches returned. Maybe there was a pattern she wasn't seeing?

Ann followed Mrs. Beaumont as she carried the tea tray into the sitting room. Captain Galeas sat in his leather chair scrolling through screens on the data pad. Mrs. Beaumont put the tray on the table and began to pour.

There was a knock on the door. Ann heard the captain greet someone and a moment later Dr. Brainard stepped into

the room. With all the excitement from the evening, Ann had forgotten the doctor might stop by.

The gentleman doctor wore a charcoal cap and a long, plum-colored driving coat. His brass, night-driving goggles made him look like a purple, mechanical owl.

"Good evening!" Dr. Brainard smiled and lifted his goggles. He pulled wire-rimmed glasses out of a coat pocket and settled them on his nose. "I'm sorry to call so late, but I thought you might still be up since it was just past closing."

"You guessed right," Captain Galeas said, giving a lopsided grin and shutting the door behind him. "Come on in."

"Would you like some tea? Ann can get you a cup if you'd like," Mrs. Beaumont said.

"That would be very nice, thank you," the doctor said, tugging off black driving gloves. "But I can't stay long. I really must get home."

Ann hurried to the kitchen for a cup and saucer and quickly poured another cup of tea before taking a seat.

The doctor took a sip and looked to Ann from his seat in front of the bookcase. "I'm afraid the medical conference wasn't a very productive trip."

Ann felt the smile fall from her face, but she tried to hide her disappointment.

"I talked to everyone there," Dr. Brainard continued. "I showed them your picture and explained how we found you. Several times I thought I might have hit on a lead only to be let down. Unfortunately, none of the cases currently open match your description."

Ann nodded. Hope drained out of her, replaced with a dreary numbness. She had been so certain that Dr. Brainard would return with good news, or even just a tidbit of information, it never occurred to her he would come back empty-handed.

"Thank you...for trying," Ann said and forced a smile.

"We know she's Andarrian, but that doesn't mean she's from the Colonies," Mrs. Beaumont said. "Maybe that's why we haven't figured out where she's from, and why no one knows who she is?"

"I thought of that already," the doctor said with a sigh. "That's why I posted her information on Andarria's data network as well as the Colonies. If she's not from the Colonies and she's not from Andarria then I'm afraid it complicates things even more."

"But why?" Mrs. Beaumont put her cup down. "Everyone needs travel documents to come here. Wouldn't there be a record of it somewhere?"

"There are ways around it. People dodge customs all the time," Captain Galeas said, leaning forward in his chair. He looked at Ann, eyes troubled. "She could have been beaten and dumped here against her will."

Ann met the captain's gaze and frowned. The same morbid thought had occurred to her more than once during her time at Siren's Cove. Curious how he had come around to the same idea.

"Good heavens," Mrs. Beaumont said. "Where your mind goes sometimes, Captain, I'll never understand it."

"It needed to be said. We have to consider all angles if we want to get to the bottom of this."

"That is a possibility," Dr. Brainard said and gave the captain a disapproving look. "But it still puts us right back to where we started. Someone needs to report her missing or respond to the queries I've already posted. Unless a report is filed with the local authorities or the consulate, we have nothing to go on. My query on the Colony's data network notified all the proper channels up to the Governor's office. If a missing person's report is filed matching her description, we'll hear something, but until then, we just have to wait."

"I guess the good news is every doctor on the Colonies now knows about you," Mrs. Beaumont said to Ann. "And they know to contact Dr. Brainard. That's got to be worth something."

"Yes, that is true." Dr. Brainard said and shifted in his chair and turned to Ann. "Er...I've been reluctant to bring this up, but I think you might need to face facts. It's been two months now and unless your memory returns, I think you need to consider the possibility you might never be able to figure out who you are or where you came from."

Ann's chest felt tight. If she couldn't figure out who she was, then she would never be able to set aside this sense of dread. The sense that she was not where she was supposed to be. *I need to know if I'm in danger.*

"I'm very sorry, Ann," Dr. Brainard said. "I know it's hard but maybe it's time you thought about building a new life for yourself. Think about where you would want to go and what you would want to do. Maybe it's time to stop looking backward and look forward." The warmth and compassion in the doctor's face did little to soften his words.

They were all looking at her. "I don't know," Ann said, hoping it would be enough to change the subject.

"There's no hurry," Mrs. Beaumont said. "No one is going to toss you out on the street."

"Of course not," Captain Galeas said. "No one said anything about tossing anyone out!"

Ann sat in stunned silence. She had thought that eventually her memory would return or someone who knew her would find her if she just stayed put, but now it looked like her memory might never return. If this dread she felt meant she was in danger, maybe it would be better to run? Run until she got to some where she felt safe? It wasn't much of a plan, but perhaps it would be better than staying in one place waiting for the threat, if there was one, to find her.

Dr. Brainard put his teacup down on the table and stood to leave.

"I really should go," the doctor said, pulling on his coat. "Thank you for the tea." He turned to Ann, his face full of sympathy. "I'm sorry I didn't have better news." Ann gave him a faint smile and nodded.

"It's all right, Doctor," Mrs. Beaumont said. "It just means we'll have to think of something else."

Captain Galeas stood and opened the door.

"Thanks for stopping by all the same," he said. "I'm sure

we'll talk to you again soon." The doctor nodded gravely and left.

Ann put her cup down and stood.

"Your tea is cold," Mrs. Beaumont said. "Let me warm it up for you."

"No. Thank you. I'm tired." Ann headed for the stairs. When she reached the guest bedroom, she could hear Mrs. Beaumont talking to Captain Galeas.

"I feel so awful. Maybe I should talk to her."

"Leave her be," he said. "She'll talk to us when she's ready."

Ann shut the door behind her. The lamp on the writing desk glowed and illuminated the papers scattered across the top of the desk. Ann took a seat and picked up a piece of paper. Looping curls filled the page from the writing exercise Dr. Brainard had suggested to help her relearn to write letters. Ann turned the page over to reveal the blank side and wrote a clumsy number one on the left margin.

Mrs. Beaumont, the doctor, and yes, even Captain Galeas had been very good to her, but they weren't her people. If she was going to leave Siren's Cove, she would need a new plan.

Ann felt the pouch of tip money heavy in her skirt pocket. Stuffed inside she found a roll of red and blue Andarrian banknotes and a handful of different sized gold and silver coins. The bills showed pictures of grand monuments or stern-looking men and women. Symbols decorated the edges—a snarling dragon's head, a stout tree, and a broadsword. The coins shared the same pictures. A shadow of a memory stirred within and disappeared.

Ann sighed. She wouldn't get far on a single night's worth of tips. She would need to save up a few weeks' worth at least. She wrote the word 'money' as best as she could at the top of the page.

*Always stay near the crash site.*

The breath caught in her throat. *Where have I heard that before?* Her memory closed again. The question echoed in the silence.

Despair welled inside her. She angrily wiped her eyes not

giving the tears a chance to fall.

*Get it together! You're not a baby!*

But the tears didn't listen. She put her head down on the desk                    and                              wept.

# EIGHT

## *THE APPRENTICE*

John rang the ship's bell above the bar and a cheer went up from the tavern. The dinner hour wound down as the evening crowd drifted into Siren's Cove. Business had been brisk. A galactic shuttle landed earlier that afternoon and tourists were making the rounds. Most were Andarrians like the Colonists, but some of the visitors hailed from farther away. A family of Maskelynes finished their dinner at one of the tables, and two slate-gray Osgaths conversed in low, guttural tones at one end of the bar.

John worked as bartender, pulling pints and settling tabs. He jumped in and out of conversations between drinks and dried fresh glasses from the cart with a towel. At the end of the bar, Duncan, Ross, Arnold, and Mike the beer man swapped dirty jokes, each one more vulgar than the last.

Laughter burst from the end of the bar, and Arnold broke from the knot of friends. He pushed back his brown checkered cap, giving a sly glance over a shoulder, just as Ross launched into telling the one about the preacher's daughter. Arnold's gaze settled on John as he leaned against the bar.

"Did you see the shipping report?"

"Leukotheans again." John nodded. He finished wiping a glass and reached for another from the cart. Freighter pirates had taken two transports in less than three weeks. Merchants like Arnold whose businesses were dependent on the free flow of goods off-world were becoming increasingly nervous. "The good news is, given their course, they're heading out of this sector."

"Blue bastards." Arnold scowled and drained his glass. "They're wrecking supply chains all over the system. It's bad for business."

"They make the same circuit through this sector about this time every year," John said. He drew Arnold another pint and slid it across the bar. "They'll be gone again in a couple months if security forces don't catch them first."

Arnold took a sip from his glass. "Any truth to the rumor on the Dramgoole raider sighting?"

"It's possible." John grabbed another glass from the cart. "The description of the ship sounded like Dramgooles, but I wouldn't worry about it even if it's true. Not yet anyway. They're still too far away."

Arnold eyed John over the foam in his glass. "And no rumors about Tyrhenians?"

John shot his friend a dark look. He muttered as he stowed the glass he'd been wiping under the bar. "No sightings. You don't have to ask. I'll tell you when to worry."

"I'm not the one who would need to worry," Arnold said. A smirk curled his mouth as he took another sip. "They wouldn't be coming to see *me*."

Before John could fire off a reply, another round of laughter burst from the men gathered at the end of the bar. Duncan set his glass down with a nod.

"So...uh...where did your pretty kitchen girl go?" Duncan glanced around.

John scowled. "She's not *my* kitchen girl." He refilled Duncan's glass and set it on the bar. "She works with Mrs. Beaumont."

Duncan shrugged and picked up his glass. "Same difference." He smiled and took a sip.

From the corner of his eye, John was discouraged to see Ann carrying a tray of desserts through the crowd to the family of Maskelynes. The men paused to watch her. Duncan moaned when she reached across the table to serve the plates.

"I'd like to undo that braid," he muttered behind his glass.

"I'd like to undo more than that," Ross replied.

"Oy!" John slammed his hand on the bar making nearby patrons jump. He leaned against the bar and pointed a finger at Duncan and Ross. "She's off-limits."

The two men blinked at John in surprise.

Duncan stammered, "But you just said—"

"I don't care." John scowled. "As long as she's under this roof, the answer is 'no' and I'll step outside with any man who tries it."

"No worries, mate," Ross said, as he cast a nervous eye in John's direction. "We were just jokin'."

John underlined his threat with another glare and snatched a glass from the hand cart. The last thing Ann needed was a couple of wharf rats hounding her.

Ann finished serving the Maskelynes and walked out of sight with a tray tucked under an arm. The men turned back to their drinks.

John took an aggravated swipe through his hair and caught the knowing smirk on Arnold's face. The corner of his mouth curled like a question mark. John ignored the look. Arnold could wonder all he wanted.

"So, the doc's given up on finding out where Ann's from?" Arnold asked, leaning an elbow on the bar.

"He hasn't given up," John said. "He just told her to think about what she'd want to do in case we *can't* figure out who she is. I guess it's all how you look at it."

"Has she said anything about what she'd want to do?"

"No. I don't think she knows yet."

Little had been said since the doctor's visit a few nights ago. Ann quietly went about her duties. The only change was her interest in learning more about the Colonies and the neighboring towns.

"She should just stay here," Arnold said. "She certainly brightens up the place."

John snorted and grabbed another glass. The conversation with Arnold reminded him of the one he'd had with Mrs. Beaumont over tea the night before.

"How would it look with her staying on with me?" John had argued with the cook. "What would people say?"

"She's been here for three months already and I haven't heard a peep out of anyone," Mrs. Beaumont said. "She has her own room. I'm still here every day. And since when do you worry about what other people think?"

John picked up his teacup and muttered as he took a sip. He wondered how long Mrs. Beaumont had rehearsed her talking points.

"What do you want her to do? Do you want her to stay?"

"Why would I want another woman in the house on a permanent basis?"

John had frowned into his cup unable to meet Mrs. Beaumont's gaze. The teacup had a silver scroll design etched just inside the rim that matched the outside. Bonnie had fallen in love with the pattern the moment she saw it, but it was this detail inside the cup that ultimately convinced her to purchase the set.

"But you just said it's been nice having Ann here," Mrs. Beaumont said, her tone softening. "She's been a big help to me in the kitchen and she's good with the customers."

"She's been good for business," John said, grateful for the change in tactic. "But why would she want to stay?"

Ann reappeared from the kitchen bringing John back to the present. He kept an eye on her over the heads of the people at the bar. She tucked a loose strand of hair behind an ear as she cleared an empty table. The sleeves of her blouse were rolled to her elbows. The bow of a white serving apron graced the small of her back. John smiled to himself. He guessed she did brighten up the place a little. He felt a tug at his arm.

"John!"

He turned back to Arnold with a start.

"You're going to polish that glass back into sand," Arnold said with a laugh. "Your cook needs you." He pointed to the other end of the bar where Mrs. Beaumont waved.

"I've been trying to get your attention," Mrs. Beaumont said when he reached the kitchen door. "What were you daydreaming about?"

"I wasn't *daydreaming*," John said. Irritation growled in his throat. "What do you want?"

"The kitchen is closed. We're down to cold sandwiches if anyone wants anything."

"That's good." John looked around at the packed tavern in surprise. "I guess we've been busier than I thought."

"We turn tables faster with Ann serving," Mrs. Beaumont said pleased with herself. "I'll start cleaning up the kitchen. Remember." She wagged a finger. "Only cold sandwiches. No special orders. I've already told Ann."

Arnold, Duncan, Ross, and Mike stood at the bar and waited for John with silly eager grins on their faces. John chuckled.

"Okay, what do you delinquents want now?"

"No more beer!" Ross said, rubbing his hands together.

"Come on! Let's have it!"

John reached under the bar and brought up a bottle and five tumblers. He pulled the cork and poured the ruby liquid into the glasses in equal portions.

"To your health." John raised a glass. The men drank deeply. Arnold put his glass down first, blew out a breath, and smacked his lips.

"You know, you could make a lot of money if you could figure out how to make more of this faster," Arnold said. "Your wine is the best in Llewelyn."

"It's just a hobby," John said and put his glass down with a shrug. "I sell enough to suit me." He had thought about converting the carriage house next to the tavern into a winery, but that had been a long time ago.

A woman's metallic voice rang out across the bar. "Colonists drink the juice of children."

John looked up. The four-eyed Osgaths laughed and watched him from their barstools. The larger of the two activated the e-polyglot clipped to an ear and spoke in harsh, guttural tones. John could see the Osgath's e-polyglot was a cheap rental from the shuttleport. The tinny, impassive female voice of the translator spoke again.

"You are a large female anatomy."

The cheap translators never could grasp the complex and subtle art of vulgarisms, which can vary greatly between languages and cultures, but the Osgath's intention was clear. John narrowed his eyes, anger beginning to burn. If the four-eyed bastards wanted to start trouble, the ion rifle under the bar would finish it. The Osgaths laughed again.

Arnold nudged John and gave him a mischievous grin.

"You know, John." Arnold spoke loud enough for the off tourists to hear. "As they are guests of our humble Colony, maybe we should buy these two fine gentlemen a drink?" John eyed his friend curiously then a broad smile broke across his face.

"You're right," he said.

John poured wine into two new tumblers, topped off his friend's glass, then his own. He put two glasses down in front of the Osgaths. Eight eyes narrowed at John in suspicion.

"To your health," Arnold said raising a glass.

The two men drained their tumblers then grinned wickedly as they watched the Osgaths hesitate. Not to be outdone, the off tourists picked up their glasses and tossed them back. A nano-second later, the smaller of the two gripped the edge of the bar with meaty gray hands, dropped his head, and stared with all four eyes unblinking at his feet. He gave a tremendous shudder. The larger Osgath panted, squinted three of four eyes and blinked back tears. His fourth eye rolled wildly then froze and twitched, staring off into the corner. His great blue tongue lolled as he made low grumbling noises. The voice of the e-polyglot struggled to translate.

"Ow! Untranslatable. Ow! Untranslatable."

"Welcome to the Colonies, pal!" Arnold jeered as the other men burst into hysterical fits of laughter. The Osgaths bellowed. Their orange eyes burned fiercely as the e-polyglot swore in the emotionless, female voice.

"You have questionable parentage. You are the offspring of one mother and many fathers."

"Colony wine the juice of children? Not bloody likely," John said with a laugh. "Next time, check your travel guide." The men roared in laughter.

***

John counted the money in his hand. The Osgaths didn't cause any more trouble and even asked him if they could purchase a couple bottles of wine. John thought he might have heard the one with the e-polyglot call him a 'rooster vacuumer' when they left. *Screw 'em.* He already had the Osgath's money. They could call him all the names they wanted.

"Forty dories. Not bad for two bottles," John said to Arnold. "You're the best salesman I have." He grinned and flipped his friend a bill.

"Can't argue with you there." Arnold chuckled and tucked the bill in a shirt pocket.

A loud yelp and a crash followed by a burst of laughter came from the other side of the tavern. John tore around the end of the bar.

***

The last few seconds blurred in Ann's mind. She remembered the touch of a hand as it reached from behind and slid under her breast. The impact of her tray as it bounced off her attacker's skull still rang in her ears. And somehow in the chaos and the ensuing shift in gravity she now stood with her foot between a man's shoulder blades, pinning him to the floor. Ann held the man's left arm with one hand as it thrust out behind him, elbow locked into place as straight as a metal bar. In the other, she held the man's wrist cocked at a painful angle.

The man groaned through clenched teeth, and Ann became

aware of the crowd that had gathered. She released the man and he rolled onto his side, pulling his arm to his chest just as Captain Galeas pushed through the ring of customers.

The captain's eyes shot to the man on the floor, then looked up and found Ann. "What happened? Are you all right?"

Ann's back stiffened. Anger set fire to the words in her mind even as she struggled to force them from her mouth. She pointed at the man at her feet. "He…!" Words failed her. Ann moved one hand into position over her right breast – her palm hovered, fingers spread wide – and gave the captain a pointed look.

Captain Galeas followed the motion of her hand. His brows shot upward as his face shone with comprehension then darkened to controlled fury. The captain's eyes darted back to the man on the floor who groaned and held the side of his head.

"Don't show the scoundrel any sympathy, Captain Galeas." Mrs. Shaw spoke up from the booth Ann had finished serving right before the incident. The elderly woman's round face trembled with anger. "I saw the whole thing. Nelson grabbed this poor woman when she wasn't looking. She had every right to defend herself." The crowd murmured in agreement.

"Reflexes like an Arkhangelsk. Damndest thing!" Captain Shaw chuckled across the table from his wife and scratched his short red and gray whiskers. "Clipped him good."

"Served him right. Disgusting behavior," Mrs. Shaw added with a sniff.

Captain Galeas took an agitated swipe through his hair with one hand and picked up Ann's serving tray from the floor. The dent in the middle of the tray was the same size and shape of Nelson's thick head.

Ann locked eyes with the captain and crossed her arms. Her mouth felt tight as she enunciated each word. "I'm. *Not.* Sorry." *If he yells at me, then so be it.*

The captain eyed her for a moment, weighing her words,

before handing back the tray.

"Go get a new one."

Ann blinked in surprise. Did she hear him right?

The captain's mouth slipped into a grin. "You haven't done anything wrong. Bar room etiquette. Grope from the left, cold cock from the right." He reached down and grabbed the scruff of Nelson's jacket and hoisted him to his feet. "Go on and get a new tray. You can't serve with that one. The glasses will wobble."

The tension left Ann's shoulders. She returned the captain's grin with a bright smile of her own.

Captain Galeas glared down at Nelson as he helped him to the door. "Be grateful I didn't get to you first."

Ann headed to the pantry, the dented tray tucked under an arm, grinning to herself. The look on Nelson's face... He certainly hadn't expected her to react the way she did. Ann put the dented tray in the recycler and grabbed a new one from the stack on a pantry shelf. She looked at the tray in her hands. *How did I do it?* Ann closed her eyes and went through the motions again in the privacy of the pantry. Ann pivoted her hips and turned, feeling the sweep of her body. She remembered the strength in her limbs as she grabbed Nelson's arm and forced him to the floor.

"Ann! Are you coming?" Mrs. Beaumont's voice called from the kitchen.

Ann looked down at her hands. A shiver of excitement ran down her spine. *I've been trained to do this!* Questions flooded Ann's mind. *Where would I have learned such a skill?*

"Ann?"

"I'm coming!"

Ann hurried back through the kitchen to the tavern.

\*\*\*

Cool sunshine streamed through the window as John walked into the kitchen the next morning. The crisp fall air nipped at his heels and made him eager to get his chores started.

Mrs. Beaumont cooked eggs and sausage on the large

griddle on the stove. A plate of warm biscuits sat on the counter. Her cropped white hair practically glowed in the light from the window.

"Morning," John said with a lopsided grin. He helped himself to a plate of eggs and took a seat at the table. He looked around the kitchen. "Where's Ann?"

"I asked her to take a few things over to Mr. McTaggert." Mrs. Beaumont poured a mug of coffee and set it in front of him. "She should be back soon."

"A bit cold for a walk," John said with a frown. He dug into his food.

"I think she wanted to get out and about." Mrs. Beaumont looked out the window above the sink and smiled. "Here she comes."

The kitchen door opened, and Ann stepped in wrapped in a large plaid shawl and carrying an empty market basket. Dr. Brainard followed close behind.

"Sorry to pop in on you," the doctor said grinning. "I ran into Ann and I have an idea I wanted to share with you all, so I thought I'd tag along."

John chuckled to himself. The doctor had been popping in for as long as they'd known each other.

"You're always welcomed," Mrs. Beaumont said. "Let me get you some coffee."

Ann unwrapped the shawl and said good morning in her odd way. John nodded and smiled to see her cheeks and nose rosy from the cold. Mrs. Beaumont set the coffee mugs down then brought heaping bowls of egg, sausage and biscuit to the table.

"So, what's this idea you wanted to talk about," John asked the doctor after they were all seated.

"I feel absolutely dreadful I haven't uncovered any information about Ann's past," the doctor said.

"No, no!" Ann frowned and patted his arm.

"She's right. It's not your fault, doctor," Mrs. Beaumont said, adding a scoop of eggs to the doctor's plate. "Sadly, there's only so much we can do."

"I still feel badly about it." Dr. Brainard turned back to Ann. "And I still firmly believe you should start thinking about your future. I would be happy to use my connections to help find a suitable, more permanent position for you."

John's insides winced. "That's a good idea." He picked at the egg on his plate. "It's the most logical next step."

"That sounds all right," Mrs. Beaumont said, glancing to the captain and back to Ann. "But it's really not up to us."

Ann thought for a moment, eyes somber. She turned back to the captain and worked the words from her mouth. "I would...like to stay *here*. And work *here*."

A flicker of happiness lifted John's gloom. He quickly smothered the spark before it could catch into a flame. John mulled the question and took another bite of egg. There were more than his own feelings to consider. If he let Ann stay, she would be his responsibility. And possibly a liability if his former comrades came looking for him.

He looked across the table. Ann watched him, waiting patiently for an answer. A wisp of hair had loosed itself from her braid and trailed gently down a cheek. The spark in his chest flickered to life again.

John dropped his gaze to his plate and fiddled with his pigtail. It had been more than ten years since he last saw the Tyrhenians. *Maybe...?* He blew out a sigh. "Seeing as you're already here, if you want to stay and work with Mrs. Beaumont then I guess that would be okay with me."

Ann beamed back at him and the spark in John's chest threatened to burst to flame.

"Thank you!"

Mrs. Beaumont clapped her hands together. "How wonderful!"

"I suppose that does make the most sense," Dr. Brainard said as he congratulated Ann.

John pushed back his chair. "I have some chores that can't wait."

He left the celebration in the kitchen for the quiet of the tavern. John opened the trap door to the wine cellar behind the bar and walked down the wooden steps. His words to Mrs. Beaumont came back to him, 'You're getting overly attached.'

The dank smell of the cellar wrapped around him and clung to his clothes. John paused at the bottom of the steps. He closed his eyes, breathing in the musty scent.

*"John Galeas. What have you done?"*

*"I haven't done anything…yet. I wanted you to have a look at the house first."*

*Bonnie stood in the middle of the room and looked around at the varying states of decay. A pervasive smell of dust and mold hung in the air. The solicitor had described the house and tavern as a grand dame in graceful decline, but as John looked at the broken spindles on the railing and the stained wallpaper he thought the old gal had slipped into a state of imminent demise. He took a step toward Bonnie and the floorboards bowed under his weight.*

*"There are other houses," he said. "A few outside of town."*

*Bonnie turned her blue eyes to him. She wore a colony dress belted around her slim waist. A blue and gray skirt concealed long legs. She looked at him, brow furrowed.*

*"I told you the room at the boarding house is fine."*

*"No, it's not," John said. "I found out Mrs. Waller has a key to all of the rooms. We can't take the chance she'll go snooping, especially while I'm away."*

*"We can find someplace else," Bonnie said. "We don't need a house."*

*"We'll be in Llewellyn for a while. A house will make it easier to fit in." John watched Bonnie as she picked her way across the room to the kitchen. She leaned on the doorframe and peered into the adjacent room. "I want you to have a proper home while we're here."*

*Bonnie looked back at him and smiled. Dark hair cascaded to her shoulders. "Home is where you are. How else would you have been able to talk me into marrying you and moving to the Colonies?"*

*John chuckled and stepped toward her, taking her hand in his. She wrapped her arms around him.*

*"Mmmm. A house would have its advantages," Bonnie said. She gave him an arched look from under dark lashes. "It would be nice to have more than a few inches of wall between our bedroom and our neighbors."*

*John laughed and pulled her closer. "I hadn't thought of that, but yes that would be nice."* He bent down to kiss her, but she turned away *suddenly, stifling a sneeze.*

*"Ugh…Sorry!" She sniffled, made a face and laughed. "It's the dust."*

*"Let's go," John said, taking her hand and turning toward the door. "It was worth a look, but I think we can write this one off."*

*"Wait a minute."*

*Bonnie crossed the room to the staircase. She rested a hand on the banister as she peered up the steps to the second floor. Her face turned pensive as she dusted her hand on her skirt.*

*"You said we need to try to fit in while we're here."*

*John nodded. "We have to do more than try. If we fail…" He felt a tightening in his chest. If I fail.*

*Bonnie's eyes swept back to John. "The house is huge. Every inch of it falling apart. It would take a battalion of tradesmen to make it livable again." The line of her mouth tweaked into a smile. "But this house is also a tavern, a legitimate business."*

*John stared at Bonnie in amazement. "You want to run a tavern?"*

*"Why not? It's perfect," she said. "A good way to keep up with the news and gossip." Bonnie took a step toward him and stood up on her toes to kiss his cheek.*

John shuddered and opened his eyes. He could still feel the soft touch of her lips on his skin. He pulled out the data link pad and started counting beer kegs in the flat light of the wine cellar.

# NINE

## *OVER A BARREL*

The wind blew cold from Llewellyn's harbor as shimmering frost crept up the windows of Siren's Cove. Burgeoning gray clouds filled the sky and threatened snow. The changing weather only heightened the air of excitement as the Colonists prepared to celebrate one of their few national holidays, and for the influx of tourists who would arrive for the Founder's Day celebrations.

A week before the official holiday, inns all over the Colonies were bursting. The local merchants were rushed off their feet with events and celebrations leading up to the big day. Each tourist was a business opportunity, and Colony goods and services were in high demand. Captain Galeas read the current business climate like a sailor reads the stars and came up with the brilliant idea of selling pre-made, self-heating boxed meals to the revelers and busy Colonists.

Mrs. Beaumont organized and prepared hundreds of extra meals. Ann helped pre-cook and package, while Mrs. Beaumont dashed about the kitchen stirring pots and checking dishes. The captain delivered large orders or sold individual boxes from behind the bar. The popularity of the meals added to the demands of the usual lunch and dinner service and stretched the kitchen's and Mrs. Beaumont's capacity for efficiency to near-breaking.

"We might have to do this every year," John said one night while reviewing the daily receipts. Mrs. Beaumont simply closed her eyes and pressed an index finger to a temple.

\*\*\*

Ann stood at the kitchen table while Mrs. Beaumont washed and prepped chicken on the cutting board by the sink. A large baking pan full of raw cut chicken sat on the table in front of Ann. Glass shaker jars each with a different colored spice clustered around the table.

"Boo," Ann said as she sprinkled seasoning over the chicken.

"Not boo, dear." Mrs. Beaumont paused, cleaver in hand, and turned to look at Ann. It's 'Boh' like a hair bow."

Mrs. Beaumont had tried to teach Ann to say everyone's proper name with little success. Mrs. Beaumont was still 'Missus' and Dr. Brainard was still 'Doctor.' Ann could not say 'Captain' at all and relied on a hand sign for his name.

"Say it with me. Boh."

Ann squinted her eyes and watched as Mrs. Beaumont made an 'O' shape with her mouth. She tried her best to mimic the sound.

"Boh?"

"Good! Now say 'Mont.'"

"Mah-nt..." Ann said, stumbling a little over the double consonant.

"Very good! Now put it all together."

Ann took a deep breath. She screwed up her face in concentration, shutting her eyes tight.

"Missus Boomoo!" Ann unclenched her eyes and collapsed into a fit of laughter. Mrs. Beaumont hung her head in mock despair and chuckled along with her.

"You're hopeless, child!"

"It might be easier to change your name to Mrs. Boomoo,"

Captain Galeas said as he walked into the kitchen from the tavern. "It has a nice ring to it."

The captain had worked in the cellar all morning getting ready for the beer delivery. He wore a ratty blue sweater and work trousers. Dirty work gloves flopped out of a back pants' pocket. Black bangs hung untidily on his forehead.

"You're no help at all." Mrs. Beaumont scolded him good-naturedly. "Mind your dirt!"

Captain Galeas rolled his eyes but did pull the chair a little farther away from the kitchen table before taking a seat.

"Good…morning." Ann greeted the captain from across the table. He cocked a grin and watched her sprinkle more spice on the chicken.

"Why don't you show the captain what you've been practicing," Mrs. Beaumont said.

Ann looked to him, uncertain. She screwed up her face again with the effort.

"Good…after…noon."

Ann looked apologetically to Captain Galeas. He raised an eyebrow in amused disbelief. "I think I liked the old way better."

"You have to admit she's improving," said Mrs. Beaumont. She cleaved another chicken leg from its thighbone with a crunch.

The captain harrumphed behind Mrs. Beaumont's back, but when Ann looked his blue eyes smiled at her.

Ann had noticed a change with Captain Galeas ever since she had decided to stay and work at Siren's Cove. He still growled and stomped around the house, but his eyes seemed softer, more at ease. Ann guessed the reason was that he was her employer and no longer her benefactor. She was a full, contributing member of the household and no longer a problem that had to be solved.

As for herself, Ann could not be happier. She had a purpose again and a sense of belonging. A restlessness sometimes came over her when she wondered if she would ever discover who she was, but she'd long given up hope that anyone would come looking for her. In her room, she had hidden a small travel bag with a change of clothes, money, and a few other essentials, but the urge to run had all but left her. Every time Ann thought about leaving Siren's Cove an instinct pressed down on her, like a hand resting on top of her head. In her mind, Ann would hear an insistent voice whisper, *Wait! Always stay near the crash site.* She did not know what she was supposed to wait for. Was it an old memory trying to break through? Did it even matter anymore? With every day that passed, Siren's Cove felt more like home, and Mrs. Beaumont and Captain Galeas became more like family.

*Home.* It was a beautiful word.

Ann finished seasoning the chicken and lifted the baking pan. The tray bumped one of the shakers, knocking it off the table. Glass shattered on the floor.

Ann set the pan down. "Bloody hell."

Ann looked up in time to see Mrs. Beaumont's and the captain's stunned faces. Ann cringed and hurried to fetch the autosweeper from the pantry.

John struggled to contain his laughter. "When did you teach her that?"

"I didn't," Mrs. Beaumont said and gave him a disapproving frown. "I can't imagine where she picked that up."

Ann returned and gave them a rueful smile.

The tavern's front door jingled, and Mike appeared in the kitchen doorway. Blond hair poked out from under a dark knit cap, a ubiquitous grin on his face. The beer man was dressed for the cold weather in a tan jacket and coveralls.

"Are you ready?" Mike clapped John on a shoulder.

"Yup, I just finished setting up the track," he said, pulling on work gloves. "The service hatch is unlocked."

"I don't understand why you don't use an anti-grav unit to move the barrels instead of rolling them," Mrs. Beaumont said over a shoulder. "Seems like it would be a lot easier and faster."

"Anti-gravs change the taste of the beer," John said with a

shrug and left the kitchen with Mike. Mrs. Beaumont gave an exasperated sigh and looked at Ann.

"That's just an old wives' tale," she said. "He's so stubborn. Ropes and pulleys." She rolled her eyes. "No wonder the tourists think we're all a bunch of barbarians." With that, she chopped an entire chicken in two with a single thwack of her cleaver.

Rolling the beer kegs by hand would keep the men busy until lunch. Mike and his assistant worked from street level and operated a mounted pulley, while Captain Galeas worked in the cellar. An hour passed and Mrs. Beaumont gave Ann metal flasks of hot tea to take to the men.

Ann pulled the cast iron handle that opened the trap door to the cellar behind the bar. Her shoes clattered on the stairs. Directly underneath the tavern, the cellar stored beer, wine and other spirits, but like most basements it had become a convenient catch-all for Siren's Cove. Trunks and boxes were stacked chock-a-block next to racks of wine and crates of whiskey bottles. The captain kept his tools and a few spare parts needed for general maintenance in a workbench at the bottom of the stairs. The cellar extended all the way under the carriage house, but that part of the tavern had sat empty for years.

Ann hugged the warm flask and shivered in the flat light. The cellar was colder than usual with the front service hatch open. She turned at the bottom of the stairs and walked to where the beer barrels were kept. As she rounded the second corner, a large barrel as tall as a man and as stout as a horse came into view through the service hatch. She waited patiently, not wanting to distract Captain Galeas from his work.

The service hatch extended several feet up to street level like an underground chimney. The captain had set up a long sloping metal track a few feet below the hatch. As Ann watched, the captain stood to one side and shouted instructions through the opening to the men working above.

"Slowly! That's it! A little more! Almost got it! HOLD!"

The barrel dangled a few inches above the track. Captain

Galeas stretched up over his head and unclipped the two safety straps that supported the barrel. The barrel, free of the straps, dropped with a thud onto the track. Gravity rolled the barrel down the slope to the other end of the cellar. The captain followed the barrel as it rolled and gave it an extra push with his hand. When it reached the end of the track, he pulled a lever and the barrel lifted to a vertical position, slid off the track, and set down next to its brothers. Captain Galeas looked up and smiled when he saw Ann.

"You read my mind. It's bloody cold down here." He unscrewed the flask and took a sip of tea. "Thanks."

Ann smiled, pleased he liked the tea. The captain put the flask on top of a nearby keg and stepped over the track. Another barrel was already on its way down through the hatch.

"Tell Mrs. Beaumont we're almost done. Just a few more to go."

Ann nodded and walked back toward the steps. She heard the captain shouting orders through the hatch.

"Easy! Easy! Keep going!"

CRACK!

"LOOK OUT!"

Another bang shook the basement followed by the crack of metal on the stone floor. Ann ran back to the service hatch. Her heart hammered in her chest. Broken pieces of wood and safety straps dangled from the hatch opening. The pulley must have broken and the barrel slipped free of its straps. The track collapsed when the barrel crashed into it. Captain Galeas lay on the ground, trapped under an enormous barrel. Ann tried to push the barrel, but it wouldn't budge. He grimaced in pain. His breath came in short, wheezing gasps.

"Get...help!"

The captain's eyes looked wide into Ann's as his breath slowly squeezed out of him. The barrel rested squarely on his chest. A pool of beer spread on the cobblestones beneath him.

Ann's heart pounded. He would not last long with the full weight of the barrel on him. Where were the other men? Were they injured when the pulley broke? She raced back toward the stairs and yelled for help. She had one foot on the bottom step when she saw an ax handle leaning against the workbench. Ann grabbed the ax and ran back to Captain Galeas. He saw her coming, ax raised high.

"No! Wait!"

Ann swung the ax hard and struck the barrel broadside with a deep thud. The captain groaned from the shock of the impact, face pinched with pain. The wood splintered but held. A fresh spray of beer erupted from the barrel's side. Ann could hear shouting and running footsteps above her. She raised the ax again and swung with all her strength. The blade plunged into the wood, striking the same spot, and the barrel burst open with a gush of foamy beer. The cold wave washed over her feet. Ann slipped on the cobblestones and fell, dropping the ax just as Mike and his assistant rounded the corner.

The captain's face was ashen. His head slumped against his chest as the men carried him into the kitchen. Ann shivered from more than cold as she followed the men. Mrs. Beaumont directed the men to the master bedroom upstairs.

"Left at the top of the stairs. End of the hall." Mrs. Beaumont grabbed Ann's arm and kept her from following the men into the sitting room. "Stop! You're not going anywhere. Are you hurt?"

She steered Ann to a chair at the kitchen table. Ann's teeth chattered.

"Barrel! Fell! Hurt! N-need help! D-doctor!"

Mrs. Beaumont checked Ann's head and limbs for broken bones. "I've already sent a message to Dr. Brainard. He'll be here soon. Just sit a moment and catch your breath."

Ann closed her eyes and wrapped her arms around herself to try to stop shaking. She could feel her wet skirt and blouse clinging to her back and legs. She heard the familiar click and whistle of Mrs. Beaumont's teapot followed by the usual sting of a headache. *Captain Galeas will be all right,* she told herself. *But what if he's not?* Was he even breathing when they carried him upstairs? Ann felt something warm and soft drape over her shoulders. She opened her eyes with a grateful sigh and soaked in the blanket's heat.

Mrs. Beaumont set a cup of tea on the table. Ann wrapped her fingers around the cup, breathing in the steam, and took a sip. The tea tasted stronger, burning as it went down, but then the sweet taste of fully ripened summer berries filled her mouth. The vapors lifted and warmed her from the inside. Mrs. Beaumont must have added a generous shot of the captain's wine to the tea.

***

Ann and Mrs. Beaumont waited in the sitting room for news of the captain's condition. The women stood when they heard Dr. Brainard on the stairs.

"How is he?" Mrs. Beaumont spoke before the doctor reached the last step. "Is he all right?"

Dr. Brainard smiled and held up a hand to soothe them.

"He's going to be fine. He had a couple of cracked ribs and a broken arm. I mended the bones, but he should stay in bed two, maybe three days. He'll be bruised and sore for a while."

Ann sighed with relief and sat down on the footstool. It felt like the deepest breath she'd taken since she saw the barrel resting on the captain's chest.

"He was lucky the barrel broke when it did," Mrs. Beaumont said, hand to her heart. "It could have been much worse."

"It wasn't that. The captain told me Ann broke the barrel with an ax." The doctor turned to her with a look of admiration. "That was quick thinking. You saved his life."

Ann didn't know what to say. She did what anyone would have done. It was dumb luck she even spotted the ax.

"We should discuss his care," Dr. Brainard said, turning back to Mrs. Beaumont. "I've given him something for the pain. Is there anyone who can help you while he is recovering? I know you've been extra busy with the holiday coming up."

Ann tried to get the doctor's attention, but he was already deep in conversation with Mrs. Beaumont.

"Ann and I can manage the kitchen, and I can ask Arnold to fill in behind the bar in the evenings," said Mrs. Beaumont.

"The problem is all these boxed meals. We'll need help delivering them else we'll have to cancel the orders."

It frustrated Ann not being able to speak her mind when she wanted to. She was tired of being left out of conversations and people talking around her. She knew they didn't mean to, but she sometimes felt forgotten even when she was sitting in the same room. She struggled to form the words and repeated the sign with her hands.

"Well, if a delivery boy is all you need, I'm sure that can be arranged," Dr. Brainard said, gathering up his bag. "I'll deliver them myself between house calls if I have to."

Ann stamped a foot in frustration. She would yell at them if only she could make the words come out of her mouth.

"Oh, doctor. I'm sure I can get one of the boys from town. There's really no need for you–"

"CAPTAIN!"

They turned with a start.

"Captain." Ann pointed to herself then upstairs. "I want…to see him."

The doctor smiled and nodded. "Of course, you may go and see him. I'm sure he would be very happy to see you."

*** 

Ann stood with Dr. Brainard as he knocked on the master bedroom door. Ann had been in the captain's bedroom before, but never while he was there and only to deliver or gather laundry.

Captain Galeas laid in bed propped up on pillows, eyes closed. A blue brace wrapped his left arm. A brass lamp cast a warm pool of light from the bedside table.

Dr. Brainard whispered, "John, you have a visitor."

The patient stirred and turned his head as Ann and the doctor came around the foot of the four-poster bed. He blinked and a broad smile spread across his face.

"He might be a little…er…foggy," the doctor said. "The pain medication, you know."

Ann nodded. She could see the captain's eyes had a bright glassy look, but his face had a much better color.

"Don't stay too long. He needs rest." Dr. Brainard left, shutting the door behind him.

Ann sat in the chair next to the bed. She glimpsed the captain's injured left arm. Swollen fingers poked from the end of the brace like thick, purple sausages. She winced. Captain Galeas watched her, still grinning, three sheets in the wind on pain medication.

"You are very handy with an ax," he said, speech slurred.

Ann gave him a tight, worried smile. Captain Galeas was always so commanding – giving orders, chucking troublemakers out of the tavern. He looked different lying in bed, his black hair tousled, dark circles under his eyes. How close had the barrel come to killing him? Ann tried to swallow the lump in her throat. She looked down and fussed with the covers, straightening and pulling them up a little higher on his chest. The captain reached for her hand.

"Leave it be."

Their hands rested together on the bed. Ann's face blazed with heat. She wished he would let go, and at the same time she liked the touch of his hand and how hers curled gently in his. She looked up at the captain. His blue eyes appeared glassy, but his face was open and as clear as a sunny day.

"You saved me. Thank you."

A wave of loyalty and affection forced Ann to look away.

"What's wrong?" He held her hand more tightly. Ann composed herself and gave the captain a genuine smile.

"Nothing. Worried for you."

The captain eased back into the pillows and smiled as his eyelids began to droop.

"Don't worry. It will take more than a barrel...to drag me under for good."

His eyelids flickered and closed, his breathing deepened. After a few minutes when the captain didn't speak or open his eyes again, Ann gently removed her hand from his and left him sleeping.

# TEN

## *FOUNDER'S DAY*

Captain Galeas stayed in bed all the next day, meek and mild and floating on a billowy cloud of heavy narcotics. Ann took him meals and made sure he had a fresh pitcher of water by his bedside. Arnold took charge behind the bar in the evenings, and Mike the beer man, feeling misplaced guilt perhaps over the accident, offered to make deliveries.

By the end of the second day, Dr. Brainard's medicinal cocktail wore off and the captain became restless and surly when told he wasn't allowed to get up yet. He resorted to bellowing orders from his bed and demanding regular updates.

"Well, at least we know he's feeling better," Mrs. Beaumont said to Ann that night after he demanded his data link pad.

The tenderness Captain Galeas showed Ann faded along with the effects of the pain medication and his usual demeanor returned—happy to see her when she brought him meals—but nothing more. Ann felt relieved and at the same time the incident put curious thoughts in her head: the warmth of his hand against hers, his blue eyes beneath dark bangs. She chided herself. Feelings of loyalty and maybe even affection toward the captain after all he had done for her were completely natural, but the fact remained he was her employer and nothing good ever came from foolish thinking.

***

Ann sat on the settee and rummaged through the sewing box, searching for a spare button for the captain's favorite maroon waistcoat. It would be his first night back behind the bar since the barrel accident and the timing was excellent. With Founder's Day only two days away, the crowds at Siren's Cove had steadily grown. Arnold was a good substitute, but no one could replace Captain Galeas behind the bar. Mrs. Beaumont was also concerned if Arnold stayed in charge much longer the captain would get riled when he saw the depleted wine reserves. A small price to pay for Arnold's help, but she didn't want to give the captain another reason to grouse.

Ann sighed and poked a finger around in the sewing box. Bonnie Galeas, like all good housewives, saved buttons—perhaps too many buttons. Ann had already found several, but the buttons were either too large, too small, the wrong shape, or design. A pile of rejected gold buttons huddled together on the table.

Another flash of gold caught Ann's eye and she pinched the button between her index finger and thumb. The button was the right size and shape. She peered more closely and saw a picture of a large, spreading tree. Another dud. Ann almost put the button aside then paused and rolled the bauble onto her palm. A tree was an odd thing to have on a button, and yet it seemed familiar. An image formed in her mind. *Gold buttons on a field of blue.* Ann blinked. She tried to grasp the image, but the memory sparkled briefly like sunlight on water only to vanish just as quickly.

Ann frowned. Insignificant bits and pieces would come to her and she didn't know what they meant, and now damn gold buttons on a blue background. She wanted to remember, but she needed a solid memory to latch onto.

"Where's my vest?" Captain Galeas shouted from upstairs. "Has anyone seen my maroon vest?"

"Coming!"

Discouraged, Ann put the tree button in the discard pile and kept searching. Another gold button surfaced from the jumble in the sewing box. A match. Ann quickly loaded the button into the stitcher and sewed it to the front of the waistcoat.

\*\*\*

A cheer went up from the bar as Ann followed Captain Galeas into the tavern. Arnold wouldn't allow the captain behind the bar and insisted he take a seat of honor on a chair made especially for the occasion. Mike had made a barstool using pieces from the barrel that had caused all the trouble. Ann could still catch the scent of malt and roasted grain as it lingered about the chair.

"Consider it poetic justice," the beer man said as Ann helped the captain settle onto the stool.

"What better revenge than for you to park your ass on the barrel that almost killed you," Ross chimed in.

"Thanks a lot!" The captain winced at the pain in his ribs and gave the men a lopsided grin.

"Always knew drink would do you in but I figured it would be your wine, not beer," Arnold said and poured drinks. The captain grunted agreement and picked up a glass.

Ann turned to leave.

"Wait one moment, Miss Ann," Arnold said.

Ann looked back and was surprised to see all the men holding their glasses in a toast.

"And now gentlemen," Arnold said. "Raise your glasses to the heroine of the hour. To the lovely Miss Ann, for saving our favorite barkeep for without whom we would all go thirsty!"

"Here, here!"

Ann smiled, face flushed. Captain Galeas raised his glass with the other men, and she felt her blush deepen. She laughed to hide her embarrassment then turned to serve a table of customers.

***

Siren's Cove was thick with Founder's Day revelers. The rhythms of the music filled the tavern and pulled the dancers to their feet. The atmosphere was as intoxicating as the beer and it bubbled and flowed over everyone, dancers and wallflowers alike. Ann danced with some of the regular customers in between waiting on tables. Even Mrs. Beaumont took a turn around the dance floor, pulled from her haven in the kitchen by Duncan.

Ann collapsed onto a barstool laughing and gasping for breath, having just finished a spirited jig with Oz. She rested against the bar, content to watch the other dancers. She felt the touch of a familiar hand. She turned and saw Captain Galeas smiling down at her, his gaze so intense she thought her heart would stop. Ann felt her face burn scarlet, but she smiled and nodded. He took her hand and led her to the floor to join the dance already in progress.

"Be gentle with him, lass," Ross catcalled from the bar. "He's still on the mend." The other men hooted and whistled their approval.

The captain didn't seem to hear them as he put his injured arm around Ann's waist and took her left hand firmly with his right. Ann placed her other hand on his shoulder, and they were off, spinning and moving in time with the other dancers. Ann's heart pounded. She kept her eyes on the captain's shoulder, afraid to look up and see his blue eyes again. His hand on her waist and the scent of whiskey and smoke on his clothes sent a flutter through her quite different from any feelings of loyalty or gratitude.

Ann was barely aware of the other dancers, their moving shapes and colors blurred and blended with the music. Her feet moved and her body turned and bent under the captain's firm, steady hand as he guided her around the dance floor. Then all too soon he released her. He pressed a hand against his side, wheezing. Captain Galeas led her back to the bar and took a

84

seat, grimacing.

Before Ann could ask if he was all right, Mike the beer man took her by the hand and twirled her away back toward the dance floor. She looked at the captain over Mike's shoulder. A thrill ran down her spine. Captain Galeas watched from across the room. A smile touched his mouth. For an instant his eyes narrowed, smoldering with a heat Ann had never seen from him before. *Was that jealousy?* The captain turned back to his beer. Ann swallowed and looked away. *Nothing good ever came from foolish thinking.*

***

Founder's Day arrived and Mrs. Beaumont suggested Captain Galeas close Siren's Cove so they could watch the festivities. The captain wanted to stay open for the lunch crowd.

"Why stay open?" The cook argued with him over breakfast. "You know everyone will be at the parade. Ann wants to go, don't you?" She looked to Ann for reinforcements.

"Yes! Can we?" Ann had heard about the parade for weeks.

The captain eyed them for a moment. "Oh, all right." He stabbed a sausage with a fork. "But we're not staying all afternoon. There's plenty to do around here."

They wrapped themselves in warm cloaks and hats for the walk to Vernon's Bluff and joined the other Colonists sitting on picnic blankets eating lunch. Large gray clouds hugged the horizon. A steady breeze blew from the ocean.

A few yards away, Captain Shaw and his wife trudged up the hill.

Captain Galeas called out to them. "Whatcha know, Larnie?"

Shaw stood from straightening a picnic blanket and turned to face them.

"Red sky this morning, John. Gale coming. Big one."

"When do you think it will hit?"

Captain Shaw looked to the ocean and sniffed the wind. He thought for a moment scratching his whiskers.

"Prolly hold off till tonight. Better batten down. I already secured the fleet."

"Thanks, Larnie!" Captain Galeas turned to Mrs. Beaumont and Ann. "We better keep an eye on that. His predictions are better than the weather service."

"I wonder if they'll have to raise the sea wall," Mrs. Beaumont said.

"It's possible if the storm is big enough," the captain said, wiping his mouth on a napkin.

"What wall?" Ann had been around the harbor several times on errands, but never saw anything that looked like a wall.

The captain leaned toward her, their shoulders almost touching. Ann drew in a quiet breath, suddenly reminded of the night they had danced and the feel of his hand around her waist. He pointed to the horizon. From their vantage point on the bluff, Ann could see Llewellyn and the entire harbor stretched out below.

"See where the harbor opens to the ocean right past the breakers?"

Ann nodded and tried to focus her attention to where the captain pointed and not to how she could almost feel the warmth of his skin against her cheek. She could just make out twin cement structures on either side of the mouth of the harbor.

"That's where the wall is," the captain said, leaning back again. "Right now, it's under water. If the gale is big enough, they'll raise the wall to protect the harbor and the town from the storm swell." He gave a reassuring smile. "Nothing to worry about. It's only a precaution. Odds are the storm won't be big enough to raise it."

A squawk came from the public address system.

"Ladies and gentlemen." The announcer's voice began amid shouts and whistles. "Happy Founder's Day to you! Please welcome the 408th Flying Dragons!"

Ann felt the vibration before she heard the sound. Four low-flying aircraft screamed over the top of the bluff from behind with an earsplitting shriek. Ann let out a yell and covered her head with her hands.

*Deep bass throbs thrummed Ann's body. Cold dread filled her heart as the ship shuddered underneath.*

The crowd erupted into cheers and whistles. Ann lifted her head. A group of twin-engine fighters dropped over the harbor below and released bursts of fireworks into the air.

*Gravitational forces pulled her insides.*

"Sorry about that," Captain Galeas said. "We probably should have warned you. They do that every year."

Ann's heart pounded in her chest. She could still feel the vibration of the engines. Not the high-pitched scream of the fighters, but a deeper thrumming coming from inside her. Her hands shook. Beads of sweat broke across Ann's forehead and the back of her neck. The fighters accelerated into a steep climb. Their metallic v-shaped wings gleamed in the sun. Ann caught her breath and quickly wiped her brow with the corner of her shawl. The thrumming faded.

Ann glanced to Mrs. Beaumont and Captain Galeas. They were too busy watching the fighters to notice her distress.

The captain gave Ann a curious look when he felt her watching him. She forced a smile and gestured to the retreating fighters. "Who are they?"

"The pilots are cadets from the military prep school in Idlewild," he said and grabbed another chicken leg from the picnic basket.

An uneasiness shifted inside Ann. *Military pilots. Always stay near the crash site.* She turned to watch the fighters, but they were already mere specks on the horizon. The parade had officially begun.

*** 

Just as Captain Shaw predicted, the wind began to howl fiercely during the dinner service. Emergency tones blared from the comm in the kitchen announcing Llewelyn was under a severe storm warning and the sea wall had been raised. The customers did not stay after that and hurried home before the gale hit. With no one to serve, Captain Galeas closed early and insisted Mrs. Beaumont go home, arguing kitchen clean up would keep until another day. Within an hour, the full fury of the storm broke, bringing half the ocean with it as rain.

Wind and water lashed relentlessly at the house and rattled the windows. Ann sat on the settee with the captain's data link pad and a cup of tea. She had tried to search for information on airship crashes near the colonies, but the storm had played havoc with reception, making a proper search impossible. Captain Galeas sat in his chair, listening to the comm announcer broadcast storm warning updates or paced back and forth between the sitting room and the kitchen. He glanced nervously at the lights whenever they flickered.

A sudden pounding on the door made them both jump. Incredibly, someone was out in the storm. Whomever it was continued to hammer and shout, their words lost in the tempest outside. Captain Galeas opened the door. A gust of wind and rain blew a crouched figure through the entryway and into the sitting room. The captain quickly closed the door, shutting out the storm.

Arnold wore an olive-green hooded slicker and rubber boots. Dark wet curls were plastered to his forehead. His face was pale and tight with worry as he wiped the water from his eyes.

John saw the look on Arnold's face. "What are you doing out? What's wrong?"

"It's the *Girwine*," Arnold panted. "She's lost power. Listing. She's drifting toward the sea wall."

Ann saw the captain flinch. She had heard the men in the bar talk about the *Girwine*, a large cargo vessel too big for Llewelyn's harbor.

"Captain Shaw offered up the fleet, but we're short pilots," Arnold said with a grimace. "His crew went through a couple kegs of beer after the parade, and most of the pilots can't walk a straight line let alone climb into a cockpit. Can you fly a Shovelhead?"

Ann felt a jolt run through her. *Shovelhead.* The image of a boxy, blunt-nosed airship filled her mind.

John nodded. "It's been awhile, but I can fly one." He looked at his friend, doubtful. "Shovelheads?"

Arnold nodded. "I know, but it's the best we have."

The image of the Shovelhead continued to burn in Ann's memory. The airship made her anxious. Why? Memories swirled and floated just out of reach, gleaming like minnows in shallow water as they flitted between her fingers. She struggled to hold on to them as the memories came into focus.

The memory of an instructor barking statistics through the cold silence of a classroom burst into her mind. She could almost feel the weight of the pen as she scribbled in a notebook. The words shone black on the gleaming page. *P38 Shovelhead. Tough workhorse. Hovering capabilities. Grappling hook.*

John pulled his rain gear out of the closet at the foot of the stairs as the lights flickered again.

"How many do we have?"

"Five. Guthrie, Cameron, Faragher, and Shimmin are flying, too," Arnold said. "Storm's too thick for tractor beams. You can secure her with grappling lines and hold her while air rescue gets the crew."

"We'll be threading a damn needle." John's voice growled as he threw on a rain slicker.

"We don't have a choice. You can tow her out to sea and scuttle her if you have to."

John glanced toward Ann. "Evacuation?"

Arnold shook his head. "There's no time. This either works or it doesn't."

Ann frantically fought to remember. What was she missing? It was like trying to catch a reflection in the palm of her hand. Another gust buffeted the house. She closed her eyes and the memory of the classroom returned. She heard the instructor's voice and watched as the notes written in her own hand filled the page.

*Shovelheads fly with all the elegance and grace of a brick thrown through a window. Slow to respond in high wind shear.*

*The storm.* Fear flowed over Ann like icy water. She shook off the image and turned to Captain Galeas. She had to warn him about the Shovelhead, but he had already crossed the room. He gripped her shoulder with one hand, his face hard as stone.

"Captain, the *wind!*" Her throat constricted with fear.

"I've got to go. You'll be fine. The house can take the wind." The captain barked orders rapid-fire. "Listen to the emergency channel. If you hear the wall has been breached, you'll only have minutes. Get upstairs. Get to the attic. You can reach it through the door in your bedroom closet. Break all the windows. Do you understand?"

Ann nodded. The captain's intensity overwhelmed her. His blue eyes were dark and shadowed, his jaw clenched. Then for a split second his features softened. He looped an arm around and pulled her close. She was in his arms, his mouth pressed warm against hers. Ann threw her arms around him and melted into his embrace.

# ELEVEN

## *WIND AND WATER*

Her lips were soft just as John imagined and tasted of sweet orange blossom and cinnamon from the tea. Ann let out a gasp of surprise when John pulled her into him, but then as his lips found hers her mouth opened willingly, and he felt her bend supplely in his arms. He loved the feel of her arms around his neck. His hands ran up and down her back and brushed the braid hanging between her shoulder blades. How it taunted him all those months, gently swaying in time with her hips wherever she walked.

"John!"

Arnold's voice wrenched John back to the present like an ion cannon blast. He released Ann, and she took a step backward. Her hand flew to her mouth. Her eyes looked like those of a frightened doe just before it bounded over a hedge. John felt his world crash and he silently and angrily cursed himself. *What have I done?* All this time he had denied himself and now one moment of selfish weakness would ruin everything. And yet, she kissed him back—he was sure of that.

"John, we've got to go!" Arnold opened the door and the wind blew spray from the rain into the entryway. "They're waiting for us at the hangar!"

John held Ann in his gaze a second longer, his mouth set.

His hands clenched at his sides. She did not look away and continued to stare back at him with the same startled expression. He knew the danger, but no words of comfort came. He turned and walked out into the storm, shutting the door behind him.

***

The fleet of air rescue vehicles fought through the wind and the rain flying low over heavy seas. The ships' forward searchlights skimmed the white caps below. The five Shovelheads' afterburners flared bright blue ovals of flame behind them. Thirty-foot storm swells rose to meet the air ships as they raced across the ocean then dropped into dark, cavernous troughs.

John corrected his course and scanned the ship's instruments, watching for the Girwine on the scope. The ship was half the size of Llewellyn itself. If they couldn't secure her in time, she would hit the sea wall and cut through without so much as a shudder. He tried not to think of the wall of water that would pummel the harbor, how high the water would reach, or of the taste of cinnamon that still burned sweetly on his lips.

A downburst of wind pushed his ship toward the water. John pulled back on the yoke to gain altitude and remembered why he hated Shovelheads. They didn't slice through the air, they pushed it out of the way like a broad-shouldered bully muscling his way through a crowded bar. John logged most of his flight time on space freighters or smaller spacecraft much sleeker in design. That was a long time ago—another life. He would still rather plot a course around a black hole using breadcrumbs than fly air ships. Gravity was a constant—predictable. Weather conditions were not.

Another swell rose up, and John pulled the yoke back. This time the ship didn't respond. A microburst of wind pushed him downward. John pulled harder and without warning the ship shot higher into the air, setting off the proximity alarm and almost bumping into the other Shovelhead flying above and a little ahead of him. John leveled off and cursed himself for the rookie mistake. Guthrie's deep voice crackled over the ship's comm.

"Whoa! Getting a little frisky back there, Galeas."

"Sorry, my fault," John said. "Damn wind!"

"No harm done," Guthrie said. "Remember, flying a Shovelhead is like bedding a virgin. Slow and easy, mate!"

The other pilots, Cam, Farg, and Shim, laughed.

John grinned. "I'll try to remember that!"

A few minutes later, the Girwine appeared on his scope. The great ship listed twenty-five degrees to its port and drifted parallel with the swells, riding the waves like a sleeping leviathan. The conning tower jutted from the aft deck, dark and deserted. John could see some of the crew had taken shelter against the shipping containers on the starboard side. Other emergency craft hovered nearby.

"All right, lads!" Guthrie's voice sounded again through the comm. "The air is going to be crowded so fly with your heads. Shim and I will take starboard. Cam and Galeas, wait till we right her, then take port. Farg, take the bow and turn her into the swells. We'll hold this position, then once the crew is evacuated, we'll tow her out to sea."

John and Cam swung their ships around and hovered off the *Girwine's* port. They watched as the other team fired their grappling hooks from the aft sections of their Shovelheads. Metal clamps punctured and dug deep into the *Girwine's* starboard side. The airships' engines flared from blue to orange then red as they throttled up, the grappling lines tightened, and the *Girwine* slowly righted back to even keel. John and Cam fired their grappling hooks into the ship's port side, while Farg took his place at the bow. Working together, the pilots revved their engines, maneuvered with their side thrusters, and slowly turned the large ship into the swells.

John watched the pressure gauges on the control panel and listened uneasily to the engine strain against the grappling line, while air rescue evacuated the crew. The Shovelheads took a beating, holding their positions against the sea and the wind. A trickle of sweat ran down John's temple. He dropped his head and wiped his face on a shoulder. His hands had begun to cramp from gripping the yoke and his shoulders ached, but it was nothing compared to the pain that bloomed in his side from his sore ribs. Several bursts of wind rattled the ship right down to his bones.

The view from the cockpit had not changed, but John could see on the scope they were only ten miles from the sea wall. Rolling gray swells rose and fell under the ship's forward searchlight, and rain and sea spray covered the windows so thickly even the ship's water repellant glass had difficulty clearing. The pilots had slowed down the *Girwine's* drift and bought themselves more time, but they would need to get underway soon.

"That's the last of the crew." Guthrie's voice burst through the comm. "Wait for air rescue to clear, then on my signal, we'll start towing."

A few minutes later, the Shovelheads began pulling the *Girwine* out to sea. Farg's airship was at the bow, his afterburners flared dangerously from orange to red then back to orange. John led on the port side with Cam behind him, while Shim led on starboard.

John could see the Girwine through the starboard window as she slowly plowed the sea. At this rate, it would be another hour before they would be far enough from shore to safely turn her loose.

"Shim, watch your gauges." Guthrie's voice crackled with the static. "Your flare looks hot from back here."

"I'm trying. The wind is too strong. I back her off and I lose altitude."

"You have the air space. Ease her off!"

"She's overheating! I can't hold her!"

John saw a flash from the corner of an eye and heard a muffled bang. He turned in time to watch Shim's engine flare sputter and wink out. The crippled Shovelhead slowly tipped its blunt nose skyward then fell backward, pushed by the wind, toward Guthrie's ship. Guthrie tried to swerve out of the way, but Shim's airship hit his grappling line. The force whipped

Guthrie's ship around, and the two collided with a sickening crunch of metal and dropped out of sight into the black ocean below.

"What happened!" Farg's voice broke through the comm.

"Shim! Guthrie!"

John didn't have time to respond. His Shovelhead jerked violently backward and he heard Cam yell through the comm. John's airship lurched down and back, engine screaming, and suddenly he saw only clouds through the cockpit window. With tension lost on the starboard side, the *Girwine* rolled back to port, pulling the grappling cables below the waterline.

"CAM! LET OUT YOUR LINE!"

John worked the grappling controls to let out more slack and pulled back hard on the yoke. The Shovelhead shot forward then swung precariously from side to side before leveling off.

"Cam! Are you okay?"

John looked out the window and saw the *Girwine* had returned to her previous list. A bare patch of deck gleamed where shipping containers once stood. Snapped cables and a broken metal railing told of the missing containers' fate. The *Girwine* looked like a drunk splayed up against a bar.

"I'm okay," Cam said, voice shaking. "I think I bounced off a wave, but I'm still flying."

"Did anyone see if they ejected? I'm calling air rescue," Farg said.

John felt the bottom drop out of his stomach. Everything happened so fast. No one spoke, then Farg's voice sounded again on the comm.

"What are we going to do? We can't tow a crippled ship."

"Maybe we can let her go," Cam said. "Maybe she won't hit the sea wall?"

"Do you really want to take that bet? We're not far enough out."

The *Girwine* turned again with the swells. John knew they didn't have enough power to tow her against the current with only three ships, but what else could they do? There had to be another option. He pulled up the map on the ship's nav computer and quickly cross-checked their position.

"We'll have to beach her," John said.

"What? Where?"

"Sandy Point is closest."

"Didn't you hear me?" Farg snapped. "We can't tow her! We don't have enough power."

"We don't have to tow her," John said, running the calculations and plotting a course. "The current is already taking us there. We just need to nudge her a little and she'll run aground on the point before she hits the sea wall."

"That's cutting it fine," said Farg. "The wall is only two miles past the point. If we miss—"

"You got a better idea?" John cut him off. They were wasting time.

The comm fell silent. John knew what the other men were thinking. The cold dark waves beneath them would unnerve the most experienced pilots, and they just watched two of their own disappear into the depths. If either one of them cut their lines, it was hopeless. Cam spoke first.

"What about our engines? Shim's engine blew when there were five of us. How are we going to do this with three?"

"We'll be riding with the current, not against it, so we won't have to go full throttle the whole time," John said. "We can drift with the *Girwine* and throttle up every now and then to keep her on course."

Another few seconds passed then Farg spoke.

"All right, Galeas. I'm in. You can navigate?"

"Course already plotted and set," John said. "Cam?"

"Yeah, sure! I'm in." said Cam, voice steadying. "This is crazy! What would Guthrie say?"

"That's easy," Farg said. "He'd tell us to fly with our heads."

\*\*\*

The sky above Sandy Point brightened as they made the long, slow haul to its shores. The storm eased but left choppy seas and a dusky, purple haze in its wake. The current swept the ship and her escort along as planned, but then was reluctant to give up its prize as they neared the point. John and Cam flew their grappling lines across the *Girwine's* deck and pulled her from the opposite side. John breathed a sigh of relief when he finally felt the *Girwine's* keel brush the sandy shoals and shudder to a stop. The pilots throttled up one last time and the *Girwine* stuck fast, indifferent to the dying swells as they continued to rock her but no longer moved her with the current.

The ground crew exploded into cheers and mobbed the three pilots as they climbed down from their cockpits back at the hangar. John was pulled into the crowd with Cam and Farg. Everyone wanted to slap their backs and shake their hands. John saw Arnold's brown-checkered cap bobbing in the swarm then his grinning face appeared from the crowd.

"You guys did it! You really did it!" Arnold cuffed John's shoulder. "When air rescue brought back Guthrie and Shimmin, we weren't sure if you'd be able to pull it off."

John felt a weight lift when he saw Guthrie pushing forward wearing a broad smile on his weathered face and a red rescue blanket around his shoulders. Brown epidermal wrap bandaged the left side of his face and neck.

"Nice flying, lads!" The airship commander grasped their hands in turn. "I couldn't be prouder."

"Thanks! Good to see you're still with us," John said grinning.

"How's Shim?" Cam asked.

"He took the worst of it, but he's gonna pull through," Guthrie said. Seeing the pilots' grave faces, he added. "Don't feel too sorry for him. They took him to medical where he'll have wall-to-wall nurses."

"Well done!" Captain Shaw jostled through the crowd and handed out bottles of beer. "I know it's a bit early, but you've earned it."

John wanted to get back to Siren's Cove, but Guthrie, Captain Shaw, and Arnold wanted to hear the full story. The pilots took turns, each adding details from their vantage point.

Finally, when all the questions had been answered and the men were all talked out, Cam and Farg shook hands with John and drifted off into the thinning crowd. Guthrie took another sip of beer and turned to John.

"You flew really well today, Galeas. Genius to think of Sandy Point," he said. "I never knew you were such a hotshot pilot."

Before John could answer, Captain Shaw slapped him on the back laughing loudly.

"Captain Galeas is top drawer," he said, eyes shining from the beer. "I always say the best pilots around are freighter pirates!"

John's face burned. He tried to take a sip of beer but couldn't unhinge his jaw. Guthrie looked confused for a moment as if unsure he heard correctly.

"Er...he means freighter pilot..." Arnold said, stepping in quickly. "John used to fly space freighters."

Captain Shaw, oblivious to the awkward silence he caused, laughed again.

"And a damn good one from the stories I've heard. You could learn a thing or two from this one, Guthrie," the grizzled captain said before staggering off to talk to some of the other crew.

"It was a long time ago," John said to Guthrie with a shrug. "I don't talk about it much."

"Well, thanks again for your help." Guthrie eyed him curiously as he shook John's hand again. "Good pilots are hard to come by. You can bet we'll call you next time we're in a jam."

"Anytime," John said and forced a smile.

John snatched up his rain slicker and headed toward the hangar door. To most in town, he was the quiet, sometimes scowling bartender of Siren's Cove, but others would always remember him as something darker.

"I swear I didn't say anything," Arnold said, catching up to him.

John stopped and looked hard at his friend.

"You know the only thing in Llewelyn older than McTaggert is the gossip. Folks still talk about Owen Bogie running off with the Collister girl and that was twenty-five years ago. They have four daughters of their own now." Arnold scratched under his cap. "Talk about poetic justice."

John sighed. Arnold was right. The old gossip reared up every now and then.

"Do you think if I live as long as McTaggert they might forget?"

"Well, maybe," Arnold said. "And even if they don't, you'll be so old you won't remember so what does it matter?"

John chuckled and gave Arnold a smirk. "I better go home and check on the house."

"Say hi to your...er...house for me," Arnold said with a wink.

***

John walked up the steps to Siren's Cove, pausing on the stoop before opening the door. The long night and the walk from the hangar had done him in. He could have asked for a ride home, but he wanted time to think. It felt so long ago when he had held Ann in his arms. It was foolish and reckless, a moment born from fear. What would he find when he walked back into his house?

John pushed open the door and stepped into the empty sitting room. Ann appeared in the kitchen doorway as soon as the front door latched behind him, a mixture of relief and worry on her face. Her braid was ruffled and coming undone, dark circles smudged her eyes. John's heart filled with a familiar ache. How many times had Bonnie worn the same haggard look while waiting for him to come home?

"Captain, I thought I heard you come in," Mrs. Beaumont said as she stepped into view from behind Ann. "Thank heavens you're back! We heard on the comm two Shovelheads went down. I was just about to contact Arnold."

"It was Guthrie and Shimmin," he said, taking off the rain slicker. "They're both banged up, but they're going to be all right."

"What a relief!" Mrs. Beaumont pressed a hand to her heart as she turned to go back into the kitchen. "You must be exhausted. I have breakfast started if you're hungry, but after a night like you've had…"

Mrs. Beaumont continued to chatter over a shoulder and fuss in the kitchen, but John only had eyes for Ann. She looked like she might take flight at any moment, perched between the kitchen and the sitting room.

"And Ann, would you please go get some sleep now?" Mrs. Beaumont popped back into the kitchen doorway, one hand on a hip. She turned to the captain. "She stayed up all night listening to storm warnings on the comm." The cook's voice trailed off again as she walked out of sight to the pantry. "I've tried to tell her to get some rest, but she won't listen to me."

Ann didn't move. Hope buoyed John like an ocean swell. *She waited up for me.* He took a step toward Ann, and she flew straight into his arms, flinging her arms around his neck. He kissed her and she covered his face with sweet kisses of her own. Fingers tangled in his hair and caressed the short pigtail and the soft fringe at the back of his neck.

"I doubt we'll see many customers today," Mrs. Beaumont continued as she walked back into the kitchen from the pantry. "When I walked over this morning, it looked like everyone had their hands full with storm clean-up…"

The cook's chatter died as she stood in the kitchen doorway holding a large tin of sugar, gaping at them. John didn't care. The whole Colonies could burst into flames and it wouldn't matter as long as Ann was in his arms.

Mrs. Beaumont gave a cough. Ann started and tried to step back, but John held tight. The impossible had happened twice in less than twelve hours and he wasn't going to let her go this time.

"My goodness, I completely forgot I wanted to stop by Tonnag's Bakery this morning." Mrs. Beaumont's voice trilled as she put the sugar tin on the counter and grabbed a wrap. "I'll be back in a little while."

"No worries. Take your time." John cupped Ann's face in

his hands. She looked up at him, eyes anxious.

The kitchen door closed, and John pulled Ann to the settee. They sat wrapped in each other's arms. He kissed the top of her head and smoothed his hands down her back. She sighed and buried her face in John's neck, whispering words he didn't understand, but he loved the sound of them as they rolled off her tongue.

After a moment, Ann leaned back. John immediately missed the warmth of her body. A smile touched her mouth, but her eyes were troubled.

"Captain."

He brushed a strand of hair behind her ear. "Maybe, you should call me John."

A pretty shade of pink dotted Ann's cheeks. She nodded but then her mouth pressed into a thin line. She reached into an apron pocket and handed him a folded sheet of paper. John opened it and saw a picture that looked like a child's drawing of an airship. The sketch was rough, but there was no mistaking the ship's boxy shape. John looked up from the paper and into Ann's eyes as comprehension broke over him.

Ann tapped the drawing with a finger, eyes solemn. "P38 Shovelhead."

# TWELVE

## *FAIRLEAD*

"You wouldn't win any prizes for artistic composition," Dr. Brainard said with a smile to Ann. He tapped his mouth with a finger as he studied the sketch. "But it's definitely a Shovelhead."

Two weeks after the storm, the doctor sat hunched on the tavern steps, his plum driving coat drawn tightly around him. The cold air held a strong bite, but the bright winter sun warmed the drive in front of the stoop. Dr. Brainard's mechanized horse, Equuleus, pawed the ground between the shafts of the carriage and shook his large copper head.

Ann sat next to the doctor on the stoop. A shawl draped around her shoulders. She lifted her palms in a hopeless gesture.

"I see it…in my head."

The doctor refolded the paper and pushed his glasses up more firmly on his nose. "It makes sense that the image would pop into your mind when you heard the captain and Arnold talking the night of the storm."

Ann frowned. "I felt…more." How could she explain what she'd seen? The images of the classroom. How she'd felt watching the fighters on the bluff. Again, words failed her, and she was left with only emptiness. She looked to John for help.

John picked up a ratchet from his toolbox. "The memory was strong enough she thought she should draw a picture. That doesn't sound like an everyday kind of memory to me." He patted the metal plating covering the horse's broad hindquarters and it made a sound like an empty metal drum.

The doctor pursed his lips and looked to Ann. "Do you think you've flown in one?"

Ann searched her memory of the Shovelhead. "I don't think so. But...classroom."

"You wouldn't have had to flown in one to know them." John lifted the horse's back right foot and straddled it between his knees. The hoof was as large as a pie pan and as black as a smithy's forge. He loosened the bolt just above the hoof, speaking rhythmically as he worked the ratchet back and forth.

"You could have worked around them. Maybe someone close to you did. It's a clue." He slipped the ratchet into a coat pocket. "Good boy, Equuleus. Steady now."

The horse held his position while John removed the entire hoof, exposing the underlying structure and sensor wires. He poked inside with his fingers, removed a large rock, and chucked it into the bushes.

Dr. Brainard stood and leaned his back against the side of the carriage, hands in his coat pockets. A thoughtful expression crossed his face and he turned back to Ann.

"There are Shovelheads being used in shuttleports all over the Colonies. I'll add to your description on the data network that you may have worked around aircraft and seem familiar with Shovelheads. Maybe that will turn up something." He handed Ann the drawing.

Ann sighed and slipped the picture back into a skirt pocket. The image of the Shovelhead and her experience on the bluff had been her strongest memories to date and still she felt lost.

"Don't give up," Dr. Brainard said, smiling. "This may be a sign you're on the verge of a major breakthrough. Let's give it some time and see if you remember more. It proves your memories are still there. They just need to be coaxed out a little more."

Ann nodded. She knew the doctor was right, but the mystery continued to gnaw at her. *Who am I? Where did I come from?* And if she suddenly remembered who she was, what then? Her eyes darted to John.

John finished fitting the horse's hoof back into place and stood, patting Equuleus again as he stepped away. He glanced over a shoulder. Dr. Brainard busied himself by feeding Equuleus a few rusted nuts and bolts from the treat can he kept in his carriage. John reached for Ann's hand, stroking her fingers as she passed. Her smile warmed him as she turned to walk up the steps.

John watched Ann walk back inside. He ached to hold her again. Mrs. Beaumont was out running errands for the morning. If not for Dr. Brainard, he would have grabbed Ann and carried her to the master bedroom.

When John turned back to the drive, he saw the doctor watching him, a knowing grin on his face as he walked back toward the carriage. John tried to gather a neutral expression and dropped his eyes. He had dreaded this moment.

"Did Equuleus need any other work done?" John turned his back to the doctor and dug the ratchet from his coat pocket. He pretended to examine the horse's front legs.

"He's fine. I'd rather talk about you. Mrs. Beaumont tells me you and Ann are getting along rather well these days."

John grunted. He hated the cheerful intonation in the doctor's voice.

"Remind me later to fire her."

John avoided the doctor's gaze as he walked around to the horse's other side to check for loose bolts. It bothered him, everyone knowing his private business.

"Mrs. Beaumont wasn't gossiping. She's happy for you. She thinks it's good for you, and I think it's wonderful."

"I'm so glad you two approve." John came back around to the steps and tossed the ratchet into the toolbox. "If you have a point to make, would you mind getting to it?"

"Does Ann make you happy?"

John wiped his hands on a rag. He wasn't sure if happy was

the right word. The last couple weeks with Ann, even with all the passion between them, had been peaceful. It felt as if he had poured all of his rage and grief into a bottle and put it on a shelf. The bottle was still there, waiting for him—a bitter vintage. John could tip it back and drink it all again if he chose. The temptation remained. Ann made him forget about the bottle. If that was happy, then yes. She made him happy.

"Yes." A smile brightened John's face before he even knew it was there.

"Then maybe it's time," Dr. Brainard said. His voice lost its teasing tone and his eyes softened. "Make the call."

John shook his head. He swept hair from his eyes. He should have known where the doctor led him. All the old pain and doubt clamped down on him again.

"I don't understand. If you care for her..." Dr. Brainard lowered his voice. "Go to Andarria and finish what you started."

"No. I don't have to finish anything," John said and snapped the lid of the toolbox shut. "I've told you it's in the past. I run a tavern." He didn't have to see the doctor's face. John could feel his disapproval. Why couldn't he just leave it be?

"You can't dodge it forever," Dr. Brainard said. "You need to set the record straight. Bonnie wanted you—"

"DON'T!"

John's anger jolted him like an electric shock. He turned on the doctor. "Don't tell me what Bonnie wanted!"

Dr. Brainard stood his ground, but his eyes showed unease behind his glasses. Regret doused John's anger.

"I overstepped. I'm sorry. I should be going." Dr. Brainard tried to move past John to the carriage door, but John placed a heavy hand on his friend's shoulder.

"I'm sorry, Rupert. I didn't mean..."

Dr. Brainard shook his head. "It's all right." He gave John a sad smile. "Just promise me you won't close the door on Andarria completely. Think about it."

The doctor clambered up into the carriage. Equuleus raised

his head and waited for his master's orders. John watched as he pulled on his driving gloves. The doctor always liked things to be neat and tidy, but life was full of torn edges and missing pieces.

"How can I go back? I'm not who I was."

The doctor gathered the reins and looked down at John.

"Of course you aren't and you are still not who you are. You were never supposed to run a tavern. Remember that."

John watched the carriage pull out of the drive and onto the main road. Equuleus broke into a smart trot. The horse's metal hooves threw sparks as they clipped the gray cobblestones. John picked up the toolbox and started up the steps.

The meeting on Andarria had always been part of the plan. It was their path and their future, but then Bonnie died. John couldn't see his way without her. If he had a future with Ann, it would have to be a different path and a better one than what he could offer working in a tavern.

The heavy scent of meat roasting made John's mouth water as he entered the kitchen. The wall ovens hummed. Fat drippings sizzled in the pans. Ann sat on a stool at the counter engrossed in the pages of a cookbook. She rested her chin on one hand as she absentmindedly twirled a wooden spoon between her fingers with the other. The spoon spun so fast it blurred and created complex patterns in the air.

John lifted the toolbox onto the counter and looked over Ann's shoulder. "What are you reading?"

Ann caught the spoon in her hand. "Looking for a recipe." She pointed with the spoon. Cookbooks lay scattered on the counter, their pages held open with kitchen utensils. All the books opened to recipes for Leukothean Chowder.

John chuckled and kissed the tender spot on Ann's neck just above the shoulder.

"I think you found a few."

Ann leaned back into his embrace and rested her cheek against his. John straightened and glanced around the kitchen.

"Is Mrs. Beaumont back yet?" He had no desire to be the subject of any more loose talk.

"Not yet. Oh!" Ann's eyes brightened. "We need wine."

"A bit early in the day for wine," John teased.

Ann laughed. "No. For cooking." She handed over an empty wine bottle. "Used the last bottle for the roast."

"That's all right," he said, setting the bottle back on the counter. "I'll bring more up from the cellar."

Ann smiled up at him. The light from the window danced in her eyes. Anxiety overtook John like a fever as he remembered the doctor's words. John dropped almost to his knees in front of her. He gripped the seat of the kitchen stool and looked directly into her eyes.

"Are you happy here? Are you happy here with me?"

Her eyes widened, startled by the sudden outburst. "Yes?"

John looked away and wiped his brow. Cleaved by necessity, his life had not been whole in years. Could he tell her? Would she understand?

"John?" She touched his arm.

"I haven't always run a tavern," John said. "Bonnie and I came to the Colonies—" His throat closed and he could say no more.

Ann murmured in sympathy and pressed her fingers to his lips. John smiled and took her hand, touched by her concern.

"It's all right. I don't mind talking about her. We came to the Colonies to start over. The tavern was Bonnie's idea. We—" John felt the invisible chain he wore tighten. He wrestled against its authority until in agony he gave into its demands once more.

"I was worried you would want to leave if you knew that."

Ann relaxed and gripped his hand. "It's all right," she said with a bewildered smile. "Happy to stay."

John hung his head and groaned inwardly with frustration. No matter how hard he tried or how much he grieved, he could not speak the words until he was free of his oath. But freedom would come at a price. He looked up. Worry pursed Ann's mouth. John smiled and kissed her.

"I'm sorry. I didn't mean to upset you."

John's eyes strayed over Ann's shoulder. The empty wine

bottle sat on the counter behind her. John picked up the bottle and wiped his hand over the smooth glass. He never bothered with labels. Arnold always nagged him about it. Swore he was leaving money on the table, but his wine always sold well enough by word of mouth, so it didn't seem to matter.

Ann watched him with a cautious expression. "What's wrong?"

"Nothing's wrong."

John lifted Ann's chin and looked into her eyes. He thought how the stars would never hold the same fascination for him. He could finally see the future, and Andarria could go to hell.

# THIRTEEN

## *TIME ENOUGH*

*The crystal goblet glowed in the light of the chandelier. Bubbles sparkled like gemstones as they rose to the top of the glass and broke on the surface. The steady hum of an unseen speaker floated toward her from the opposite end of the banquet hall.*

*A burst of laughter and applause broke through the crowd. Ann looked at the man sitting next to her. He wore a formal suit coat as black as ink. He turned to face her, but as she watched, his eyes glowed with an inner heat. They grew brighter like two searchlights until they merged and blotted out his entire face.*

*The applause thundered. Ann covered her head with her arms to block out the deafening sound, but it continued to grow until she thought her eardrums would burst. She opened her mouth to scream, but the roaring poured from her mouth in a horrible torrent.*

\*\*\*

Ann sat up in bed shaking and gasping for breath. Her heart raced as she tried to shake off the remnants of the nightmare, but she could still feel the echo of the sound inside her as easily as she felt the pounding of her own heart. John rolled over and mumbled in his sleep next to her. Ann pulled the covers up and curled into his side, careful not to wake him. She was glad to see him sleeping and not pacing the house like he sometimes did. She looked at the clock on the nightstand.

The pale moon face said she still had several hours before she needed to get up.

Ann listened to John's comforting snores and replayed the events of the dream. The image of the Shovelhead had dislodged more than a single memory. The veil over the past had thinned, and through its gauzy shroud, she could see shadows and hear snatches of voices. The terrifying noise in the dream was the same sound she remembered when she watched the fighters on the bluff the day of the parade. The sound was from her accident. An airship crash. It was the only answer that made sense, but the clues didn't fit. Where was the wreck? There would have been house-crushing debris and casualties, not just her in a rubbish heap. If by some miracle she'd somehow jettisoned from a ship and it crashed elsewhere, it still would have been found and reported, with a list of missing crew and passengers.

But if it wasn't a crash, then what was it?

Ann fought the panic rising from the pit of her stomach. She had not felt the urge to run since her first few weeks at Siren's Cove, but now as she remembered the man from her dream the fear came back to her. She still had the emergency travel bag and money hidden in her room. She could leave. Catch a shuttle to the next star system. No. It was only a dream. Nothing had changed. It didn't make sense to run headlong into the unknown if she wasn't certain from what direction the danger might come or even if she was in danger at all. The clock downstairs in the kitchen chimed the hour and sent Ann's heart racing again.

\*\*\*

Ann walked into the kitchen. John stood at the counter, pouring a mug of coffee. He smiled when he saw her and poured a second cup.

"Good morning," he said and handed her a mug.

Ann breathed in the coffee's aroma in the hope of clearing her head. She looked at John, puzzled by his appearance. He seldom beat her to the kitchen in the morning and making coffee came only once in a proxigean tide.

"Up early," Ann said and took a seat at the kitchen table.

"Well, why not?" John leaned toward her. Ann's heart skipped as his lips pressed against hers. "Nothing wrong with an early start."

Ann stirred her coffee as John sat down across from her. The images from her dream rested heavy on her mind. She wanted to tell him all her fears, but words were still clumsy. How could she describe things she hardly understood herself? She would have to try. Ann looked up at John. He seemed unusually bright and cheerful for that time of the morning, or for any time of day for that matter.

Ann tilted her head. "What?"

John glanced at the clock on the wall. "I have a surprise for you." His blue eyes shone with a secret.

"Hmmph!" She raised an eyebrow in disbelief. She'd heard that before. "Tell me?"

"When Mrs. Beaumont gets here," he said taking her hands in his. "It's a surprise for both of you."

Ann smiled curiously at him. He acted like an eager puppy. What was he up to? The kitchen door opened, and Mrs. Beaumont appeared carrying her basket.

"Good morning," she said. She looked at John sitting at the kitchen table. "You're up early, Captain."

John frowned. "You two make it sound like I'm never up before noon."

"He has a surprise," Ann said, sipping coffee.

"Oh, well that's another story." Mrs. Beaumont hung up the wrap and put the basket away. "Don't keep us in suspense. What is it?"

John looked at the kitchen clock again. "You'll have to wait a few more minutes." The bell over the tavern's front door rang. "There he is!" John jumped up, rubbing his hands together.

"Good morning everyone," Arnold said, as he walked into the kitchen with a generous grin and tipped his cap.

"Arnold is the surprise?" The older woman rolled her eyes. Ann laughed.

"And it's lovely to see you too, Mrs. Beaumont."

John frowned with impatience and turned to Arnold. "How are we doing on time?"

Arnold pulled out a pocket watch. "Five more minutes. Ten at most."

"Good." John looked at the two women. "Well, come on! Do you want to see or not?"

The men walked out of the kitchen. Ann looked at Mrs. Beaumont bewildered and followed.

Instead of walking into the tavern, John turned sharply to the right and led them down the hallway toward the carriage house door. For as long as Ann had lived at Siren's Cove, the door was always bolted and locked, but now she saw the padlock had been removed. John opened the door and passed through without pausing. Arnold, Mrs. Beaumont, and Ann trooped through after him.

Ann walked down the wooden steps into the three-story carriage house. The structure was empty except for a few broken wooden crates pushed up against the walls. Deep scratches in the wood floor wrote a history of hard use. Enormous rafters crisscrossed overhead, and dust danced and floated in the shafts of light pouring through the tall glass block windows. Paint peeled from the walls, and years of dirt and grime covered the windows and floor.

John and Arnold stood in the middle of the empty room beaming at Ann and Mrs. Beaumont, clearly loving the confused looks on their faces.

John spread his arms wide. "What do you think?"

Ann wrinkled her nose and watched a particularly large spider scurry under an old crate.

"Very dirty." Ann lifted the hem of her skirt to keep it clear of the floor.

John chuckled. "Come on. I need you to think bigger than that."

"If you think we're going to clean this place up, you're crazy," Mrs. Beaumont said, hands on her hips.

Arnold scratched the side of his head. "They really don't

have any vision, do they?"

Ann scowled. Mrs. Beaumont opened her mouth to object, but Arnold was saved from the verbal assault by a loud pounding coming from the double doors at the opposite end of the carriage house. Ann and Mrs. Beaumont watched as the men unlatched the doors and slid them apart.

Five copper blurs zoomed between the doors, clicking wildly and flying in all directions. Mrs. Beaumont shrieked and ran for cover. Ann dodged as one came dangerously close to brushing the side of her head. The strange objects whizzed past them, circled and landed, attaching themselves to the walls and windows.

One of the objects landed on a nearby windowpane. Ann stepped closer for a better look. An enormous copper beetle the size of one of Mrs. Beaumont's saucepans chirped and buzzed. Sunlight reflected on its rosy metal body as it flicked and folded its wings. A single, yellow-domed sensor rotated back and forth where the beetle's head should have been and blinked as if examining its new surroundings. After a few seconds, the beetle lowered itself onto the glass and glided down the window, humming in a high-pitched key as it went. In its wake, the glass shone spotlessly clean. Ann looked around astonished. The other beetles did the same—some cleaned the walls while others polished the windows—filling the warehouse with a melodious hum.

Recovered from her fright, Mrs. Beaumont stood breathless next to Ann and watched the beetles work.

"You bought mini-bots?"

"The captain didn't buy them," Arnold said. "He rented them for the cleanup and renovation. More cost-effective that way. Our plan is to get things up and running as quickly as possible. The mini-bots are a one-time business expense."

The humming grew louder and deeper as two bots, the size of John's leather footstool, lumbered through the open warehouse doors and began a meticulous route of the floor, sweeping it clean.

"What renovation? What business?" Mrs. Beaumont's voice

jumped an octave and sounded as if she was about to pop a button.

"My new winery."

Ann looked to John who stood near the double doors at the opposite end of the warehouse. He finished scrawling his signature on a digital pad and handed it to a workman in blue overalls.

"I'm expanding my wine business," John said. "Arnold finally talked me into it. I wanted to see if I could really make a go of it." Mrs. Beaumont had asked the question, but it felt to Ann as if John spoke directly to her.

Ann looked past the double doors into the yard and saw more workmen outside unloading crates from a flatbed carrier. A steel tank, as tall as a house, gleamed in the sun. It lay on the carrier next to the other cargo. So that was the big surprise. She looked back to John, and he gave her a sheepish grin.

"But Captain, what about Siren's Cove?" There was no hiding the worry on Mrs. Beaumont's face.

"Nothing will change," John said. "I can work in the winery during the day when I'm not busy with the tavern."

"But how will you possibly have time to do both? There's more to a wine business than just making wine."

"The captain will make the wine and I'll handle distribution," Arnold said. "I have contacts through my import-export business and I can work on commission."

Mrs. Beaumont looked doubtful.

"We've figured it all out," John said. "The winery will be fitted for a one-man operation, and I have a few ideas to help keep things on an even keel with the tavern while I'm busy with the winery."

Mrs. Beaumont sighed. "All right then. I'll leave you and the workmen to it. Ann, I'll need you in a few minutes to help make pies." She shook her head as she walked back to the kitchen.

Ann stayed out of the way of the bots as they completed a slow circuit of the floor and watched as teams of workmen pushed and maneuvered the crates using anti-grav clamps. The crates hovered a few inches off the ground and moved through the air as if sliding on ice. The workmen moved the crates to where the bots had already cleaned and released the clamps, setting the cargo down hard. Arnold hurried over to talk to the workmen.

John stepped behind Ann and wrapped his arms around her waist.

"What do you think? Am I crazy?"

Ann leaned back into John and placed her hands on top of his. "Yes, but I like your crazy."

"It will take time to get the first full batch going," John said. "And then to build up a decent business."

Ann turned to look at John. Black bangs fell low on his forehead. A question lingered in his eyes. John wanted her approval. Ann blinked in surprise. The winery wasn't just a selfish whim. He was doing it for her—for both of them. Ann had wondered if John's affection for her was another one of his passing moods, but now she saw his sincerity. Ann fought against her feelings. She had not expected this. And yet... Ann's heart ignored the caution in her head and swelled with happiness. She thought again of the nightmare, but standing there wrapped in John's strong arms, her fears felt small and so very far away.

"We have time enough," Ann said with a smile.

***

The labels had barely dried on the wine bottles when John carried the crate into the tavern. The bar erupted into catcalls and whistles. Arnold, Ross, Duncan, Mike, Oz, Gil, and Rennie clustered around their usual spot and pounded empty glasses on the bar's wooden top. John cringed. They were his friends, but they were also his toughest customers. He'd know soon enough if the wine was a bust. John's lungs felt as if someone had shoved him in an airlock and opened the hatch.

Ann finished serving a table. She walked to the front of the bar and took a seat when Oz gallantly offered one of the high stools. John set the wine crate behind the bar and pulled out a bottle amid 'ooohs' and 'ahs.'

"I've never seen anything so beautiful in all my life," Duncan said and pretended to mop his eyes with John's bar towel. The men laughed.

"Quit messin' around," Arnold said. "This is serious!"

"Come on! We're thirsty," Ross said.

John pulled the cork and the men shoved glasses forward, each clambering to be first.

"Hold it!" John pulled the bottle back. "You're not here to get drunk. You're here to taste and give me your honest opinion. This is my business we're talking about. I need to know if I got it right. Can you do that?"

"We're just jokin' with you," Gil said. "You can count on us." The men nodded.

John eyed them silently for a moment. "All right then. Put your glasses down."

John filled Ann's tumbler first then the others before pouring his own. The wine glowed like a red jewel. The men waited and held their glasses up for a toast. John racked his brain, trying to think of something appropriate for the occasion, but nothing came to mind. He looked to Ann and she came to his rescue.

"Fair winds?"

John smiled and raised his glass.

"Fair winds!"

John closed his eyes and took a sip. He rolled the wine over his tongue, releasing the sweet taste of ripe berries before he swallowed. It smoldered down the back of his throat—a good burn—before the familiar vapors caressed his senses. He opened his eyes. The others finished drinking and looked around at each other. John frowned. He thought the wine was good. Why did they all look so indifferent? John cleared his throat and set his glass down on the bar.

"So...how was it?"

The men shuffled their feet and wouldn't meet his eye. John didn't understand it. He looked at Ann.

"Very good, I thought," she said and looked across the bar at the men, confused.

John picked up his glass to take another sip and saw Arnold and Duncan break into wicked grins. The men burst out laughing. Arnold reached across the bar and slapped John on the back.

"I think you have a winner!"

"Just for that, I shouldn't give you any more," John said with a grin.

The men groaned and pleaded until John finally gave in with a laugh and refilled their glasses. John took Ann's hand as he poured another drink. She beamed at him, and John felt as if the wine's vapors flooded his brain once more.

\*\*\*

Ann wandered off into the crowd balancing a tray of wine samples on a shoulder. John finished pulling a pint for a customer and looked up in time to see Dr. Brainard trying to excuse his way past the dancers to get to the bar. Every time the doctor tried to move forward another couple twirled in front of him blocking his path. John could see the scowl on the doctor's face from across the room. He gave Arnold a nudge, interrupting his conversation with Mike.

"I think Dr. Brainard could use a hand," John said, and gestured to the dance floor.

"Huh? We can fix that. Come on, Mike."

The two men waded into the dancers, parting them as easily as wheat stalks. They each took one of the doctor's arms and escorted him to the bar, plopping him down on one of the stools.

"Good to see you, doc. Have a drink with us!" Mike said and clapped Dr. Brainard hard on the shoulder, almost knocking his glasses off his face. The doctor continued to scowl as he adjusted his glasses and smoothed his wrinkled jacket. John poured him a glass of wine.

"Might as well," Dr. Brainard said, picking up the glass. "So, this is what my good advice led to?" He gave John a reproachful look and took a sip.

John ignored the look and picked up a towel to wipe down the bar. He knew the doctor wouldn't be happy with his decision, but he hadn't guessed he would be this angry. Arnold turned to Dr. Brainard in surprise.

"So it was you? I wondered what changed John's mind. I've been trying to get him to open a winery for years."

"It would seem so, although a winery wasn't really my intention," Dr. Brainard said. "I merely suggested he needed to think about his future."

"No worries there, doc," Arnold said. "With as good as this first batch came out, I think he has a very bright future ahead of him."

John saw how his friend's optimism had the opposite effect on Dr. Brainard. The doctor's face sagged into a deeper frown the more Arnold talked.

"Arnold, would you mind getting me another crate from the winery? I'm running low back here."

"Sure. I'll be back in a few."

Arnold disappeared into the crowd. Dr. Brainard sipped his wine and continued to frown. John broke the silence.

"I'm moving forward," he said. "It's what you wanted, isn't it?"

The doctor put his glass down and leaned across the bar.

"You know what I meant." Dr. Brainard whispered, "You're playing a dangerous game. You've been lucky so far, but if you don't go to Andarria and they come looking for you what then? What will you tell Ann?"

John glanced down the bar. Mike had wandered off to talk to Gil and Rennie. The old friends were too busy to pay any attention, and the noise from the band gave them cover. John picked up a few empty glasses from the end of the bar.

"They won't come," John said. "I have to contact them. Those are the rules." He put the dirty glasses on the pushcart and went back to wiping the bar.

"So you're okay with living this fantasy you've created and lying to Ann? She deserves better. You need to go back to Andarria. She deserves the truth!"

John felt his anger begin to burn as he stared into the doctor's face.

"The truth?" John barked out a laugh. He leaned across the bar until he was inches from the doctor.

"I was court-martialed. Humiliated." John felt his voice begin to shake as anger boiled away all sense of caution. "I left my home. I became something I wasn't. They hunted me just like the rest of the thieves and murderers. I stayed here year after year and when it was finally time to go home, it was too late!"

John felt his throat tighten around Bonnie's memory. He broke away from Dr. Brainard's gaze and wiped his brow. He glanced toward the other end of the bar. Gil and Rennie were laughing at some barroom antics. A few other customers milled about, but everyone was either too preoccupied with their own conversations, or too drunk to notice the outburst.

John took a deep breath. He turned back to the doctor and lowered his voice. "I gave up everything for them. I did my job. I've kept my oath." John grabbed the wine bottle sitting on the bar and put it in front of the doctor. "I did this for Ann," John said. "Andarria doesn't matter anymore. We can have a perfectly good life here. I don't need to go back. Why should it matter to you?"

Dr. Brainard's eyes flashed. The color slowly rose to his face. He pointed an accusing finger into John's chest.

"The truth still matters. You're lying to yourself and to her. And the longer you continue with the lie the harder it will be to find your way back. You of all people should know that by now."

Dr. Brainard took a swig of wine, draining his glass. John knew exactly when the vapors hit him from the spasm that exploded under the doctor's right eye. Dr. Brainard grimaced and tried to catch his breath, eyes squeezed tight. John poured the doctor a glass of water and set it on the bar. The doctor picked up the glass, took several deep swallows, and set the glass down hard.

"Damn you, Galeas!"

Dr. Brainard wiped his mouth. He pulled a few bills from a pocket, turned and strode back through the crowd.

John snatched up the water glass and slammed it onto the pushcart. The glass split on impact. John swore as a shard of glass sliced open his palm.

\*\*\*

"Come, Rennie. Closing time."

John wiped the bar and watched as Ann tried to coax the old cavalier off his barstool. Most of the tavern's customers had already meandered out into the night. Everyone who tasted John's wine said it was just as good or better than his old wine. He even sold ten bottles—the most ever in a single evening. Arnold was ecstatic.

"Once word gets out, you'll be selling wine as fast as you can make it," Arnold said as he stumbled out the door. "Make sure you save one of those bottles from the first run. It'll be a collector's item someday!"

John grinned at the thought. Arnold had the head of a businessman and the heart of a preacher, converting the doubtful one business opportunity at a time.

John picked up an empty wine bottle with his bandaged hand and winced. The cut on the palm wasn't deep, but it still nagged him all evening. He changed hands and grumbled to himself as he finished stowing the empty bottles in the collection bin under the bar. Dr. Brainard didn't know what he was talking about. John could go to Andarria but then what? If it meant giving up Siren's Cove, he already knew his answer would be no.

Rennie remained stubbornly on his stool and stared at Ann through watery eyes. His gray hair was as rumpled as his tattered brown jacket.

"The misses has a terruble, terruble temper," Rennie said, shaking his head. "You don't know her."

Ann smiled and patted the old man's arm. John put down his rag to give her a hand. He looped an arm around Rennie to help him off the stool.

"I know her and I know she'll be worried sick if you don't go home," John said. "I'm sure she's forgiven you by now." John turned to Ann. "I've got him. Tell Mrs. Beaumont to start the tea and I'll be there in a minute."

Ann nodded and left for the kitchen. John couldn't wait to see the look on Mrs. Beaumont's face when she finally admitted maybe the winery wasn't such a bad idea after all.

"You there," John called to a young couple heading to the front door. "Are you walking past Hillside? Would you mind letting him walk with you? He'll be fine the rest of the way." The couple nodded and took Rennie between them as they stepped out into the night.

John hurried back behind the bar. He'd left his data link pad under the counter. As he bent down, he saw a crate of wine sitting on the floor. Maybe he would save one. John pulled out a bottle and put it in a place of honor on the shelf behind the bar. His wine looked good with the other high-end liquor. The bell above the tavern door jingled and John cursed himself for forgetting to lock it.

"Sorry, we're closed," he called out and straightened a few bottles on the shelf.

"Captain John Galeas?"

John's back stiffened. The tenor of the man's voice made him uneasy. He turned. Two strangers walked toward the bar. The man was tall and thin. Bony wrists protruded from the sleeves of a dark suit jacket. A white pocket square peeked out from a breast pocket. The woman wore large, wraparound glasses, the lenses tinted a golden yellow, and a short pea green jacket. The yellow and green combination of the woman's outfit reminded John unpleasantly of the three weeks he'd spent in sickbay with Titovian pox.

"Yeah, I'm Galeas and we're still closed," John said, glaring at the off tourists. Neither shied away.

"I'm Agent Drake," the man said. "And this is my partner, Agent Knox. We're with the Andarrian Ministry of Investigations. We'd like a few moments of your time."

John kept a steady bead on the two agents, face stony. He thought of the ion rifle under the bar, but experience told him to wait.

"What do you want?"

"Is there someplace we can sit and talk?"

"Come back tomorrow," John said and headed toward the kitchen.

Agent Knox stepped in front of him. She pulled her jacket open to show a black and steel laser pistol strapped to her side.

"We can either sit and talk, or you'll have to come with us."

# FOURTEEN

## *KNOX AND DRAKE*

John looked at Agent Knox without flinching, while his heart skipped into double time. The agents had called his bluff. John hoped he could talk his way around whatever they came to talk to him about. Luck came in limited quantities and he had already used up a fair share over his lifetime.

"Fine. We can talk here." He pointed to a table.

The agents held their ground.

"We would also like to speak to your kitchen staff," Drake said. "Do you have a Miss Ann working for you?"

John's insides winced. *Why would they want to talk to Ann?* One fear was suddenly replaced by another.

John walked into the kitchen with the agents close behind. Mrs. Beaumont and Ann looked up. Their smiles faded when they saw the unexpected company.

"We're needed in the sitting room," John said to Ann.

Ann gave him a searching look. John ran a hand through his hair and shook his head. She glanced at the two agents behind him and disappeared into the sitting room.

Mrs. Beaumont's gaze bounced from the captain to the two agents and back again. "What's wrong? What's all this?"

Drake pulled a data pad from a pocket and looked at the screen. "Just an inquiry. You are Mrs. Claire Beaumont?"

The cook drew up stiffly. Her mouth pinched. "Yes."

The agent dismissed her with a wave of a hand. "You're free to go. This doesn't concern you."

John stopped the cook before she could unsheathe her sharp tongue. "Go home. We'll see you in the morning."

Mrs. Beaumont's glare scorched the air surrounding the agents, but for once she didn't argue. She grabbed her things and left through the kitchen door.

\*\*\*

Ann sat in the chair in front of the bookcase. Anxiety knotted her insides. *Who are these people?* John took a seat in his leather chair but said nothing, his face grim.

The woman made herself comfortable on the settee, crossing her legs. Chin-length strawberry-blond hair swung free and curled under at the ends.

The man sat next to her, perched on the edge of the seat cushion in his inky black suit. The skin stretched over the bridge of his large nose looked paper thin. Ann's muscles tensed as she remembered the black suit worn by the man in her nightmare.

"I'm sorry for the late-night call, Captain Galeas." The man's words sounded friendly enough, but his voice was as cold as a corpse. The stranger turned to Ann and gave a tight, humorless smile. "You are Ann, correct?"

Ann glanced to John, but he stared straight ahead. She could see the muscles working in his jaw. She narrowed her eyes at the man and nodded. The stranger looked down at the data link pad in his hands. His fingertips flew over the screen. He didn't look at Ann again until he finished.

"My name is Agent Evan Drake and this is Agent Fionna Knox. We've come all the way from Andarria to follow up on some leads on a case. We hope you and Captain Galeas might be able to answer a few questions."

Ann's chest felt tight. She couldn't tear her eyes away from the two agents. She swallowed hard and nodded.

"Six months ago, a test flight was conducted for a new spaceship, the *Kairos*. The test was performed on the far side of

Andarria's moon, but something went wrong. The *Kairos* was destroyed, and the pilot was presumed killed. I have a picture of the pilot." Drake handed the data pad to John.

John's mouth jerked. The color drained from his face. He closed his eyes for an instant before handing Ann the device. Ann looked at the picture on the screen. Her hands shook as if a knife had sliced open her heart.

Ann stared at herself in a picture she couldn't remember being taken, wearing a uniform she didn't recognize. The woman had her face, her eyes, her smile. She even wore her braid the same way. Ann tried to swallow the queasy feeling rising from her stomach.

"Is there any chance this could be a mistake?" John said, his voice thick.

"I know this must come as an incredible shock," Agent Knox said. "But we are certain Ann is the missing pilot, Lieutenant Anaya Chapman."

Ann's eyes darted to the other agent. She thought when she heard her real name for the first time it would speak to her, that she would know it instinctively, but this name sounded hollow. Agent Knox looked at Ann through her yellow-tinted glasses with a note of concern.

Ann looked away. She didn't want sympathy from a stranger. She collected her thoughts and turned to Agent Drake. "How?" Ann's hand shook as she handed back the data pad.

"At this point, we are not entirely sure what caused the initial explosion," Drake said, scrolling through a few screens. "The flight went as scheduled on the twenty-sixth and everything looked fine right up until the accident."

"That can't be right," John said. "We found Ann six months ago on the twelfth."

Ann's heart leapt. She was already on the Colonies two weeks before the test flight even took place. She couldn't be the woman in the picture no matter how much they looked alike.

Agent Drake held up a hand. "Let me explain. The *Kairos*

was the prototype for a new time ship. Andarrian Special Forces was testing a new time coil design. When the ship exploded, we thought it had been completely destroyed, but we were wrong. Half of the ship along with the cockpit time jumped at the moment of the explosion, creating a second crash site."

Ann heard the agent's words but couldn't wrap her mind around what Drake was saying. *Time travel?* He couldn't be serious. "Not possible."

"Yes, it is," John said with a sigh. "That's what Special Forces does. For them, it's as easy as skipping a stone across water."

"No. It's a mistake. It can't be," Ann said. It was all too incredible to believe.

Agent Drake frowned. His black eyes narrowed. "The Ministry of Investigations doesn't make mistakes." He flipped to a new screen on the data pad and read from the notes. "You have complete memory and identity loss, disrupted speech patterns, and you used to suffer from frequent headaches and vertigo. Six months ago, on the twenty-sixth, exactly fourteen days after you were found, your headaches and vertigo increased. At approximately seventeen hundred hours Colony time, you experienced an event involving nausea, migraine, loss of motor control, seizure and or temporary paralysis. You lost consciousness and afterward exhibited a gradual return to a more normal speech pattern as your headaches and vertigo decreased." Drake looked up at Ann as if daring her to contradict him again. "These are all symptoms of anachronosis, or time sickness, a common brain injury among people who have experienced a traumatic time-teleportation event."

Thoughts raced through Ann's head. Her memories of the accident. The sound from her dream. The clues finally fit, and try as she might, she couldn't find fault in the agent's logic.

John turned on Drake, anger coloring his face.

"If you KNEW all this, then what took you so long? She's been here SIX MONTHS and you just now show up?"

Drake opened his mouth to respond, but Agent Knox cut him off.

"I'm afraid that is a complicated answer," Knox said, looking to Ann. "It wasn't until the discovery of the second crash site two months ago that we had any hope you were still alive. Our computer models showed the possibility of a second time jump, so we started looking for your time signature to see if we could track you and bring you home, but no one knew how the new time coil design would react in a crash. There was no way to know where or when you would turn up. Our big break came when we found the query on the Colonies' data network."

"The time rift transported you a total distance of ninety-seven million kilometers," Agent Drake said, reading from his data pad again. "You reappeared exactly fourteen days, six hours, twenty-three minutes, and forty-two seconds prior to the first explosion."

"It may seem like a long way, but in time travel terms you barely moved an inch from where you started," Knox said. "You reappeared in your own timeline so close to the initial jump your time signature was hidden. We weren't one-hundred percent sure who you were until we saw you standing in the kitchen a few minutes ago." Knox shook her head. "All the advanced technology trying to track you, and it came down to good, old-fashioned detective work."

Ann sat in stunned silence. The walls of the sitting room pressed in. Ann swallowed hard. Her head reeled but she knew the agents spoke the truth.

"It's all right," John said. His voice rumbled in his chest. "We've wondered for a long time and now we know."

Agent Drake looked at his watch and stood.

"We have a ship waiting for us back at the shuttleport. Thank you, Captain, for your hospitality. Lieutenant Chapman, you'll need to come with us. We can send for your things later."

"Wait just a minute," John said. "Where are you taking her?"

"Back to Andarria. She needs therapy to restore her memory and identity."

The agent's words snapped Ann's thoughts back into focus. "No."

"Lieutenant Chapman, this isn't open for debate," Agent Drake snapped. The name made Ann cringe. "We have orders to bring you back to Andarria. There are still questions about the crash only you can answer. If you don't come willingly, it could mean a court-martial."

Anger flared in Ann's chest. She didn't care what Drake said. For six months, she had lived at Siren's Cove and no one had come. No word of any kind. And now based on the word of two strangers she was expected to follow their orders and leave the only place she remembered and the only people she trusted?

"No." Ann stood and faced down the agent, hands clenched at her side. "I'm staying here!"

"Is that what you want me to tell your family?"

Ann eyed Agent Knox still sitting on the settee.

"You have a brother. He's your only living relative. He was devastated when he thought you died," Knox said. "Do you really want me to tell him you would rather face a court-martial than come home? That you don't want to see him?"

Ann stared at the agent and felt her anger waver. *I have a brother...*

"Does she have to go back to Andarria for the memory therapy?" John stepped between her and the agents. "Couldn't it be done here?"

Ann stared at John in disbelief. His eyes met hers. "You have family. You owe it to your brother."

Agent Knox thought for a moment and turned to Drake. "The therapy is most effective when the subject is relaxed and in comfortable surroundings."

"Those are not our orders," Drake said, shaking his head. "We were told to confirm her identity and take her back to Andarria."

"That's true, and we have confirmed her identity, but she is not willing to accept it yet," Knox said. "I think it would do more harm long-term if we forced her to return to Andarria."

"Fine!" Drake sneered as he straightened his jacket and glared at Knox. "You stay here and file the report for the change in orders, explaining to Montressador Chapman why his sister won't be returning home. I'm taking the shuttle back to Andarria."

# FIFTEEN

## *THE MONTRESSADOR*

Montressador Sean Chapman ignored the stares of the other travelers as he walked through the Llewelyn shuttleport terminal. A clipped beard accentuated a square jaw and pointed nose. A large sword hung at his side. Andarria hadn't been ruled by a monarchy in two thousand years, but tradition demanded the King's Champion carry a sword at all times so Sean bowed to the custom.

The automated luggage carrier scuttled along behind as Sean watched the video feed on a data link pad. The picture was fuzzy, but the audio was clear. His assistant, Josephine, ran through the daily messages and reminders.

"Minister Pollux called again. I told him you were out of the office, but he is becoming quite insistent," she said, pursing red lips and running a hand down a list just below the viewscreen. "Your report on new recruit selection is now three days past due. I don't think I can keep the committee at bay much longer. You have an invitation to Ambassador Aldebaran's dinner party on the sixteenth, but I wasn't sure when you would be back." The woman paused and looked directly into the viewscreen. A few dark curls escaped a loose bun and framed a round face. "I know it's not really your thing, but you declined last time so you might consider going if only to make an appearance." Josephine turned back to the list. "The usual messages piling up. The rest can wait until you have more time. Hope you had a pleasant flight. Sorry for the recorded message. I couldn't get a direct signal. Let me know when you arrive. Good luck, Montressador!" She signed off with a smile.

The message ended, and the screen asked if Sean wanted to record a video response. The spotty reception between Andarria and the Colonies was legendary. The communication lag was inconvenient, but it wasn't all bad. Jo could use it as an excuse while he was off-world. Sean pressed the reply button without slowing his gait.

"Thanks, Jo. Just landed. Tell the minister I will try to contact him once I'm settled. Send me the file on his nephew. I'm sure that's what he wants to talk to me about," Sean said, rolling his eyes. "My report is mostly finished. I will send it to you later for a quick proof before you forward to the committee. Tell the ambassador yes." Sean paused and gave a playful smirk. "Maybe something else will come up. Thanks for juggling. I'll be in touch."

Sean stopped recording and pressed send. He tucked the data pad in a pocket. Jo was the best assistant—admittedly, the only assistant—he'd ever had. Initially, Sean argued against needing administrative help, but now he wasn't sure he could function without her. It still felt strange. His predecessors fought dragons, assassins, and invading forces. Montressador Chapman fought politicians, diplomats, and military brass— more glorified administrator than defender. The data pad beeped, signaling another incoming message. Sean sighed. How he longed for a dragon.

The terminal doors slid open, and Sean walked from the sterile artificial air of the shuttleport into the warm sunlight. He slowed and took a deep breath, turning toward the sun for a second before walking on. Six months ago, Sean wouldn't have noticed. Three months ago, he wouldn't have cared. Now, on the other side of his grief, he could finally feel the sun and take pleasure from it.

Agent Fionna Knox leaned against a maroon roadster as it idled at the curb. The hover car gleamed, all chrome and fenders. The roadster's convertible top was rolled back for the spring weather. Fionna played the part of tourist, dressed in crop pants and sandals. A peasant blouse showed the paleness of her shoulders. She watched lazily through yellow-tinted glasses as the crowds of shuttleport travelers hurried past. Fionna smiled when she saw the swordsman walking toward her.

Sean grabbed his bag from the luggage carrier and tossed it into the backseat of the car without taking his eyes off Agent Knox.

"Glasses off," he said with a frown and stood at the curb, waiting for her to comply.

Fionna grinned at Sean before lifting her Bio-Vision glasses to reveal stunning violet eyes.

"Touchy. Rough flight, Montressador?" Fionna rested the glasses on the top of her head.

"How else am I supposed to have a conversation with you without thinking you're psychoanalyzing me the entire time?"

Sean opened the passenger door and climbed in. Fionna chuckled and walked around to the driver's side. She slid easily into the bucket seat and put the car in gear.

The roadster's engine hummed as the car glided down the winding country road past fields and orchards. The air smelled of freshly turned soil and tender shoots. The sunlight splashed on the meadows and every flower sparkled with the newness of an early spring.

Sean Chapman had lived without hope since the accident. He had cut optimism from his body like a cancer, purged himself of it so completely that even now after reading Agent Knox's report he couldn't believe his sister, Anaya, was alive. Not only alive but also living with an expatriate on the Colonies and working as a kitchen girl. It reminded Sean of a quote from one of his favorite Earth authors. 'While many things are too strange to be believed, nothing is too strange to have happened.' Sean then thought of another old Earth saying, 'There's a sucker born every minute.'

"Who is this Galeas? What does he want? Could this all be a big con?"

Fionna glanced at the swordsman from the driver's seat. "Everything checks out. No one had any idea who she was until we showed up. The tests confirm she really is Anaya," she said. "I did a Level One background check on Captain Galeas. The only item of interest was four years of military service in the National Air Guard. His term was cut short when he was given dishonorable discharge."

"What for?"

"Drunk and disorderly and striking an officer," Fionna said. "Galeas was court-martialed and served six months. Shortly after that, he moved to the Colonies with his wife and opened a tavern."

Sean grunted acknowledgement. "You said he was widowed. What happened to the wife?"

"Complications due to Procyon Fever."

"Anything else?"

Agent Knox stiffened. "Montressador, are you asking the Ministry to perform a Level Two background check?"

Sean studied the side mirror as Fionna took the roadster through a sweeping curve. A preliminary background check would only cover time spent living on Andarria or the Colonies. A Level Two report would include any time spent outside of Andarrian territory. Certainly more thorough, but there could be political blowback if it was ever made public that he had used a governmental investigative agency for what could be viewed as a purely personal matter. Not to mention a guaranteed tongue lashing, and worse if his sister found out about his snooping, assuming Anaya ever remembered who he was.

"Any evidence Captain Galeas traveled outside of Andarrian territory after his discharge?"

Fionna shook her head. "No."

"Then I guess not," Sean said with a sigh. "What about Anaya? Does she remember anything about what happened or who she is?"

"A few disjointed memories, but not much. She's a good candidate for therapy, but she's still refusing treatment. I'm hoping Anaya might change her mind after meeting you."

Fionna changed lanes to pass a delivery van. Sean admired the quaint cottages and sprawling estates as they rolled past. Every so often he saw houses with wash lines strung through the backyards. Clothing and household linens floated in the breeze like strange, multicolored garlands.

A man riding a chestnut horse in the field next to the road tipped his hat as the car approached. Fionna lifted a hand from the steering wheel in salute as they passed. Behind the man, two laughing children rode a squat, spotted pony with a bristled mane. As Sean looked closer, he saw a padded safety bar bolted to the pony's metal withers. The youngest child sat in front and clutched the bar with chubby hands. An older sibling sat behind and helped the child balance. The pony's smooth, high-stepping, hydraulic action barely jostled its riders. The two children shouted greetings and waved enthusiastically. Sean couldn't help but turn in his seat and wave back. He had read about the Colonies but had never visited. Sean smiled to himself as he felt the pull of its charms.

"Galeas loves her," Fionna said, spoiling Sean's daydream. "and Anaya is in love with him."

Sean turned to face forward, a small pinch between his brows. He rested a hand on the hilt of the sword next to him.

"That could be a problem," he said. Sean thought briefly of the message he needed to write. He'd been looking forward to sending it, until now.

"These things usually work themselves out on their own," Fionna said.

The roadster crested a hill, and Sean looked down across the town to the shimmering, blue harbor below. He could smell the salt in the ocean breeze. White sea birds drifted in the air currents above and called to each other. Between the peaked brown- and red-roofed houses, Sean saw more wash lines dotted with laundry.

"I thought they had a power grid here," Sean said. "Why are they drying their laundry outside?"

"They have a power grid," Fionna said. "and all the houses you see probably have a perfectly modern laundry facility inside, but it's a beautiful day."

Sean cocked an eyebrow and turned to the agent, perplexed. He failed to see the connection. Agent Knox gave him a smile as peaceful as unbroken water.

"They're a little different here."

The country roads blended into cobblestone streets and the tidy houses grew more tightly packed together. Fionna steered the roadster past an odd assortment of horse-drawn wagons, tour busses, and other hovercraft until finally slowing in front of an old tavern.

The wooden sign hanging above the door showed a picture of a bare-breasted mermaid with tangles of flowing red hair. She welcomed patrons to Siren's Cove with a coy smile. Agent Knox turned down the rutted drive next to the tavern and parked the roadster in front of the stoop behind a battered flatbed truck. Sean climbed out of the roadster and eyed the other vehicle. A combustion engine? The rattletrap looked like it violated a half a dozen safety laws just sitting in the drive.

Sean turned his attention to the tavern. Nothing distinguished Siren's Cove from the other houses and businesses except for the sign out front. He looked at the windows and imagined his sister peeking unseen from behind the curtains. Sean's heart shuddered and he brushed the feeling aside.

He followed Agent Knox up the wooden steps and knocked on the large, polished wooden door. A face appeared for an instant through the beveled glass and the door flung open wide. An older woman with cropped white hair looked at them with a startled expression.

"Agent Knox, you're here already? Come in! Come in!" She stepped back to let them into the sitting room. The woman kept wiping her palms on her skirt as if unsure of what to do with her hands. "You don't have to knock, dear. You're welcomed any time."

"Thank you. That's very kind," Fionna said. "Mrs. Beaumont, I would like you to meet Montressador Sean Chapman."

"It's very nice to meet you," Sean said and gave a small bow.

Mrs. Beaumont's eyes flicked to the sword hanging at his side. The older woman drew herself up stiffly.

"Montressador Chapman, with all due respect, I hope your plan is not to simply swoop in and take Ann away. We have all grown very fond of her."

Sean's eyes widened briefly. The grandmotherly woman stood in front of him with all the strength of a corsair. He offered a diplomatic smile rather than strike his colors.

"I assure you that is not my intention," he said. "There are questions that only Anaya can answer, and it is her responsibility to address them, but after that, it is her decision whether or not she returns to Andarria." Sean took Mrs. Beaumont's hand with chivalrous concern. "I hope if my sister does choose to stay on the Colonies, I might be allowed to visit from time to time."

Mrs. Beaumont's features softened into a blush. "Oh, well, of course." She quickly withdrew her hand. "It's an honor to have you here, Montressador."

Agent Knox peered past Mrs. Beaumont into the kitchen. "Is Captain Galeas home?"

"Yes, the captain and Ann…" she glanced to Sean. "…I mean…Anaya…are in the courtyard. You can go out the kitchen door. I was on my way to the market, but I could get you something before I leave?"

"We'll be fine," Fionna said. "Don't let us keep you."

"All right, as long as you're sure," Mrs. Beaumont said as she grabbed a basket from the table. "Help yourselves to anything in the kitchen. I won't be gone long."

Sean opened the door and stepped aside to let the older woman pass.

"It was nice meeting you. I'll see you when you get back."

Mrs. Beaumont blushed again and tittered a quick thank you as she left.

"You're not what she expected, Montressador," Fionna said with an amused smirk. "And she likes you. No wonder the tabloids crowned you one of Andarria's most eligible bachelors."

Sean looked at Agent Knox, doubtful. "If manners make me a ladies' man, then that is a very sad commentary on society."

"Manners? Is that what that was when you barked at me to take off my glasses?"

"You're a special case," Sean said, eyeing the agent. "But since I offended you, a pox on me and may an Uwibami piss on my grave." He finished with a dramatic bow.

Fionna regarded him as a smile playfully curled the corner of her mouth.

"I believe flowers are a more traditional apology, but the Uwibami was a nice touch." She turned and walked toward the kitchen. "Apology accepted."

Sean grinned and followed Fionna. She was almost to the kitchen door when Sean rested a hand on her shoulder.

"Wait, not yet."

Sean suddenly couldn't shake the feeling that maybe Agent Knox was wrong. What if he had traveled to the Colonies for nothing? He peered out the window above the kitchen sink. The vantage point gave a clear view of the courtyard and garden outside.

Like so many of the other houses in town, Siren's Cove had strung a wash line. Clean white sheets drifted in the breeze. At first, that was all Sean could see. Then as the breeze lifted the sheets, a pair of woman's shoes came into view. He could not see the woman's face, only her silhouette as she moved behind the sheets. Sean caught a glimpse of a long brown skirt, then briefly the back of her head. The young woman turned and walked back toward the house, and in that second Sean's breath stopped. His heart shouted for joy and he was forced to blink back tears. Sean dropped his head and steadied himself on the counter. When he could finally draw breath, he exhaled what felt like the weight of a thousand years. Sean saw Fionna watching him. He wiped his eyes with the back of a sleeve.

"Are you ready to talk to her?"

The agent's voice was a comfort. Sean swallowed hard and nodded.

"What do I say? How much do I tell her if she asks me?"

"Try not to share too much," Fionna said. "It's better if Anaya remembers on her own."

"But the memory therapy…she will remember everything? Everyone from her past?"

"Yes, in time." Agent Knox looked at Sean and smiled. "I told you these things work themselves out. You worry too much."

A bare patch of ground enclosed the courtyard at the far end, staked and ready for planting. Behind the garden, a fence with a small gate opened to the road. A broad-shouldered man sat on a bench under the budding shade trees and stared intently at a data link pad. He looked up and stood when he heard Agent Knox and the Montressador approach.

"Good morning, Captain Galeas," Fionna said. "Mrs. Beaumont told us we'd find you out here."

"And so you have." The captain stowed the data pad in a pocket. His eyes focused on Sean.

"This is Montressador Sean Chapman," Fionna said.

Sean stepped forward. "It's nice to finally meet you, Captain Galeas. I owe you a huge debt. Thank you for everything you've done."

The captain tossed a token smile and looked at him as if examining an interesting pebble he'd found in the road. Sean kept his gaze steady. If the man wanted to intimidate him, he'd have to do better than a stare down.

"It seemed like the right thing to do," Galeas said, his face a mask of indifference.

Anaya ignored their arrival and continued hanging sheets at the other end of the courtyard. Sean thought it strange to see his sister dressed as a Colonist. The last time he saw her she wore a black flight suit.

Fionna watched Anaya hanging sheets. "How is she this morning?"

"The same." Captain Galeas looked to Montressador Chapman. "I hope you weren't expecting a warm welcome." He turned and called to her. "Ann, your brother's here."

Anaya put the basket down and walked toward them. She stood next to Galeas, shoulders squared and her mouth set. When the captain looked at her, Sean saw his mask slip and the warmth from the man's eyes shone through. Chalk up another point for Fionna, not that Sean was keeping score.

The breeze had loosened Anaya's hair from its tidy braid. Fine strands played about her face, catching the light and creating a fiery aura. She met Sean's gaze with defiance as if daring him to say or do the wrong thing. Sean wanted to wrap his sister in a bear hug, but the look she gave him was as welcoming as razor wire and just as impenetrable.

"Hello, Anaya," Sean said, his voice barely above a whisper. He held out a hand. His mouth felt like he'd eaten a bag of cotton balls.

Sean hoped no one saw how his hand shook and silently begged his sister to take it. He wanted to feel the warmth of Anaya's hand, further proof she wasn't simply a shadow from his imagination. Anaya's eyes narrowed, face darkened.

"My name is Ann."

Strike one.

Sean mentally kicked himself and withdrew his hand with an awkward cough. All right. Ann it is. He regrouped and tried again.

"Happy to see you doesn't even begin to cover it," Sean said with a lopsided grin. He thought for a second and his face brightened. "Rumors of your demise have been greatly exaggerated."

Anaya stared at him in silence, the joke shattered at her feet. The look she gave him reminded Sean of the day she discovered he had used her dollhouse for target practice. That conversation hadn't gone well for him either. Light banter obviously out, Sean decided to play it straight.

"I brought you some clothes from home."

"I am home."

Strike two.

Fionna Knox whispered, "Agent Drake spooked her during our first—"

"Don't speak for me," Ann said, cutting across Fionna.

"Ann!" Captain Galeas fingered the pigtail at the back of his head.

"It's all right," Sean said, trying to loosen the tension coiled around them. "My fault. Agent Drake never should have been assigned to the case." He shot a dark look to Fionna. Drake's involvement in the investigation of his sister's disappearance had always bothered him. Sean turned back to Ann. "I can give you your things whenever you want."

Another few seconds of tension-filled silence passed, then Galeas spoke.

"I have work to do." The captain turned and gave Ann a hard look. "Talk to your brother." He walked off toward the kitchen door.

Ann shot Galeas a look that would have turned him to stone had he looked in her direction.

"I'll see if Mrs. Beaumont is back from the market," Agent Knox said. She hurried after Captain Galeas.

Sean smiled to himself. Cowards. At least he wasn't the only one in trouble. He realized his mistake when Ann caught him smirking. The anger in her eyes burned as bright as a solar flare. Sean cringed.

Strike three.

"Er...so I guess we should..." Sean tried to change the subject, but Ann walked past him toward the wash line before he could finish.

Sean blew out a sigh. Whatever memories his sister had lost, her temper remained. Ann grabbed another wet sheet from the basket and pinned it to the line.

"No one is going to force you to go back to Andarria if you don't want to," he said. "I promise."

"An empty promise," Ann said with a shrug. "I don't know you."

"You're right. I guess a promise wouldn't mean much to you right now." Sean adjusted the weight of the sword on his hip and drummed fingers on the hilt. "I guess I'll just have to tell you about me."

Sean watched Ann out of the corner of an eye. She picked up the basket and moved to another stretch of clothesline by the garden fence.

"Let's see," he said, pacing behind her. "I'm incredibly handsome, but you can already see that. I am extremely generous. I give all my money away to charity." Sean picked up the basket and held it for Ann. She gave him a dark look as she pulled out another sheet. "I rescue orphans from burning buildings. I'm modest. I have a scar on my left bu—"

"What do you want?" Ann snatched the basket from Sean's hands, and dropped it onto the grass.

"I want you to remember who you are. You're the only one I know who understands Earth jokes." Ann's mouth twitched. How could he get through to her? "You are my sister and I want you to be happy."

"I am happy," she snapped, but her anger had lost some of its fury.

Sean sighed and looked across the garden fence to the fields and hills beyond. Spring crept across the landscape. He imagined what it must look like in the full bloom of summer, tall grasses bending in the breeze, rustling with the sound of women's skirts.

"I can understand why. It's beautiful here."

Sean looked at his sister. Ann had gone back to hanging sheets. Anaya was alive and well and stood only a few feet away, and yet it felt to Sean like death still separated them.

"I'm not asking you to give any of this up," Sean said, voice soft. "If you want me to call you Ann, I will. If you want to live here, that's fine. I just want my sister back."

Ann let the sheet drape from her hands. Her eyes quietly examined the swordsman, dissecting every word.

"Our family is gone. We're the last of the unlucky. I want you to remember who you are because..." Sean struggled to explain. "...because without you, nothing holds me to this life." He smiled sadly, surprised by his own words. Sean scratched his beard. "I guess I should add selfish to my list."

Ann looked at him a moment like a judge about to pass sentence. She finally spoke.

"Agent Drake—"

"—is an ass," Sean said cutting her off with a growl. "Don't take anything he says personally. He hates me."

"Why?"

Sean hesitated. Agent Drake had been assigned to the investigation along with several other ministry agents immediately after Anaya's disappearance. Nothing unusual, but from what Fionna had told him, Drake had demanded that he travel with her to the Colonies to help confirm Anaya's identity when reports of a woman matching her description came through the ministry's network. Drake's insistence in involving himself so directly seemed odd to Sean given their mutual dislike for each other. Sean sighed. His personal history with the agent had no bearing here, but perhaps he could use it as a way to build Anaya's trust. He remembered Fionna's instructions about not sharing too much, but in this instance, it was his story to tell so maybe there was no harm in it. Sean shifted his sword and took a seat on an overturned garden bucket, elbows on knees.

"I was a first-year at the Academy," he said, plucking at some new blades of grass. "Drake was a graduate student. At the end of each spring term, students are selected to demonstrate hand-to-hand combat techniques for prospective recruits. It wasn't supposed to be a competition per se, but that's how the students always looked at it. Everything was going fine until I drew Drake's name for the Gladius bout."

Ann paused as she hung another sheet on the line and looked at the swordsman.

"It wasn't dangerous," Sean said. "We used practice swords—not steel." Ann continued pinning sheets. "The bout began, and Drake scored the first few points."

Sean heard Ann chuckle behind a drifting white sheet. He called out, "I was a first-year, remember?" He shook his head. "Anyway, Drake started getting cocky. Showing off for his friends in the stands. I noticed after every point he scored Drake would turn to look at them. That's when I got the idea of how I could beat him."

Sean looked up. Ann had stopped hanging sheets and stood listening intently. It felt strange telling the story knowing she had been there at the time, a precocious twelve-year-old cheering him from the stands.

"I feinted to draw him in and let him strike me for a half point," Sean said. "It seemed like a good idea at the time. I didn't plan for him to break my wrist. When Drake dropped his guard to mug for his friends, I wanted to draw my sword across his middle. A belly slice would have given me enough points to tie, but I was off balance because of my wrist, so I swung with my opposite hand, straight up for a lateral cut. Drake turned back toward me at the last second and stepped into my swing. Instead of his belly, I caught him lower..." Sean coughed into a fist. "...between his legs." Ann cringed. "Drake dropped like a corpse. I was told later there was enough force behind my swing that I shattered his protective cup. That pretty much ended the bout."

"What happened after?"

"I was disqualified for an illegal hit, and Drake was declared the winner. A rumor went around at one point that he had complications from his injury and Drake...er...lost one of his testicles." Sean shrugged and scratched his beard. "I'm sure it's just a rumor, but either way, he still holds a grudge. He went on to accept a position with the Ministry of Investigations, and I was recommended to begin training for the Royal Guard. Turned out they liked my swordsmanship in spite of everything. I completed my training with the Guard and five years later I was appointed Montressador. Now every time Drake sees me," Sean patted the hilt of his sword. "I guess I kind of remind him of...things.

"So you see, Drake doesn't hate you," Sean said, standing and stretching. "He hates me because I humiliated him all those years ago and possibly, unintentionally, altered his anatomy." Sean saw Ann hide a grin behind a handful of clothespins. "What did he say to you?"

Ann's expression turned serious as she let the sheet in her arms fall back into the basket.

"He thinks I know why the crash happened."

Sean raised an eyebrow. "Do you?"

"No, Drake said memory therapy would help."

"He's guessing," Sean said, shaking his head. "You might be able to tell us more about what happened, but no one knows for sure."

"He said court-martial. If I didn't go back to Andarria."

"Let me worry about that," Sean said with a sigh. "I might be able to pull some strings."

Sean watched as Ann turned back to the basket. She looked at the clothespins bunched in her hand.

"Will I still remember Siren's Cove?"

Sean smiled. "The therapy doesn't erase memories—it only helps you remember what's already in your head," he said. "You will still remember everything since the accident."

Ann clipped another sheet to the line. "How long are you staying?"

Sean thought of all the messages piling up for him at the office.

"As long as you want." He'd have hell to pay with Jo. "I promise I won't get in the way."

Ann shrugged and started to reply. Sean waved her off.

"Okay, okay, promises don't mean anything until you know me." He gave Ann a wicked sideways glance. "Do you want to see my scar?"

Ann burst out with a laugh. "No!"

Sean chuckled. How he had missed that sound. Ann leaned against the fence and gave the Montressador a genuine smile.

"How did you get it? Your scar?"

Sean looked at Ann with a wide grin.

"I got it from you."

# SIXTEEN

## *SURFACING*

Montressador Chapman was as good as his word, visiting often without overstaying his welcome. Sean ate at Siren's Cove every day, laughed with the men in the bar, and retired in the evenings to the inn down the road. Ann watched his routine and after a few days agreed to let Sean spend time with her, talking in the kitchen or walking to the market.

The usually busy tavern became even more crowded. Town gossip, which under normal circumstances gurgled as steadily as a creek, nearly burst its banks when the Montressador joined in the after-dinner revelry, and again when he learned a few of the local dance steps. This news delighted scheming mothers with eligible daughters. The latter became permanent fixtures in Siren's Cove, sitting in groups of three or more and giggling behind their hands whenever the swordsman passed.

Not everyone was pleased. Ann noticed John spent as little time as possible around the Montressador, even as he encouraged her to visit with him. The captain was always polite, never growling or argumentative, but still guarded or in a solitary mood when Sean came to see her. When Ann asked John for advice on the matter, he remained noncommittal and told her, "Do whatever you think is best."

As for Ann, at first she doubted whether Montressador

Chapman could be her brother, but as she looked closer she saw the truth in the shape and color of his eyes and the curve of his mouth. Ann heard it in the timbre of Sean's laugh. Even the word 'brother' nudged and tweaked her much in the same way he teased her when he visited. Soon, Ann knew Sean was her brother as certainly as she knew her left from her right even without any tangible memories as proof. This knowing without knowing troubled Ann and would not let her rest until finally she agreed to submit to the memory therapy.

***

"Ow!"

Ann rubbed her arm. She breathed through the steady burn that followed as it traveled the length of her arm like a flash fire. Dr. Brainard sat next to Ann on the settee and helped massage her arm.

"I'm sorry. I wish there was another way, but the injections are the most effective method for strengthening your neural pathways."

Ann nodded and gave the doctor a weak smile. She sighed with relief and leaned back against the cushion as the tongues of fire reached her fingertips and flamed out.

Dr. Brainard made a few quick entries in the digital pad on his lap. He then picked up a pair of black goggles from the table. The doctor muttered to himself as he crosschecked his calculations and worked the external control panel. The goggles hummed each time he entered a new set of variables.

"I'm almost finished," the doctor said with a glance to Agent Knox sitting in the captain's chair. "The neural stimulator needs to be calibrated by hand." The control panel gave two angry beeps as he made the next entry. "Damn!" The doctor scowled. "Well, I was almost finished." He bent over and peered intently at the medical pad.

Dr. Brainard took the news of Ann's diagnosis hard even though everyone assured him there was no possible way he could have suspected time sickness. All attempts to console him failed and the doctor would only shake his head and say, "Doctors should know these things."

"Take your time, doctor," Agent Knox said. The morning sun through the bay window glinted on the edges of her yellow glasses. She looked at Ann. "Why don't you have another go with the memory box while we wait?"

Ann nodded. She'd gladly take the memory box over injections any day.

Montressador Chapman sat in front of the bookshelf. Every time Ann looked at the swordsman she had a nagging sense she knew him, but without any memories it was like having a word just on the tip of her tongue but never able to say it. Ann hoped the memory therapy would change that. The Montressador always wore the same expression – one of slight amusement. Today, he also wore a bright orange shirt. The color didn't suit him. It clashed with the reddish coloring in his beard and made him look like an emergency flare.

Ann reached into the box sitting on the table next to a plate of Mrs. Beaumont's sweet rolls. She rummaged around until she found a familiar shape. She opened her hand and saw a pin in the shape of a bird. The creature's body sparkled with blue stones. The white stone that was the bird's eye winked in the light. The first day Ann pulled the pin out of the box she couldn't make any connection, but it soon became a favorite.

"Mom," Ann said and smiled as she traced the length of the bird's feathered tail with one finger.

Montressador Chapman chuckled. "That's an easy one. Pick something else."

Ann laid the bird pin in the growing pile on the table: a golden metal ball slightly bigger than an apple, a leather hair band, several dog-eared paperback books, and the picture of a beautiful mountain lake.

She reached back into the box and pulled out a small moonstone ring. The creamy stone glowed like a drop of moonlight on a silver ribbon. Ann had chosen the ring several times before without any luck. It still didn't speak to her. She shook her head and put the ring on the table next to the glittering bird pin and was reminded of the time she looked for a button to sew on John's maroon vest. All of those golden buttons clumped together in a little pile. *Gold buttons on a field of blue*. Ann frowned.

Agent Knox leaned forward. "Did you remember something?"

Ann shook her head. "No...not the ring. Gold buttons. From my uniform?"

Montressador Chapman rested his head on a hand and looked deep in thought.

"Damn and blast!"

Dr. Brainard scowled and jabbed at the control panel with an angry finger.

"I think we have time for one more," Agent Knox said with a glance in the doctor's direction.

Ann reached back into the box. This time her fingers found something long and thin. The simple green wooden stick was heavier than it looked, twelve inches long and balanced perfectly in her hand. An impulse came over Ann and she began to twirl the stick between her fingers. The stick spun faster until it became a green blur. Ann surprised herself when she found she could easily pass the stick to her left hand then back again without dropping it or slowing its spin.

"Very good," Montressador Chapman said. "Can you make it do anything else?"

Ann caught the stick in her hand and looked at it more closely. Nothing came to mind. What else could you do with a stick?

"It's a stick," Ann said with a shrug.

"Hmmm, you might have to relearn that," Chapman said scratching his beard.

Ann saw Agent Knox give him a warning look.

"Why not tell me?" Ann sensed a conspiracy and it sharpened her curiosity.

"Because," the Montressador said looking to the agent for approval. "If I told you, you wouldn't be remembering." He gave Ann a clever smile.

Ann smirked and rolled her eyes. She liked the Montressador, but he could be annoying. She wondered if that was how you were supposed to feel toward a brother.

The neural stimulator's control panel struck a four-note chord, and Dr. Brainard unfolded from his bent position with an exclamation of triumph.

"I think it's finally ready."

Ann shifted in her seat and wished John was there. He always disappeared into the winery whenever Montressador Chapman visited.

"Would you like me to get Captain Galeas for you? We could wait for him."

Ann shook her head at Agent Knox. "No, I'm fine." If John didn't feel the need to be there, then why should she interrupt his work she thought with annoyance.

Dr. Brainard cleared his throat and held the goggles out in front of him.

"I consulted with my colleague, Dr. Oribasius. He said the neural stimulator is not a magic bullet, if you will pardon the expression, but it will reverse the effects of the anachronosis." The doctor turned to Ann. "Some memories may come back to you quickly, while others will require more time and it may take more than one session to achieve the best results." His face took on a regretful cast. "Memory loss from time sickness can be unpredictable."

Ann smiled and squeezed the doctor's hand. Dr. Brainard gave a grateful look and patted her hand in return.

"Right then. Let's get started." The doctor fitted the goggles over Ann's head and adjusted the straps.

"Doctor, are there any risks?" A note of concern crept into Montressador Chapman's voice. "Anything we should watch for?"

"The neuropsychiatric side effects are temporary and generally mild," Dr. Brainard said. Ann's stomach flipped and the doctor paused when he saw the look in her eyes. "Nothing to worry about. The hallucinations are usually confined to a brief period immediately following treatment."

*Hallucinations?*

Ann's stomach flipped again, but Dr. Brainard had already

lowered the goggles into place, blotting out all light.

"You'll feel a bit disoriented and tired after, so you'll want to rest."

The thick goggles covered most of Ann's face and her ears. Her pulse ticked faster. She strained to see into the black void in front of her.

"Just try to relax." Dr. Brainard's voice came from somewhere beyond the void. "The stimulator will do the rest."

Ann heard a beep and a kaleidoscope of flashing color exploded in front of her eyes. A series of deep monotones filled her ears. Ann's jaw went slack. She tried to blink but couldn't. A curious sensation tingled deep within her skull. Warmth and contentment wrapped around Ann as she felt her mind pulled into the pulsing light.

The screen went blank. Ann felt Dr. Brainard remove the goggles from her head. She blinked. A shimmering haze played about the edge of her vision. Ann slumped against the back of the settee, arms at her side. Unseen fingers continued to root around in her memory like a pencil box.

Sean peered down at her, his face framed in a misty aura. Ann's head lolled to one side and he righted her again with a gentle push of his hand. Ann giggled. Sean gave her a dopey grin.

"How are you feeling?" Dr. Brainard read Ann's vitals on the digital pad.

Ann felt as if her body had melted into a puddle of buttery goo. Descriptive words darted through her mind like flocks of birds.

"Soft." she said. It was the best she could do.

The doctor chuckled. "Why don't you sit there for a moment and let the effects wear off."

Dr. Brainard had such a kind face. Ann never noticed before how his eyes were the exact shade of toffee-brown as Mrs. Beaumont's sweet rolls.

Ann looked at Sean sitting next to her. His shirt made him look like he could burst into flames any moment. *That damn shirt, she thought. I told him not to buy it, but he never listens to me.*

"I...hate...that...shirt," Ann said. Her mouth contorted into a strange shape with every word.

Sean gave a broad grin and patted her shoulder. "I know."

It was too much effort to talk. Ann felt as if she could ooze into the cushions and trickle through to the other side. Sean stood to speak to Agent Knox. The sunlight from the bay window reflected in the haze and swirled around them in golden pools. Their words slipped past too quickly for Ann's mind to catch.

*Twas brillig, and the slithy toves did gyre and gimble in the wabe.*

The poem spooled effortlessly from Ann's memory then stopped, interrupted by the smell of the sweet rolls on the table. It was a loud smell. Ann could see a smudge of icing left on the edge of the serving plate and taste the syrupy scent of the rolls in the back of her throat.

*All mimsy were the borogoves.*

Ann giggled as the bird pin hopped up from the table and ruffled its feathers, sending a cascade of sparkling blue stones bouncing and scattering in all directions. The bird gave a few cheeps then took flight, gliding through the glass pane of the bay window without a sound. It made Ann sad to see the bird leave. She hoped it would come back and at the same time knew it never left.

Mimsy. Ann giggled again. A funny word and yet it was exactly how she felt. Ann wished when Dr. Brainard asked how she felt she had said mimsy and not that other word she could no longer remember. Ann searched for the lost thread of the poem.

*Beware.*

The next line slipped from Ann's grasp. *Beware of what?* Maybe if she started again from the beginning she would remember.

The woman's eyes glittered like the golden buttons on her blue uniform. Ann thought it odd she did not notice the woman sitting in front of the bookcase before and watched as the stranger stood and drew closer. The woman, Ann realized, was Lieutenant Anaya Chapman from the picture Agent Drake had showed them.

*That's me! How strange to be sitting here and standing there,* Ann thought.

The Lieutenant leaned over Ann with a look of disdain.

"You're still here."

The Lieutenant picked up the green stick from the table.

*I must remember to tell Sean. He will think my dreams are so odd.*

Hatred zigzagged across the Lieutenant's face as she raised the stick.

*She's going to kill me, then I'll wake up.*

Ann closed her eyes. Something sliced past her face, cutting the air. She felt a trickle of blood in her nose and tasted copper as it pooled in her mouth.

*I'll wake up now. It's just like in a dream when you fall off a cliff. You always wake up before you hit the ground.*

Something soft pressed against Ann's nose and mouth. The Lieutenant was trying to smother her. *Why won't I wake up?* Panic stampeded through her chest. Ann flailed and clawed at the cloth. Hands grabbed her. Ann kicked hard and struck with the heel of her foot. She heard a crash. She pulled her left arm free. She balled a fist and swung, connecting somewhere with a meaty slap. A woman shrieked. Hands grabbed her arms and pinned them. More shouting and scuffling and through the chaos she heard Agent Knox's voice.

"Ann! Wake up!"

Ann opened her eyes. Agent Knox released her. Dr. Brainard stood over Ann panting, his glasses askew. He held a towel in his hand. To Ann's horror, she saw the towel stained with blood. She touched her mouth and nose and saw fresh blood on her fingertips. But it was a dream! Ann looked around. The Lieutenant had disappeared along with the shimmering haze.

"WHAT'S GOING ON!"

John burst into the sitting room with Mrs. Beaumont at his heels. His eyes locked onto Ann's and she saw the color drain from John's face. He rushed to her side.

"Are you hurt? What happened?"

Before Ann could answer, John rounded on the doctor and started to see the bloody towel in his hands.

"What the hell did you do to her?"

"The doctor didn't do anything," Sean said from across the room. He pressed the back of a hand to his busted lip, his face no longer cheerful. Ann cringed. "Obviously, Ann wasn't the one in danger!"

"It was just a bloody nose, Captain," Dr. Brainard said, dabbing at Ann's face with the towel and trying to regain his composure. "It happens sometimes with the neural stimulator. There's no need to—"

"Mrs. Beaumont said there was yelling!"

"There was a bit of a scramble, but everyone is okay," Agent Knox said. Sean grunted and took the tea towel offered by Mrs. Beaumont. Fionna glanced in the swordsman's direction. "Well, mostly everyone. Ann is fine."

"I'm okay," Ann said. It pained her to see the fear in John's eyes. "My fault….I…" She didn't know how to explain the Lieutenant. "I fell asleep. I had a bad dream."

"A bad dream did all this?" John waved a hand to the overturned table and the scattered objects on the floor.

"Yes. A bad dream. Nothing else," Ann said.

John scrutinized her another second. For an instant, Ann saw a deeper pain flicker across his face before he regained control. John looked away and ran a hand through his hair.

Ann took the towel from Dr. Brainard and stood, wiping the blood from her face. She pushed her way to the stairs. "No more today."

# SEVENTEEN

## *SECRETS*

Ann climbed over the fence stile and traveled the well-worn path through McTaggart's orchard back to Siren's Cove. Fluffy white and pink spires towered over her. The apple blossoms' heady perfume filled the orchard.

She took the green stick from a skirt pocket, twirling it between her fingers as she walked. The spinning stick looked like the fluttering wings of a large green moth. Ann still couldn't figure out what else the stick did. She kept the oddity with her and played with it whenever she could to see what else it might do.

The vision of the Lieutenant had not returned, but the threat of another encounter made Ann think twice about another round with the neural stimulator. She continued to work with the memory box but refused to do more therapy sessions. Both Agent Knox and Dr. Brainard tried to get her to reconsider. Knox was the most persistent and cornered Ann that morning after breakfast.

"What did you see?" The agent appeared so suddenly in the kitchen Ann almost dropped a stack of plates.

"What? What are you talking about?"

"You told the captain you had a bad dream after the therapy session," Agent Knox said. "What did you see?"

"I...I don't remember...it was a dream..." Ann said and stepped to the kitchen door. "I have to go. I have errands."

"If it was just a dream, then what are you afraid of?"

"I'm not afraid! I'm busy!" Ann grabbed the market basket from the counter and darted out the kitchen door.

Ann frowned and stepped over a fallen branch lying across the path. Agent Knox was probably waiting back at the tavern, hoping for another chance to talk. The agent always wanted to talk about what Ann was thinking, what she was feeling, and always at a time when Ann wanted to keep her thoughts and feelings to herself. Ann knew Knox was disappointed with her decision, but how could she explain the reasons why?

The Lieutenant was just a hallucination, or was she? The look of hatred on the Lieutenant's face unnerved her. Ann's insides twisted as she remembered what the Lieutenant said. *'You're still here.'* It was a threat. If Ann remembered everything about her former life, if she became the Lieutenant again, what would happen to her? Would she know herself or would she change into someone she no longer recognized? Ann knew it sounded crazy. She didn't expect the others to understand. Until she knew for sure, the neural stimulator would have to wait.

Even without additional therapy sessions, Ann sensed a change. Words and ideas flowed together instead of emerging from her mouth in lurching, broken sentences. Her mind felt clearer. Images from Ann's childhood came to her as quietly as a cat slinking into a room. The few seconds she remembered from the accident, however, split open her memory so violently Ann dropped an entire tray of food in the middle of the dinner rush. The look on John's face when he rounded the bar was so full of angst Ann quickly made up a story about a plate shifting the load and tipping the tray. The story was mostly true. The plate did shift, but Ann left out the part about seeing a fireball engulfing the outside of the cockpit and the sensation of the ship disintegrating around her.

Ann noticed John kept a closer watch since the incident with the neural stimulator, a constant shade of concern in his eyes. It was sweet he worried about her, but Ann didn't want him to worry too much. Every night, John asked if Ann remembered anything new. Ann thought maybe he could tell when she edited out some of the scarier images. They never talked about why she stopped the therapy sessions. Ann smiled to herself. They didn't always talk. Her cheeks flushed, remembering the taste of his mouth and the feel of his thick hair tangled between her fingers.

The path curved, dropping down into a gully, and continued across an open field. Tired of twirling the stick, Ann reached up to tap the branches of the last of the apple trees as she passed underneath.

"You're still not doing it right."

Ann stopped. Sean stood in the field a few yards down the path, watching with an amused grin. Ann pressed her lips together as she remembered how she accidentally punched him in the mouth. As far as she could tell, her brother held no grudge against her.

Ann continued down the path toward him. "What are you doing?" Sean wore a short sleeve shirt and long work pants. A ring of sweat darkened his brow.

"Just wanted to get out for a while. If I don't practice, I'll never hear the end of it."

Sean swung his sword over his head in a graceful, two-handed arc then lunged and brought the blade down with deadly force, slicing through an invisible foe. The sword flashed like heat lightning.

"Your sword is beautiful," Ann said, then felt foolish thinking how silly she must sound. She watched him work the blade through the air.

"Each Montressador is given his own sword. No two are alike," he said. Sean held the sword out for Ann to see. The weapon's golden hilt sparkled in the sunlight. "Some day, when I'm dead, my sword will hang under my portrait in the Montressador's Hall and will never be used again." He looked at the blade, his expression darkening with regret. "Bit of a pity, really." Sean returned the sword to the leather sheath strapped across his back.

"So what am I doing wrong?"

"You've got the right idea, but your execution is off." Sean picked up a water jug from the grass and took a swig.

"Will you show me?"

Sean shook his head. "I can't make it work."

Ann frowned. What did he mean? If Sean couldn't show her what the stick did, then how was she ever going to figure it out?

"Then give me a hint."

"Don't think, just concentrate. Good advice for most any occasion."

Ann rolled her eyes with exasperation. "That doesn't make sense. You can't not think and concentrate at the same time."

Sean chuckled. "Fine. Close your eyes."

He put the stick in Ann's hand and made her grip the middle. Ann felt a small vibration as it traveled up her arm.

"Can you feel it humming?" Ann nodded. "Good. Now unlock it."

Something clicked inside Ann's head, an instinct, like releasing a deep breath. The stick quivered and she opened her eyes. Instantly, the stick expanded, stretching to four times its original length.

"Once you find the power source, you can activate it," Sean said. "And stop calling it a stick. It's a quarterstaff."

After a few more tries, Ann could open and close the staff at will.

"The body remembers what the head forgets," her brother said, grinning. "And you thought it was just a stick."

Ann laughed. Sean was right, but she doubted she would have figured it out without his help. Ann twirled the quarterstaff in front of her, captivated by how easily she could maneuver it.

The ends of the staff blurred as it spun. A dark halo encircled the edge of Ann's vision. The halo grew thicker, reducing her line of sight to a pinprick as another image ruptured her memory. Ann saw a teenage boy, her brother.

Sean's bangs brushed his eyes, his face clean-shaven. The image of her brother smiled and reached to take her hand. Deep, penetrating sadness engulfed her.

"What's wrong?"

Ann shook off the image and looked up. Sean had grabbed her arm, his face pinched with worry. Suddenly, Ann knew the reason for her overwhelming grief.

*We're the last of the unlucky.*

"Mom's dead and dad, too," Ann said. Sean flinched, his eyes troubled.

"It was a long time ago," he said.

"I thought so." Ann knew her brother told the truth and yet the grief she felt was still tender.

"Dr. Brainard and Fionna are worried some of your memories might be disconnected from your emotions," Sean said. "If you would just try the neural stimulator one more time it might help you make sense of everything."

Ann collected herself and shook her head. "I'm fine. The memory caught me off-guard." She picked up the quarterstaff from where she dropped it. "I better get back. Mrs. Beaumont will wonder where I am."

\*\*\*

Ann walked down the steps into the winery, a mini-bot trapped under an arm. John had purchased three refurbished bots to help with cleaning around the tavern and to silence Mrs. Beaumont's complaints he spent too much time in the winery.

The mini-bots required maintenance on a weekly basis. The bot Ann carried was nicknamed Port. Its left wing routinely needed tightening to keep it from flying in left-handed circles. Ann walked to John's toolbox sitting next to the winery's main control panel and placed the mini-bot on the tall stool.

"Stay," Ann said and gave Port an affectionate pat.

Ann opened the toolbox and searched for a wrench. She found it in the second drawer, but before she could pick up the bot, it flicked its beetle-like wings and took flight, spinning off in tight circles toward the wine tank. Ann sighed and chased after it.

"Wait! Come back!"

Ann hurried to where Port had disappeared. She found the mini-bot attached to the back of the gleaming metal tank, blinking and humming to itself.

"Come on, Port. You don't want to be back here."

The bot sat like a golden bump on the otherwise smooth, metallic surface. The tank reflected the blue sky from the glass block windows.

Ann heard the maintenance room door open and footsteps as they echoed through the winery. She detached Port from the tank and turned to walk back to the control panel.

"Aren't you worried? He's the Montressador. He could have you arrested!"

"For what? A rumor? Gossip?"

Ann froze behind the tank. The voices came closer.

"It's ancient history. He has better things to do," she heard John say. "Besides, if he was going to arrest me, he would have done it by now."

Ann could have stepped out from behind the wine tank. She could have pretended not to have heard, but she hesitated. Why would anyone want to arrest John? It must be a mistake. Ann quieted her breathing and strained to hear. She heard switches flipping on the control panel and edged her way back farther behind the tank. Port struggled in her arms. Ann gripped the bot tighter against her chest to silence its clicking wings.

"Maybe this is a good thing," Arnold said. "You could talk to him. He seems like a nice guy. Maybe he could get you a pardon?"

"I don't need his help."

"I know it's none of my business," Arnold said. John snorted. "I'm just worried, that's all. You can't make wine in a jail cell. What if he hears something? What about Ann?" Ann jumped at the sound of her name. "You've got a big problem."

"Look, why don't you stick to selling wine and let me worry about me," John said, his tone softening. Ann heard John rummaging in the toolbox. "Where did my spanner go? It's gotta be around here somewhere."

Ann looked at the wrench in her hand, her heart in her throat. If John started looking around the winery, he would find her for sure and then how would she explain? Ann heard the lid of the toolbox snap shut.

"You said you had a sales update for me," John said. "What are the numbers this week?"

Footsteps retreated across the winery to the maintenance room.

"Numbers are up and I signed another distributor," Arnold said. "At this rate, you're gonna need another tank."

Ann heard the maintenance room door latch. She waited a few seconds and hurried back to the kitchen.

\*\*\*

John sat at the desk in the master bedroom and looked over the column of figures by the glow of his lamp. Ann had already gone to bed, choosing to sleep in the guest room while he worked. He promised to join her as soon as he finished, but that had been over an hour ago. He wanted to walk through the figures one more time to make sure. John scratched a few more numbers on the paper with a pencil and compared them to the numbers on the data link pad. Arnold was right. John would need to buy another tank. The winery was doing better than he'd hoped.

John leaned back in the chair, stretched, and yawned. He picked up his glass and gulped the last swallow, grimacing even as he savored the burn down the back of his throat. John flicked off the lamp. The moonlight through the window would be enough to find his way.

A flash of light rippled across the windowpane. John frowned. It wasn't moonlight. He looked out the window. The sliver of moon was bright enough for him to see the courtyard below and the shadowy outline of the carriage house as it jutted from the side of the tavern. Everything was quiet. Then from the corner of John's eye he saw another strobe of light. A faint orange beam flickered from the carriage house windows.

Adrenaline shot through John's veins like an alarm bell. He reached for the laser pistol in the nightstand.

***

John squatted in the hallway by the carriage house door, one hand on the doorknob. He could hear the occasional sandy scrape of footsteps on the wooden floor inside. John shifted his grip on the laser pistol. He had prowlers before, but they'd never made it over the threshold at least not any still breathing.

John turned the knob and opened the door a crack to look inside. The winery was dark except for the soft puddles of moonlight in front of the windows. The towering silhouette of the wine tank dominated the carriage house, a silent presence in the darkness. John slipped into the winery using the shadows by the stairs as cover. His ears pricked for the slightest sound. The orange beam flickered again from behind the wine tank. John trained his gun toward the beam and tripped the light switch by the door, flooding the carriage house in bright light.

"Give yourself up and I might let you walk out of here alive." John's voice broke the stillness and echoed off the high ceiling. "I've shot enough men in my life, one more won't make much difference to me," John said. "Come out. NOW!"

No response. John clenched his jaw. A bead of sweat trickled down the back of his neck. He took a few cautious steps toward the wine tank. A heavy blow across his back knocked him to the ground. John lunged at his attacker's ankle and missed, catching only a glimpse of the gold and turquoise of a shiny boot buckle as the assailant hurtled past.

John staggered to his feet, took aim, and fired at the retreating figure. The blue plasma bolt sliced through the air. The prowler yelled and swore as the bolt ripped past an ear and impacted on the door at the opposite end of the winery, scorching the wood. John raced across the winery, but by the time he reached the sliding doors the intruders were gone.

John cursed himself for his stupidity. He'd only heard one set of footsteps. The smell of burnt wood from the door filled

162

the winery. John pulled the door shut and saw the lock had been cut clean through with a laser saw. A new lock would have to wait till morning.

\*\*\*

John rolled out of bed bruised and exhausted. He stayed up half the night to repaint the winery door where the plasma bolt scorched the wood. He hoped Mrs. Beaumont and Ann wouldn't notice the fresh paint. At least the paint fumes covered the tinge of burnt wood.

John replayed the incident over in his mind as he got dressed. He never saw the prowlers' faces, only a close up of his attacker's boots. The gold and turquoise buckle seemed like an oddly decorative touch for a man's boot. John frowned. A coincidence? It had to be. The more John tried to push the thought away the more his anxiety burrowed under his skin. He decided to ask around town just to make sure. Dr. Brainard had a talent for discreet, casual inquiries. John sighed. He hadn't spoken to the doctor much since their argument in the tavern. He could already picture the I-told-you-so look on Dr. Brainard's face. Maybe it would be better to talk to Arnold first.

John walked into the kitchen. Ann stood at the counter cutting thick slices of bread. She looked up and smiled when she heard John walk in. John gave her a kiss on the cheek on the way to pouring himself a large mug of coffee.

"Mrs. Beaumont says the number three oven still isn't working," Ann said. "She really wants you to look at it today."

"I know...I know..." John tried to rub the fatigue from his eyes. "She told me yesterday."

"She told me if you don't do it this morning, I should cut off your pigtail," Ann said with a mischievous smile.

Her eyes teased and stirred him from his weariness. John pulled Ann to him and buried his face in her neck. She smelled of fresh wildflowers.

"You would miss my pigtail as much as I would," John murmured, his lips brushing Ann's neck. His hands wandered across the gentle curve of her hips.

Ann sighed and wrapped her arms more tightly around John's shoulders. He flinched when Ann touched the welt on his back.

"Are you hurt?" Her mouth puckered with concern.

"I guess I lifted one too many wine crates yesterday. Nothing serious." There was no need to worry Ann until he had more information.

"Hello? Is anyone home?"

John heard Agent Knox calling from the sitting room and the sound of Montressador Chapman's boots in the entryway. Ann slipped from John's arms, much to his disappointment.

"They have impeccable timing," John muttered. He tolerated them for Ann's sake, but his hospitality was wearing thin.

"I'm in the kitchen! I'll be there in a minute!" Ann turned to John. "Sean wanted me to try the memory box again before Agent Knox left for Andarria this afternoon." Ann looked at him, a question in her eyes. "You don't have to sit in. I know you're busy."

John wavered. He wanted to be there when Ann worked with the memory box, but he needed to send Arnold a message on the comm.

"I better fix the oven first before Mrs. Beaumont starts sharpening knives," John said with a sigh. "I'll be in here if you need anything. I'll pop in when I'm done."

Ann gave him a tight smile and hurried to the sitting room.

John fired off a short message to Arnold using the comm's access terminal in the kitchen. He knew the data network was reasonably secure but kept the message as bland as possible just in case. John hoped Arnold would understand.

*Ran numbers last night. Go ahead with new tank purchase. How are sales to off-tourists? Old friends visited last night for tour of the winery.*

John worked on the oven while he waited for Arnold's reply. Thankfully, the repair job was a simple problem and only took a few minutes.

"The oven is fixed," John told Mrs. Beaumont as he wiped down the front of the oven door. "You won't be cutting off my pigtail today. Sorry to disappoint you."

Mrs. Beaumont finished programming one of the mini-bots. It took flight from her open hands and settled on the windowpane above the kitchen sink. She turned to the captain, perplexed.

"Pigtail? I never said anything about cutting off your pigtail." Mrs. Beaumont gave John a wicked grin before walking to the pantry.

John chuckled. The comm beeped, signaling a new message. John checked the screen and glanced over a shoulder to the pantry before opening Arnold's reply.

*Tank is ordered. Expect delivery in a few days. Tourist sales are steady. Spoke to sales assistant. Off-tourist with lots of questions about local wineries stopped by shop two days ago. Assistant has been reassigned to stockroom. I hope tour went well?*

John's internal alarm bells went off again, this time louder and more urgent. He sent Arnold a quick reply.

*Tour went well but was cut short. Will talk more later.*

John deleted the string of messages. He needed to get a description of the off tourist who visited Arnold's shop before he could know for sure, but the late night visit felt less and less like a coincidence. John tried to rub the tension out of the back of his neck.

He'd taken every precaution, but they still found him, and now they were all in danger.

\*\*\*

John walked into the sitting room, his thoughts heavy. Montressador Chapman stood when John entered, his hand resting on the hilt of his sword. The gesture always put John on guard although he knew the motion was only a habit of the swordsman and not an active threat. Agent Knox and Ann sat on the settee. Ann clutched her hands, eyes squeezed tight. John frowned and started to speak, but the agent held up a hand for silence.

"It's all right," Knox said, speaking to Ann. "Don't try to fight it."

Ann opened her eyes and unclenched her fingers. John saw a silver ring resting in Ann's hand. Half-moon indentations marked her palm where fingernails had dug into the skin. Ann stared at the ring.

"Who gave me this ring?"

John's heart lurched in his chest.

Agent Knox touched Ann's shoulder. "What do you remember?"

"No. Tell me now." Ann turned to Knox, eyes steady. "Who gave me this ring?"

"Tell us what you see."

Ann looked up. Her eyes widened when she saw John, the color rising to her cheeks. She looked away and shook her head. John felt his insides shrivel with cold fear.

"Fionna, we need to tell them," Montressador Chapman said.

"Ann needs to remember on her own. It could compromise her therapy."

"Damn it, Fionna! He'll be back in Andarrian space in three days!"

Knox narrowed her eyes and pressed her lips together. She finally relented and nodded.

Montressador Chapman took a deep breath. "It's an engagement ring."

The wooden floor reeled under John's feet. He sank onto the leather footstool and sat like a puppet whose strings had been cut. Nothing mattered any more—not the winery or the prowlers—John's worst fear had come true.

Ann looked at her brother. Her hazel eyes burned into him. "You son of a bitch. You told me about the quarterstaff, but you didn't tell me about *this*?"

"You told her about the staff?" Agent Knox's tone prickled with irritation.

"Give it a rest, Fionna," Chapman said and glared back.

"TELL ME WHO HE IS!"

The Montressador sighed. "His name is Commander Vincent Lazar. He wouldn't speak to anyone after your accident. He accepted a deep space assignment and left two weeks later. I sent Vincent a message after we found you, but we had no way of knowing when he received it. He's only been in communication range for a couple weeks." Chapman looked at Ann with a pained expression. "I hoped you would have remembered Vincent sooner. I'm sorry."

"You're sorry?" Ann looked at her brother with disdain then down at the ring as she rolled it between her fingers. "I'm engaged to a man whose face I can't remember!"

Montressador Chapman stared at his boots, his face a picture of misery.

"Give it time."

Ann's eyes flashed to Agent Knox.

"You're just beginning to remember," Knox said. "Commander Lazar wants to see you." She waved off Ann's attempt to object. "Your brother told him about your memory loss. Vincent will be at Navis Command in three days. Your brother and I can go with you." John saw Agent Knox give a glance in his direction. "I thought it would be best if you met him there."

"Ann, you don't have to go if you don't want to," Chapman said.

Ann looked up and stared at her brother.

Agent Knox frowned. "Montressador—"

"She can meet with him another time." Montressador Chapman looked hard at Ann. "If you want to give the ring back, I can take it to Vincent for you." Sean sighed and shook his head. "I'll explain it to him...somehow."

Knox stiffened. "With all due respect, Montressador, you've lost sight of the bigger picture."

"This is between my sister and Commander Lazar."

Montressador Chapman said, his tone more a command than a statement. "If she doesn't want to see him, I won't force her to go."

"It's not that simple." Agent Knox turned to Ann. "The crash investigation committee expects you to make every effort to regain your memories from the accident. I believe meeting the commander in person will help just as meeting your brother did." The agent's words lit a fuse inside John and roused him from his stupor. "Refusing to meet with him could make you look bad in the eyes of the committee." Fionna sighed. "I realize this is a delicate matter with personal consequences for all involved but remembering what caused your accident is too important not to try."

Ann looked down at the ring as she turned it over in her hands. John's heart wrenched when it slipped onto the tip of her finger before rolling back onto her palm.

"Fine." Ann's face darkened. "I'll meet with him. I'll give him his ring back. And then it will be done." She turned her glare on her brother then to Agent Knox. "Will that satisfy everyone?"

John stood and clenched his hands to keep them from shaking. "I'd like to speak to Ann. Alone." He turned to her once the others had left for the kitchen. "What if Agent Knox is right? What if you meet this commander and you remember who he was to you?"

"It won't change how I feel about you."

"You don't know that."

Ann looked down at the ring. "It's the right thing to do." A shade of anxiety or doubt passed over her features. "Come with me."

John's heart twisted in his chest. He swallowed hard, hating his decision. After the break-in at the winery, Ann would be safer away from Siren's Cove, and until he was certain the threat had passed, he couldn't leave.

"I can't."

Ann blinked in surprise. John saw the hurt swelling inside her like a bruise. He hated the thought of lying to her, but what choice did he have?

"Someone tried to break into the winery last night."

Ann's eyes opened wide. "What?"

John cautioned her to stay quiet and led her to the settee. "I discovered it this morning," He said in a whisper. "I didn't want to worry you. I haven't even told Mrs. Beaumont. Whoever it was tried to cut through the lock on the outside doors, but they never got inside. I already replaced the lock."

"Why would anyone want to break into the winery?"

"I don't know. I'm sure it's nothing, but I don't feel right leaving so soon after," John said. He reached for Ann and cupped her cheek. "Can you understand?"

Ann nodded. Her brow knotted with worry. "Maybe I should stay, too. I can give the ring to Sean to take back." She blew out a sigh of frustration. "Damn the committee. I don't care what they think."

"No."

Ann looked at him, a question in her eye. John's heart jumped. He rifled through his thoughts to come up with something that sounded like a reasonable excuse.

"Like you said, it's the right thing to do."

Ann frowned at the ring. "Yes...I suppose..."

John breathed a quiet sigh of relief. "Don't say anything to Mrs. Beaumont about the prowlers. She's never been a big fan of the winery, and I don't want to give her more ammo."

Ann squeezed John's hand. "You'll be careful while I'm gone?"

John wrapped his arms around her and caught the scent of wildflowers in her hair.

"I'll be fine." John felt a familiar hole opening up inside him. He knew he must not yield to despair with the work ahead. "You'll only be gone a few days, and by then everything will be back to how it should be."

# EIGHTEEN

## *THE COMMANDER RETURNS*

The stars streaked past, filling the canopy window above Ann with ribbons of blue and silver light. Flight attendants in black vests navigated between islands of overstuffed chairs and offered drinks to shuttle passengers in the dimly lit lounge. Conversations droned around Ann just as the shuttle's engines hummed under her feet. Ann felt strange surrounded by so much technology. She fidgeted in her chair and tried to concentrate on her book.

The shuttle would make its final approach soon. The thought made the breath hitch in Ann's chest, and she blew out an anxious sigh. Returning the ring in person was the right thing to do, but why did the thought of seeing Commander Lazar make her tremble? What reason did she have to be afraid?

John had kept to himself, distant and brooding, until the day of her departure, worried about the prowlers Ann supposed. He hadn't shown any more concern about her returning the ring in person, but when the time came to say goodbye the grief he bore on his face made his thoughts painfully clear. Ann asked him again to go with her. She offered to send the ring with a letter, but each time John refused and insisted she go, all the while maintaining that the prowlers were nothing to be concerned about. But then if that was the case why wouldn't he go with her?

Ann tossed the book aside in disgust. The constant hum and noise around her had given her a stinging headache. She looked at her brother sitting across from her. Sean wore his black uniform jacket as an afterthought with the silver buttons undone and his shirt collar open. Even in this casual state, the uniform gave the Montressador an air of authority Ann had not seen when they were on the Colonies.

Sean stared out the window, strangely quiet. A digital pad rested in his lap. They had traveled together for over twelve hours, first on a galactic shuttle to Andarria then changing to a shuttle reserved for military brass and diplomats. Traveling with him had been pleasant enough, but Ann's anger sparked whenever she remembered how Sean had kept the ring a secret. What else had he not told her?

Ann remembered the conversation she overheard between John and Arnold in the winery. The threat of possible arrest explained why John always seemed to avoid being in the same room with her brother, but she did not sense the same avoidance from Sean. A mild reluctance perhaps, but nothing more. Whatever secret John kept, Sean seemed as much in the dark as Ann was. Maybe it was this secret and not John's concern for the prowlers that kept him from accompanying her?

Ann felt the shuttle decelerate and the stars above shrunk back to pinpricks of light. A woman's voice sounded from the invisible speaker overhead.

*"Attention passengers…Beginning final approach to space station Navis."*

Ann blew out another impatient sigh, nerves humming. Her hand went to the pocket of her traveling cloak. Ann rolled the ring between her fingers and the images came again. Gold buttons on a field of blue. Ann felt the stranger's arms around her, his body pressed against hers, but when she tried to see the stranger's face his features appeared as smooth and as formless as melted wax. Two days had passed since Ann's first encounter with the memory and she could not add any details to the faceless horror in her mind. A nervous bubble trembled inside Ann. She shivered and left the ring in her pocket.

"Mon-TRESS-ador!"

The loud synthesized voice jolted Ann and Sean in their seats. A man stepped forward from a group of passengers in business attire. He wore a stiff leather and brass collar that encased his neck from his shoulders to just below his jaw. A squat metal implant protruded from the side of the man's skull. Wispy white hair covered a pink scalp like fuzz on a peach.

"I didn't real-ize you were fly-ING with us to-day. Are you HERE for the security brief-ING?" The collared man raised his eyebrows with each word he emphasized. His mouth didn't move except to smile or purse his lips. The computerized voice came from a speaker on the front of the man's collar.

"Nice to see you, minister," Sean said and stood to shake the man's hand. "I've already been briefed this month. I'm just here for a quick visit...er...family business. You remember my sister?" Sean whispered discretely to Ann. "This is Minister Greffenius."

The minister turned stiffly to Ann. The man's appearance was so extraordinary that even with her memory loss Ann wondered how it was possible she could not remember meeting him before.

"Hello, Minister."

"AH, yes! A plea-sure to SEE you again." Minister Greffenius smiled broadly as he shook Ann's hand. "Sooooo glad to see you BACK among the liv-ING. Time jumpers are the pri-ide of the re-pub-LIC!"

Each sentence the man uttered was an adventure in facial gymnastics. Ann began to suspect the minister used his expressions to control the inflection of the computer's voice.

"So how are you?" Sean lowered his voice to a discreet level. "I heard you were at the veteran's hospital."

"VERY well! The new tis-sue grafts are re-mark-able!" Greffenius said, raising his eyebrows and opening his eyes wide. "I tas-ted food for the first time in two years!"

Minister Greffenius looked up and waved to the other members of his group waiting for him at the lounge entrance.

"Well, I bet-ter get go-ING. Good to see you both!" The minister left to rejoin his traveling companions.

Sean read the question on Ann's face before she could ask it. "Partial decapitation." Ann cringed. Sean watched the minister as he left the lounge. "He's looking much better these days."

Ann gathered up her things and put them in her carpetbag. She remembered what Minister Greffenius had said.

"What's a time jumper?"

Sean looked up from the digital pad.

"It's just as the name says. Time jumpers travel through time. They're trained to observe and fix things." Sean nodded in the minister's direction. "He was a time jumper before his accident and it's what you used to do before you had yours."

Ann could not imagine she did anything as dangerous as Sean described. She still found it difficult to believe she had once piloted a time ship. A million questions tried to exit Ann's mouth simultaneously, but she was interrupted by one of the flight attendants.

"We'll be docking soon. You're welcome to stay here until we open the gangway," the attendant said. "You can watch the docking procedure on the view screen if you'd like."

The flight attendant touched a panel on the smooth, black surface of the table. A monitor unfolded from its center. The screen flickered and space station Navis appeared. The station gleamed silver against the black velvet of space. Solar panels fanned from its rounded head and glittered like jewels. Ann saw several shuttles docked along the station's central column. Larger star ships, more impressive than the shuttles, crouched in the lower berths. Ann leaned forward to get a closer look.

Seeing Ann's interest, the attendant pointed to the star ships. "This one is the *Virginia Dare* and that one's the *Ricochet*...and oh, look!" She turned to Ann smiling. "That's Commander Lazar's ship, the *Peregrine*. His crew must be on shore leave."

Ann swallowed hard and felt the bubble tremble inside her again.

***

Ann and Sean joined the other passengers on the gangway. A large metal door at the end of the corridor dilated with a blast of cool air. A steward stood at a thin, metal podium at the entrance to the main concourse, checking off items on a digital pad. The passengers continued past into the concourse and blended with the other visitors. The steward looked up as Sean and Ann approached. He straightened his black vest and stepped from behind the podium in one crisp motion.

"Hello, Montressador. Lieutenant Chapman."

Ann frowned at the mention of the Lieutenant's name. The steward noted her displeasure and shrewdly changed course.

"Ann Chapman?"

Ann nodded approval. The steward smiled and continued.

"Welcome to space station Navis. My name is Janus, Senior Steward." The words rolled expertly from the steward's mouth, each syllable as round as a ripe cherry. "I have been instructed to escort you immediately to the reception area. Commander Lazar and Agent Knox are waiting for you. I arranged for your bags to be taken to your quarters."

Seeing Ann's carpetbag, Janus snapped his fingers and a second attendant standing nearby stepped forward and took the bag before Ann could object. She felt awkward without something for her hands to do.

"If you will come with me please." Janus turned and beckoned.

"Wait just a minute," Sean said. "We've been traveling for fourteen hours. We'd like to go to our cabins before meeting with the Commander."

"I understand, sir," Janus said. "But the Commander is anxious to meet with you. I assure you the reception room has been prepared with your comfort in mind."

Sean scowled and straightened his jacket. "Is there any particular reason why Commander Lazar is insisting on time and tide?"

Ann looked up at Sean, surprised by the commanding tone in his voice.

Janus pulled a thick silver watch from a vest pocket and pressed the button on its side. The watch clicked and fanned like nesting spoons in the steward's hand. Three glowing watch faces illuminated the deep frown lines around his mouth. Janus clicked the button again and the three watch faces retracted to form a single watch.

"I can't say, sir," the steward said, returning the watch to a vest pocket. "I only know my orders."

Sean narrowed his eyes. "Your orders? What if I gave you a new order? Or do stewards outrank me on this tin-plated—"

"Sean, it's all right," Ann said, taking his arm. The bubble of anxiety fought its way up the back of her throat and trembled more urgently. "Let's just get it over with."

"Are you sure?"

Ann nodded and wondered when the next flight to the Colonies was scheduled to leave.

"Fine," Sean said, turning to the steward. "But I'm not happy about it."

"Of course, sir. I will make note of it." Janus waved an arm in the direction of the main concourse. "This way please."

Ann whispered to Sean as they followed. "What did you mean by time and tide?"

"It's from an old expression. Time and tide means something can't wait, or that we can't bend or change the rules." Sean smirked and leaned toward Ann so Janus could not overhear. "Even Andarrians must obey the laws of the physical universe occasionally."

The main concourse stretched in both directions as far as Ann could see. Grand metal arches connected high overhead. Large observation windows positioned near the shuttle gates showed the bulky exteriors of star ships docked outside or into the starry field beyond.

Janus guided them through the crowds of passengers to a waiting tram car. He touched the sensor on the side of the tram and the double doors swung open. Ann and Sean took a seat on the cushioned bench inside. The dim interior lighting brightened by a degree as the car powered up. Janus sat in the cockpit and worked the control panel. Ann felt the pressure in her ears change as the double doors sealed shut.

"Please remain seated until the car comes to a complete stop."

The steward touched the controls and the car leaped down the track with a burst of speed that took Ann's breath away. Air thundered past. The tram zipped through a tunnel and the interior lights went out, throwing its passengers into near darkness. The only light came from a strobe effect through the windows before the car burst into the open on the other side of the tunnel and the interior lights came back on. Another few seconds and the tram slowed to a stop.

"Welcome to Navis command," Janus said. "Please watch your step exiting the tram."

The steward touched the control panel and the double doors unsealed with a sucking sound. Ann followed Sean, stepping out of the tram and onto the platform.

Ann stopped in her tracks and gaped at what she saw. A giant armillary sphere rose fifteen stories through the center of the space station's atrium, reaching almost to the observation windows on the upper decks. Its large brass rings rotated, each ring moving at a different speed and in an opposite direction of its closest neighbor. The outer rings crept slowly while the smaller inner rings spun faster. Their reflections moved across the surface of the black polished floor in waves.

"I remember this," Ann said, heart racing.

The hours Ann spent as a cadet manually pouring over star charts and filing practice flight plans came rushing back to her. Every Andarrian star ship comm used a miniaturized version of the sphere as a navigational device. If you couldn't make sense of the sphere, you couldn't find your way home.

"The sphere. It's *Time!*"

Ann moved closer, eager to take in the whole scene. Words etched in gold lettering in the black obsidian floor read, *Andarrians weave what the Fates spin.* A statue of three women stood at the base of the sphere and spun golden thread from a spinning wheel. The thread trailed through the women's hands down to the polished black floor and transformed into a brook. The stream widened to a golden river as it flowed away from the base of the statue. The river glittered and moved past Ann's feet, its swirling water trapped under the glass. Eddies of water looped backward or tapered into narrow inlets. The effect made Ann dizzy.

Ann followed the path of the river. Smaller tributaries led into and away from the main channel, sometimes pooling into a lake then continuing through a sluice gate to rejoin the riverbed. Ann looked closer. Animated figures stood here and there along the bank and helped the water flow—unblocking brambles, making the channels wider, opening or closing gates. Some figures sailed the water in boats. The river ran completely around the base of the sphere in a continuous flow.

"All these people. They're time jumpers," Ann said gesturing to the river at her feet. "They're fixing time." Ann turned to Sean who stood quietly watching her while she gazed at the monument. "You said I was a time jumper like Minister Greffenius, but I still don't understand how that's even possible."

Sean looked up at the sphere.

"Andarrians are the stewards of time. We were given the knowledge and the ability over every other race to watch over and manage time. It's not easy. It's like trying to braid water." Sean pointed to different scenes along the riverbank as he spoke. "Time is messy. It slips away from you. It's easily diverted. It loops back on itself without warning. If you're not careful, the currents can be treacherous."

Sean pointed to a time jumper who had fallen into the river and was in danger of being pulled into a whirlpool. Another figure in a nearby boat reached out to pull him from the water. Ann looked down at the two figures, face grim. Her heart pinched with sympathy for the time jumper in the water.

Ann looked at her brother. "But why would time need to be fixed?"

"Lots of reasons," he said and shrugged. "For one thing, every race, every culture in the universe eventually, sometimes accidentally, develops the ability to travel through time. An amateur time traveler with good intentions can do just as much damage as someone who is only acting in their own selfish interests." Sean shook his head. "Time is difficult enough to control. Imagine if we just let everyone run around causing chaos."

Ann nodded. She could see his point.

"But why Andarrians? And why would all the other people in the universe let us control time? That would make us—"

"—the most powerful race in the universe?" Sean chuckled. "Not exactly. We're more caretakers than masters."

Sean motioned for Ann to follow as he walked toward the statue of the three women.

"We didn't make the laws," Sean said, gesturing toward the spinning wheel. "We just enforce them."

The wheel sat on an old stump of a large tree. Ann looked closer and saw carved into the stump pictures of men and women stooped under a heavy burden. Written on the stump was a single phrase in simple block letters, *Cursed, we serve.*

An old memory of dusty books and history lessons slipped from the shadows. "We're being punished." Ann looked up at her brother. She didn't need him to confirm it. Ann knew it was true.

Sean nodded, his eyes downcast but a smile still curled his mouth. "It's a long story."

"Ahem."

They looked up and saw Janus waiting for them a discrete distance away.

Sean looked at Ann. "We better get going. Old Time and Tide over there has us on a tight schedule."

Janus escorted them down a corridor leading away from the atrium. Ann grew more anxious with every step. The noise and bustle of the station faded in the quiet corridor with the only sound the muffled clanking of Sean's sword and belt as he walked beside her.

The steward passed several rooms, finally stopping at a metal door midway down the corridor. The steward touched a sensor next to the door and it slid open. Agent Knox and a man wearing a blue uniform sat in plush chairs grouped around a low table. The commander stood and tugged at the bottom of his uniform jacket when he heard them enter.

"Commander Lazar and Agent Knox. The Montressador and Ann Chapman have arrived," Janus said. He turned to Sean. "If you require anything else during your stay, please do not hesitate to ask." Sean nodded and the steward left, the door sliding shut behind him.

Sean and the commander greeted as old friends, slapping each other on the back.

"Vincent, it's good to see you."

Ann looked away and swallowed hard, trying to master the nervous bubble stubbornly pushing its way up the back of her throat.

"Anaya, is it really you?"

The sound of the commander's voice startled Ann. She looked up. A single row of gold buttons marched up the front of his blue jacket. Ann looked into his face. His features crashed into focus in her memory. Vincent's eyes were the color of a distant blue horizon. Short, wavy blond hair crowned his head. Tall and slender, he wore the uniform without fault. Vincent stood beaming at Ann, and doubt swallowed the certainty of her task.

Vincent's face fell with sudden embarrassment at Ann's silence. "I'm sorry. Sean told me you prefer to be called Ann. I forgot."

Ann could not speak. She stared wide-eyed, her mind frozen in shock as Vincent's features stripped the faceless stranger from Ann's memory.

"I want to hug you, but I'm afraid if I touch you, I'll wake up and discover this is all a dream." Vincent's hand twitched as if to reach out to Ann, but then his face lost its radiance and the commander stood stiffly, hands clasped behind his back. "Thank you for coming. I hope you had a pleasant journey."

Ann blinked, remembering herself and gave a small nod.

"Why don't we all sit down and have a drink?" Agent Knox eyed Sean who had already helped himself to the sideboard.

"Yes, of course." Vincent sprung to life with a nervous laugh. "You've been traveling. You must be tired."

Ann willed her feet to move. She sat on the edge of her seat next to Agent Knox, hands in her lap. The bubble swelled inside her, threatening to burst. The conversation turned to strained pleasantries with Vincent and Sean discussing their flight. Agent Knox smiled at Ann from behind yellow glasses and sipped her drink. The agent wore the same pea green jacket from the first night she and Agent Drake arrived at Siren's Cove.

Ann took the ring from a pocket and put it on the table. Vincent stopped in mid-sentence. His eyes searched her face. Ann fought to maintain a blank expression as she looked into his blue eyes.

Agent Knox leaned forward and put her drink on the table. "Commander, I know you have something you would like to say to Ann."

Ann frowned. She returned the ring. What more was there to say?

Vincent cleared his throat and shifted in his seat. "Yes, I do have something I wish to say." He leaned forward and looked into Ann's eyes. She wanted to look away but couldn't.

"I still care very deeply for you," Vincent said, all his formality melting away. "When I thought I lost you I never felt pain like that before. I needed to get away, as far away as possible." His face darkened. "I know things are different now. Maybe it doesn't matter anymore? I never intended...I never thought I would..." Vincent took a deep breath. "I met someone and I asked her to marry me."

Ann's mouth stiffened. What did it matter to her? Sean coughed in surprise as he took a sip of his drink.

"You were on deep space assignment," Sean said, brushing droplets from his pant leg. "How do you meet someone?"

"Her name is Mirina Canopus. She's an ambassador. I was

assigned to escort her home. If I'd known, I never would have," Vincent rubbed his face with his hands. "Oh, what have I done?"

Sean narrowed his eyes and mumbled as he took another sip. "You could have told me and saved us the trouble of the trip."

"I needed to tell Anaya...Ann...myself."

Agent Knox looked to Ann. "Ann, do you have anything you would like to say?"

The deed was done, but instead of relief Ann's anxiety grew, quaking in her chest. She shook her head and clamped her mouth shut. She tried to swallow the bubble rising in her throat but this time it wouldn't budge.

"Yes, you do," the agent said. She lifted her glasses, violet eyes full of sympathy. "My glasses can read your vital signs. They help me interpret what you're feeling. Ann, I can see your anger. Please...you're not doing yourself any good holding it in."

Ann stared at her hands curled in her lap, breath coming faster. She remembered the time jumper struggling in the whirlpool from the monument. No one reached out for her. No one tried to pull her back into the boat. All those months waiting and wondering and no one came. The bubble burst, unleashing a tidal wave. The torrent pulled Ann under and she closed her eyes as images ripped from her memory.

*The cockpit shifted underneath. Metal strained—the sound of a death moan. Cracks stretched across the damaged canopy window, obscuring the view of the debris field. Ann gasped for breath, choking on the tainted air. Arcs of electricity sparked from the shattered control panel. She couldn't move. Pain stabbed from every direction. Ann looked down at her blistered hands. A few singed pieces of her gloves remained and clung to raw flesh. A flash of blue light reflected on the window of the cockpit. Ann turned her head a fraction to look out the side window.*

"Ann?"

Agent Knox's voice pulled Ann back to the reception room. She opened her eyes and saw her hands clutching the folds of her skirt. Her hands were perfect without a trace of a scar or blemish, but at that moment she could still feel them burning. Ann's memory lay open, as bloodied as a fresh wound.

"You left." Ann said, hating how her voice squeaked. "You left and you didn't come for me. I waited for someone to come find me and no one came."

"We searched for two weeks," Vincent said. "I would have stayed if I thought there was any hope you were still alive. I thought...we all thought...you were gone." He reached out to take her hand, but Ann pulled back.

"Sean thought I was dead, but he still tried to find out what caused the accident." Ann's voice rose with anger. "Maybe if you stayed, maybe if you helped him, Sean would have found me sooner?"

"Ann, it's all right."

She rounded on her brother. "NO, IT'S NOT!" She looked to Vincent. "You left and didn't even try to find out what happened to me!"

"That's why we're here now," Agent Knox said. "We want to understand what happened, but you need to tell us what you remember."

Ann closed her eyes and clenched her hands. "I was trapped in the cockpit. I don't know for how long." She spoke through gritted teeth. "I wanted to blow the hatch and end it before bio-support shut down, but I couldn't." Ann opened her eyes and looked at Vincent. She felt her face twist with rage. "And I was so angry! I was angry at you! You said you would always be there for me and you didn't come. *And how I hated you for it!*"

Vincent stared at Ann, his face white with shock. His eyes wavered and his voice broke as he whispered, "I'm so sorry."

"We did a full sweep of the area after the accident and didn't find anything," Sean said. "We didn't even know about the second crash site for four months. It's not Vincent's fault." Her brother's tone was gentle, but Ann still felt the sting of a rebuke.

"It *is* my fault," Vincent said in disgrace. "I should have stayed. I left because I was a coward. I couldn't face the thought…" The commander looked down at the ring on the table. He reached out to take it then slid it back across the table to Ann. Vincent looked into Ann's eyes and his tears cut her where Sean's reprimand only stung. "I can't take the ring back. I gave it to you. You can do whatever you want with it. I do still care for you even if we can never be together. It's my fault. You have every right to be angry with me. I hope maybe someday you can forgive me."

Vincent stood and walked to the door. Ann heard the door slide open and shut, and her heart tore in two.

# NINETEEN

## *THE MONKEY'S FIST*

"Are you sure he's in there?"

Arnold squinted through a gap in the stacked crates, the heavy mist beading on his slicker.

"Mike said he would be and he knows the habits of every barfly in town," John said. He tucked a laser pistol in his belt.

John and Arnold had taken cover between the wall of crates and the edge of the pier. John could hear the black water of the harbor as it slopped against the pilings under the dock. Given the darkness and lateness of the hour, stealth was most likely unnecessary, but he didn't want to be seen out in the open until he was ready.

"Are you sure he was the one Lena saw?"

Arnold straightened and pulled his cap down. "That's what she said. Your boot buckle chap and Bernie McKenna were talking in the park the day your winery was broken into. Lena thought it was a strange pairing at the time but forgot about it until now."

"You trust her?"

"I think she's hoping to redeem herself and get out of stockroom duty," Arnold said. "But I've never known her to make up stories."

John unzipped the canvas duffel bag sitting on top of the crate in front of him. It made sense. McKenna had a slightly shady reputation. He'd bet a keg of beer the con man was the second prowler in the winery that night. John took the laser cutter from the bag and shoved it into a coat pocket. The cutter's clamp was too large even when fully retracted. The square handle showed a few inches above the top of the pocket. John tore the pocket lining to make more room. The minor alteration did the trick and the entire handle disappeared deep within his coat.

Arnold frowned. "What are you going to do?"

"I need to know where our boot buckle friend is," John said. No one had seen him since John's encounter in the winery. John took a second laser pistol from the bag and handed it to Arnold. "Here."

Arnold cringed and took the pistol. "How many of these do you have?" John shot his friend a hard look as he turned up the collar on his coat. "Right, I don't want to know." Arnold took a deep breath. "What do you want me to do?"

"Nothing for now. Just wait here. You'll know if you need to do anything."

John practiced pulling the laser cutter out of his pocket until he could pull the clamp free in one, clean motion.

"Be careful," Arnold said, his mouth tight as he watched John. "I'm not sure how I could explain all of this if anything goes wrong."

"Don't worry. This won't take long."

John checked to make sure nothing showed under his coat and stepped from behind the crates. He tucked his chin against the mist. The streets were empty except for the scurries of rats in the shadows. John gripped the metal handle in his pocket and held it tight against his leg as he walked. His thoughts drifted to Ann and what she was doing at that moment. John gripped the handle tighter and buried his feelings. He couldn't afford any distractions.

The windows of The Monkey's Fist threw squares of light onto the wet cobblestones. The bartender looked up when John walked in, but then went back to reading the dog-eared pages of his book. The bar smelled of stale beer and old piss, or maybe it was the other way around. It was hard to tell. John scanned the room, searching faces in the dim light. Hunchbacked men huddled in mumbled conversations or stared with empty eyes into their glasses of beer.

John spotted McKenna's shock of red hair sticking up from a booth toward the back. The con man had an arm around a serving girl. She giggled as McKenna pressed his lips to her ear and tried to slide a hand lower on her bosom, his fingers tracing the neckline of her blouse. John moved quickly, pulling the clamp out of his pocket.

McKenna looked up and broke into a nervous grin when he saw John.

"Captain Galeas! What a pleasant surpri—"

John grabbed the big man by the collar and yanked him to his feet. He raised the laser cutter to McKenna's neck and pulled the trigger.

CRACK!

The clamp's jaws opened wide and shot forward. The serving girl screamed and scrambled to get out of the way, scattering beer bottles as she went. The clamp closed around McKenna's throat. The con man gasped and grabbed at his neck, his eyes the size of dinner plates. John gripped the clamp's handle. McKenna squirmed like a dog on a leash.

The bartender reached under the bar. John pulled the pistol from his belt with his free hand and swung it toward the bartender.

"I'm settling a bar tab!"

The bartender raised his hands and backed away. The few patrons who jumped to their feet during the commotion settled back down and watched with uneasy eyes from behind their drinks.

John backed into the hallway behind the bar pulling McKenna after him. He pushed open the door to the storeroom with a shoulder. The door banged open and John swung his captive inside. He kicked the door shut and turned to McKenna.

"Do you know what this is?" John jerked the clamp's

handle.

The big man struggled to keep his feet and collapsed onto a beer keg. His face was as gray as a weathered topsail. McKenna's eyes flicked to the clamp around his neck and nodded as best he could, given the circumstances.

"I once saw someone cut through twelve inches of steel in ten seconds with one of these," John said. "I wonder how much faster it could take your head off."

McKenna swallowed hard and turned a sickly shade of green.

"You were in my winery. Why?"

The con man hesitated. John flipped open the plastic cover on the side of the handle with a thumb. A red button glowed underneath.

"Okay! Okay! Please d-don't!" McKenna said, voice raspy. "We didn't take anything. I swear! He just wanted to look around. He needed my help to get inside!" He wheezed with every breath.

"What was his name?"

"Scrivani!"

John's jaw clenched. He already suspected as much, but it was strange to hear the name spoken out loud after all those years.

"Where is he?"

"I don't know!" Beads of sweat trickled from McKenna's hairline. "He was hurt real bad. I think he left the Colonies."

"Was he with anybody? Did he talk about anyone else?"

"No! I swear. I don't know anything else! It was a one-time job! Please!"

John leaned in close and stared into the man's gray eyes. "If you see him again, you tell him to stay the hell away from my tavern."

McKenna nodded and licked his lips.

John released the clamp.

The con man dropped to his knees, gasping for air.

"Anybody asks, you tell them you settled your bar tab with me," John said. "If you say anything else about this conversation, I'll know."

John slipped the laser cutter back into his coat pocket and left the storeroom. He pulled out a small wad of bills and left the money on the bar as he passed. No one stopped him or made eye contact as John walked through the bar and out into the empty street.

John's footsteps echoed as he hurried to the end of the pier. His encounter with McKenna wouldn't do much for his reputation around town, but it had to be done. John felt for the pistol in his belt as his eyes darted to the shadows. He hoped McKenna was right and Scrivani had left the Colonies with his tail between his legs.

Arnold was on John as soon as he rounded the crates.

"What happened?"

"I'll tell you everything, but not here."

John and Arnold slipped from behind the crates and headed back to Siren's Cove. They took the long way around, dodging streetlamps. John told Arnold about his conversation with McKenna as they weaved through the crooked streets. Arnold listened quietly until John finished.

"So you know this Scrivani fellow," Arnold said and panted as he tried to keep up with John's long strides. "So was he...?"

John hesitated and weighed how much to tell Arnold.

"Scrivani was our front man. His job was to look for opportunities and report back to the Tyrhenian syndicate. He was captured in one of the early raids."

"I thought they were all sentenced to life without parole."

"Not all of them," John said. "Scrivani was always a smooth talker. I heard he earned early release a few years back and disappeared."

"So did McKenna say what they were doing in your winery?"

"No. He said they were just looking around."

John had turned the question over in his mind since he left The Monkey's Fist. Was Scrivani simply paying him a visit out of curiosity, or did the front man see something else that interested him?

"Well, the good news is, it sounds like you scared him off," Arnold said.

John couldn't share Arnold's optimism. McKenna's word offered no guarantee. John's only option was to keep his eyes open and hope Scrivani had gone back into hiding.

The two men rounded a corner and walked down another street to Siren's Cove. They stood in the shadow of the house. All the windows of the tavern were dark. Arnold handed the laser pistol back to John.

"It certainly has been an interesting evening," Arnold said. He grinned and inclined his head in the direction of the tavern. "Should we raise a glass to our courage?"

John chuckled. "Maybe tomorrow." He took the laser cutter out of his pocket. "I promised Oz I'd have this fixed and back to him at the salvage yard by tomorrow morning."

John pushed the red button on the metal handle. The clamp clicked, buzzed loudly, and stopped. Arnold lifted the brim of his cap and looked at the clamp, perplexed. He looked up at John, eyes wide in disbelief.

"You bluffed McKenna?"

John smiled and shrugged. Arnold tossed his head back and laughed.

"You are without a doubt the craziest person I've ever met!"

# TWENTY

## *ADRIFT*

*The crowd burst through the doors of the banquet hall, spilling into the courtyard like shiny coins. Vincent took Anaya's hand. He smiled and her heart leaped. She loved how the light from the windows danced in his eyes. Vincent pulled Anaya through the crowd toward the tree line. She didn't resist. She knew where he led her and why – the ring box nestled deep inside a jacket pocket.*

*Anaya's feet skimmed the path as she walked. The trail skirted the trees and they came to a stone bridge spanning a creek. I know this place. The creek swelled. The water churned and boiled between the banks.*

*Anaya stepped onto the bridge and felt it shudder from the water as it carved through the creek bed below. She looked over the side of the bridge. Her gait slowed. Voices chattered beneath the roar of the water. Anaya tried to grasp the words, but they bounced along with the current, impossible to catch. A peculiar feeling knotted her stomach and coursed through her arms and legs. The currents are treacherous.*

*Anaya shook off the voices and forced herself to turn away from the water. Vincent had dropped her hand and continued across the bridge without looking back. Anaya hurried to catch up and stumbled, landing hard on her hands and knees. Beneath her outstretched hands the bridge's cobblestones split apart. Terror shot through Anaya as the mortar between the bricks disintegrated to dust before her eyes. She looked through the widening gaps to the water rushing below. The water roared. The voices grew louder.*

*"Please!" She begged the stones to hold together. "Please let me cross!" She screamed to Vincent, "Help me!" But Vincent was gone. Anaya reached for the side of the bridge to steady herself. The stones crumbled under her touch. Great blocks toppled into the water and opened a gaping hole in the side of the bridge.*

*The sky darkened and the air thickened. The sound of the water filled her head, pulling her toward the gap in the side of the bridge.*

*Anaya clawed at the cobblestones with her hands. "LET ME GO!"*

*The heels of her boots scraped the stones, but the bridge tipped and twisted under her. Anaya slid toward the edge of the bridge and fell. Her body stretched toward the water. The wind rushed past. Anaya screamed as the water reached out and pulled her under the churning waves.*

\*\*\*

Ann sat up in bed gasping for air. She wrapped her arms around her shoulders to slow her breathing. She looked around at the room's unfamiliar gray and chrome furnishings and remembered she was in the cabin on the space station Navis. Ann kicked off the covers. She needed to get back to the Colonies.

\*\*\*

"Do you remember being in the water?"

Ann glanced to Agent Knox sitting across from her. The drab blue and gray furniture of the cabin's common area made her miss the sitting room back at Siren's Cove all the more. Ann had spent the last fifteen minutes telling the agent about her dream. She needed someone to help her make sense of the images and Agent Knox seemed the logical choice. Fionna smiled and waited patiently for Ann to answer.

Ann shifted in her chair and nodded. She remembered the water all too well – the sensation of the water filling her mouth and ears clung to her like a wet sheet.

Fionna made a few notes on the digital pad balanced on a knee. Her bio-vision glasses rested on top of her blond-bobbed head. She had offered to remove her glasses as long as Ann promised to be honest and answer all of the questions.

Agent Knox finished taking notes and looked up at Ann.

"You said you heard voices." It was strange to see the woman's violet eyes without the yellow glasses to obscure them.

"This wasn't really a dream, was it?" Ann thought of Vincent's ring sitting on the nightstand in the next room. Her heart winced.

"You were dreaming about events leading up to your accident," Fionna said and brushed a strand of hair from her eyes with the end of the stylus. "Your brother told me Vincent proposed to you one week prior to the test flight." Ann's face flushed with the realization. "We need to separate the dream elements from actual memories. There may be clues as to what caused your accident. Can you remember what the voices said?" Fionna gave Ann another coaxing smile.

Ann narrowed her eyes in thought. The voices had grown strongest when she was in the water, but she had only been in the water a second or two before she woke up.

"I couldn't understand most of what the voices were saying, but I'm certain I heard the word vibration."

"Are you sure?"

Ann thought for a moment. "Yes, I'm sure that's what I heard."

The agent's stylus flew across the digital pad. "Is that all you can remember? Anything else?"

Ann shook her head. "That's all."

Ann heard the door to the common area slide open.

"Ann, are you up? I brought you something."

Sean stepped into the sitting room carrying a thin metallic case in one hand. He stopped short. His eyes brightened as his gaze darted to Agent Knox then back to Ann.

"Sorry, I hope I'm not interrupting."

Fionna tucked the stylus into the side compartment in the digital pad. "We were just finishing up." She turned to Ann and stood to leave. "If you remember anything else, you know how to get a hold of me."

Sean watched Agent Knox leave, then looked at Ann.

"So you and Fionna had a good talk?"

"She just stopped by for coffee." Ann took the empty

coffee mugs to the kitchenette. Now that she knew Sean and the Commander were friends it felt weird to talk to him about Vincent. "When's the next shuttle back to the Colonies?"

Sean's smile collapsed into a frown.

"I'm in meetings this afternoon. We'll fly to Andarria tomorrow morning and catch a shuttle to the Colonies from there."

"I could fly back by myself. I don't mind."

"Sorry. Protocol," Sean said. "You arrived here with me as my guest. I'm afraid you're stuck with me as your chaperone until your status and privileges are restored."

Ann let out a growl of frustration and dropped back into her chair. She had hoped as soon as she completed her task they would fly back to the Colonies.

"Stop being such a baby about it."

Ann looked up expecting to see her brother's teasing smile and instead met a stony gaze.

"I had hoped coming here would have reminded you of your responsibilities, but I guess I was wrong."

Ann stiffened. Sean had never used that tone with her before.

"I have responsibilities at home too," Ann said, eyeing him. "You said you had something for me." Ann gestured to the metallic case still in Sean's hands, hoping a change of subject would lighten the mood.

Sean looked down, brow furrowed. He opened the case and removed a black half-moon disc.

"Put this in your ear," Sean said and handed her the device.

The disc was smaller than Ann's palm and reminded her of the e-polyglots the off tourists wore on the Colonies. A metal clip curved outward from the disc's rounded side. Two lights blinked in tandem in its center.

"What is it?"

"It's a keravnos implant," Sean said. "Your memory wasn't the only thing damaged during the accident."

Ann lifted the implant to an ear and the image of Minister Greffenius and all his mechanical accessories came to mind.

She hesitated.

Sean let out a weary sigh and rubbed his eyes. "Why is everything such a battle with you? Just put the damn thing on."

Ann glared. "Before I stick this in my ear, I would like to know exactly what it does."

"It's another piece of your past." Ann shot her brother a dubious look. "You are a time jumper. You seemed curious enough yesterday." Sean shrugged. "I'm just trying to give you some of your old life back. The keravnos implant is kind of hard to explain, so you'll just have to trust me on this one, okay?"

Ann frowned and looked at the implant. The disc looked harmless enough. She looped the piece around the back of an ear. The disc settled into place and Ann felt a hum. The vibration grew stronger, reaching inside her head – an odd, twisting sensation. She scrunched her eyes tightly, grimaced, and lifted a hand to shield herself from the pain she was sure would follow. But it never came. The humming stopped. The blood pounded in Ann's ears and she opened her eyes.

Ann let out a soft moan. She could feel the space station's power as it cascaded all around her. The station hummed its own unique song, rising and falling in pitch like a massive orchestra tuning its instruments. Ann gazed about the room in amazement and discovered she could focus her attention toward any power source in the room, sharpening the intensity of the electrical notes or letting the music fade into the background until the song disappeared entirely. The implant chirped periodically in Ann's ear.

"It's beautiful," Ann said and didn't try to hide the amazement in her voice. "What is it?"

"Electro-perception." Her eyes swept back to Sean. He tossed a pillow off a chair and slumped into the seat. "You're a Vego. You can sense power sources like other people can see and hear. It's what makes you so good at your job as a time jumper."

Ann looked away, distracted by a tremolo coming from behind a bulkhead.

"The ancients thought Vegos could map and interpret the meaning of lightning in the sky," Sean continued. "They thought the lightning bolts were messages from the gods. You can sense electrical pulses, and in some instances manipulate energy, but as far as I know you're not taking dictation from deities." He made a sweeping gesture with both arms. "If you'd stuck with the memory therapy you would have figured this all out on your own. Didn't you wonder how you could sense and activate the power source in your quarterstaff?"

Ann had wondered, but at the same time it had felt so natural she accepted it. She closed her eyes and rested her head against the back of the chair. She could still sense the electrical pulses coming from the kitchenette as they rolled and tumbled toward her like notes descending on a scale. She touched the implant in her ear with her fingertips. Sensing the energy around her was as familiar as a favorite blanket and as comfortable as an old pair of shoes. *How could I have forgotten?* Ann pulled her focus away from the electrical symphony and opened her eyes. Her brother watched from his chair with a self-satisfied smirk.

"The implant stimulates the areas of your brain that control your electro-perceptive ability and gets them firing again," Sean said, his voice still sharp with irritation. "I would have given it to you sooner, but you've been such a pain in the ass about everything there was never a good time."

Ann's cheeks warmed with embarrassment. Sean was right. All he'd done since finding her on the Colonies was to try and help her remember who she was. Would it hurt to trust him a little? Ann sighed and met his gaze. "What was I like before the accident?"

"No different from how you are now—aggravating and stubborn as hell."

Ann took a deep breath and told him about the vision of the Lieutenant after the session with the neural stimulator.

"The Lieutenant threatened me like I wasn't supposed to be here. The look on her face…" Ann suppressed a shudder. "I know it sounds ridiculous, but I thought she was going to kill me. I didn't want to be that person, to become someone I wouldn't recognize."

"You were never cruel or vicious," Sean said. "You are still the sister I remember."

Ann breathed a sigh of relief. "I'm sorry about Vincent. I know he was your friend."

Sean shrugged and smiled. "He still is and he's still your friend too if you'll let him be."

Ann felt a rush of anger.

"If Andarrians can control time, why couldn't anyone see my accident coming? Why couldn't someone have fixed time or prevented the accident from happening in the first place?"

Sean rubbed the back of his neck. "No one could have predicted your accident, and once it occurred there was no way we could have undone it. The First Law of Ineluctabilis—Andarrians cannot knowingly tamper with their own timeline." Sean shrugged. "We don't get do-overs."

"How come I never heard about any of this on the Colonies?"

"The colonists are civilians. Only Andarrian special forces are allowed devices to time travel." Sean handed her the implant's metallic case. "You should try to wear it as much as possible. You won't sense as much on the Colonies as on a ship or space station, but it will still be good practice for you. It will retrain your brain until you won't need to wear it anymore."

Ann turned the case over in her hand, relieved the implant was only temporary.

"You know, you could live on the Colonies and still be a time jumper," Sean said. "They could still use you."

"I don't know," Ann said. It was all too much to think about.

"It's your choice. A lot of people think women make better time jumpers. I agree." Sean propped his feet up on the table and leaned back in the chair. His mouth curled into his familiar smile. "The right woman can make hours feel like minutes. The wrong woman can make minutes feel like a life sentence."

*\*\**

Sean's meetings kept him occupied most of the day. Before he left their quarters, he suggested Ann explore the space station on her own.

"But I thought you were my chaperone? Don't you have to be with me?"

"That's only if you try to leave the station," he said as he pulled on his uniform jacket. "If you stay in the public areas, no one will give you any trouble. Tell them you're with me if anyone asks, but if you're caught hijacking a starship back to the Colonies, leave me out of it." Ann smirked and rolled her eyes. Sean finished with the top button of his jacket and adjusted his sword belt. "Wear the keravnos implant. It will be good practice for you." Sean tossed her a grin and left the cabin.

*\*\**

Ann wandered through the crowded atrium. Groups of visitors hurried under the armillary sphere as the monument's rings completed circuits high overhead. With the implant tucked in her ear, Ann could sense the deep, brassy notes of energy radiating from the center of the monument.

She had explored the space station's corridors and observation decks for over an hour, delighting in each new discovery: the reedy notes of the tram cars, the trills and pops of unidentified power sources hidden nearby. Ann smiled to herself. Sean was right. *This is who I am.* She tried not to think about how close she'd come to refusing the implant.

Ann stopped to look at the golden river at the base of the monument. A few people muttered their displeasure as they were forced to walk around her.

"I'll be staying in Palladium Beta if you need to reach me."

Ann snapped her attention away from the monument and back to the crowded atrium. The implant chirped a single note and the energies she sensed faded into nothing. She spun around to look for the source of the familiar voice and saw Vincent hurrying toward the tram platform. Janus walked rapidly at his side, carrying a travel bag.

Ann sprinted through the crowd after Vincent. They were almost to the platform.

"Commander! Commander Lazar!"

Vincent and the steward stopped and scanned the crowd. Ann cringed. She'd called out before she'd thought through exactly what to say.

Vincent found Ann as she stepped from the crowd. His mouth stiffened and she saw in his eyes the same sorrow from the night before.

"I…I just wanted to…" Ann's voice trailed off. The Commander's blue eyes reminded Ann so much of John's, or had John's eyes reminded her of Vincent's? Her chest felt tight.

"I wanted to say good-bye."

Janus excused himself a few discreet paces and talked to a young military officer waiting to board the tram.

"Ann, I'm so sorry. I didn't think you wanted to see me, else I would have left word. My shuttle leaves in a few minutes."

Ann looked around, unsure of what to do. Did it even matter anymore?

"It wasn't your fault. I know that now." The words tumbled out in a rush. "There was no way you could have known what happened to me."

Vincent blinked in surprise. For an instant, Ann saw the anguish of his heart etched in his face. Vincent took a step towards Ann, but then stopped and collected himself, as if remembering the crowds of people milling around them.

"Ann…"

"I didn't want to see you. I was afraid if I remembered my old life, I would lose everything I have on the Colonies. Sean says I don't have to give up anything, but he's wrong. Even if all my memories come back, it will never be like it was before. It's my life here in this world that I've lost."

Vincent reached out and took Ann's hand in his. He wore the same hopeful expression he wore in her dream. Gravity shifted under Ann's feet and a deep sense of longing welled up inside of her.

"You haven't lost me. I'm still here," he said. "Just tell me what you want me to do."

The light from Ann's smile faded as a dull sadness crept across her heart. Vincent cared for her, but his love was fragile. Even now, he hesitated. Had it always been this way? The longing Ann felt was only a memory and it disappeared like a curl of smoke. She looked away.

"I remember you. I remember us." Ann shook her head. "But I'm in love with someone else. I'm sorry."

Vincent sighed, a strangely deep and lonely sound for the crowded atrium. He stared at the floor deep in thought, his mouth set, but he did not let go of her hand. Janus returned and stood expectantly.

"Commander, I'm sorry for the interrupt—"

"Yes! Yes! I'm coming!"

Vincent's eyes darted to Ann's. His face pinched. "If you ever need anything. If there's anything I can do." Ann nodded and blinked the tears from her eyes. He took a deep breath. "Be happy."

Ann's fingers slipped from his grasp. Vincent turned and walked toward the tram platform.

***

Ann walked back to her quarters. Her heart felt heavier with every step. The flight back to the Colonies would not come soon enough. The cabin door slid open and Ann stepped into the common room.

"Do you realize what you've done!?"

Ann stopped in her tracks. Sean paced the common room. His hand gripped the hilt of his sword, so the knuckles shone white against the gold. Agent Knox stood in the middle of the room, arms crossed, with a very uncharacteristic scowl as she glared at the Montressador. Her bio-vision glasses rested on top of her head. They hadn't heard Ann enter the common room.

"Why are you so surprised? This is an active investigation," Fionna said as she watched Sean pace. "I've been filing reports since day one. I did my job!"

Sean turned to Fionna and spoke through gritted teeth. "It was a private matter. You had no right!"

"Ann *remembers* being in the wreckage! She *remembers* events prior to the crash and she is showing signs of *remembering* what caused it! I did not include in my report details of Ann's relationship with Commander Lazar, but I did have an obligation to report my findings!"

Ann stepped the rest of the way into the room, heart pounding. "What's going on?"

Sean and Fionna froze, their eyes locked onto Ann. The agent opened her mouth to speak, but Sean was quicker.

"The crash investigation committee read Fionna's latest report," Sean said, his mouth twisted in resentment. "They're now demanding you return to Andarria immediately to testify."

Sean's words hit Ann like a blow to the stomach. Agent Knox had been assigned to investigate the accident, so of course she would send reports along with anything else Ann said back to her superiors. Ann felt foolish for ever trusting her.

Fionna stiffened. She looked at Sean, her face sharp with her own bitterness. "Montressador Chapman, I have no control over how my reports are interpreted or what actions the committee chooses to take." She turned to Ann. Her eyes softened. "They ignored my recommendations. I'm sorry."

Ann glared back. She was in no mood to forgive. She looked to Sean.

"What good am I to the committee if I can't remember what caused the accident? It doesn't make sense."

Sean continued pacing and scratched his beard. "I think they've already made up their minds. Your testimony is only a formality. The committee will rule pilot error unless we can provide evidence it wasn't."

Ann swallowed hard. "If they say it's my fault, what happens to me?"

Sean's brow knotted. "The *Kairos* was a valuable prototype. If they can prove negligence, it could mean five years in a penal colony."

Ann's knees wobbled. For a moment, she felt like she stood on the bridge from her dream with everything crumbling around her. She gripped the back of a chair to steady herself.

"I wasn't the only investigator," Fionna said. "If we can delay the committee, I can find out what evidence they have and give Ann more time to remember."

Sean looked at the agent, his face steeped in anger. The data link pad beeped in his pocket.

"It's Jo," he said, looking at the screen. "I'll put her on the viewer."

Sean activated the comm station on the table. A large panel on the wall glowed and a woman's face appeared. Dark curls draped from the loose knot pinned to the back of her head.

"Tell me you have good news, Jo," Sean said.

"I'm sorry, Montressador." The image of the woman watched him pace in front of the viewer. Worry creased the corners of her eyes. "I'm still trying to reach the Minister, but I did leave a message with his aide. I've also been researching protocols but haven't found a way to delay the committee."

Sean shook his head. "We need a legal precedent. If the committee followed protocol, they wouldn't require Ann to testify while she was still on the injured list."

Jo's image touched the screen. An information box opened, filling one half of the viewer as the box with her image slid to the other side. Jo scrolled through the pages of electronic documents with a flick of a finger.

"The committee is arguing that only applies to physical injuries and not to loss of identity or memory aberrations," Jo said and enlarged a paragraph for the others to read.

"But her memory loss was caused by anachronosis," Fionna said. "It is a type of brain injury. Couldn't we argue on those grounds?"

Jo looked to the agent and shook her head. "The committee said if Ann was well enough to travel to a space station, she is well enough to testify." Sean muttered to himself and rubbed his eyes. Jo glanced in his direction. "I'll keep searching."

"Keep the comm line open," Sean said. "We'll keep working on the problem here."

Jo nodded and touched the screen. The information box cleared and was replaced by a rolling field of data that changed as quickly as her fingers skimmed the control panel.

Ann heard the door to the common room slide open. She spun around in time to see Agent Drake stroll into the room followed by two station guards. Drake wore the same dark suit and white pocket square from their first meeting at Siren's Cove. The skin on his nose stretched so tight the capillaries stood out like red lines on a star chart in the artificial light. Drake looked around at their stunned faces, wearing a cold dead smile.

"Drake." Sean spat out the name as if it were a curse. "Two guards? Don't you think that's excessive?"

"Good evening, Montressador Chapman," Drake said. "Please forgive the interruption. This will only take a moment." Ann's insides twisted as Drake's eyes found hers. "Lieutenant Chapman, you are ordered to come with me to Andarria and submit to questioning."

"The Lieutenant is in my charge," Sean said, stepping forward. "You can't take her from this station without my permission."

"My orders come directly from Commander Rectrix," Drake said. He regarded Sean with a sneer. "Your antiquated office holds no authority here." Drake motioned to the guards. "Remove her."

The guards stepped forward to obey. Ann raised her hands to defend herself.

"No!"

Sean threw an arm across Ann, knocking her backward into Agent Knox. Ann heard the sharp ring of metal as her brother drew his sword and leveled it at the two guards. Fionna grabbed Ann's arm and yanked her out of the way.

"Montressador, *wait*!"

Ann wrenched her arm free from Fionna and looked at the

viewer. She had forgotten about Jo. Maybe there was a chance she could get out of this mess after all.

"Kind of busy, Jo," Sean said, voice taunt. "If you have something, you better make it fast."

Agent Drake's eyes flicked toward the viewscreen and back to the Montressador's blade in front of him. The guards exchanged nervous glances as they contemplated their next move.

Jo's mouth tightened. She took a breath to compose herself and enlarged the image of an ancient legal document on the screen for all to see.

"*Ex Concessis, Nolo Contendere.*"

Sean's shoulders drooped and he lowered his sword. Drake broke into a broad grin.

"I don't understand," Ann said. "What does it mean?"

Jo looked to Ann. Her eyes conceded defeat.

"It means you accept the committee's evidence and resign your commission." The color rose to Ann's face in hot, prickly waves. "As long as you have no memory of the accident, it's your only option. Your career as a time jumper would be over, but by pleading no contest they could not force you to testify in front of the committee. You should be able to avoid prison." Jo sighed. "I'm sorry. I was saving it only as a last resort."

Sean returned the sword to its sheath. He stepped back, keeping a hand on the hilt and his eyes on the guards. Agent Drake looked at Ann with a self-satisfied smirk.

"All that's needed from you, Lieutenant, is to verbally state your plea and your intent to resign in the presence of three officers," Drake said. "And as luck would have it," his eyes flicked to Sean. "Agent Knox, your brother, and I make three. One simple statement from you and all your problems disappear."

Fionna whispered in Ann's ear. "We don't even know the committee's evidence yet. You could still remember what caused the accident."

"And if I can't remember?"

"If you resign now, you would give up any chance of continuing your career," Fionna said. "You could never be a time jumper again."

"It would make my job easier," Drake said. He dabbed at the beads of sweat that had gathered on his forehead with a pocket square. "Although I did enjoy the thought of dragging you in front of the committee."

Ann felt everything crumbling around her again, but this time anger burned inside. How could she admit fault for something she could not remember doing? But if she didn't resign, the committee might still find her guilty. Ann thought of John waiting back at Siren's Cove and remembered what Sean had said. *If they can prove negligence.* She tried to swallow the lump in her throat and pushed the thought away. The committee would have to convict her first. Ann clenched her hands and met Drake's gaze.

"No." The single word gave her courage. She took a deep breath. "I won't resign. I will go with you to testify."

Drake smiled in triumph and turned to Sean. "Well, well. It looks like baby sister has some backbone after all."

"Amazing, isn't she?" Sean said. "She's twice the man you are...or were." Sean looked at Drake, his mouth slipping into a wicked grin.

Drake's face reddened as he scowled back. He motioned for the guards.

Sean turned to Ann. His face glowed with pride, but his eyes showed concern. "It's going to be okay." He attempted to bolster Ann with a smile. "I'll get it sorted out somehow."

Ann tried to hitch a smile on her face in return. The guards had clasped her arms and ushered her towards the door.

"Wait!" Jo's voice rang out again from the viewer. "Montressador, I have an incoming communication. Transferring."

Sean blocked the doorway to keep the guards from leaving with Ann. The screen flickered and Minister Greffenius' face appeared. He blinked and looked around at everyone in surprise.

"I can SEE why your assis-tant said it was an emer-gency, Mon-TRESS-ador." The Minister's computerized voice blared from the view screen.

Agent Drake stepped forward with a bow. "Minister, with all due respect I am expected urgently on Andarria with—"

"Then I WILL be brief," Minister Greffenius said cutting him off. Drake narrowed his eyes and nodded to the minister to continue. "I spoke to AD-mir-al Dhow. I ex-plained the sit-ua-TION and he con-tacted Com-MAN-der Rectrix. The committee has agreed to POST-pone Lieutenant Chapman's TES-timony."

Ann gaped at Sean, but his eyes cautioned her to stay quiet.

"I don't believe you," Drake said, his face coloring. "I won't believe it until I hear from Commander Rectrix herself!"

Minister Greffenius frowned and peered at Drake from the screen. "A-gent Drake, isn't it? You should be receiv-ING word any mo-ment."

Drake's front pocket of his coat beeped. His face turned a deeper shade of red. He yanked the data link pad from his coat and scowled at the message on its screen. He jammed the device back into a pocket, turned on his heel, and stormed out of the common room. The guards released Ann and followed Drake.

"Thank you, minister," Sean said and breathed a deep sigh of relief. "If there is ever anything I can do for you."

Minister Greffenius smiled and shook his head. "There is NO need to thank me." He looked to Ann. His eyes twinkled. "You have three weeks, Lieu-ten-ant. Make me PROUD."

# TWENTY-ONE

## *THE TROUBLE WITH PIRATES*

Rumors of John's excursion to The Monkey's Fist spread, and before the sun sank below the planet's rim, everyone in Llewelyn had heard at least one version of the evening's events. One story claimed he'd gone on a drunken rampage. Another said he'd fought with Bernie McKenna over a barmaid. John did not realize how far the stories had traveled until Mrs. Beaumont returned from her afternoon shopping. She dropped the packages on the kitchen table and advised him in a frosty tone, "Respectable tavern owners get drunk in their own establishments and not among thieves and layabouts down by the docks." John said nothing and did his best to look guilty for her benefit. The wilder the tale, the further from the truth.

John looked in the bathroom mirror and worked the straight-edge razor in short brisk strokes. Ann would be returning on the late afternoon shuttle, and John had happily agreed to Mrs. Beaumont's suggestion of a welcome home dinner. She then suggested John consider making himself more presentable before Ann got home—hence the shave.

A rap on the master bedroom door made John jump. The razor slipped and bit into his cheek. John cursed the mother of the person responsible and dabbed at his face with a piece of tissue to stop the flow.

"Come!"

The bedroom door opened and Dr. Brainard appeared in the bathroom doorway, his face uncertain.

"Mrs. Beaumont invited me for dinner," the doctor said, hands in pockets. "I hope you don't mind."

John winced. He knew he'd been standoffish with the doctor since their argument in the tavern, but he never intended for their friendship to suffer.

"Of course not," John said, his voice gruff. "I'm glad you came."

Dr. Brainard's face brightened a degree only to turn somber a second later.

"John, I've heard some unsettling news."

"Save your breath," John said with a sigh. He drew the razor upward along his neck. "Mrs. Beaumont already lectured me."

The doctor looked confused a moment then shook his head. "No, not that. I heard your winery was broken into. Is it true?"

John finished with the razor and wiped the remaining traces of foam from his face. Dr. Brainard read his silence like a medical journal. His eyes narrowed.

"Who was it?"

John grabbed a shirt from the wall hook and pulled it on. "Arnold and I took care of it." He pushed past the doctor into the bedroom.

"This is exactly what I was afraid of! Who was it?"

John hazarded a glance in the doctor's direction as he buttoned his shirt. The man's face was red and well on its way to crimson. There was no use denying it.

"Scrivani."

Dr. Brainard's face blanched.

The muscles in John's jaw tightened. "I've had close calls before."

"Not like this." The doctor's face crumpled with worry.

John tucked in his shirt. "He's gone back into hiding.

Unless you have information I can use, there's nothing more I can do about it."

The doctor's eyes flashed behind his glasses. "Captain Galeas, you and I both know that's not true!"

"Don't start!"

"Fine!" Dr. Brainard leaned sulkily against the dresser. "How much does Arnold know?"

"He knows what I told him," John said. He wished the doctor would stop asking questions. He had enough to worry about with Ann coming home.

"John, they've never tracked you this far before. What are you going to do?"

"Nothing."

John slumped into the desk chair and tugged at his pigtail. Hope was the strategy of fools and little children, but the lack of information gave him few options.

"I can't do anything if I don't know where he is and I can't pick up and run." *Not without a good enough reason.*

"What if he comes back?"

The tension between John's shoulder blades felt tight enough to snap him in half. "I'll be ready for him this time."

\*\*\*

"You two chatter enough for a sewing circle," Mrs. Beaumont said, eyeing John and the doctor as they came down the stairs.

Ann had removed her traveling cloak. Her braid, windblown from the drive, fell loose and soft against her neck. John's heart ached at the sight of her, and as much as he tried not to show it, he still felt himself grinning like a fool.

Montressador Chapman and Dr. Brainard went out to the drive to collect Ann's trunk from the roadster. Mrs. Beaumont excused herself to check on dinner, a sly grin on her face. John didn't waste time. He scooped Ann up in his arms and kissed her. The warmth of her in his arms chased away all the worries that had haunted him the last few days.

Ann released John and eyed him with a worried expression. "The prowlers. Is everything all right?"

"Everything is fine," John said. "Just some teenagers on a lark. I don't think they'll give us any more trouble."

John felt the tension leave Ann's body and he became suddenly aware of every curve beneath her dress. His pulse quickened and he wished the house was empty.

Ann's lips strayed across his cheek. "Mmmm. You smell nice."

John chuckled. "Let's keep that our little secret."

He brushed Ann's cheek with the back of a hand and heard a high-pitched chirp. John's eyes darted to her ear where a black metal implant blinked. He frowned and tucked Ann's hair behind her ear for a closer look.

"What's this?"

Ann's eyes turned anxious and she touched the implant. John braced himself.

"A lot has happened."

*** 

"Three weeks?" Mrs. Beaumont passed the salad bowl to Dr. Brainard. "If Ann hasn't remembered by now, what could she possibly hope to remember in three weeks?"

They had all gathered around the kitchen table for dinner. John tried to enjoy his food, but after listening to Ann and her brother describe their encounter with Agent Drake, his anger and the cold fear he felt for Ann made it impossible.

"She made some progress while we were on Navis," Montressador Chapman said and helped himself to some more pot roast.

Ann nodded. "I remember more than I did a week ago. Maybe it's a good sign."

John stabbed a potato wedge with a fork and wondered darkly if Commander Lazar was the catalyst for her breakthrough.

"I don't want to discourage you," Dr. Brainard said. "But it's common for anachronosis patients to recover lost memories in random, non-linear bursts."

"That doesn't do us much good when we are trying to find a single memory," John grumbled. He put his fork down and looked at Ann. "It's more than remembering the accident. You'll have to remember the exact moment that triggered the crash. It could be only a fraction of a second, or it may have been caused by something you were completely unaware of at the time." John sighed. "Maybe you should just..."

Ann cocked her head and looked hard at John. "You want me to resign and plead no contest?"

John met her gaze but couldn't open his mouth to answer. How could she remember so much in so little time? And even if Ann did, would the committee take her testimony into consideration or were their minds already made up?

"Would resigning be so awful?" Mrs. Beaumont fixed her eyes on Ann. "I mean, considering the alternative if you can't remember? It just seems like such a gamble."

"I have to try," Ann said. "I don't know if I want to be a time jumper again, but I'm not ready to give it up either. I've lost too much already."

John swallowed his fear. Forward seemed the only way out. He looked at the Montressador. "So what do we do now?"

"Fionna is getting access to the committee's evidence. We're hoping it might trigger Ann to remember more details from the crash. Either way, we'll know what the committee's game is and what we're up against." Montressador Chapman turned to the doctor. "What about trying the neural stimulator again?"

Dr. Brainard shook his head. "I'm afraid not. When I returned the stimulator, Dr. Oribasius told me the longer you wait to administer follow up sessions the less chance you have for an improved result. It's most likely been too long since the original session for us to try again."

"So I guess we're down to remembering the old-fashioned way," Chapman said. He looked at Ann, his mouth tight. "Fionna says that at this point the trial is more important than memory therapy protocol. I'll round up all the memorabilia I have at home and send it to you. Maybe looking through old pictures will help move things along."

"And I'll talk to Dr. Oribasius again," Dr. Brainard said

with a sympathetic smile. "He might have other ideas."

The doctor picked up his wine glass to take a sip and hesitated. A curious expression crossed his face as he looked at Ann's keravnos implant.

Ann touched her ear. "What?"

"I was just thinking," Dr. Brainard said. "All this time your electro-perceptive abilities have been dormant, but you said when you used the keravnos implant for the first time it felt familiar."

"Yes...it surprised me at first but then..." Ann paused. She fixed eyes on the doctor. "It was like when I practiced with the memory box."

John stopped in mid chew, looked at Dr. Brainard and swallowed. "You think the implant might help Ann regain more of her memories?"

"It's possible," the doctor said and contemplated the wine in his glass. "Our senses involuntarily trigger memories all the time. A familiar sound or smell and you instantly remember, or even relive an event that happened months or years before." John looked down at his plate. He knew all too well the phenomenon the doctor described. "As Ann's electro-perceptive abilities grow stronger, she might find her memories coming more clearly into focus."

"It's an interesting theory," Montressador Chapman said and scratched his beard. He glanced up at the kitchen clock. "I better get going."

"So soon?" Mrs. Beaumont looked up. "Can't you stay for dessert?"

"I'm sorry, Mrs. Beaumont," Chapman said. "Dinner was wonderful, but I need to leave for Andarria tonight. Fionna might need my help." He stood and turned to Ann "I'll be in touch and let you know as soon as I find out anything."

Dr. Brainard pushed back his chair. "Where will Ann be testifying?"

"Palladium Beta. The committee meets at the Ministry of Investigations."

Ann looked to John. "Will you go to Andarria with me? I'd

really like you to be there when I testify."

John felt like he'd plunged into icy water. A knot tightened in his chest.

"Of course, I will," John heard himself say. He could see Dr. Brainard watching him from across the table.

Ann frowned. Disappointment shaded her eyes, and John knew she'd seen his hesitation.

"It's okay if you can't. Sean will be with me."

John could feel Montressador Chapman's eyes on him and the knot in his chest doubled in size. Ann was a time jumper. Her brother was the Montressador. John's situation was complicated enough, but this new development presented a different challenge.

John forced a smile. "I can go. I'll need to ask Arnold to cover for me, that's all." Ann smiled and followed her brother to the sitting room.

Dr. Brainard caught John's eye and gave him a peculiar look. John ignored the doctor and followed the others.

***

The news over the next week was grim. The accident investigation committee flooded Agent Knox with red tape and prevented the release of the evidence to the Colonies citing the confidential nature of the *Kairos* prototype. Forced to change course, Sean and Fionna focused their attention on getting permission to view the evidence at the Ministry of Investigations.

Ann grew more anxious as the date of the hearing ticked closer. Sean sent journals from home. He even found a few of Ann's old textbooks. Ann studied the flight manuals and poured over the pages in her journals, trying to absorb every word. Once or twice a memory came to the surface, but without shape or context, the memories felt more like random pages torn from a book.

The last communication Ann received from Sean came as two cryptic lines through the tavern's comm station.

*Find the gold metal ball in the memory box.*

*Don't think, just concentrate.*
*- Sean*

Ann remembered the metal ball from memory therapy but had never been able to figure out what it was. Nothing on the ball's shiny smooth surface gave any clue to its purpose.

Ann cupped the cold metal orb and felt the power source humming deep inside. The vibration tickled her fingers and traveled upward almost to her elbows. Ann took a deep breath and closed her eyes. In her mind, she sensed a circle of locks. Ann imagined unlocking the first one just as she had with the quarterstaff and blew through pursed lips. The lock clicked, the ball quivered, and Ann opened her eyes.

The ball had changed from a shiny golden color to as black as ink. Excitement swelled inside her. Ann closed her eyes again and concentrated on the next lock. The second felt larger than the first. Ann turned the ball over in her hands for several minutes but could not find a way to open the second lock. Discouraged, she shoved the ball in a drawer in the writing desk and went back to chores.

\*\*\*

Ann stood behind the bar and restocked glasses while the three mini-bots swept and scrubbed the empty tavern. John usually restocked the glasses, but he left after lunch to take care of winery business.

A loud buzzing made Ann look up. She rolled her eyes when she saw two of the bots fighting with each other in one of the corner booths. The bots had become increasingly territorial and argued with each other over chores. Port and Jib squabbled like siblings.

Ann chucked a wet bar towel at the table. The rag landed with a heavy splat, missing Port and Jib by inches. The mini-bots fell silent, their sensor domes fully dilated.

"Port! Clean windows! Jib! Wash tables!"

The bots gave two low whistles of acknowledgement, flicked their copper wings, and took flight.

Ann finished restocking the glasses and walked to where

the third mini-bot swept. The sweeper bot hummed to itself as it turned and made another pass across the tavern's wood floor.

"Luff, stop."

The mini-bot gave a cheery whistle and waited as Ann squatted to clear away the trash from the bot's sweeper arms.

The sensation began as a tickle on the back of Ann's neck and spread to the top of her head. Ann shivered as the notes of a thousand strings played across her skin and shimmered down her spine. The energy cascaded all around for several seconds then stopped.

Ann looked up at the ceiling perplexed. Somewhere in the room above a power source had switched on then off again without any explanation. Ann had grown accustomed to sensing random energy, but most of the power sources at Siren's Cove centered in the kitchen or in the winery. This power source came from directly above the tavern in the master bedroom. Stranger still, Ann knew she was alone. Mrs. Beaumont had left several minutes before to run errands.

Ann stood, wiped her hands on her apron, and headed to the kitchen to investigate when the bell above the tavern door jingled.

A man entered the tavern dressed in traveling clothes. Honey-blond hair slicked backward from his forehead. The jagged edges of a fresh skin graft stood stark against tanned skin and extended from his right cheek down the side of his neck, disappearing underneath the man's shirt collar. The scar crisscrossed the traveler's face and stitched the new and old skin together like a quilt.

A twinge of sympathy tweaked Ann's insides. "I'm sorry, sir, but we don't open for dinner for another couple hours."

The man turned brown eyes toward Ann and flashed a brilliant smile.

"My apologies, miss." His voice was deep and pleasant. "I was actually here to speak to Captain Galeas about purchasing some wine." The man paused as his eyes skimmed Ann's silhouette. A smile played on his mouth. "But I could be persuaded to stay for dinner."

"Captain Galeas isn't here." Something about the man's presence made Ann wary. She glanced at the bar clock. "He should be back within the hour. If you give me your name and how he can reach you, I'll tell him you stopped by."

The man's eyes narrowed. "I have nowhere else to be at the moment. I would like to wait for him. With your permission, of course."

Ann hesitated. She didn't like the idea of the man waiting in the tavern, but a new customer, especially an off tourist, would be good for the winery's reputation. Ann nodded and the traveler took a seat in one of the booths.

The man watched her as she carried an armload of clean towels behind the bar. She looked up when he cleared his throat.

"Could I trouble you for a glass of water?"

The tip of the man's index finger stroked the insignificant patch of whiskers beneath his broad bottom lip.

Ann poured the water and set the glass on the man's table.

The blow across Ann's face knocked her backward and sent stars shooting across her vision. Another blow slammed her against the bar. Ann gasped for air. The man pinned her with his body. Hands grabbed and tore at her blouse. The man's breath blew hot on her neck.

Ann fought to keep her feet. She twisted an arm free from the man's grasp and raked fingernails across his face. The stitches in his face pulled under her nails and snapped. The man shrieked and jerked backward in pain. Ann yanked her other arm clear, reached behind, and grabbed the neck of a wine bottle from the top of the bar. She swung hard and heard a grunt as the bottle shattered on her attacker's head. Ann scrambled backward and rolled over the top of the bar.

"You *bitch*!"

Ann landed behind the bar, her back on fire. Her head reeled like the floor underneath. *Get up! Get out of there!* Ann struggled to a sitting position. From the corner of an eye, she saw John's ion rifle. The weapon shone like black ice under the bar. Ann pulled the rifle from its moorings, planted her feet and stood. Ann leveled the weapon, the butt of the rifle tight against her shoulder.

The man stood a few feet away on the other side of the bar and held his head in his hands. His face black with rage dripped with wine and blood from the gash on his head. The skin graft flapped open and hung limply. The man locked eyes on Ann and barred his teeth in a snarl.

The cool steel in Ann's hands gave her courage. "Get out!"

The man froze. He looked at the rifle and chuckled. A wolfish smile spread across his face.

"You left the safety on." He took a step to walk around the end of the bar.

Ann fought panic as her hands fumbled across the bridge of the rifle. She found the safety and snapped it off.

"Get out *now*!"

Ann kept the rifle trained on her attacker as she advanced around the end of the bar. The man retreated a few steps to the middle of the tavern.

He gave Ann a mocking smile. "Are you going to shoot me?"

Ann tightened her hold on the rifle and cocked the handgrip. The weapon released a high-pitched whine as the power cells charged to full strength.

The man chuckled and took a step toward Ann. "I don't believe you. I think it was a lucky guess you found the safety. I bet you've never held a gun before in your life."

Fury coursed through Ann. The rifle tingled in her hands. A prickling sensation spread up her arms. Another step and the man would be close enough to reach the rifle.

"Stay where you are!"

The stranger laughed. "Should I stay, or should I go? Decisions...decisions...." He lunged for the rifle barrel.

\*\*\*

BOOM!

The explosion rattled shop windows and sent passersby scurrying.

John yanked the ion pistol from his belt and dropped to a crouched position, taking cover in an open doorway.

A few people pointed to a puff of black smoke drifting across the rooftops. John stood and shoved the pistol back in his belt. He hurried through the crowd in the direction of the smoke. A sick feeling filled his stomach. Whatever the cause, the blast occurred close to Siren's Cove. John reached the end of the block and broke into a run.

Sweat poured down John's face as he sprinted the three blocks back to Siren's Cove. His lungs felt ready to burst. He rounded a corner and his heart sank. Splintered wood and broken glass littered the street. The blast shattered one of the tavern's front windows and gouged out the wooden frame like an eye from its socket.

A blackened figure lay crumpled in the street. John raced to the blast site, sick with fear. The stench of burning hair and flesh filled the air. The blast victim's hair had burned away, leaving raw flesh on the scalp. Deep gashes on the victim's face and hands were the only other visible injuries.

The injured man sucked in a ragged breath as John put his coat under his head. The man's eyes opened to slits.

John checked for a pulse. "Hang on! Help is coming!"

The man's mouth curled into a familiar sneer. "I'm touched, Galeas."

John's heart nearly stopped. He peered at the injured man's face. The man reached a trembling hand into a jacket pocket, pulled out a scorched piece of paper, and pressed it into John's hand.

"Your old friends send greetings, captain," Scrivani said. The wolfish smile John remembered so well returned. "If I'd known you had such a delightful serving girl, I would have come to visit much sooner."

Fear turned John's guts to ice. The blast had originated from inside Siren's Cove, not from the street.

John burst through the tavern's front door and stopped. The breath caught in his throat. Ann sat on a bar stool and gripped the ion rifle across her knees. The rifle's barrel had split open like the petals of a flower. Ann stared out the broken front window with wide and vacant eyes. The sight of her torn blouse and the angry red welt rising on her cheek sparked a murderous hatred inside John, and he fought the urge to go back outside and shoot Scrivani on the spot.

Ann blinked and looked at John. "There was a man here." Her eyes grew more perceptive as she focused on his face.

"I know." John's voice shook. "I'm sorry." He put an arm around Ann to help her off the stool, but she refused.

"Is he dead?"

John hesitated, unsure of how Ann would react. He swallowed hard.

"No."

Ann frowned. Her eyes regained their faraway look.

"I used to be a better shot."

\*\*\*

John paced in the cool darkness of the winery. His footsteps traced the arc of light on the floor thrown from the lamp above the control panel. The intermittent gurgle and hiss of the wine tanks joined the sound of footfalls and echoed off the high ceiling.

The note from Scrivani burned in John's pocket. The message printed on the scorched paper appeared in stiff block letters.

*Winery—midnight.*

John glanced at the clock on the control panel. He blew out an impatient sigh and resumed pacing.

He'd had no choice but to board up the damaged front window of the tavern and send Mrs. Beaumont home early. John hoped he could clean up the mess in time to reopen for dinner the next night. Incredibly, Ann suffered only cuts and bruises from the encounter with Scrivani.

"The man who attacked me asked to speak to you," Ann had said after John convinced her to handover the damaged rifle. "Do you know him?"

"I didn't recognize him," John said, choosing his words carefully. "I'm sorry you got caught in the middle. I should have been here."

Ann insisted John didn't need to call Dr. Brainard and went to bed early. John's conscience mocked him. It was his fault Scrivani had found Siren's Cove, and John was the reason why Ann suffered now.

John's ears pricked at the sound of the doors opening at the far end of the winery. The scuffle of boots on the wood floor drew closer. Figures emerged from the darkness. Former comrades and foes fanned out and stood between the black shadows of the wine tanks and the pool of light from the control panel: Xebec, Zabra, Polacca, Razzia, Vago. Hard faces stared at John through the gloom.

Chohon-Lo stepped from behind Xebec. John drew himself up to face his former commander and tried to rein in his pulse.

The Tyrhenian's hair was rolled into thick, gray ropes, and gathered with a cord at the back of his neck. The coarse mane hung past Chohon-Lo's shoulders. Ribbons of graceful Tyrhen script flowed across the raider's muscled arms and chest. John suppressed a shudder as he saw how far the tattoos had spread across Chohon-Lo's body. Hidden among the intricate loops and curls were the names of the Tyrhenian's victims, men and women he saw fit to personally put his blade to. His weapon of choice—the curved, talon-like knife that hung from the raider's belt.

Chohon-Lo peered at John, black eyes burned like two coals in a grate. He unclipped the e-polyglot from an ear and dropped it into a vest pocket.

"Brevity is good for business. We will speak in your tongue. I am much improved since we last met." The soft roll in his Rs gave the Tyrhenian's voice the texture of rough silk.

John did not speak. It was not a question, therefore it did not require him to answer.

"It has been a long time, Galeas. You look well," Chohon-Lo said. His eyes examined John with penetrating curiosity. "Why did you leave the syndicate? You were not captured or injured."

John steadied himself. His life depended on how well he played his part.

"The market was no longer profitable."

Chohon-Lo tipped his head back and gave a full-throated laugh. "Agreed! We lost many associates...but the syndicate is growing. Profit can be ours again."

The Tyrhenian moved to the closest wine tank and pressed a hand to the polished steel.

"You've done well for yourself." Chohon-Lo looked at John. "I wish to renew our business association. I am in need of a navigator."

The tightness in John's shoulders spread to his chest. The raider continued to survey the winery. He pulled a wine bottle from a crate and admired the label. John fought to keep his expression blank.

"My winery business is still new," John said. His mind worked frantically, searching for a way to buy himself more time. "I'd have to sell it and take a loss to join the syndicate."

"You are passing on a lucrative opportunity," Chohon-Lo said. "If you prefer to be a silent partner, I'm sure we can reach an agreement." He shoved the bottle back into the crate and eyed John. "But it will be a more costly and a much less profitable arrangement...for you."

John swallowed hard. "The winery isn't profitable enough. Maybe in a few months...a year from now...."

The raider advanced, erasing the distance between the two men with startling speed.

"You misunderstand me! I offer you two choices! You will join my syndicate as my navigator, or you will pay for the privilege of remaining here! What do you choose?"

Chohon-Lo stood close enough John could smell the Tyrhenian's breath. The stench of rotting fish filled the air between them. John held his ground, his face like iron. If he stepped backward or flinched, the raider's knife would open his belly with a single slash.

John checked himself before answering. "What are your terms?"

The Tyrhenian blinked in surprise. "A silent partner?" He eyed John carefully. "Very well. I will honor it." He gave John a cold smile. "A standard contract. I assume you want protection for your extended liabilities?" Chohon-Lo gestured to Vago who handed him a worn leather book.

John's anger burned. He thought of Ann, Dr. Brainard, and Mrs. Beaumont.

"I will need guarantees. What happened with Scrivani—"

"Ah, yes, Scrivani," Chohon-Lo said. He dropped the book open on top of a stack of wine crates and flipped through the pages. "I should charge you for the loss of his services, but I am told Scrivani will recover. It is a small matter."

The image of Ann and her torn blouse filled John's mind.

"I should have killed him and paid full price!"

The Tyrhenian paused. His mouth puckered in thought then spread to a wide grin.

"The woman is of special value?" Chohon-Lo looked up from the page. Black eyes glittered.

Fear pierced John's heart as he realized his mistake. He tried to regain his composure, but it was too late. The raider saw through him.

"Her price will be greater of course."

Panic twisted John's stomach, his confidence shattered. If he failed to make the payments on time, more than his own life would be threatened.

Chohon-Lo scribbled a few lines onto the page. "If you were my navigator, you would be a full partner and the cost for your liabilities would not be as high. Are you sure I cannot persuade you?"

John hesitated and shook his head. Chohon-Lo made another quick notation and motioned for him to approach. John held out his right hand, palm up. The Tyrhenian drew the knife from his belt and grabbed John's wrist. John ground his teeth as the blade made a slash from the tip of his thumb downward and curved across his palm. He pressed his bloody hand to the page in Chohon-Lo's book. John hung his head in defeat.

The pirate commander returned the knife to his belt. "Perhaps in a few months you will see it is more profitable to be a full partner."

# TWENTY-TWO

## *PALLADIUM BETA*

*"John!" He searched through the empty rooms. "JOHN!" He followed the sound of her voice and hurried upstairs, but she was not in the bedrooms. He walked back to the kitchen. Her voice whispered so close it tickled the back of an ear. John spun around, but he was alone. He wandered through Siren's Cove in despair, searching as her voice flitted from room to room.*

\*\*\*

"John, wake up!"

He struggled to open his eyes. Ann's face came into focus. Her hand rested on his cheek. John tried to speak, but someone had replaced his face with a rubber mask. He sat up, pulse racing.

"S'matter?"

"I'm sorry to wake you," Ann said, a pinch forming between her brows. "We're on final approach. They'll shut off the synthofood ports soon. Did you want breakfast before we land?"

John unstuck his tongue from the roof of his mouth.

"Coffee."

Ann worked the food service port on the wall next to the cabin door. John wiped the corners of his mouth and tried to rub some feeling back into his face. Dr. Brainard's sleeping tablets worked as they always did, which was why John rarely took them. His head felt like it was stuffed full of mash.

John leaned back in the seat and stretched his legs as far as the sleeper berth's limited space would allow. He closed his eyes and felt anxiety twisting up inside him again. Montressador Chapman's message had come without warning and knocked everything into confusion. The accident investigation committee finally granted Ann permission to review the evidence with only three days to spare before her testimony. John had just enough time to give instructions to Mrs. Beaumont and Arnold before running out the door to catch the overnight flight to Andarria. God help him if they couldn't keep the tavern and the winery running while John was gone. *God help us all.*

Ann set his coffee on the table. John opened his eyes and looked with suspicion at the inky liquid in the plastic cup. The bitter smell of synthetic coffee made John's throat constrict.

"Are you all right?" Ann touched John's arm, her mouth puckered with concern.

John swallowed hard. He managed to lift one corner of his mouth and gave a sleepy smile.

"I'm okay." John swept the bangs back from his eyes. "I guess I was really out."

"Are you sure you don't want anything to eat?"

John's stomach clenched in dissent.

"No. Coffee will do."

The overhead speaker crackled with an announcement.

*"Passengers, prepare for entry."*

John picked up his cup and looked out the cabin's oval window at the distant ribbon of stars that ringed Rudnick's Expanse, an enormous swathe of empty space that at its widest stretched six billion light years. The void was without a single galaxy, nebula, or astrological body for a traveler to take notice. Most starships avoided the area because of its navigational challenges, but John and Ann had flown twelve hours to this hole in space to reach the jump point.

The shuttle lurched and a rush of orange flames pressed against the window. John cradled his cup to keep the coffee from slopping over as the ship punched through the spacetime bubble into the Andarrian universe. Turbulence rocked the shuttle for several seconds. The orange light faded, and John felt the ship disengage its time coils. When he looked through the window again, the stars in the distance had rearranged themselves and the planet Andarria loomed where before showed an eternity of emptiness.

Ann gazed at the bright blue and green planet and ate cereal in silence. Andarria's rim reflected in her eyes. John watched, amazed by how calm Ann appeared in spite of what waited on the planet below. He took a sip of coffee. His stomach tensed then relaxed with grudging acceptance.

"Do you ever miss living on Andarria?" Ann peered out the window, a hand tucked under her chin.

"I used to when Bonnie and I first moved to the Colonies." Tenderness and grief welled up inside John as he looked at his home planet.

He wished he could tell Ann everything, but now with Chohon-Lo back, all he could do was play the game until he could think of a way out. John lifted the cup to take another sip. Anxiety ratcheted his nerves another turn.

"I'll be back in a minute."

John left the sleeper berth and hurried down the narrow corridor to the washrooms. The brisk vomiting session cleared his stomach and his head.

\*\*\*

John and Ann stepped off the gangway and were engulfed by the swarm of passengers in the shuttleport's concourse. The crowd moved back and forth as travelers buffeted each other, eager to get to their destinations. The resulting chaos would have classified as a near riot by Llewelyn standards.

Montressador Chapman stood by the attendant's counter in the only empty patch of ground in the concourse. The passengers and shuttleport attendants standing nearby gave him a wide berth. *Wearing a sword on your hip has its advantages,*

John thought.

Ann gave her brother a quick hug, drawing looks from some of the waiting passengers. The back of John's head prickled. He didn't like being out in front of so many pairs of eyes.

Chapman clasped John's hand in his. "You look a little rough around the edges, Captain Galeas. Overnight flights not agree with you?"

"I've had worse." John had to shout to be heard over the noise of the crowd. A passenger banged into John from behind, knocking the duffel bag off his shoulder. John grumbled. "All of Llewelyn could be in here."

"You landed in the capital city in the middle of morning rush hour. What were you expecting?" Chapman gave John a wry smile. "Let's get out of here."

The Montressador grabbed Ann's bag and waded into the crowd. John shouldered his duffel and kept a bead on Ann's back as he pushed through the crowd after them. He was almost on top of the security checkpoint when he saw the guards. Shuttleport security stood along the wall in a gray line, black ion guns strapped to their sides, scanning the crowd as the travelers funneled past. John's pulse cranked up a notch, the forged passport rested heavy in his coat pocket. Beads of sweat formed under his shirt. He hadn't had time to come up with a backup plan for the return trip. He would have to hope the forgery was good enough to get him home. John put his head down and quickened his pace.

The crowd thinned as the trio walked through the grand promenade of the shuttleport. Tempus Hall had not changed since John's last visit. Reproductions of confiscated time machines hung high overhead and filtered the sunlight pouring through the windows. Smaller displays on loan from the national museum were encased under glass on marble pillars, each with a brass placard explaining their origins and other points of historical significance. Patriotic banners and murals of important events in Andarrian history decorated the walls.

A bruise swelled in John's heart. He remembered how

Bonnie insisted they arrive early for their flight to the Colonies, so she could gaze into every glass case and marvel at the strange configurations of the renegade time ships. The diversion had been an hour well spent as the couple held hands and wandered the sunlit hall.

Montressador Chapman didn't break stride until he reached the sleek, black hover car waiting in front of the shuttleport. He gave instructions to the driver before climbing into the seat across from John and Ann. The car lifted from the curb and joined a thick ribbon of hovercraft winding through the heart of the capital city.

Palladium Beta towered all around. Spiraling structures sparkled like quartz in the morning sun. To John, the city looked cold and alien. He turned away from the window.

Montressador Chapman undid the top silver button of his jacket. "Sorry for the short notice. We wanted to get you two here as soon as possible to review the evidence."

John studied Chapman. His mouth looked tight under his beard, and without a trace of his usual humor.

"You've seen the evidence?" Chapman nodded. "How bad is it?"

The swordsman considered the question for an instant before answering. "It's not good, but it's not hopeless."

"How far is it to the Ministry of Investigations?" Ann stared out the window. If she heard her brother's assessment of her situation, she didn't show it.

"We've had a change of plans. We're not going to the ministry right away."

The keravnos implant in Ann's ear gave a low whistle. "Why not?"

"The committee gave us permission to view the evidence at the Veterans Hospital. You'll stay there until it's time to give your testimony at the ministry."

John couldn't believe his good fortune. He quietly breathed a sigh of relief and relaxed into the seat.

"Why the hospital?" Ann looked at her brother perplexed. "I thought memory therapy wasn't an option."

"Fionna has an idea that might help. It'll be easier to have her explain once we get there."

The hover car slowed and gently touched down in front of a cluster of white, rounded buildings. The hospital campus stretched the full block. Multiple sky bridges served as walkways between buildings. Glass panels refracted the morning light into brilliant arcs. John turned and shaded his eyes against the sundogs as he followed Ann and Montressador Chapman up the steps.

A man's gravel voice boomed at a decibel unsuitable for that time of morning.

"Montressador Chapman, wonderful to see you! We are ready for you inside."

John's heart twisted. A chill swept over him as fresh beads of sweat broke across the back of his neck. John blinked, his eyes still dazzled by the reflection of the sun. He could see a short, heavyset man wearing a blue medical coat standing by the front entrance.

"Good to see you again, Colonel," Chapman said and shook the man's hand. "I'd like you to meet my sister, Ann Chapman, and Captain John Galeas. This is the hospital administrator, Colonel Gideon Wick."

Colonel Wick turned to extend a hand and the blood in John's veins ran cold. The lines on the Colonel's face were deeper than John remembered, and a touch of gray showed in the black goatee. Wick arched his brows in surprise as his eyes focused on John. Recognition swept across the administrator's face. John held his breath. The Colonel brightened as he shook John's hand.

"A pleasure to meet you, Captain Galeas."

John swallowed hard and forced a smile of his own. It looked like he would have his long overdue meeting with Colonel Wick after all—ten years too late.

Wick led them through the doors into the main reception area, a wide rotunda decorated in dark wood and marble. Hospital staff in blue walked briskly without seeming to hurry. Ann and her brother greeted Agent Knox on the opposite side of the rotunda. John felt a tug on his sleeve. Wick slowed his gait and pulled John to a stop.

"Have you made contact yet? I could tell A.K. you're here." The administrator kept his eyes forward. The hushed tone added another layer of gravel to the colonel's voice.

John clenched his jaw. "No. That won't be necessary."

Wick gave John a searching look. His countenance fell and he looked away in dismay. "You're taking a hell of a risk."

"You're one to talk," John muttered. "You don't have the clearance to speak to me."

Colonel Wick puffed out his chest. "Military hospitals are considered safe houses. I'm completely within my authority." Wick nodded to Ann and Montressador Chapman talking to Agent Knox. "Do they know?"

"No." Anxiety rocketed through John's chest again. If Wick blew his cover, Arnold, Mrs. Beaumont and Dr. Brainard would still be in danger. "Are you going to turn me in?"

"There won't be any record of you being here, but my influence only extends to the front doors. All protocols are still in place."

John nodded. As usual, it would be trickier to get out than it would be to get in.

"What about the accident investigation committee? Will anyone recognize me?"

Wick's eyes darted to the stiff pigtail at the back of John's head. "I almost didn't recognize you." The administrator gave a heavy sigh. "You should be okay."

John brushed bangs out of his eyes. He didn't want any more surprises on this trip.

"I'm sorry about Bonnie." Wick's tone softened. "But why didn't you come back?"

John didn't answer. The conversation had gone on long enough. He took a step forward, but Wick caught his arm. John turned, surprised by the administrator's boldness.

"Captain Galeas, you're not the first person to struggle with re-integration," Colonel Wick said, his face full of sympathy. "There are people here who can help you."

Anger boiled up inside John. He ripped his arm from the colonel's grasp.

"I'm here for Ann. Help her, not me." He turned and stalked away.

\*\*\*

Ann stared at her image on the viewscreen. The image of herself wore a black flight suit. The visor of the helmet was open, and Ann could see eyes and the bridge of a nose through the gap. The image peered from the helmet and scanned from side-to-side. Sometimes the eyes seemed to stare directly out of the viewscreen.

In the next screen, the angle reversed and Ann could look down on the control panel of the *Kairos*. Digital displays spread out before her like a table setting. In the bottom center of the screen, gloved hands held the ship's yoke. The left hand darted to the control panel—a minor adjustment—before darting back and gripping the yoke again. Ann heard her own voice through the conference room speakers.

"Initiating flight pattern rho beta."

Ann watched the screen as her image turned the yoke and executed a forty-five degree turn, holding the wheel in position for several seconds before leveling off. Ann's heart skipped as she imagined the pull of g-forces. Command control chattered through the comm.

*"Well done, Lieutenant. How does she feel?"*

"Solid. Not a wobble." On the screen, the image smiled, eyes crinkled, and her cheeks bunched. Ann felt herself smiling as she watched. "Command Control, did you want to see anything else? I could run that last sequence again."

*"That's all for today. Stand by for approach coordinates and we'll bring you home."*

Ann watched as her image narrowed her eyes then opened them wide. Safe in the conference room, the hair prickled on the back of Ann's neck. *Something's wrong.*

"Wait a minute...I'm picking up a vibration."

The image moved her right hand to the side of the screen and hovered for an instant over a bank of switches. The screen froze and cut to black, the signal from the cockpit lost. A chill ran down Ann's spine. She didn't need to see what happened next to know the fate of the *Kairos*.

The viewscreen dimmed, and the lights of the conference room brightened. Ann sat in silence and tried to make sense of the final seconds of the flight of the *Kairos*. She remembered the flight manuals Sean had sent and the bank of switches her image had reached for prior to the signal cutting out. Ann swiveled in her chair to face the others.

"They think I hit the kill switch?"

"Did you?"

Ann looked across the table at Agent Knox. She peered at Ann through her yellow Bio-Vision glasses.

"No. That's not how it happened." Ann rubbed a temple, feeling the first pangs of a headache.

The agent slid a metal tin across the table. Ann glowered but opened the tin and popped the pain tablet in her mouth anyway. She decided the first chance she got she was going to snap Agent Knox's Bio-Vision glasses in half.

"It feels wrong...like the timing is off." Ann chased the tablet with a gulp of water. "I don't think the explosion happened right after the vibration. There was more time in between."

"What happened after the vibration? What did you do?"

"I don't remember." Ann let her hands drop to her lap.

"Lieutenant..." Ann looked up. Colonel Wick leaned forward and rested his arms on the table. "Can you tell me what the kill switch is for?"

Ann caught her breath. She almost answered no, but then realized she knew the answer to the colonel's question.

"The kill switch cuts power to the engines. A cold shut down. If you hit the kill switch while the engines are engaged you run the risk of blowing up the engines." Ann paused and another thought occurred to her. "A vibration isn't a big enough of an emergency to warrant hitting the kill switch."

"And what would have been the proper procedure in this case?"

Ann felt like a student called on to recite in front of the classroom. She struggled for an instant, but then the answer became clear.

"A controlled deceleration and disengage the engines."

Colonel Wick broke into a broad smile that added more wrinkles to his cheeks and crinkled the corners of his eyes. Sean sat next to the Colonel, his face lit up like a firework.

Ann smiled and breathed a sigh of relief. *How am I remembering this?* Her mind had been a blank screen for so long and now it gave up information almost effortlessly.

Agent Knox scribbled on the digital pad. Short blond hair fell forward across her cheeks.

"So...is that what you did?"

Ann's smile faded as a sense of dread came over her.

"No..."

She hadn't followed procedure. *But why not? What did I do?*

"I don't know what I did. I just know I didn't hit the kill switch." Ann gestured to the blank viewscreen. "The visual log is wrong."

"The committee's theory is bullshit."

The group turned to look at John sitting at the other end of the table. He had hardly spoken since entering the conference room. John leaned back in his chair arms folded.

"The kill switch could cause an explosion in the engines, but it doesn't mean it will. And even if it did, it wouldn't have been big enough to take out the entire ship. The committee is out of their bloody minds."

Sean nodded. "The kill switch theory also doesn't explain how the time jump occurred. There were two crash sites—the first from the initial explosion, the second from when the ship reappeared after the jump. You can see the control panel on the visual log. The time coils weren't engaged."

Agent Knox put her stylus down. "The committee will argue the time coils were a new design, and we don't really know what could have happened if the kill switch was triggered. If the engines exploded, the committee will say a time event was possible."

"But I didn't hit the kill switch!" Ann stared around the table in frustration. Even Sean looked doubtful. "Something else caused the explosion."

Dread filled Ann's stomach like a lead weight. She knew what a ruling of pilot error would mean. They were back to square one.

"Lieutenant Chapman is an experienced pilot," Colonel Wick said. "If she says she didn't trigger the kill switch, I believe her. She even recited the proper procedure for responding to the vibration. It seems ridiculous the Lieutenant would have used the kill switch under the circumstances." The administrator's voice carried the full weight of his authority as if determined to settle the matter once and for all. He looked at Ann. "If you are convincing in your testimony, it might be enough for the committee to rule in your favor."

"It's still Ann's word against the visual log," John said. He pinched the bridge of his nose, eyes closed in concentration. He looked up at Ann with weary eyes. "If the signal had held on a few more seconds, we might have an answer."

Ann saw Agent Knox look sideways to Sean. He nodded and the agent turned back to Ann.

"There is one more thing we could try," Knox said, her tone cautious. "Colonel Wick has offered the use of the hospital's new mental imager."

"We're the first hospital to have access to the technology," Wick said. "Our therapists have used it with patients recovering from traumatic events. It allows us to view memories and talk the patient through what they're feeling. We've had some luck with uncovering repressed memories."

"But I still need to have a memory of what caused the accident," Ann said.

The Colonel nodded. "And you will need to be actively engaged for the imager to work."

Ann cocked a brow. *Actively engaged?*

"I know it's a long-shot," Knox said, a pleading note crept into the agent's voice. "But I thought if we could see what you see, then maybe one of us might see something that will help us piece together what happened. I've already cleared it with the committee." She gave Ann a coaxing smile. "We'll be able to submit anything we find as evidence."

Ann pressed her lips together and nodded. What did she have to lose? She looked across the table at Sean. He cringed as if expecting a slap across the face. Ann narrowed her eyes.

"What's the catch?"

Sean gave an apologetic smile. "You're not going to like it."

# TWENTY-THREE

## *MENTAL TRIALS*

*Bio gel.*

Ann shuddered. The memory of bio gel oozing across flesh and absorbing into her skin was as real as the cold tile floor that sent daggers of ice into her bare feet.

The red gel pulsed and moved in slow waves across the surface of the pool. Ann curled her lip in disgust as the viscous substance gathered into a mounded peak. A glistening, tongue-like appendage reached out to explore the edge of the metal exam table before sinking back into the trough. More bio gel swelled and clung to the underside of the exam table's rounded lid.

Ann's breath quickened as the purpose of the table became clear. She folded her arms and shivered in the thin, hospital-issue t-shirt and shorts.

The med tech positioned a step stool next to the table. "Come on. Let's get you settled." He patted the edge of the table. "Think of it like swimming in cold water. Best to jump in and get it over with."

Ann shot the tech a dubious look. She would prefer a cold swim. Bio gel felt like warm spit crawling with maggots.

"You're not scared, are you?" The med tech watched Ann, hands on hips. "Bio gel won't hurt you. Watch."

Ann cringed as the tech rested his open hand on the surface of the pool. The gel gathered under the man's palm, bulged upward between his fingers, quivered and dropped slowly back into its own mass. The med tech held out his hand for Ann to see.

"The gel reads your vital signs and neurological activity through a synthetic membrane."

Hope threw Ann a lifeline. "I don't have to touch it?"

The tech chuckled. "No, that's only for tissue reconstruction. This bio gel relays synaptic function to the mental imager in the next room."

Ann took a deep breath and shook off her fear. She stepped onto the stool and sat on the table's narrow ledge.

The gelatin quivered underneath its membrane. The faint smell of maple syrup wafted up from the pool. Ann swallowed hard, pushing disgust into the pit of her stomach. The faster she found the missing memory, the sooner she would be done.

The med tech looked up and gestured to Ann's ear. "You'll need to take that off."

Ann raised a hand and felt the keravnos implant. She'd forgotten all about it. Ann handed the black, half-moon disc to the med tech. The pulses she had sensed with the help of the implant faded and disappeared. The exam room felt hollow without its electrical symphony.

Ann laid back and sunk deep into the warm cushion of gel. The tech closed the lid of the exam table, sealing her tightly between two thick layers of gelatin and membrane. Ann fought panic and stared through the observation window at the ceiling of the exam room, her breath coming faster and fogging the glass. The alien substance oozed all around her. The thin membrane molded to the shape of Ann's body and made it difficult to sense where her body ended and the gel began. Ann had never been claustrophobic that she remembered. Now would not be a good time to start.

Ann's toes tingled. The feeling grew stronger, crept up her legs, and over her hips, chest and arms. The tingling reached the back of Ann's head, traveled across her face and lips and finally the tip of her nose. The blood pounded in her ears. The med tech smiled through the observation window and flashed a thumbs up.

"You're doing great!"

Ann could only grimace. Her breathing and pulse locked in a foot race as a string of curses tore through her mind. Sparkles of light danced in front of her eyes. The tingling became a frenzy. Ann squeezed her eyes shut and gave her mind over to the gel.

***

Montressador Sean Chapman peered over Agent Fionna Knox's shoulder with a frown. The mental imager's control panel lit up like a city skyline.

"I told you this was a bad idea. Ann hates bio gel."

The agent continued making adjustments to the sensors. "What choice did we have? You prefer the committee find her guilty?"

Sean ignored the remark and watched Fionna work. Her yellow Bio-Vision glasses rested on top of her head and swept her blond hair behind her ears. The corners of Fionna's mouth turned down. While not quite a frown, the expression was far from the tranquil smile the agent usually wore. Over the last three weeks, Sean had watched Fionna fight bureaucrats and lobby the investigation committee on Ann's behalf. She had pulled every string, called in every favor, and snubbed him at every opportunity except when duty or necessity required otherwise. Sean almost felt guilty for coming down so hard on her. *Almost.*

Captain Galeas paced the gallery, glancing to the metal door at the far end of the room. "What's taking so long?"

Fionna looked up from the control panel with a patient smile. "Ann's just a little keyed up. We can't engage the imager until she settles down." She turned back to the control panel and touched the comm link. "Ann? I want you to take some deep breaths. We need you to relax before we can get started."

Sean watched Captain Galeas from the corner of an eye. This bartender from the Colonies was still a mystery. He obviously cared for his sister, but why did Galeas hesitate when Ann asked him to come with her to Andarria? Sean had tried to get to know the captain, tried to befriend him at least on some level, but Galeas remained distant and distracted. Not to mention moody as hell. Sean never questioned his sister's choices when it came to men and yet... Sean drummed fingers on the hilt of his sword. *Why would an experienced pilot waste time tending bar?*

"You're doing wonderfully, Ann," Fionna said, speaking into the comm. The warning lights on the control panel had lost some of their urgency. "I'm going to try to engage the imager."

Sean looked out the gallery window. The curved, black-paneled walls of the imaging room formed a backdrop to the round platform. A low hum filled the air, and the lights on the bottom of the platform glowed white hot. An image melted into view, beginning with a pair of feet then arms, legs, torso and head. The lights dimmed as the image coalesced and solidified into a three-dimensional likeness of Ann, barefoot and wearing hospital shorts and a t-shirt. The avatar stepped into a fighter's stance, fists raised, glancing into the shadows on either side of the platform.

As Sean watched, a red teardrop appeared under the avatar's right eye. Ann's image brushed the drop away with a finger. Her expression changed from wonder to horror as the sticky globe slid down her finger, leaving a stain. The stain became a ribbon, wrapping around the avatar's wrist and continuing up her arm.

Captain Galeas jumped to his feet. "What in the bloody hell is that?"

"Ann isn't in any danger," Fionna said. "The mental imager interprets the readings from the bio gel and creates an avatar. The ribbon is symbolic of Ann's emotional state." Fionna glanced in the avatar's direction. "She's still a little tense."

Sean cocked an eyebrow and watched the avatar's pantomime. Tense was not the word he would have chosen. The avatar stood stiffly with her mummified arm extended.

Her free hand gripped the end of the ribbon as it drew closer to her throat.

Ann's avatar suddenly straightened, releasing the ribbon. The curl shot forward, but she ignored the ribbon as it looped around her neck. The image cupped her hands and a golden metal ball appeared. The tips of her fingers flew around the smooth arc of the ball, pausing for an instant before turning it in a different direction. The ribbon, looping around the avatar's neck, faltered then fluttered to the floor and disappeared. The ball in the avatar's hands changed in color from gold to black then red then back to gold as she worked. Sean chuckled to himself.

Fionna looked up perplexed and followed Sean's gaze to the avatar.

"What's she doing?"

"It's a puzzle ball," Sean said. "I told Ann to dig it out of the memory box so she could practice using electro-perception."

Fionna sighed. "Well, now she's using it to mentally distract herself from the bio gel." She touched the comm link and spoke with forced cheerfulness. "Okay, Ann, I need you to focus on my voice." The avatar continued to concentrate on the ball. "Ann, I need you to stop thinking about the puzzle ball." Still no response. Fionna closed the comm link. "Great. She's blocking."

Colonel Wick pushed past Agent Knox to the control panel and spoke into the comm.

"*Lieutenant!* Put the puzzle ball *down!*"

The avatar's head snapped to attention, and the golden ball dropped from her hands. The image of the ball scattered like sand, disappearing before it reached the tops of her bare feet. The avatar ceased fidgeting and waited wide-eyed and alert.

Wick closed the comm link and gestured toward the avatar with a smile. "She's all yours, Agent Knox."

Sean cocked a grin as he watched the colonel return to his seat. He would have to remember that trick.

"Ann, I'm going to ask you to think about people or places

you know," Fionna said, speaking into the comm. "I want you to picture them in your mind and imagine how they make you feel."

Captain Galeas sat up straighter in his chair. "I thought we were using the mental imager to look for memories. Why not just ask about the accident?"

"We need to take a few baseline readings first," Colonel Wick said. "If her brainwaves break from the baseline during the memory search, we'll know we hit on a false memory."

"Let's get started." Fionna leaned toward the comm and spoke in a clear voice. "Show me Siren's Cove."

Fionna put Ann through her paces for several minutes, asking about people and places that would draw the strongest emotional responses and recording the actions of the avatar.

"You're doing great, Ann. Show me Commander Vincent Lazar."

Two chairs folded up from the floor. Ann's avatar took a seat. From the side of the platform, another image formed. Vincent's avatar took a seat in the second chair. A thick carpet of white wildflowers sprung from the floor. Sean smiled. *Friendship flowers.*

Sean heard Captain Galeas shift in the seat behind him. He glanced over a shoulder and smirked. Galeas scowled at the avatars, arms across his chest. Sean could almost see the jealousy rippling out from him. Sean gave Fionna a nudge. She looked in the captain's direction. A smile tweaked her lips. Fionna turned back to the control panel and spoke into the comm link.

"Show me Captain John Galeas."

Ann's avatar stood. Vincent's image and the two chairs folded into the floor as the captain's avatar appeared. Ann's image greeted the new avatar with a wide smile and the two embraced.

Sean looked over at Galeas and chuckled to see the change in his demeanor. The captain's face flushed with embarrassment, but he also wore the grin of a love-struck schoolboy. In spite of all of Captain Galeas' bluster and gloom,

Ann had wrapped him around her little finger.

The two avatars swayed together, still locked in an embrace. Ann's avatar shifted, her body turned and gave a glimpse of her back. Sean sucked in a breath. The captain's avatar wore a black glove on his left hand while the right remained bare.

Sean whispered to Fionna. "The glove. Do you see it?"

Fionna nodded, her face pinched. "It doesn't mean Galeas is lying to her. It just means Ann thinks he might be."

Sean cast a glance over a shoulder. Colonel Wick and Captain Galeas didn't seem to have noticed the avatar's appearance. Sean looked back at Fionna and cocked his head toward the agent's Bio-Vision glasses resting on the control panel.

Fionna gave her head an almost imperceptible shake. "I can't see the avatar with my glasses on. I'll try to talk to Captain Galeas after we're done."

Sean looked through the window at the two avatars, the image of the captain's left hand now hidden from view. Sean's anger uncurled and growled in his chest. The mental imager sensed the captain's deception through Ann. A response like that would take more than a little white lie. Sean gripped the hilt of his sword. Maybe the time had come for him to take a closer look at Captain John Galeas.

***

Ann tugged at the high, stiff collar of her uniform jacket and waited outside of the committee's chamber. Failure hung in the hallway, silent and suffocating. For two days, the mental imager had plowed the barren field of Ann's memory, ripping up everything in its path, but no new evidence surfaced to counter the visual log. Images of the final seconds of the flight of the Kairos played in Ann's head, but always stopped at the same instant with her hand hovering over the bank of switches. The memory of what caused the accident, if it existed at all, remained hidden.

"You could still plead no contest. You don't have to do this."

John's voice rumbled in Ann's ear. She looked up. The dark

241

shadows under his blue eyes suggested lack of sleep. Ann's heart ached. The intensity of John's gaze had made him appear almost menacing when Ann had first met him, but since then she'd seen how John's face could brighten when he laughed or smiled. It was only when his clouds rolled in and his shadows of grief lengthened did he look anything like those early days at Siren's Cove.

Ann looked away, the ache in her heart too much to bear, and stared at the ornate silver door that led to the committee's chamber. It would be so much easier to accept the committee's evidence and admit fault. The committee would put an end to their investigation and Ann could return to the Colonies. No one was asking her to be a martyr. One simple phrase would release her.

Ann blew out a sigh of frustration as her insides knotted up again. *But what about the truth?* Memory or not, Ann knew in her gut she did not hit the kill switch. To plead no contest would mean admitting fault for something she didn't do, and her release would come with a greater price. Resigning her commission and giving up status as a time jumper would be one more piece of her life stolen.

Ann took John's hand and held it tight. There was so much she wouldn't change, but the desire to hold on to what little she had left of her old life was just as strong.

The silver door slid open and Agent Knox stepped into the hallway. Ann heard Sean's sword clank as he stood from the bench behind her.

The agent's violet eyes locked on Ann. "They're ready for you."

Ann looked at John, her heart suddenly in her throat. If the committee convicted her, would she see John again before the authorities took her away?

"I'll be watching from the gallery." John's arms folded around her. His lips pressed against Ann's for an instant before he stepped away.

Sean rested a heavy hand on Ann's shoulder, eyes bright. "Tell them what you told us. You may not be able to answer all of their questions but be confident in what you do know."

Sean mustered a smile under his beard, and for a second Ann thought her brother might say more. Instead of making a joke, he turned and clanked down the hallway to the gallery entrance with John at his side.

Ann took a deep breath to stifle her nerves and followed Agent Knox into the committee's chamber. The brightness of the room made Ann blink. The high ceiling and curved walls of the chamber were dressed all in white. Blue and gold diamonds of light showered the room. A round decorative glass window in the middle of the ceiling displayed the great seal of the Ministry of Investigation—a magnificent golden sun in a cobalt sky. Curved around the edges of the sun's flaming corona was written, *Let Justice Be Done, Even If the Heavens Fall.*

Ann stepped to the agent's side. Five officers of varying rank sat behind a long bench. Ann felt her skin warm under her jacket as five pairs of eyes studied her.

Agent Knox addressed the committee. "Commander Rectrix, I'd like to present to you and to the committee, Lieutenant Anaya Chapman. She's ready to submit to questioning."

Commander Rectrix leaned forward and rested a cheek against the curve of her hand, an index finger pressed against her temple. Soft wrinkles lined the woman's face and throat. Light auburn hair swept up into a large roll at the back of her head, was streaked with silver. The Commander's cheeks dimpled as her lips stretched into a thin smile.

"Thank you, Agent Knox. You may sit down, Lieutenant." Commander Rectrix gestured toward the interrogation chair facing the committee.

Agent Knox sat with a group of spectators in a row of chairs separate from the gallery. Ann hadn't noticed the group when she first entered the chamber. The three men and two women were dressed in civilian clothing. Ann wondered if they were the other investigators. Her suspicions were confirmed when she saw Agent Drake a few chairs down from Agent Knox. Drake sat with arms crossed, a cold smile on his lips.

Ann looked away. Her animosity toward Drake grew by the second. She turned her attention to the gallery and was cheered to see John, her brother, and Colonel Wick sitting a few rows up in the gallery's middle section. Most of the remaining seats were vacant.

Ann tried to relax into the curve of the interrogation chair. Her uniform felt stiff and strange. The short, buttoned jacket nipped at Ann's waist. Her skirt skimmed her knees and showed an embarrassment of bare legs compared to the colony skirt she usually wore. Ann tugged at the hem once and gave up, letting her legs lean to one side and crossed her ankles.

Commander Rectrix cleared her throat. "Before we begin...Agent Knox, I must say it is unusual for an agent of the committee to spend so much time with an officer currently under investigation." The commander leveled her eyes in the agent's direction.

Ann couldn't decide if Rectrix was accusing Agent Knox of impropriety or making a statement of fact. She thought she caught Drake smirking from his chair.

"It's an unusual case, ma'am," Agent Knox said, rising from her seat. "Given the circumstances, I thought the investigation and the committee would benefit from my direct involvement. Does the committee have any specific concerns I could help address before hearing Lieutenant Chapman's testimony?"

Ann saw the commander's eyes dart to where Sean sat in the gallery and back to Agent Knox. "No, that won't be necessary. Thank you for your service."

Commander Rectrix turned to Ann and her cool smile warmed a degree. "Lieutenant Chapman, I understand this has been a long journey for you. As Agent Knox has already stated, your case is highly unusual. The committee appreciates you being here today, and I speak for everyone when I wish you every success in your continued recovery."

"Thank you, ma'am."

Rectrix continued, shifting to a more professional tone. "The committee has been reviewing limited evidence for many months and has looked forward to hearing your testimony.

Unfortunately, we've been told you can't remember any more of the accident. We would still like to have your statement for the record."

Ann nodded. Commander Rectrix touched a panel on the bench, activating the viewing panel. Ann swiveled the interrogation chair and watched the familiar scene of her image in the cockpit of the *Kairos*. When the viewscreen darkened, Ann swiveled the chair to face the committee and explained again how the timing was off between the vibration and the explosion.

"Can you tell us anything more about the vibration?" Commander Rectrix scrolled through a digital pad. "It didn't show up in any of the data collected prior to the crash. Did the vibration appear on your ship's instrument panel?"

"No, ma'am." Ann tilted her head as she spoke, surprised by her own answer.

The commander looked up and studied Ann. "Are you certain?"

"Yes, ma'am." Ann's heart thumped harder. *It was happening again!* Her memory opened with a rush where a moment ago there'd been only a silent void.

"If it didn't appear on your instruments, then please explain to the committee how you detected the vibration."

Ann thought in desperation and tried to sharpen the vibration in her memory. *What am I missing?* The deep steady throb of the engine filled Ann's senses and the answer blurted from her mouth.

"The ship changed in pitch."

Commander Rectrix blinked in surprise. "The orientation of your ship changed?"

"No, ma'am." Ann steadied herself with a deep breath. "Pitch...like in music. The hum from the engines changed, then I felt the vibration. It didn't appear on my instruments."

Ann had the committee's full attention. Styluses that scratched notes a moment ago fell silent. From the corner of an eye, Ann saw John lean forward in his seat. The rest of the gallery, which had up to this point watched in detached silence, stirred as if awakening from a deep sleep.

"What did you do next?" Commander Rectrix's eyes never wavered from Ann's face.

Ann tried to hold open the window in her memory. Her temple throbbed with a dull ache from the effort.

Ann shook her head. "I don't remember."

"Did you hit the kill switch?"

"No, ma'am. Absolutely not."

An officer sitting next to the commander leaned forward. His round face spoke of youth, while his cropped hair showed early signs of a receding hairline.

"How can you be so sure you didn't hit the kill switch if you can't remember what you did next?"

Ann rubbed her temple and squinted against the pain. The answer slipped through just before the memory snapped shut again.

"It just wasn't an option."

"Do you have anything else you'd like to add?"

Ann thought for a moment. "No, ma'am."

"That's unfortunate," the commander said with a sigh. "Thank you, Lieutenant."

Commander Rectrix made a few notes on the digital pad and looked to her colleagues sitting on either side. They nodded and she turned to address the chamber.

"The committee will take a brief recess to consider the Lieutenant's testimony."

The officers stood, bringing Ann and the rest of the chamber to their feet. Agent Knox caught Ann's eye and gave a brilliant smile and nodded encouragement. The tension in Ann's stomach made it impossible to think positive thoughts.

The committee returned to the bench a few minutes later. Commander Rectrix waited to address the chamber until the noise of the gallery returning to their seats died away.

"We've been investigating the destruction of the *Kairos* for several months with very little evidence. We'd hoped Lieutenant Chapman's testimony would have shed new light, but unfortunately it hasn't. Based on the visual log and the lack of any new evidence, the committee has decided to rule pilot error."

A single gasp broke the silence of the chamber. Ann didn't know if the sound had come from the gallery, or if she'd been the one to draw breath. Her lungs felt as if all the oxygen had burned out of them in a flash. *It's over.* Ann fought to take a breath and her body relented with a choking shudder.

Agent Knox stood and faced the committee. "Commander Rectrix, with all due respect, Lieutenant Chapman is remembering more about the accident every day. She told you about the change in the sound of the engines. I respectfully ask the committee to give her more time."

"Agent Knox, we all have considerable time invested in this case already, and there's no guarantee Lieutenant Chapman will ever recover her memory completely. She hasn't remembered much even after several months of rehabilitation. The mental imager was our last hope."

"But Commander, if the committee would just allow—"

"Enough!" The commander's eyes blazed for an instant. "Regardless of your personal feelings, this can't be an open-ended investigation. If new evidence comes to light, Lieutenant Chapman may file a petition with the committee, and based on the new evidence we may choose to reopen the investigation. Until then, the investigation is closed."

Commander Rectrix turned to Ann. A flicker of remorse passed over her features.

"Lieutenant Chapman, the committee will reconvene tomorrow morning for sentencing."

# TWENTY-FOUR

## *SPIKING THE BOX*

Ann sat in the interrogation chair, numb. The shuffle of feet filled the gallery as people stood to leave the chamber, but she couldn't bring herself to stand. Someone grabbed her arm and pulled her into the hallway. Terror seized Ann for a second when she thought a guard was escorting her to a holding cell, but when she looked up she saw Agent Knox standing next to her.

Ann collapsed onto a bench, head in her hands, and stared at the floor's tiles. Panic pierced her like a thousand arrows. *I'm going to prison.* There was no doubt anymore. Ann's heart pounded against her rib cage. She should have listened to John and pled no contest, but now it was too late.

"This is crazy!" Ann glanced up at Agent Knox. "I didn't hit the kill switch!"

The agent put a hand on Ann's shoulder. "It's going to be okay. The committee said if we uncover more evidence—"

"There *isn't* any more evidence!" Anger and frustration swirled inside Ann and she clenched her hands. "If there was, the mental imager would have found it!" How could Agent Knox stay optimistic when it was obvious they had lost?

Footsteps hurried down the hallway towards them. Sean argued options with Colonel Wick, sword clanking at his side.

"Request a new committee? That could take a year or more."

John slid onto the bench next to Ann and gripped her shoulders.

"Listen. Maybe we're looking at this wrong," John said, trying to catch his breath. "You heard something in the engines. You told the committee the kill switch wasn't an option. In what circumstances would you *not* hit the kill switch?"

"We've been over this!" Ann was tired of circling dead ends. "A cadet with thirty hours of flight time knows not to hit the kill switch under those circumstances."

"I want you to tell me!" John gave Ann's shoulders a shake and forced her to look at him. His blue eyes burned into her own. The lines of his face gathered in determination.

Ann shook her head. "You don't hit the kill switch when the engines are engaged unless it's an emergency, and a vibration isn't enough of a reason."

"Forget about the vibration for a minute. What if it was an emergency?" John said, relaxing the grip on Ann's shoulders. "A big enough of one you thought about hitting the kill switch, but then realized you couldn't. The change in pitch could have been a cascade failure in the engines. Why wasn't the kill switch an option? Can you think of a reason?"

Ann slumped against the back of the bench. "Meteor showers! A Heraclitus paradox! When you're taking fire from an enemy ship!"

"Now you're just being silly! *Think!*"

Ann didn't want to think any more. She pressed the heels of her palms to her temples and tried to restrain the headache building behind her eyes.

"During take-off or reentry," Ann said. "Or any time gravity shifts are unpredictable."

"Good!" John's face turned pensive. "Gravity shifts. Could you have run into an uncharted cosmic string?"

Ann shook her head. "There weren't any gravity wells in my flight path."

John frowned and fingered his pigtail. "What else? Bio-system failure. Ion storms. When the time coils are engaged."

"The time coils weren't engaged, all ship systems were functional, and there weren't any ion storms in the area," Agent Knox said with a sigh.

*Ship systems.*

The breath caught in Ann's throat as her headache split open behind her eyes. The pain pulsed in time with her heartbeat. White flashes of light grayed Ann's vision. An image of the cockpit's control panel formed. A shudder ran though Ann as comprehension broke from the memory. She moaned and buried her face in her hands.

John grabbed her arm. "Ann? What is it?"

She blinked hard, tears leaked from the corners of her eyes. "It was the time coil!"

Agent Knox was at her side in a flash. "Are you sure? The indicator light on the control panel—"

"A faulty switch!" Ann's voice broke as another wave of pain shook her body. "The time coil in the starboard engine. I couldn't shut it down."

Agent Knox gripped her shoulder. "Do you have an actual memory?"

Ann squeezed her eyes tight. The memory burned white hot, but the pain kept her from seeing it.

"I can't see it. I just *know.*"

"That would explain why you thought there was more time between the vibration and the explosion," Knox said, her excitement growing. "For you, there *was* more time. The coil was already creating a time distortion."

Ann couldn't answer. She gritted teeth and suppressed the moan rising in her throat.

"Bloody hell." John's voice growled with anger. "Her hand didn't freeze over the switches, it just seemed that way to anyone watching the visual log. That should be enough, shouldn't it? We need to tell the committee."

"It's not good enough," Knox said. "We need the mental imager. If we don't have the actual memory, they'll just say we're grasping at straws."

***

The pain in Ann's head didn't subside until she sat shivering in the mental imager's exam room. Bio gel oozed and churned on the exam table. Ann shuddered and looked away. Only the threat of prison would make her climb up on the table again.

Ann rested against the back of the chair and rubbed her eyes. With the pain in her head fading, the memory felt further away than ever.

"What am I going to do?" Ann mumbled to herself.

The med tech glanced in her direction as he adjusted dials on the exam table. "You need to focus on what you felt right at that moment. That should help you break into your memory. Do you remember what you were feeling?"

"The time coil was going to pull the ship apart. I keep trying to tap into the fear I felt, but it's not working."

"Are you sure fear is the right emotion?"

Ann started at the suggestion. If fear wasn't the right emotion, then it meant she was nowhere near to unlocking the memory.

"Once you find the right emotion you should be home free," the med tech said, checking his data pad. "Then just do what you did last time."

Ann eyed the med tech. "What do you mean?"

The tech looked up. "That trick you did with the puzzle ball." He tapped a finger to his ear. "You're a Vego, right?"

Ann touched the keravnos implant in her ear and frowned. "Yes, but what are you talking about? What trick?"

The med tech's brows shot up in surprise. "You Vegos are always pulling stunts in the mental imager so I just assumed..." He studied Ann another moment then shrugged. "The emotional connection between you and your avatar works both ways. It's called spiking the box."

***

John entered the gallery, his long strides stiff from anxiety. Montressador Chapman stood next to Agent Knox at the control panel and stared through the observation window into the empty imaging chamber. The agent busied herself with the controls.

John looked through the glass to the imaging room and felt as if he stood on the bridge of a doomed ship. *What if we fail?* A tremor ran through him. He wouldn't leave Ann, but he also knew he couldn't stay on Andarria. John held the two thoughts in his mind. Each pressed on the other, neither giving way or offering a solution.

"What are your plans after this is over?"

John jerked his head toward Montressador Chapman, surprised how the question so closely mirrored his thoughts. Chapman's face looked as hard and as unyielding as the glass in front of him.

John glanced in Colonel Wick's direction before answering. Wick sat in the gallery. The administrator's posture hadn't changed, but John knew the older man's ears had pricked in response to the Montressador's question.

"I need to get back to Siren's Cove," John said. The words gave more weight to his growing sense of hopelessness. John struggled against despair. There was still a chance. "I hope Ann will be coming home with me."

Only a slight change in the angle of Montressador Chapman's mouth gave any indication the swordsman had heard John's words.

"I love Ann. I want to build a life with her," John said, not knowing why he felt the sudden urge to convince Ann's brother of his good intentions. "I wanted you to know."

In one fluid arc of motion, Chapman slid a data link pad across the steel ledge of the control panel. "Can you explain this?"

John trapped the device with a hand and looked down at the glowing screen. His mouth jerked. The information displayed was like a sucker punch to the jaw.

*Captain John Galeas—LEVEL 2—BACKGROUND CHECK*

John didn't need to read any further. He already knew the story. How much did Montressador Chapman know? Had he told Ann? John slid the data pad back to Chapman.

"No."

A violent emotion gripped Montressador Chapman's face. His glare was as sharp as the sword he wore on his hip. John saw in his expression the knowledge of every one of his deeds, the laws he'd broken, and the company he'd kept after the court martial. John forced himself to wear the hardened look of a mercenary, acutely aware of how the Montressador gripped the hilt of his sword. John knew the swordsman's reputation with the blade. Unlike an ion pistol, there were some wounds a blade could give that were worse than death. The sting of regret seeped into John's limbs and threatened to crack his careful facade.

Chapman pulled his anger back. He slipped the data pad into a pocket.

"I think heading back to the Colonies as soon as possible is a good idea."

Agent Knox cleared her throat. "Gentlemen. We're ready."

The lights on the platform flashed, and the familiar, barefooted image appeared. Ann's avatar stepped into a fighter's stance and looked around, breathing heavy. The avatar's eyes were lined with fatigue. Gray strands of hair threaded through her loose braid.

Agent Knox turned to the med tech next to her and muttered, "Keep an eye on her readings. This may be a short session." She spoke into the comm link on the control panel. "Whenever you're ready, Ann."

As John watched from the gallery, a steel table popped up from the platform floor in front of the avatar. An ancient-looking wooden box occupied one end of the table. The curve of the wood gleamed the color of old honey. Two golden dials attached to the front of its polished surface underneath an oval of steel mesh. John narrowed his eyes and stepped toward the glass for a closer look. The box was an antique wireless communication device or radio, a more primitive version of the comm network used by the Colonists.

Ann's avatar sat on the stool behind the table—head bowed, eyes closed—and tuned the radio dials with tight controlled movements of her fingers. Her lips parted in concentration as the image listened to the static issuing from the radio's speaker. A few loose strands escaped from the avatar's braid. The sight of the avatar bent over the table reminded John of the hours Ann spent working in the kitchen at Siren's Cove. A few minutes passed, and the avatar straightened and shook her head.

John looked to Agent Knox. She leaned over the control panel and spoke into the comm link.

"That's okay. Take a minute and try again."

John looked back to the imaging room and waited. The avatar's lifeless eyes stared at the surface of the steel table, unblinking. Not a breath stirred in the imaging chamber. The seconds crept across John's skin. He fought the urge to pace, and was about to give in, when the avatar leaned toward the radio and began to work the dials.

John overheard Montressador Chapman whisper to Knox. "How is she?"

John watched the pair from the corner of an eye and strained to hear every word.

"She's exhausted. I don't know how much more we can push her."

A loud bang sent John's heart racing. The avatar had kicked the metal stool across the platform where it rolled into the darkness and disappeared.

"It's not working," Chapman said.

"She's not done yet." Colonel Wick's gravel voice came from the back of the gallery. "She still has a lot of fight left in her."

Agent Knox leaned over the control panel and pressed the comm link. "Take a deep breath and try again." Knox turned toward the group. "Let's give her one more chance, but then I'm afraid we'll have to stop."

John watched Ann's avatar pace the edge of the platform.

The image suddenly froze in its tracks and raised her head as if pulled by a string. She took a deep breath, though John knew that was impossible, and turned back to the table. Static flowed as the avatar twisted the radio dials.

The avatar's body jerked suddenly upright. Eyes wide and empty stared down at her right hand. She pressed her palm onto the table, fingers spread. The motion of the avatar's left hand blurred as she raised her arm high overhead.

John jumped at the clatter of chairs behind him. Colonel Wick had leapt to his feet and struggled to reach the control panel.

"She's spiking it! Stop her!"

John spun back toward the imaging room. A knife flashed in the avatar's hand. The blade dropped with deadly speed and struck the table, severing the right hand at the wrist. Horror exploded across the avatar's face as she dropped the knife and clutched the bloodless stump to her chest.

\*\*\*

The scream of the avatar hit like a bomb blast, the shockwave filling Ann's head till she thought her skull would split. Lights flashed behind Ann's eyes. Her muscles tightened like cords as the bio gel forced synaptic impulses into her body. Ann screamed in terror, her voice joining the avatar's as it rebounded. Ann felt her mind collapsing, shrinking down to a single point. The avatar's scream deepened and throbbed in time with the racing of Ann's heart, transforming until the sound became the familiar, mechanical rumbles of engines.

\*\*\*

"I'm picking up a vibration."

Anaya pressed a palm to the control panel, head bowed in concentration, as she listened to the deep bass throbs coming from behind the cockpit. *There it was again.*

The engine's steady rumble had changed—perhaps only a slide of a half step sharp—but it was there...and growing worse. The *Kairos* was in the early stages of a cascade engine failure. Anaya's mouth twisted into a frown. It was the vibration underneath the sound of the engines she couldn't explain.

"Command Control, this is Lieutenant Chapman. The Kairos is in a level one cascade engine failure, and the starboard time coil has engaged." Anaya flipped the control switch back and forth to try and deactivate the time coil. Cold dread squeezed her heart. She triggered the comm link again. "Time coil is unresponsive. Attempting manual override."

Anaya's hands raced across the control panel, rerouting power away from the time coil to force a shutdown. Her mind listed options while her fingers worked. With only one coil engaged, the vibration would increase until the ship tore itself apart. She could sense the electrical notes of the time coil growing stronger as its power cells charged to full strength. The ship shuddered again as if to underscore the point. The engines were in a level one cascade failure. Anaya's eyes flicked to the power gauges. The red line crept across the display panel as she registered the slide of another half step in pitch. *Correction—level two cascade failure.* She would need to perform a cold shut down of the engines before they burned out. *But killing the engines with the time coil engaged was suicidal.*

Anaya finished rerouting power and tried to deactivate the time coil a second time. The trill of notes played on, mocking her attempt. A cold sweat broke across the back of her neck and under her black flight suit. She couldn't shut down the time coil. Anaya gripped the yoke to steady her nerves, head bowed. She was out of options. The ship would tear apart with only one time coil engaged. *But I still have two time coils.*

Anaya snapped her head up, eyes darting to the power gauges. The red line pushed across the screen, slowly overtaking the white. A quick calculation told her she only had a few minutes before the red filled the entire screen and the engines seized. Anaya routed the power back along its original path, her finger resting a moment on the last switch as she blew out a breath and activated the port engine's time coil. Anaya triggered the comm link and talked fast.

"Command Control, this is the Kairos. I can't shut the coil down. I'm going to attempt a time jump. I'm relaying coordinates now." Anaya punched numbers into the nav computer and ignored the voice in her head that screamed a time jump during an engine cascade failure was impossible. "If the engines can hold out through the jump, the time coils might disengage on their own, then I'll hit the kill switch to prevent any further damage to the engines. Kairos out!"

Anaya didn't wait for a response. She didn't have time to ask for permission. *Time...* She smirked at the absurdity. The *Kairos* was the most sophisticated time ship Andarria had ever built, capable of traveling to any *where* and any *when*, and yet she was most likely going to die for the want of a few minutes. Anaya gripped the throttle. Her thoughts turned for an instant to her brother and then to Vincent. *My God... What if...?* Anaya gritted her teeth, pushed the throttle forward, and felt like she'd pulled the rope for her own execution.

The *Kairos* leapt forward, streaking deeper into Andarrian space. Stars lengthened and rushed past the cockpit windows. Anaya watched the power gauges and listened to the time coils' flute song. The harmonics between the two coils needed to be pitch perfect before she could attempt the time jump. The notes slid over and under each other, refusing to lock. The ship bucked in protest and buffeted Anaya in the pilot seat. She grimaced and tightened her grip on the yoke. *Level 3.*

The time coils refused to sync, growing in volume, but not locking in tune. The discordant notes made Anaya's teeth ache.

*"Come on! Come on!"*

The sudden lock and ring of notes swelled the cockpit. That's it! Anaya triggered the jump.

An explosion ripped through the back of the ship, breaking one side of the cockpit harness and throwing Anaya hard against the controls. She pushed back into the jump seat and clenched her teeth against the scream of metal as the starboard engine ripped from the hull. The *Kairos* slipped and rolled right. Anaya braced her feet against the control panel. She clutched the yoke with both hands and fought to regain control of the ship.

The port time coil shrugged off the loss of its twin and

twisted open the blackness of space. Anaya could see through the cockpit front window that the portal wasn't large enough, but it was too late. The *Kairos* broke through the spacetime barrier with a roar. Orange flames pressed around the ship. Sparks shot across the control panel. Cockpit windows cracked under the pressure as the *Kairos* twisted, forcing its way through the portal.

Anaya yelled, her scream joining the chaos around her. She tried to break the ship free of the jump. The ship bucked. Her helmet slammed into the control panel. The cockpit blurred as black feathered her vision. Her cheek pressed against the controls.

Anaya awoke slumped across the remains of the control panel, the right side of her helmet shattered. Blood, sticky and warm, covered one side of her face. Ann gasped for breath. Her lungs burned in the smoky air. She tried to move and moaned at the stabs of pain coming from every direction. Ann looked down at her hands still clutching the yoke. Her gloves had melted to the wheel. Anaya pulled her hands free and cried out as the gloves tore and exposed raw, blistered skin underneath.

She laid back in her seat and cried softly. *I sent them coordinates. They should be here soon.* Minutes passed. No one came. Her pain turned to panic then to anger. *Why is no one coming? How long have I been here?*

A flash of blue light reflected on the shattered cockpit glass. Ann winced against the pain as she turned her head. The port engine drifted in the debris field. As Anaya watched, the engine emitted another blue flash then a bright explosion split open its side. The shock wave raced toward her. *Oh, God. No!* Lieutenant Chapman pinched her eyes shut. The impact shattered the cockpit, freeing her from the wreckage and throwing her into a river of white flame.

# TWENTY-FIVE

## *HOME AGAIN*

Ann blinked in the harsh light. The brilliance of the exam room made her cringe, but she preferred the light to the spiraling darkness behind her eyes. Her brain felt like a cold slab of meat. Ann looked down and saw she lay on a gurney covered by a heavy blanket. The muscles in her arms and legs jumped with tiny explosions, a side effect from the bio gel.

She pulled her right arm out from underneath the blanket. Just like with the puzzle ball the bio gel had relayed the false emotion from the avatar back to Ann, doubling the intensity and creating an emotional feedback loop. When the knife touched the avatar's wrist, it had felt like a strand of a spider's web breaking across Ann's skin. Pressure and the crunch of bone followed, but with the curious absence of pain.

Ann flexed the fingers of her right hand. *Sacrifice.* That had been the key emotion. From the moment she first realized the time coil had engaged, every action Ann took had been to save the ship, not herself. The fear for herself was secondary. Ann never expected to live, but if she could have saved a portion of the ship, then that would have been enough. Ann laid her arm across her chest. She curled her fingers around the folds of the blanket, taking pleasure in the motion.

The door of the exam room slid open and Colonel Wick

burst in. His eyes swept over Ann.

*"What the hell did you think you were doing?"*

Ann thought of the med tech and tried to assume a blank expression. She didn't want him to get in trouble for helping her.

"What do you mean?"

*"Who told you to do that?"*

"No one told me..." Ann paused to take a breath. Her head reeled from the effort of speaking. "I guess I was so angry about not finding the memory...it just...happened."

"Do you know what kind of a risk you took? How dangerous that was?" Wick had stopped yelling, but his voice still thundered in the small room. "Do you know we have patients with brain damage from trying the same stunt you just pulled?"

Ann's spine stiffened. The med tech hadn't said anything about physical risks. No. She wouldn't blame it on him.

"Did Agent Knox get the memory?"

The colonel's jaw jutted forward. His mouth slanted in grudging admission. "Yes. She's taking it to the committee right now."

"Will it be enough?"

"More than enough. They'll probably give you a damn medal."

Ann closed her eyes and rested her head against the pillow. "Then it was worth it."

The room began to spin again, her stomach rolled dangerously, and Ann was forced to open her eyes. Wick continued to stare down at her, holding Ann's gaze.

"Go home, Lieutenant."

Colonel Wick picked up a steel basin from the counter and put it next to Ann on the gurney. "When you're ready to be a time jumper again, give me a call." Wick turned and left the exam room.

***

Commander Rectrix and the investigation committee didn't hesitate to drop the charges after viewing the memory. Ann's role in the investigation of the Kairos was over, and she was free to go home to the Colonies.

"Goodbye, Captain," Colonel Wick said as he shook John's hand on the steps of the hospital's main entrance. "If you're ever on Andarria again—"

"I don't have much reason to come to Andarria," John said, jaw tight. "But if I do I'm sure we'll see each other."

Wick nodded. His stern features offered a warning.

"Safe travels."

John walked in silence between Ann and her brother. The surrounding buildings reflected the blues and grays of the clouds. The knot in John's chest grew tighter with every step. Watching Ann's avatar mutilate herself in the mental imager had left John shaken, but now the question of how to get past shuttleport security for the trip home loomed large in his mind. With Ann safe and the trial behind them, the seriousness of John's situation came back with agonizing clarity. And, assuming John could even get home to the Colonies, there was still the matter of Chohon-Lo.

The hover car lifted from the curb and mixed with the traffic. John looked out the window, his brain racing as fast as the cars as they zigzagged through the city. He fingered the passport in his coat pocket, barely aware of Ann and Montressador Chapman sitting next to him. The document granted John permission to fly from the Colonies to Andarria—a brilliant forgery—but like most illusions, some tricks shouldn't be performed more than once. There might be a chance if security only did a routine inspection, but John needed a backup plan. He still hadn't thought of one when the car touched down at the shuttleport entrance.

John hopped out of the car. He slung the duffel bag over a shoulder just as the doors to the terminal split open. A pair of gray-uniformed security guards stepped through and headed toward him, their black ion rifles strapped across their backs. John ducked his head, his heart hammering, and pretended to search for something in his bag.

"The concourse won't be as crowded this time of day."

John looked up. Montressador Chapman had stepped in front, blocking the guards' view. Chapman nodded to the sentries and they continued their patrol.

John quietly blew out a sigh as his pulse slowed. He looked sideways at the Montressador. Was it a coincidence, or had the swordsman covered for him?

"I don't like crowds," John said. He dropped his voice and added. "But they can be useful."

Chapman frowned, drumming fingers on the hilt of his sword. He watched the guards until they were out of sight.

"Keep your head down," he muttered. "and for god's sake, stay close!"

Montressador Chapman yanked Ann's carpet bag from John's hand and walked into the terminal with Ann at his heels. John's pulse ticked faster. He never expected help from the Montressador, certainly not after their confrontation at the hospital.

The promenade was empty except for a few scattered groups of sightseers wandering among the exhibits. The clanking of Montressador Chapman's sword echoed in the open space and turned a few heads. John felt like a roach scurrying across a kitchen floor.

The concourse narrowed and angled sharply to the right. John gathered his courage as they came in sight of the security checkpoint. A tall barricade of bluish-green metal divided the concourse in half. Arriving passengers bypassed security on one side of the barricade, while departing passengers were funneled into a horseshoe-shaped area on the other. A curved row of dark sensor portals spread out before the lines of passengers like a honeycomb. Guards inspected passports and instructed departing passengers to walk single file through the narrow portals.

John pushed away the temptation of bold maneuvers. He steadied his breathing and tried to imitate the bored looks of the other passengers. With luck, he would be able to pass himself off as just an average traveler with no worries except for getting home.

Chapman walked toward the lines of passengers waiting to be processed, but instead of stopping, he continued straight for a guard's station on the opposite side of the checkpoint.

John's heart froze. *What the hell is he doing?* He grabbed Ann's hand. "Where is he going? The line starts back there."

Ann looked up and smiled. "Sean likes to use the VIP entrance. It's a lot faster."

John choked on the lump in his throat. VIP, while faster, also meant extra attention. It was too late to change course. John hitched up his duffel bag on a shoulder and tried to ignore the squirming in his stomach.

The security guard, sitting behind the VIP observation desk, stood as Montressador Chapman approached. His eyes grew round with recognition, and his arm snapped up in salute.

"At ease," Chapman said with a smile as he leaned on the guard's desk. "I'm walking my sister and her friend to their shuttle gate. Do you need to see travel documents?"

The guard's eyes darted to Ann and John then back to Montressador Chapman. John held his breath.

"No, sir. You may proceed with your guests through the sensor portal unless your guests have anything they would like to declare."

Chapman stared blankly at the guard. "Can you be more specific?"

"Produce, sir. There is a new ban on the transportation of flivver fruit."

The Montressador looked pointedly at Ann then John. His eyes danced with subdued merriment.

"You two don't have any fruit on you, do you?"

Ann smirked and shook her head. John bit back a burst of nervous laughter.

Chapman turned back to the guard. "We are fruit-free."

"Then you may proceed, sir."

Montressador Chapman touched an index finger briefly to his brow and walked toward the dark portal.

John tightened the grip on his duffel and followed Ann. He tried to restrain the amusement twitching at the corners of his mouth. *Fruit?* Of all the things security could have stopped him for and the guard asked him about flivver fruit? The euphoria of relief almost made John lightheaded.

"Here is where I need to leave you." Montressador Chapman dropped Ann's carpet bag when he reached the shuttle gate. "The Ministers are meeting in an hour and they're insisting I attend. Or maybe it's Jo who insists. Sometimes it's hard to tell." He shrugged and gave Ann a crooked grin. "Anyway, I've missed the last three meetings, so I should probably go to this one."

"I wish we could have stayed longer," Ann said. John's muscles tensed. "I would have liked to have seen more of the city."

"Maybe next time." The Montressador's expression cooled as he turned to shake John's hand. "I'm sure the Captain is anxious to get back to his tavern."

"It's not fair to Arnold and Mrs. Beaumont to leave them alone for so long," John said and gripped Chapman's hand. "Thanks for walking us to our gate."

"Captain, if it wasn't for you, my sister would be dead, or at best I would be saying goodbye to her in a visitor's lounge at a prison facility somewhere." Montressador Chapman's expression remained cool, but the gratitude John saw in his eyes mirrored his own. "Thank you."

*** 

The boarding announcement sent passengers scurrying to form a line at the entrance to the gangway. John grabbed his bag. He would finally be able to relax, maybe even sleep, after liftoff. Ann followed John to the back of the line.

"Why did you and Bonnie move to the Colonies?"

John looked at Ann in surprise. The thoughtful smile that curled her mouth was remarkably like her brother's.

John forced a chuckle and raised an eyebrow. "Why the sudden interest?"

Ann shrugged. "Just curious. You never talk about it."

"Never had a reason to." John pretended to examine their shuttle tickets.

"So...why did you leave Andarria?"

The curiosity etched in Ann's face told him she would not be easily diverted. John craned his neck to look past the line of passengers in front of him. The shuttle gate was still thirty feet away. John sighed and rattled off the standard bullet points.

"Bonnie and I were in love. Her parents didn't approve. We got married and moved to the Colonies. The End."

*Silence.* John looked at Ann. She stared straight ahead, lost in thought. Perhaps he had answered too quickly.

"You wanted to know why. That's why."

"It makes sense," Ann said, her face pulled in concentration. "You've been tense ever since I asked you to come to Palladium Beta. I thought it was the trial or my brother." Ann looked down at the mention of Sean. "Andarria reminds you of Bonnie. That's why you didn't want to come back."

John's mouth stiffened. It wasn't Andarria that reminded him of Bonnie, it was Siren's Cove, and it was the fear of her memory fading that kept John there. The line shuffled forward another step before John could trust himself to answer.

"There will always be things that remind me of Bonnie."

The old sorrow gripped his heart. John struggled against the pain and it relented. He blew out a sigh and took Ann's hand.

"It's ancient history. I love you. I couldn't let you go to Andarria without me. The thought of you not coming back home... Grief can kill a man. I don't think I could survive it a second time."

John looked at Ann. A question still troubled her eyes. *What isn't she telling me?*

"Sir, may we speak to you for a moment?"

John froze. The voice behind him was not the shuttle attendant. John looked over a shoulder. Two helmeted security guards stood behind him.

"Of course." John bolted a tight smile of cooperation to his face.

The first guard studied the comm link strapped to the inside of a forearm then looked up. "Are you John Galeas?"

Anxiety ratcheted John's nerves a final turn, locking fear into place.

"Yes."

Ann gripped John's arm. "What's going on?"

"Just a security check." John gave Ann a reassuring smile he did not feel.

"Is she traveling with you?" John nodded to the guard. "Would both of you please step this way?" The guard waved in the direction of the passenger lounge.

John steadied himself as he walked with Ann flanked by the two security guards. *Why didn't the guard ask to see our passports? Why pull us out of line?* John took a deep breath and tried to relax to give his walk a more natural gait. *Be calm. Be polite. That's how to play it. No reason to get worked up.* John reached into a coat pocket for his passport. Fingers brushed the feathered edge of a tear in the lining. His stomach clenched. John dug deeper into the pocket. Empty. John's pulse pounded as he remembered how he had torn the pocket at The Monkey's Fist to make room for the laser cutter. The hole was just large enough for the booklet to have slipped through. John's insides writhed.

The first security guard motioned to John and led him a few paces away from Ann and the second guard. John followed, nerves humming like a fully charged ion cannon. The guard stopped, reached into a pocket of his flak jacket, and pulled out a green passport book.

"Your passport was found and turned in to security by another passenger." John's heart lurched. "I have orders to bring you in for further questioning."

Hope died with the guard's last words. From the moment he'd lost his passport, John had been throwing losing dice. It made sense security would have completed a full background scan when the booklet was found. The guards had pulled him out of line to avoid making a scene in front of the other passengers when they arrested him. John felt his strength collapse, his limbs turned to dead weight.

"She checks out." The guard interrogating Ann called to his

partner from across the lounge. "Ma'am, you are free to board the shuttle."

Ann took a step toward John. The security guard raised a hand and blocked her path.

"I'm sorry, ma'am. He will have to come with us."

Ann's eyes widened. "Why? What has he done?"

"Ann, get on the shuttle." John could see the last of the passengers walking through the gangway entrance.

"I'm not leaving without you." Ann turned to the guard. The look of determination on her face made John uneasy. "I'm sure there's been a mistake. Montressador Chapman is my brother. He can vouch for Captain Galeas."

"Ann, it's okay. I can catch the next shuttle." John winced as the guard secured the wrist clamps behind his back. "Just get on the damn shuttle!"

The whistle of a plasma gun charging to full strength split the air. The guard slammed Ann against the wall, pinning her across the throat. The barrel of a plasma gun poised inches from her face.

"Get off her!"

John wrenched from the security guard's grasp. The guard grabbed his shoulder from behind, and a jolt of searing pain made his muscles snap. Fire burned a path from John's shoulder through the center of his body and down his right leg. John's legs buckled. He slammed facedown on the floor. His nose cracked on impact and sent another arrow of pain through his head. The blood roared in John's ears before darkness dragged him under.

*** 

Ann stared down the barrel of the security guard's plasma gun. The weapon's fully charged power cell cast a violent glow. The energy pulse prickled and popped against her skin. She looked past the weapon to the guard's face. His mouth hardened into a thin white line, but the young man's eyes were bright with fear. The gun quaked in his hand. If the guard's finger slipped, the light from the blast of the plasma bolt would be the last thing Ann's eyes would ever see.

"Please. I'm unarmed."

The guard didn't move or lower the weapon. Ann closed her eyes and tried to keep the terror from her voice.

"The keravnos implant in my ear. It chirps." Ann's throat and lungs burned with the effort. "That was the noise you heard."

The guard released her. Ann fell to her knees and gulped air. John lay face down and as still as death on the floor a few feet away. The security guard retreated a couple paces, but kept his gun drawn. Ann watched as the other guard clamped the anti-grav cuffs behind John's back. The guard activated the cuffs and lifted John from the floor. John's head slumped against his chest. The anti-gravs supported his upper body, while his legs crumpled underneath, as useless as a marionette's.

"Where are you taking him?" Ann's voice cracked.

"Central lockup."

"What are the charges?"

Ann's guard holstered the weapon after a signal from his partner. The two sentries grabbed John's arms and dragged him backwards from the lounge, the heels of his boots scraping the floor behind them.

Ann grabbed their bags and raced after the guards. Her suspicions had been right. The conversation with Arnold in the winery, John's reluctance to go to Andarria, how he acted around Sean. *What was John hiding?* And then there was the man who attacked Ann in the tavern. Had John lied about him too? Ann gritted teeth and pulled the strap of John's duffel over her head. She would get answers to her questions later.

Ann struggled under the weight of the two bags and tried to keep pace with the guards. She couldn't lose sight of John.

John moaned and lifted his head. Ann winced. His bloody lip swelled. The bridge of his nose jutted at an odd angle.

"John!"

Ann pushed through a group of passengers who turned to gawk at the sentries dragging a bloody and unconscious traveler through the terminal. The guards turned down a narrow corridor leading away from the main concourse. Ann rounded the corner in time to see John's boots disappearing through a security door. Ann ran to catch up and muscled her way through the door as it was about to close. The roar of engines blasted her ears as a galactic shuttle took to the sky. An armored security transport waited in a loading area behind the terminal.

The noise of the engines and the fresh air shook John from his stupor.

"Ann!"

"I'm here!"

Ann dropped the bags and sprinted toward the transport. She skidded to a stop when a sentry with an ion rifle blocked her path.

John locked eyes on Ann. "Find A.K. Max!"

The guards lifted John and threw him hard into the back of the vehicle. Ann tried to get closer, but the sentry with the rifle pushed her back.

"Who's A.K? How do I find him?"

"Avery Kildare Max. Tell him I've been arrested." John's eyes grew wide as the hatch started to close. "Tell him *genie*!"

# TWENTY-SIX

## *A.K. MAX*

The hatch slammed shut and the security transport drove off, leaving Ann standing alone. She didn't care what John told Arnold. Ancient history didn't slap you in restraints and throw you into the back of a security vehicle.

"Ma'am, this is a restricted area."

The sentry who had kept her from getting close to the transport peered from underneath a gray helmet.

"Go back to the terminal or you will be arrested for trespassing." The guard asserted his authority with a nudge from the bridge of a rifle.

Ann bristled, but she was in no position to argue. She needed to find a comm station. Ann lugged the two bags back into the terminal and through the concourse. She thought her arms would fall off by the time she found a cluster of kiosks. Her fingers trembled as she entered a datalink code. A second later, Jo's round face and tumbling curls filled the comm screen.

"Montressador Chapman's office."

"Jo? Where's Sean?"

"Ann? I thought you would have left by now. Why aren't you on the shuttle?"

"John's been arrested! I have to talk to Sean!"

Jo's expression veered from surprise to dread. "Your brother isn't here. He's meeting with the Ministers. There's no way I can get word to him until after the council has adjourned."

Ann's insides knotted. She couldn't wait for Sean to get out of the meeting. She needed him now.

Jo's fingers skimmed the control panel. "I'm sending a car to pick you up. You can come to the office and wait for your brother here."

"What? No! I need to get to central lockup. John needs my help."

Jo looked at Ann from the comm screen, brown eyes deep with sympathy. "Ann, they won't listen to you. You don't have the authority to get him released. Come to the office. Wait for your brother and let him sort it out."

"No." Ann stared hard at Jo. John may have kept secrets, but Ann trusted he had given her exactly what she needed to get him released.

"I'm going to central lockup. Send the car and keep the comm line open. I have a job for you."

***

John slumped on the bench and pressed the cold pack to his swollen face. The pain in his head pounded like a sledgehammer. The electric shock from the guard's taser glove had ripped through his body and exited his right foot. John half expected to discover his toes blasted off, but when he wriggled his foot inside the boot, he could tell all the toes remained accounted for and intact.

John sighed. He lowered the cold pack and ran his fingers down the bridge of his nose, wincing as he passed over the break. A ham-fisted med tech had set the bone after the guards processed him. Dr. Brainard was always more artful with these matters. John would have to ask the doctor to reset his nose for him. Of course, that assumed he would ever see the Colonies again. A weariness deeper than John had ever known weighed him down and he closed his eyes.

"You stupid sack of meat."

John's shoulders sagged. It was a relief to know he came, and yet the sound of the agent's voice did little to cheer him. John opened his eyes and lifted his head.

A.K. Max stood, hands in pockets, and looked at John from behind the glittering blue force shield covering the entry to the cell. The agent hadn't changed since they last met: dark pinstripe suit, brown hair swept into a crested wave. The bags under his eyes gave the intelligence officer a permanent woebegone look, and the curved white scar under his bottom lip gave shape to his chin. A.K. studied John a moment, then the corners of his mouth quirked into a smile.

"You're doing something different with your face. Not a good look for you."

John scowled. "Skip to the part where you get me out of here."

"Come on, John. Quit playing games with me. I'm tired."

John grunted and pressed the cold pack to his face. He heard A.K. take a step closer to the door of the cell.

"Do you know how hard it is to poof someone out of central lockup in Palladium Beta? I think this may be a new personal best for you."

John looked up and saw A.K. examining the force shield by running a hand along the edges of the entryway. The shield quivered and threw warning arcs that snapped and frizzled in all directions. A.K. licked a finger and tapped the shield, testing its strength. Blue sparks flew from the point of contact. He blew out frustration and locked eyes on John.

"Why didn't you come back when you had the chance? Why in hell would you come back now? And now that you're here, why won't you end this?"

"The job isn't finished yet."

"It is over, John," A.K. said, anger edging his words. "You did your duty. You were one hell of an operative. A lot of bad guys are locked up because of you. I'm sorry Bonnie died. I'm sorry you're having a hard time letting go, but it's time for you to come up for air. Just tell me what I want to hear, and we can both walk out of here and get on with our lives."

John gripped the edge of the bench. If he relented and A.K. released him from his oath, his cover would be blown, and the people he cared about the most would be dead from Chohon-Lo's blade. He could stay quiet, but if A.K. refused to spring him from central lockup, he would never be able to return to the Colonies and everyone would still be just as dead. John felt the cold creep of fear cover him like a condemned man's hood.

John shook his head. "I can't. Chohon-Lo is back." He watched A.K. tense. "If I stay here, he'll kill them all."

"What does he want?"

"Me as his new navigator. I told him no." John told A.K. about the deal he made with the raider in hopes of buying himself more time.

"You're an idiot," A.K. said. "A brave idiot, but still an idiot. What are you going to do?"

"I don't know. I'll think of something. Can you get me out of here or not?"

The agent nodded, face grim. "It's not going to be easy...not like busting you out of some dark side of the moon outpost." A.K. looked at John. His mouth slowly twisted into a smile. "I might need you to pay me back for this one."

\*\*\*

Ann burst through the doorway of central lockup and stopped cold. Dozens of uniformed officials sat behind long counters. Lines of people formed everywhere and snaked across the floor. A traffic jam had delayed Ann a full hour before the driver had found an alternate route, giving A.K. Max plenty of time to arrive ahead of her. At least, Ann hoped he had. Jo's data search had uncovered a roll call of potential matches, but when Ann finally reached the right Max, her conversation with him through the comm hadn't done much to reassure her.

"Max here."

Ann took a deep breath. "This is Lieutenant Anaya Chapman. I was told to contact Avery Kildare Max. I'm calling you for Captain John Galeas. He's been arrested and—"

"Sorry. I don't know anyone by that name."

"Are you sure? I had the impression he hasn't spoken to you in a while."

The voice sighed with impatience. "You've got the wrong Max. Look. I have to get back to a meeting."

"Wait!" Desperation welled inside Ann. "He told me to tell you—"

"Sweetheart, I don't know you and I don't know any John Galeas. You have the wrong number."

"Genie! He told me to tell you genie!"

The comm crackled in the silence. Ann held her breath.

"Where are you?"

"Palladium Beta. I'm heading to central lockup."

"I'll meet you there."

Ann scanned the dreary faces of the people around her, searching for anyone who might be A.K. Max. The question of what she had set into motion prickled in the back of Ann's mind.

A buzzer sounded. The security door leading to the holding cells dilated with a whoosh of air. John, bruised and bloodied, entered the waiting area escorted by a security guard.

Ann winced. John's nose was swollen to twice its normal size, and a dark bruise covered a cheek. Dried blood traced the gash in his lip and flecked his shirt. John looked like an early morning drunk after a night of street brawling. Ann waited for the guard to remove the wrist restraints before she rushed into John's arms. He held her for an instant then gently pushed her back.

"Are you all right?" Ann searched John's face.

"I'm okay." John's cheeks bunched into a weary smile that didn't reach his eyes.

"I got here as fast as I could. What happened? Why did they arrest you?"

A man in a pinstriped suit stepped forward and stood next to John. "A simple case of mistaken identity. It happens a lot. Captain Galeas has one of those faces," the stranger said with a smirk and looked sideways at John. "Well...not now...maybe when the swelling goes down."

Ann's heart jumped. "Are you...?"

"A.K. Max." The man nodded to Ann and flashed a calculated smile. "Here, Buttercup. You better take this in case Galeas gets in trouble again." He handed Ann a business card.

Ann looked at the stiff white card. Max's name appeared without embellishment.

*A.K. Max, Legal Counsel*

Ann glanced at the stranger over the top of the card. Except for the suit, he didn't look much like an attorney. She frowned and slipped the card into the pocket of her traveling cloak.

John sighed impatiently. "Can we get out of here? I need to get home if that's all right with everyone."

Ann felt the crowd around her shift as dozens of people turned to look in the same direction. A whisper ran past and she saw a uniformed official walk purposely toward the entrance. She turned to look in the direction of the crowd. Her insides squirmed. Sean stood near the entrance and scanned the room. The anger buckling her brother's face told Ann the Montressador had not come for pleasant conversation. Now that John had been released, having Sean there didn't seem like such a good idea anymore.

John gripped Ann's arm and whispered in her ear. "Why is your brother here? Did you contact him?"

"I tried to, but I couldn't reach him. Jo must have sent him."

The official greeted Sean and led him to a row of offices behind the counters. Sean followed, never looking in Ann and John's direction. The crowd lost interest and returned to their dismal conversations.

Max pulled two shuttle tickets and a green passport book from an inside coat pocket and handed them to John.

"You two should get going. You have a shuttle to catch. I'll let Montressador Chapman know you were on a tight schedule." Max gave Ann a wink and headed for the row of offices.

Before Ann could think, John had grabbed her hand and pulled her through the crowd toward the exit.

***

Ann slammed the cabin door behind her. John dropped their bags and pulled the med kit out from under the bench. He found a cold pack and activated it by smacking it hard against the table. John looked at Ann. His blue eyes shone like glacier ice.

"All you had to do was call A.K. Why did you call him?"

"I was trying to help you," Ann said. "I needed Jo's help. I didn't know who A.K. was. I didn't know if I could find him on my own. What's wrong with you? Why are you acting so strange?"

John scowled and flopped onto the bench, pressing the cold pack to his face. "After the day I've had, seeing your brother in central lockup was not my idea of a great place for a family reunion."

Ann sunk onto the opposite bench.

"It's my fault you got hurt. My keravnos implant chirped. That's why the security guard turned on me."

John stared glumly out the porthole at the tarmac below and muttered. "It's not your fault."

Ann watched John as he looked out the window. His features remained dark and brooding, but she was encouraged to see the anger beginning to dissipate. Maybe he would talk to her now?

"Who is A.K. Max really?" Ann spoke softly, hoping to coax the answers out. "And what is Genie?"

John tore his gaze away from the window. "A.K.'s just an old friend." He lay down on the bench with the cold pack over his face. "No questions. Not now. My head is killing me. I just want to sleep."

Ann fought the tangle of questions filling her head. She looked at John lying on the bench. His breathing grew deeper. A.K. Max wasn't the only stranger Ann had met that day.

The shuttle engines shook the cabin floor as they fired,

beginning the long flight back to Siren's Cove.

# TWENTY-SEVEN

## *WINDBOUND*

When the shuttle broke through the clouds, the early morning sky over Llewellyn was the color of a bruise. The town below looked like an old rumpled coat. Ann turned away from the window. She watched John pull their bags from the cabin's overhead compartment, his face a gathering storm in the dim light. The swelling around John's nose had improved but left him with two black eyes, and the break in the bridge more pronounced. He'd slept for most of the flight and had barely spoken since he awoke. John's indifference chilled Ann, the distance between them as great as when she first arrived at Siren's Cove.

A tinny nicker greeted them as they exited the shuttleport terminal. Dr. Brainard stood waiting at the curb. Equuleus snorted and bobbed his great copper head.

"Thank heavens you're home," Dr. Brainard said as he clasped Ann's hands. John pushed past the doctor and threw the bags into the carriage. "When you didn't arrive last night, I checked with the shuttleport steward. He told me you were on the passenger list for this morning's flight." The doctor turned to greet John. His smile vanished when he saw John's face. "Good Lord, what happened?"

John opened the carriage door and got in. "Mix-up with

shuttleport security."

Dr. Brainard frowned and opened his mouth to reply, but Ann caught his eye and cautioned him with a shake of her head as she slid into the back seat. The doctor sighed and climbed up into the driver's seat.

The mechanized horse's cast-iron hooves pounded the dirt road, demolishing the distance between the shuttleport and Siren's Cove as fast as any hover car. Before long, Dr. Brainard reined Equuleus into the drive next to the tavern.

Ann grabbed her bag and hopped to the ground. Maybe she would have better luck getting answers out of John after breakfast.

Dr. Brainard eyed the captain as they climbed down from the carriage. "Who set your nose?"

"Med tech," John grumbled.

The doctor clicked his tongue in sympathy. "The bridge is still bowed, but only slightly. I have time before my first appointment. I can reset it for you." John grunted his consent.

Ann walked up the steps. The door flung open and Mrs. Beaumont burst onto the stoop. Her eyes lit upon the captain as Ann and Dr. Brainard filed past.

"It's about time you got home." Mrs. Beaumont held the door open with one hand, the other on a hip. "Mike stopped by yesterday and said you didn't pay him for this month's beer yet."

John struggled through the doorway with his duffel bag.

"I was going to pay him when I got back."

The cook's eyes narrowed as she peered into John's bruised face. "What fresh hell have you brought on yourself?"

"Never mind!"

John put one foot on the steps to go upstairs and motioned for Dr. Brainard to follow.

"Stop right there!" Mrs. Beaumont came about with her cannons fully loaded. "Arnold is here. He's been waiting for you to get home."

Ann looked and saw Arnold standing in the kitchen doorway. He held his cap crumpled in his hands, face white with tension.

"Sorry for the early visit...I know you're busy just getting home and all," Arnold said. His fingers twisted the cap. "John, could I talk to you?" He jerked a thumb in the direction of the winery.

John paused on the step, eyes on Arnold and his teeth set. He blew out an exasperated sigh and looked to Dr. Brainard.

The doctor shrugged and adjusted his glasses. "I can work while you two talk. I don't mind if you don't."

John swiped a hand through his hair. "All right. Let's get on with it then."

John dropped the duffel at the foot of the stairs and stalked off toward the winery with Arnold and the doctor in tow. Mrs. Beaumont watched the men leave with a troubled look.

"Ann, why don't you take a moment to change, then I'm afraid I'll need your help with tonight's menu," she said as she headed back to the kitchen.

Ann put her bag down and followed the cook.

Coffee perked in the carafe on the counter. Ann's stomach grumbled as she caught the scent of ham and eggs in the skillet.

"Is everything all right?" Ann stepped over Luff, sweeping up around the table. "Why was Arnold here?"

"Oh, it's nothing to worry about." Mrs. Beaumont reached into the depths of the kitchen sink and removed Port. The mini-bot chirruped in annoyance at having his task interrupted. "The sink is clean enough," she scolded him. "Go clean something in the tavern."

She gave the mini-bot a light toss. Port opened his wings and took flight, sailing lopsidedly through the kitchen and into the tavern. Mrs. Beaumont turned back to Ann. Seeing the look of concern on her face, the cook sighed and shrugged.

"I guess you'll find out soon enough. While you and the captain were gone, Arnold had some trouble with a few customers in the tavern."

Ann tilted her head in surprise. Siren's Cove could get lively at times, but the tavern's customers were, for the most part, well behaved.

"What happened?"

Mrs. Beaumont stood at the stove and scooped eggs into a serving bowl. "A group of ruffians. Drunks, all of them!" Her mouth puckered in distaste. "I don't mind high spirits, but not when it scares off our regular customers."

Ann's spine stiffened. "What did they do?"

The older woman finished with the eggs and turned her attention to the thick slices of ham sizzling in the skillet.

"They were looking for trouble." Mrs. Beaumont stabbed at the meat with a serving fork. "They wore their pistols in plain sight. Even kept them on the table while they drank. You might see that down by the docks but not here. Arnold asked them to settle down or leave, but they laughed at him." The cook shook her head sadly. "Poor Arnold would rather bet on a fight than be in one."

"Who were they? Did you recognize them?"

"No. They looked like off tourists to me."

Ann's insides turned cold. The man who attacked her in the tavern was an off tourist. She set the bowl of eggs on the table. "Did a lot of off tourists come by while we were gone?"

"No more than usual," Mrs. Beaumont said. "But this lot came every night. Now that the captain is home, if they come back, he'll take care of them."

Ann watched the older woman as she transferred the last of the ham to the platter. While Mrs. Beaumont's words were confident, Ann detected a note of uncertainty in her tone.

"My goodness!" Mrs. Beaumont dropped the serving fork onto the platter and spun to face Ann. "Here you are standing in front of me and I completely forgot! Welcome home!" She wrapped Ann in a quick hug. "Your brother sent me a message on the comm. I'm so glad everything worked out with the investigation committee."

Ann smiled. "Thank you. It's nice to be—"

A loud yelp followed by muffled cursing came from the winery. Ann winced.

Mrs. Beaumont set the platter of ham on the table. She

glanced toward the winery with a frown. "It will be good to have that trouble behind us."

***

Ann tried to talk to John after breakfast, but he bolted his food in silence and headed back to the winery, muttering about maintenance and repairs. His mood lifted by lunch, but he continued to evade Ann's questions.

"I can't talk now," John said, grabbing a sandwich from the cutting board and almost losing two fingers to Mrs. Beaumont's bread knife in the process. "I've got to balance the books. If I don't pay Mike soon, we'll be the only tavern in Llewellyn without any beer."

Ann crossed her arms in irritation. "Maybe you could find time in your hectic schedule for me later?"

Mrs. Beaumont choked back a snort of laughter and continued cutting sandwiches at the counter.

John stopped in mid stride on his way into the sitting room and gave Ann a peculiar look. His mouth broke into a crooked grin.

"I'm sorry." He reached out to cup Ann's cheek. The touch of John's hand made Ann shiver. "I've had a lot on my mind with your trial and worrying about things here. There's a lot I need to catch up on. Give me some time to get things back on even keel, then I promise I'll give you all the time in the world."

Ann gave him a reluctant smile. "That's a pretty big promise to make to a time jumper."

John chuckled. "I know. But I can make good on it."

John gave Ann a quick kiss on the lips, hesitated, and leaned in again. His fingertips trailed from Ann's cheek to the back of her neck. John's mouth pulled Ann to him like gravity and stole her breath. When he released her, Ann caught the roguish gleam in his eyes. Before she could speak, John left the kitchen, calling back over a shoulder, "I'll be in my room if anyone needs me!"

Ann watched John leave, feeling thwarted and slightly manipulated. She sunk into a chair at the kitchen table.

"Let him go. He's happy." Mrs. Beaumont took a seat in the chair opposite Ann and passed a sandwich. "Which is more than I could say about the captain for most of the time I've worked here." The older woman regarded Ann with a smile. "You're good for him."

Ann gave Mrs. Beaumont a doubtful smirk and took a bite of sandwich. *If I'm so good for John, why is he keeping secrets from me?*

***

Ann pushed through a group of Colonists gathered at the end of the bar, a serving tray tucked under an arm. The laughter and music from the tavern followed as she stepped into the kitchen.

Mrs. Beaumont added a final plate to the serving tray on the kitchen table and side-stepped Ann to keep watch in the doorway. The cook had hopped like a bird on a perch from the doorway, to the stove, and back again all evening, certain the off tourists who had given Arnold trouble would return.

"They could be here any minute," Mrs. Beaumont said with a glance at the clock.

"How can you be sure?"

"They always come around nine."

Ann blew out a sigh and nodded. The constant hopping about made her glad she'd slipped her quarterstaff into a skirt pocket.

Ann lifted the tray onto a shoulder and took a step to the door. Mrs. Beaumont flung an arm across her path.

"Wait!"

The tray shifted. Plates clinked. Ann contorted her body to steady the load and exhaled a slow breath when the tray rebalanced. Ann's eyes flashed to Mrs. Beaumont.

"I almost dropped the tray!"

"Shhh!" The cook waved a hand impatiently and continued to peer around the edge of the doorway. "They're here!"

Ann looked past Mrs. Beaumont into the tavern. Her muscles tensed as five men strode through the front door. Snub-nosed pistols of brass and pewter rode their hips or hung buckled across the front of leather coats. The men arrived like a cold wind, chilling conversations and freezing the festive atmosphere of the tavern.

Ann put the serving tray on the kitchen table. When she returned to the doorway, the men had taken a seat at an empty booth across from the bar.

"Captain Shaw said they were freighter pirates," Mrs. Beaumont said, nodding toward the men in the booth. "I've heard the stories. The devil wouldn't take them as his own."

Ann's uneasiness grew as she watched the men. Even seated, the freighter pirates carried with them the confidence of a pack, glaring at anyone who met their eyes. The men laughed with each other as if amused by the fear they inspired. One of the pirates, a thickset man in a leather pea coat, slapped the table, making the customers closest to him jump.

"Barkeep! Bottle and five glasses!"

Mrs. Beaumont touched the back of Ann's hand. The thin line of the cook's mouth dropped into a worried slant. "Now that the captain is back, watch and get ready to duck."

Ann's heart jumped to her throat as she watched John behind the bar. Arnold leaned forward and whispered tight-clipped words into John's ear. The other men at the end of the bar sat hunched on stools as if the slightest movement would bring excruciating pain. John's eyes never left the pirates. Ann could see the tension in his back and shoulders, his face a mask of control.

John reached under the bar. Ann held her breath. Her pulse ticked faster as she slipped a hand into her skirt pocket and found the quarterstaff. When John straightened, he held a bottle and a stack of glasses. He walked to the booth where the pirates sat and set the bottle down hard.

The freighter pirate in the leather coat leaned back and watched John pour. He muttered something that made the others bellow with laughter. John stopped in mid pour and stared down at the pirate, his face as tight as a fist. The pirate looked up with a cunning smile, eyes never wavering. It seemed as if the tavern itself held its breath.

Then John picked up the bottle again and continued

serving.

A murmur rose up from the tavern as the other customers turned their backs and resumed their conversations in hushed tones. Ann's heart plummeted. Serving the men a bottle under protest was one thing, but pouring the drinks was as good as inviting them to stay.

Mrs. Beaumont sucked in her breath. "I guess that answers that."

The cook went back to the kitchen. Ann relaxed her grip on the quarterstaff in her pocket. Adrenaline gave way to despair as she looked around the tavern. A handful of customers stood, abandoning drinks, and quietly left. The looks on the Colonists' faces as they passed John made the breath catch in Ann's throat. Their eyes held the same contempt and loathing when they looked at John as when they looked at the pirates.

*They think John's one of them.*

Ann's pulse pounded in her head. The sickness she had felt at John's arrest flooded her insides.

John returned to the bar. His face twisted with the grief she so often saw hidden behind his eyes. His gaze locked on Ann, face frozen. The pain and anger she saw a moment ago disappeared behind his stone mask.

"Stay away from their table."

Ann stiffened and let his words bounce off her like a handful of pebbles. She opened her mouth to reply, but John turned away and headed back behind the bar.

*** 

Ann finished clearing tables and watched John stow glasses. The freighter pirates left well before last call along with the few remaining customers. With no one left to serve, the tavern closed early.

Ann carried a tray of empty glasses to the bar. John looked more like his old self since Dr. Brainard reset his nose.

"Your nose looks a lot better."

John grunted and continued stocking glasses.

"Does it hurt?"

"A little."

"I'm sorry."

"I told you it's not your fault."

John tossed an empty bottle into the collection bin under the bar. Ann set the tray down and pulled herself up onto one of the bar stools.

"All right. It's not my fault, but you never told me why security arrested you in the first place."

John straightened and eyed Ann sitting at the bar. He picked up his glass and took a sip before answering.

"I lost my passport." John stared down at the wine in the glass. "Damn hole in my coat pocket. Someone found it and turned it in. Security thought I looked like someone else."

"That's what I don't understand. Who did they think you were?"

"Does it matter?" John scowled and snatched the towel slung over a shoulder. He reached for another tumbler from the handcart. "I didn't ask and they were too busy throwing my ass into the back of the transport to tell me."

Ann watched John work. She supposed the missing passport could have caused all the trouble. Maybe security made a mistake?

"Why did A.K. Max pretend he didn't know you when I contacted him? He kept saying he didn't have any idea who you were until I said Genie."

"Genie is an old joke I used to kid him about. I haven't seen A.K. in a long time. I told you to say that, so he would remember who I was."

The question burned in Ann's mouth, but she wondered how far she should press John in his current mood.

"The men who were here tonight...."

John hung his head and blew out an impatient sigh.

"Are you in trouble?"

"No."

John put down the glass he had been drying and took Ann's hand. His blue eyes penetrated her own.

"If I didn't serve them, they would have torn this place apart."

Ann gripped his hand tighter. "But why did you pour their drinks? The other customers...I saw the looks on their faces. They think—"

"I know what they think," John said. Anger crisscrossed his features then faded. He looked down and ran a hand through his hair. "Freighter pirates are nomads. Raiders never stay in one place for very long. We just need to put up with them for a little while and they'll be on their way."

John picked up his glass and drained the wine in a single gulp. He grimaced against the burn and turned back to the handcart. Ann wanted to believe him. Some of what John said rang true, but she still sensed there was something he wasn't telling her. Without any proof, questions were useless.

"Captain Galeas, your tea is ready."

Mrs. Beaumont stood by the kitchen doorway with a wrap around her shoulders and a market basket on the crook of an arm.

"I'm leaving now unless there's something else I can do for you," Mrs. Beaumont said, her face pinched.

Ann blinked in surprise. She looked to John. His puzzled expression told Ann he was just as confused by the cook's formal tone.

"No, I guess not," John said. "If you need to leave—"

"Very well, sir. I will see you in the morning. Goodnight."

Mrs. Beaumont turned and disappeared through the doorway. Ann heard the kitchen door slam shut.

John's face clouded over. He shoved the handcart out of his way and started toward the winery door.

"The rest can keep till morning. I have work to do in the winery."

***

The next few days brought more of the same. Mrs. Beaumont performed kitchen duties with cold efficiency and without any of the usual scolding. The change disheartened Ann. Mrs. Beaumont didn't even slam the pots and pans in protest. Ann tried to ask the cook what was bothering her, but each time, the woman dismissed Ann with 'everything's fine' and hurried to stir a stew pot or sent Ann out on errands.

John's grim mood hung over the tavern like a thunderhead. He spent all of his spare time in the winery, sometimes working well past midnight. Ann found herself alone most nights after closing with no one to keep her company, and nothing much to occupy her time except for the puzzle ball or practicing with the quarterstaff.

***

*Don't think. Just concentrate.*

Ann sat at the kitchen table, face scrunched in concentration as she tried to block out the rhythmic clacking of the winery's bottling machine. Her hands cradled the puzzle ball. The image of the circle of locks deep inside the metal orb seared her mind. With every level Ann completed, the surface of the ball changed color: black, red, green, purple, blue, orange, yellow. Ann had focused on the yellow level for twenty minutes without any luck.

DING!

The kitchen timer sounded, and the image of the locks flickered and vanished. Ann opened her eyes and scowled at the puzzle ball.

She pulled the baking trays from the wall ovens and set the pies on racks to cool. Ann walked back to the table, picked up the orb, and took a deep breath to shake off her frustration. She knew from experience the ball was less receptive if she let emotions get the best of her.

Ann closed her eyes and stretched out her senses. She heard the keravnos implant chirp in her ear, and the image filled her mind again. Ann let the image grow until she could feel the weight of the locks. The yellow lock was different from the others—heavier and yet buoyant. Every time Ann reached toward the lock's power source, it floated away.

Ann blew out a slow breath and drew her senses around the image, circling it like a cat. The lock quivered. Ann froze. Her eyes flew open. The puzzle ball had not changed color. Then what was that? Ann closed her eyes again and searched with her mind. Hidden underneath, a crack no wider than a hair came into view. Triumphant, Ann pushed her senses toward the breech, the ball trembled in her hands, and she opened her eyes.

The metal orb changed from a solid yellow to glittering jewels of red, green, gold, and purple. Ann felt a new power source humming inside the ball. She focused on its pulse, and the lock yielded without hesitation. Ann heard a click and the ball split across its equator. Her face brightened as the notes of a familiar tune flowed from the gap. She lifted what she assumed to be the top half of the ball and found a yellowed piece of folded paper laying on top of a divided jewelry compartment.

> *Congratulations, cadet! Or should I say, Lieutenant?*
> *Never doubt that only a true time jumper*
> *could have opened this puzzle ball.*
> *-Sean*

A smile spread across Ann's face as tears pricked the corners of her eyes.

The bell above the tavern door jingled. Ann's hand darted to the quarterstaff in her skirt pocket. She peeked through the kitchen doorway and was relieved to see the town baker standing in the tavern.

"Mr. Tonnag, what can I do for you?"

The baker met Ann as she passed the end of the bar. He shook hands with his usual businessman's air.

"Hello, Miss Ann. I stopped by to see Mrs. Beaumont." Tonnag's eyes flicked in the direction of the winery. The noise of the bottling machine grew louder in the empty tavern. "Is she here?"

Ann knew John had never been on friendly terms with Tonnag, preferring to let Mrs. Beaumont handle bakery business. With Mrs. Beaumont out on errands, it would be up to Ann to help keep the peace.

"She's not here right now, but I could give her a message."

Mr. Tonnag pulled an envelope from an inside pocket of

his baker's coat and handed it to Ann.

"Would you give her this message?"

Ann eyed the envelope with a sense of unease. This was not the usual bakery invoice. She looked up at Mr. Tonnag and mirrored the false politeness she saw on his face.

"I'll make sure she gets it."

Ann walked the baker to the tavern's front door.

"Thank you very much! Oh, I would appreciate it if you didn't mention to the captain that I was here." Tonnag winked as he inclined his head toward the winery.

Ann nodded and gave the baker a knowing smile in return. Tonnag left and she turned to walk back to the kitchen.

Ann was halfway across the tavern when an energy burst poured over her. The notes of a thousand strings rained down for several seconds, raising the hair on the back of her neck, then stopped. Ann shivered. She looked up at the ceiling and rubbed the goose bumps from her arms. She remembered the first time she encountered the energy burst. It had been right before the man attacked her in the tavern. With all the excitement and traveling to Andarria so soon after, Ann had forgotten all about sensing the strange energy. The burst had come from the master bedroom. Ann glanced to the winery door as she walked to the kitchen. She laid the envelope from Mr. Tonnag on the windowsill above the sink and headed for the stairs.

***

Ann balanced the laundry basket on her hip—a ready excuse—as she stood outside the door to the master bedroom. She listened for the approach of footsteps on the stairs. Hearing none, she slowly opened the bedroom door.

Ann looked around as she padded to the center of the room, searching for the exact spot where she sensed the energy in the tavern below. She scooped up a loose shirt and tossed it into the laundry basket. More *camouflage*. When Ann reached the middle of the room, she put the basket down and stood with her feet shoulder-width apart. Ann closed her eyes and concentrated, arms loose at her sides. The keravnos implant chirped in an ear as the bedroom's energy pulses sharpened into focus.

The ion pistol John always kept in the nightstand tweeted breathy notes, while the comm station on the desk plucked out deep bass rhythms. There was nothing in the room that matched the energy she sensed in the tavern. Ann grumbled in frustration. The electrical symphony dimmed. Ann took a deep breath to refocus, and the energy pulses sharpened again. With nowhere else left to search, Ann pushed her senses toward the bedroom ceiling.

Ann froze and opened her eyes. Senses flew back toward her at a rate that made her head spin. In the attic directly above, she had sensed an energy pulse, a grave timpani as slow and as steady as a heartbeat. Ann shuddered. She blew out a breath and scolded herself. There was nothing alive in the attic. The energy pulse was mechanical, of that she was sure. Ann looked back up at the ceiling. The pulse was not the energy burst she originally sensed in the tavern. This power source was almost beyond her range of detection, even standing in the bedroom. Ann picked up the laundry basket and headed for the bedroom door.

Ann had never been in the attic before, but she remembered John telling her once about the trap door in the guest room closet. She hurried down the hallway to the guest room, closing the bedroom door behind her. She ditched the laundry basket on the bed and flung open the closet door. In the dim light, Ann could just make out a trap door in the ceiling. She pushed all of the hanging clothes to one side and spotted narrow wooden slats bolted to the back wall. The makeshift ladder almost blended into the dark wood paneling.

Climbing around in the attic would be difficult while wearing her long colony skirt. Ann thought for a moment, then crossed the bedroom to her dresser. The bottom drawer overflowed with clothes Sean had brought her from Andarria. Ann had never worn them, thinking she would look out of place on the Colonies, but the clothing might be useful now. She dug through the piles until she found a pair of loose-fitting black exercise pants and matching shirt. She quickly stripped off her colony blouse and skirt and pulled on the lightweight training clothes. The loose pants hung to Ann's knees. The short-sleeve shirt clung to her upper body but didn't restrict movement. Ann grabbed a pair of running shoes from the drawer and slipped them on.

She pushed open the trap door in the ceiling with one hand. The wooden panel fell open with a bang. Ann listened for sounds from the hallway outside the bedroom, then pulled herself up through the opening.

Light from the attic windows on either end of the house cut through the darkness and pushed the deepest shadows to the far corners and to the eaves above. Ann stood and wiped her palms on a pant leg, leaving a smear of dust. She looked around. Unlike the basement with its crates and boxes, the attic above Ann's bedroom stood practically empty. Ann's nose twitched. Thick layers of dust covered the attic from floor to rafters.

Ann ducked under a beam and moved toward the opposite end of the house. Light from the attic window silhouetted a woman's shape. *Damn it!* Her heart rate rocketed out of control. Ann stared at the figure, the quarterstaff clenched tightly in her hands. She blew out a sigh. A dress mannequin stood motionless in front of the window and showed no sign of attacking her.

Ann cringed and muttered to herself. "When did you become such a coward?" She made a mental note to never mention the incident to Sean.

Ann picked her way across the attic, ducking beams and treading lightly on the floorboards until she stood over the master bedroom.

The attic at this end of the house contained a few scattered trunks. The dress mannequin guarded a pile of boxes stacked waist-high in the middle of the floor. Ann cleared her mind and pushed her senses outward, searching for the energy source. She locked onto the faint pulse coming from somewhere deep within the pile of boxes. Ann gritted her teeth. *You thought this was going to be easy?* She got to work shifting boxes, searching for the power source as she went.

Ann sweated through her shirt within a few minutes in the stagnant attic air. She reached for another box when an old picture frame tucked inside caught her eye. The images behind the glass twisted at her heart. John looked at Ann from the picture, eyes bright with laughter as his arms wound round the young woman standing next to him. Strands of the woman's dark hair blew across her smiling face as she gazed up at John.

Ann looked around as if seeing her surroundings for the first time: the dress mannequin, the boxes, the trunks. *These were Bonnie's things.* Her face burned with shame. What would John think if he knew what she was doing right now? Ann cast a nervous glance behind her. The keravnos implant gave a low whistle. Ann gritted her teeth. She couldn't give up now. If the power source was worth coming all the way up here to investigate, then it was worth seeing it through. Ann glanced down at the picture frame. *Forgive me.* She returned the picture to the box and resumed searching.

The pulse grew stronger. Ann stepped forward to move another box and felt the energy pulse tickle the bottom of her foot. The source of the energy was not in one of Bonnie's boxes, but rather hidden under the floorboards. Ann dropped to her knees. Her own pulse quickened with excitement She hooked a finger into a notch in the wood and lifted the plank.

A metal cylinder two feet in length nested in the compartment under the floor. The lights on its control panel winked in time with the energy pulse. Ann frowned. A lithium generator? Ann blinked hard to clear the memory and leaned in for a closer look. Lithium generators were designed to be covert power sources. Difficult to detect, even for time jumpers.

Ann touched the generator's control panel, awakening it from standby mode. She scrolled through the panel's screens until she found the manual settings and activated the generator.

A few feet away, the shimmering notes of a stringed orchestra poured from an old steamer trunk underneath the attic window. Ann's hands shook as she lifted the trunk's lid. Her heart landed like a lead weight in the pit of her stomach. An armillary sphere sat on its base in the bottom of the trunk, a miniature replica of the monument on space station Navis. Below the sphere's brass rings, a display panel showed navigation screens for entering space-time coordinates.

Ann's head reeled as the full implication of the discovery crashed down. Only military personnel were allowed to have time travel devices. Civilians who used space-time navigation beacons were usually up to no good – smuggling or worse. A beacon could be used to travel long distances without being tracked.

Ann rubbed a temple. Didn't John know the penalty for just having a device like this in his possession? A sick feeling filled her stomach. *He knew.* The beacon must have been what John meant when she overheard him talking with Arnold that day in the winery. The arrest at the shuttleport. Freighter pirates in the tavern. A picture of John's past sharpened into focus.

Ann looked around. A second trap door lay partially hidden in the shadows. She lifted the door a few inches and saw it led to John's closet in the master bedroom. The bedroom gave easy access to the beacon, but judging by the layers of dust and cobwebs around the trap door, no one had disturbed the attic in many years.

Ann looked at the armillary sphere. John called it ancient history. Her stomach clenched as she remembered the freighter pirates. If only she could be as certain.

# TWENTY-EIGHT

## *HISTORY LESSONS*

"Ann? *Ann, where are you?*"

When she heard Mrs. Beaumont's voice, Ann skipped the last couple ladder rungs and jumped to the closet floor.

"I'm in my bedroom! I'll be down in a minute!"

She pulled the lightweight shirt over her head as she crossed the bedroom. The trip to the attic had taken longer than planned. Her heart pounded as she considered her options. The discovery of the space-time beacon made talking to Sean out of the question. If her brother knew John had an illegal time travel device, he would be bound by the duty of the Montressador's office to report it. Ann needed to talk to John. She cringed as she stepped into her skirt and secured it around her waist. She would have to admit to overhearing John's conversation with Arnold in the winery and snooping in the attic, but if there was any possibility of another explanation for the beacon, she would have to take the chance. Ann finished buttoning her blouse and did a quick check in the dresser mirror before heading downstairs.

"There you are!"

Mrs. Beaumont jumped up from the settee as Ann raced down the steps and turned the newel post. The cook tossed John's coat she'd been sewing and the hand stitcher back onto the cushions. The sewing box sat open on the table.

"I need you in the kitchen." The woman looked at Ann then narrowed her eyes. "What have you been doing? You look like you've been pushing chickens in the creek."

Ann tried not to wither under Mrs. Beaumont's accusing stare. Given the cook's mood the last few days, there was no telling how she would react if she knew about the beacon in the attic.

"I was just putting some things away." Ann shrugged and gave what she hoped was a convincing smile. Before Mrs. Beaumont could question her further, Ann quickly added, "Mr. Tonnag stopped by earlier and left an envelope for you. I put it on the kitchen windowsill."

"I found it. Thank you," Mrs. Beaumont turned and headed for the kitchen. "I need you to prep vegetables."

"I just need to run to the winery for a moment. I'll be right back."

"Fine. But make it quick."

Ann followed Mrs. Beaumont into the kitchen. The cook glanced toward the winery as she stepped to the counter.

"Thank heavens that's over with," Mrs. Beaumont said, grabbing a spoon. "The noise from that bottler was getting under my skin."

Ann stopped on her way to the winery and turned to look at Mrs. Beaumont, perplexed. The only sound in the kitchen was the hum of the rotisseries coming from the wall ovens. The clacking from the winery's bottling machine had stopped.

Ann frowned. "It's only been a couple hours. He can't be—"

The winery door slammed shut, followed by the sound of John's heavy footsteps in the hallway. He strode into the kitchen carrying a bottle of wine, his face hard.

"I need a glass. *Now!*"

John snatched the tumbler from Ann's outstretched hand and stepped to the kitchen sink. He poured the wine into the glass. The late afternoon sun through the window illuminated the liquid. Ann's insides twisted. The wine's rich ruby color was lost in a swirl of clouds.

John closed his eyes. Ann could see the muscles in his jaw clench as he lowered the glass. He hung his head and leaned against the counter, gripping the edge of the sink with both hands.

"Is it the entire batch?" Ann thought her voice sounded small and flat in the quiet kitchen.

John poured the rest of the bottle down the drain, his face awash with despair.

"The whole tank." He rubbed his eyes and mumbled about faulty lines and contamination.

Ann's heart pinched to see his anguish. "I'm so sorry."

"It doesn't matter..."

Ann's eyes grew round with surprise. "What?"

John looked out the kitchen window, his expression hardened. "It doesn't matter," he said, his voice stronger.

"What do you mean it doesn't matter?" Mrs. Beaumont's voice cut the air. She stood by the kitchen table, hands clenched at her sides. The cook's gray eyes burned black as she glared at the captain. The intensity of her anger threatened to crack the foundations of the house.

"Of course, it matters," Mrs. Beaumont said. "What are you going to do about it?"

"I'm going to do my job," John said, his tone even. He avoided the cook's gaze as he turned to walk back toward the tavern. "I suggest you stick to doing yours."

"I have been doing my job! It's *you who*..." Mrs. Beaumont bit back the next words and lifted her chin in defiance. "Captain Galeas, *I quit!*"

John stopped at the kitchen door. Ann's heart froze as she stared at the cook. The words struck her as hard as a frying pan.

"Mr. Tonnag made me an offer and I accepted. I can give you the customary two weeks while you look for a replacement, but no more."

"Mrs. Beaumont, please," Ann said. "Let's talk this out. John, you can't let her go!"

John leaned against the door frame with one hand, shoulders sagging. When he looked up, Ann saw his pain and grief again before anger exploded across his face.

"Anyone who would work for that arrogant son of a bitch!" John gritted teeth and pulled the anger back, narrowing his eyes. "I don't need two weeks! You're done!" John turned and stormed out of the kitchen.

Ann stood with her feet locked in place, unable to move. *What just happened?* Her insides tightened until she thought her stomach felt pressed flat against her backbone.

Mrs. Beaumont's face looked white with shock. Her mouth began to tremble, the lines of her face sagged, and her eyes cast downward. It was like watching a mountain crumble into the sea.

"John didn't mean it," Ann said. "He was just mad about Mr. Tonnag. Can't you see he doesn't want you to leave?"

The cook blinked moisture from her eyes and looked away. "The stew meat needs another hour in the pressure cooker." She moved past Ann to the stove. "Don't put the vegetables in until the last fifteen minutes, else you'll cook them into oblivion." Mrs. Beaumont lifted a lid from one of the pots and frowned at the bubbling sauce inside.

"Mrs. Beaumont, I'll talk to John. You don't have to go."

"If you don't stir the gravy, you get lousy gravy," Mrs. Beaumont said, reaching for a whisk. "You have to remember to stir it every five minutes." She attacked the gravy with a few flicks of a wrist.

Ann trailed after the cook, helpless. Panic grew inside her like a shrill whistle.

"You won't have time to do the carving." Mrs. Beaumont peered through the oven doors at the rotisseries inside. "Make *him* carve the chicken before he opens. You can keep the meat in the warming trays." She straightened and surveyed the kitchen, mouth set like a steel rod.

The whistle inside Ann reached its peak and burst from her mouth.

"You can't leave!"

"I will leave when my job is done." The cook untied her apron and tossed it over the back of a kitchen chair. "And I'll be damned if that man runs me off before I finish what I started." She stepped into the sitting room with Ann at her heels.

Mrs. Beaumont scooped up the discarded sewing and took a seat on the settee. Her face gathered in concentration as she sewed the pocket of the captain's coat. She wielded the stitcher as if cutting the heads off snakes.

"Let me do that." Ann reached for the stitcher.

Mrs. Beaumont's hands fell to her lap as Ann laid the sewing aside. The woman stared down at her idle hands. Tears spilled onto her cheeks as she started to tremble.

"Stupid, stupid man! He's gone and let it all go!"

Ann sat and rested a hand on Mrs. Beaumont's shoulder. "I'll talk to John. We can get this straightened out."

"No. I'm all right," she said, brushing her eyes. "I knew what the captain was when I started working for him." Mrs. Beaumont's eyes flickered downward. She swallowed hard and pressed her lips together.

Ann's eyes widened as she looked at Mrs. Beaumont. What is he? She took the older woman's hand.

"I know it's not the job offer from Mr. Tonnag," Ann said. "Why are you really leaving Siren's Cove? What has John done?"

Mrs. Beaumont pursed her lips. Shades of guilt and uncertainty passed over her features, knotting her brow. Her eyes flickered to Ann's then turned away shamefaced and stared into her lap. She took a deep breath.

"He used to be just like those freighter pirates," Mrs. Beaumont said. "He'd be gone for weeks at a time. Bonnie Galeas had to run the tavern by herself. She never said where the Captain went or what he did, but we all knew. We saw how worried Bonnie was when he was gone. You can't hide something like that. Not in Llewellyn." Mrs. Beaumont looked across the sitting room to the captain's leather chair. "Then he just . . . stopped. He changed . . . I think for her. They worked the tavern together. They made Siren's Cove shine and they were happy.

"When Bonnie died, it broke him. Some days, the captain wouldn't even come out of his room. Something had to be done, else he would have lost the tavern and everything he and Bonnie had worked for. Nobody wanted to see that. It was Dr. Brainard who hired me. Told me to keep the house clean and do a light dinner service, nothing fancy, just enough to keep a little money coming in. The doctor paid me out of his own pocket until the captain was well enough to run payroll. I think it was the guilt."

Ann frowned. "What do you mean?"

Mrs. Beaumont looked at Ann. "Bonnie was Dr. Brainard's patient." The older woman shook her head sadly. "It was a simple infection...a child's ailment...but she was allergic to the medicine the doctor prescribed and it destroyed her. She couldn't fight any more. There was nothing anyone could do. Bonnie died a few days later."

"But it wasn't Dr. Brainard's fault."

"No, it wasn't, and the captain never blamed the doctor for it. But you know how men are. They think they balance the world on their backs, so they take the blame for things they have no business taking the blame for."

Ann nodded. She remembered how Dr. Brainard had blamed himself for not diagnosing her anachronosis.

"Those first few weeks the captain never spoke to me," Mrs. Beaumont said. "I'm not even sure he knew I was here most of the time. It took a couple months, but he gradually came out of it. He started working the bar and taking an interest in the tavern again. The captain had his moments, but we made a good team." The cook smiled at the memory as her eyes filled with fresh tears. "Early on we all thought he might leave the Colonies...go back to his old life. With Bonnie gone, what did he have to hold him here?"

"But he stayed," Ann said, remembering the dust and cobwebs in the attic around the beacon.

Mrs. Beaumont nodded. "The tavern seemed to be enough

for him...but I knew he wasn't happy...not like he was before. I think the captain did it out of habit when before he did it out of love."

Ann frowned, thoughtful. "Why didn't you tell me any of this before?"

Mrs. Beaumont turned away. "I saw the way he looked at you those first few weeks. I wanted him to be happy, and you were so good for him. You were good for each other. I thought if you knew about the captain's past, you would leave."

"And the rest of the town?" Ann felt a rising resentment at being kept in the dark for so long. "All the time I've been here and I've never heard anything about any of this."

"I don't know about everyone, but the ones I spoke to saw what I saw," Mrs. Beaumont said. "And we made sure you never heard a word of the captain's past."

"But I still don't understand," Ann said. "Why leave now? What has John done to make you so angry?"

"I thought...we all thought...." Mrs. Beaumont covered her mouth, eyes glassy with tears. "I've put you in a terrible position. I'm so sorry. It's been so long, we never thought he would do it."

Fear gripped Ann. "Do what?"

"The freighter pirates! You saw how the captain was with them."

"But that doesn't mean—"

"Skulking around The Monkey's Fist down by the docks and getting into fights?" Mrs. Beaumont nodded at Ann's astonishment. "While you and your brother were gone. The man who attacked you in the tavern...you said he came to talk to the captain. Why?"

Ann's pulse pounded in her head. *Was it all connected?*

"There's more," she said, voice trembling. "I looked at the books. I wanted to make sure the captain paid Mike for the beer. He had, but I also saw large sums of money transferred out with no explanation. And now he's as good as given up on the winery." The older woman's eyes opened wide, expression near panic. "He's going to leave with them."

A chill swept over Ann. She swallowed hard, remembering what John said about the freighter pirates never staying in one place very long. Ann pushed her fear aside. John didn't act like a man getting ready to make a run for it, but the money transfers confused her.

Mrs. Beaumont leveled her eyes. "Are you going with him?"

"No!" Ann looked at the cook, stunned. "I'm not going anywhere until I get some answers."

Mrs. Beaumont sighed with relief then turned thoughtful. She reached for the stitcher and coat on the table and pulled them back to her lap. She sewed in silence for a few seconds before speaking again.

"I think deep down, Captain Galeas is a good man." Mrs. Beaumont tied off the last stitch. She smoothed a hand over the finished work, her brow furrowed. "But maybe not good enough." The older woman turned and looked at Ann, eyes brimming with affection and concern. "I'm sorry for all this." She gave Ann a quick hug. "Be careful." She stood and headed to the kitchen.

Ann heard the kitchen door open and shut. She sat with her hands gripping the cushions and tried to get a hold on her thoughts. How many times had John lied to her? Ann believed John when he said he was biding his time, waiting for the pirates to leave, but now...

Her eyes strayed to John's coat tossed on the cushion next to her. Ann pulled the coat toward her and ran a hand over Mrs. Beaumont's stitching, measuring the length of the tear. The hole in the coat pocket had been large enough for his passport to slip through, just as John had said. Ann sighed. At least he hadn't lied to her about that. Her hand lingered on the neat stitches. Since she sewed the inside of a pocket, Mrs. Beaumont hadn't bothered to change the bobbin from the last time Ann used the stitcher. The maroon thread looked strange against the gray fabric of the pocket. Ann recognized the color. The thread matched the vest John always wore when he tended bar.

Ann pulled in a breath as the room reeled. She upended the sewing box. Buttons poured onto the table. Ann cupped her hands around the rolling pile to keep the buttons from spilling onto the floor. Her fingers scrabbled, pulse racing, until finally she held her prize. Ann sprinted up the stairs to the guest bedroom.

Ann burst into the bedroom and crossed to the closet. She stripped the jacket from its hanger and flung it across the bed. The button felt slick between her fingers. Ann sucked air through her teeth. *Gold buttons on a field of blue.* The buttons on her uniform jacket glittered—on each, the picture of a sturdy tree with spreading branches. Ann sunk onto the bed and stared at the button in her hand. The button from the sewing box was older and in want of polish but otherwise it was a perfect match.

Bonnie Galeas hadn't saved random buttons, only the most important. The one Ann held was the one button that could have been sewed onto an Andarrian special forces jacket. She clenched the button in her hand. *Damn him!* Ann hopped up from the bed and headed for the bedroom door.

\*\*\*

Ann's shoes clattered down the wooden steps into the winery. The bottling machine idled and vented a hiss of steam as she passed.

"John? Are you in here?"

The sliding wooden doors at the opposite end of the winery slammed shut. The captain came into view from behind the wine tanks, head bent low over the piece of paper in his hands.

"John, I need to talk to you."

His mouth twitched as his eyes darted across the paper.

*"John!"*

John looked up. His face paled as he focused on Ann. He stuffed the paper into a trouser pocket.

"Get your cloak."

"What?" Ann stared in disbelief.

John walked past to the control panel and flipped a few

switches. "You're flying to Andarria tonight."

The bottling machine released another jet of steam as gears ground to a stop.

"Why?"

John jerked his head to look at Ann. His face contorted. "They've changed the time. They're coming tonight. Not tomorrow—*tonight*!"

Fear tripped down Ann's spine as John paced in front of the control panel. His arms and legs moved in spasms as he tugged at his pigtail. Ann had never seen him so shaken.

"I don't have the money," John said, as if to himself. "I can't even give them the *damn wine*!"

John grabbed a wine bottle from the top of a nearby crate and threw it against the far wall. The glass shattered, staining the wall a deep burgundy. John buried his face in his hands.

"Who's coming?" But Ann already knew.

John's arms fell to his sides, limp.

"Who do you need to give money to?"

John avoided her gaze as he stalked past to the tavern door. Ann followed him through the kitchen to the comm station. He leaned over the keyboard. His face looked as hard as marble in the flat light of the screen.

"Are you working with the freighter pirates?" Ann detonated the words, hoping to provoke some kind of a reaction. John didn't look up as his fingers tapped the keys.

"The overnight shuttle to Andarria leaves in less than hour."

"I'm staying. You're in trouble."

John continued to work the keys.

"*Look at me!*"

Ann grabbed the keyboard, ripping it from the comm station and knocking over a stack of cookbooks on the counter. John jumped back in surprise. Ann threw the keyboard aside and advanced, pointing a finger at John's chest.

"I *know* you used to be a freighter pirate! I found the beacon in the attic! I found this!"

Ann thrust the button forward. John's eyes grew round, his

mouth hitched sideways. He stared at the button pinched between her fingers. Ann wavered. *He's afraid?*

John's eyes flicked from the button to Ann's face. "Where did you—?"

"In Bonnie's sewing box." Ann's confidence grew. She finally had his attention. "Bonnie was a time jumper. Is she why you gave up being a freighter pirate?" Ann felt sick to her stomach as she came to a realization. "Or, were you just using her beacon the whole time?"

John's face hardened into a sneer. Before Ann could react, he snatched the button and marched toward the sitting room. He tossed the button into the trash.

"I don't have time for this! You're leaving *now!*"

Ann followed close behind. "I'm not leaving until you *answer me!*"

John pulled Ann's traveling cloak from the closet at the foot of the stairs and tossed it to her. Ann crossed her arms and let the cloak fall to the floor.

"I'm getting the truck." His voice sounded as cold as sea ice. "When I come back, you're going to walk out of here, or I will drag you out by your ankles." John left, slamming the door so hard it rattled the pictures on the walls.

Ann tried to slow her pulse to a manageable rate. John would remove her by force – she could see it in his eyes. She tried to think of a plan. Could she overpower John? And even if she could, then what? The freighter pirates were still coming. Could she take John with her and get away from Siren's Cove in time? *Doubtful.* Ann had to keep him talking and hope she could make him see sense.

The sound of a truck's engine rumbled up the drive. Ann reached into a skirt pocket for the quarterstaff. *Gone.* Panic rushed in. She had left the quarterstaff in her pants pocket after the trip to the attic. Ann gave a glance to the stairs as she heard John at the door. Ann steadied herself, planting her feet shoulder-width apart.

John stepped into the sitting room. He stared at Ann, eyes dark. The muscles in his jaw clenched.

"Let's go."

"John. Please."

John dropped his head and raked a hand through his hair.

"Mrs. Beaumont was right." Ann tried to swallow the desperation in her voice. "You're throwing everything away. Are you leaving with the freighter pirates tonight? Is that why you want me to go?"

John took a step forward, towering over Ann, hands clenched.

Ann raised her fists, muscles taunt, as adrenaline pulsed through her like an electric current. She didn't want to strike him.

"I'm not leaving." Ann shifted her weight and prepared to block. "You can go with them if that's what you want. I won't stop you. If you don't have the courage to tell me goodbye, I'll wave to you from the stoop."

John stared at Ann. The intensity of his face shattered. He dropped to his knees and grabbed her waist. Ann tried to push back, but John's grip was too strong. He leaned against her and clasped his hands behind her back.

"I can't protect you anymore." John's voice broke as his shoulders began to shake. "Please! You have to go now!"

Ann looked down, stunned, and suddenly everything clicked. She rested her hands on his shoulders. "They're blackmailing you."

"Chohon-Lo has your name in his book. I couldn't let him—"

Ann sunk to her knees and pressed her lips to John's. She released him and brushed the hair from his eyes. "What about the beacon in the attic? We could both get away."

John sighed. "It doesn't work."

"What do you mean? I turned it on."

"I broke it after Bonnie died. I couldn't risk anyone else using it, so I pulled the beacon's rocker. It's at the bottom of the harbor. The beacon's lights will come on, but it can't take you anywhere."

"Then let me stay and help you."

John shook his head. "They will use you against me."

"What are you going to do?"

"I have a plan, but I need to know you're safe."

Ann opened her mouth to argue.

"No!" John's eyes flashed. "Can't you see you will make this harder for me if you stay?"

Ann looked at John. Determination creased the corners of his eyes, but Ann could also see fear. Her heart wrenched. How could she leave, knowing he was in danger?

"All right," she said. John breathed a sigh of relief. "Just let me get my bag."

The kitchen clock chimed the hour.

John sucked in a breath and stood, pulling Ann to her feet. "Hurry!"

When Ann headed back downstairs carrying the carpet bag, John stood at the door holding her traveling cloak. The old truck rumbled to life again as John turned the key. Tires spun on slick cobblestones as they headed out the drive.

# TWENTY-NINE

## *CUT AND RUN*

The sun burned like a drop of molten glass as it sunk behind the distant hills. Shadows of trees and farm cottages stretched across the fields as John's truck bounced and rattled down the country road. The truck's combustion engine rumbled loudly in Ann's ears. Surely, anyone within fifty miles of Llewellyn could hear them. Ann glanced in the truck's side mirror. The dirt road wound out behind them without another ground or air vehicle in sight. Ann pulled her cloak tighter to ward off the ocean breeze blowing through the truck's cab. John kept his eyes on the road and hands on the wheel except to force the truck's headstrong stick shift into a higher gear.

The truck roared up to the shuttleport entrance and skidded to a stop. Ann grabbed the carpet bag and ran with John into the terminal. The line of passengers waiting to board had shrunk to less than a handful by the time the two reached the gate.

"I'll send you a message as soon as it's safe," John said, breathing hard. "They can't get to you once you're on the shuttle."

"I'm not worried about me," Ann said, leveling her eyes.

"I'll be fine," John said, pulling her close. "I promise you'll have a message waiting for you when you get to Andarria."

Ann held John tighter. *But a message from whom?* Would word come from John, or from someone else saying he was dead.

"You need to go. The attendant is about to close the gate."

John's blue eyes, no longer brooding, looked into hers, wide and anxious. His mouth set in a worried line. He kissed her, hungrily for an instant, then pushed her back.

"Go!"

Ann picked up her carpet bag and hurried through the gate out onto the tarmac. When she reached the top of the gangway and looked back toward the gate, John was gone.

Ann took a step to walk back down the ramp, but a shuttle attendant blocked her path.

"Please head directly to your cabin," the attendant said, swinging the gangway door closed. "We'll be taking off shortly."

Ann's pulse ticked faster. There had to be another way off the shuttle. She pushed her way down the central aisle, past passengers and stairwells. The lights dimmed and the lilting voice of a shuttle attendant floated from the overhead speakers.

*"Attention, passengers. Please make yourselves comfortable in your cabins. Attendants, prepare for departure."*

Ann reached the metal bulkhead at the back of the shuttle. Three doors clustered in an alcove, two marked lavatory and the third, Galley Lift: Attendants Only. Ann stepped toward the lift, but the door refused to open. A buzzer sounded and a computerized voice spoke from the security sensor.

*"Access denied. Authorization required."*

Ann grimaced. She didn't have time for this. She threw a glance behind. The attendants were busy helping the other passengers. Ann pressed a hand against the security sensor and closed her eyes. The keravnos implant chirped in her ear. Ann felt the power source pulsing within the door's security system. She caught the energy pulse and pushed back hard. In her mind, Ann saw a blinding flash. When she opened her eyes, a wisp of ozone drifted up from the sensor panel and the door slid open.

Ann stepped into the lift. Her stomach fluttered as the elevator dropped into the belly of the shuttle. For one terrifying instant, Ann feared she had short-circuited the entire operating system, but then the descent slowed and stopped. The opposite wall slid open and Ann stepped from the lift into the shuttle's galley.

The galley spread out before Ann like a ballroom. Mini-bots swarmed the air carrying parcels. Larger bots wheeled containers of heavier cargo and walked on legs like metal men, their skeletal, blueish-green bodies gleamed in the white lights of the galley. Fresh air poured into the scullery from a large open hatch at the opposite end. A lift loader had just finished delivering a pallet of supplies and slowly backed away from the opening.

The rear hatch started to close. Ann tightened the grip on her carpet bag, lifted her skirt with the other hand, and charged through the galley, ducking and dodging bots as she ran.

Mini-bots squawked and scattered at the intruder's approach. A tall two-legged bot stepped in Ann's path and reached with grasping, metal fingers. Ann swung the carpet bag, hitting the metal man hard in its square head and knocking it off balance. She reached the edge of the open hatch and leapt across the widening gap toward the lift loader's platform, now several feet from the back of the shuttle.

Ann felt the rush of cool air as she fell. Her skirt ballooned to the waist. The black tarmac beckoned from three stories below. Ann landed hard on the edge of the platform, pitched forward, and rolled with the carpet bag clutched to her chest.

Ann lay face down in a tangle of skirt. Her exit from the shuttle hadn't gone exactly to plan, but the end result was what mattered. She propped herself up on one elbow, gasping for breath, and turned to look at the broad back end of the galactic shuttle. It was then Ann allowed herself a little tremble of fear. The enormous black maw of the afterburner hung high overhead. Had Ann seen the leap from her current position, she might have lacked the courage to jump.

The shuttle's galley hatch sealed shut. Maneuvering thrusters jetted and whined as the craft began to taxi toward the runway. The lift loader continued backward for several yards before lowering its platform to the ground.

Ann hopped off the platform and ran across the tarmac toward a group of outbuildings next to the shuttle terminal. She reached the edge of the tarmac out of breath and perspiring under the cloak. The crescendo of the shuttle's engines rattled the air as the craft raced down the runway. She turned and watched the shuttle lift into the sky and wink against the rays of the setting sun.

When Ann reached the front of the terminal, John's truck was nowhere in sight. She breathed a sigh of relief. *All right, Lieutenant. What now?* Ann looked around. With the major incoming and departing flights done for the day, the public transports wouldn't make their runs again until morning. Ann was about to start the long walk back to town when she saw a familiar green and white delivery van parked in front of the shipping warehouse. A figure wearing tan coveralls and a knit cap wheeled a half-barrel from the back of the van and dropped it next to a growing pile of beer kegs.

"Mike!"

The beer man looked up and smiled as Ann trotted toward him. He glanced down at the carpet bag in her hand.

Mike's ubiquitous grin widened. "Where are you just getting back from?"

Ann hesitated. How much could she trust Mike now that she knew the townsfolk had hidden John's past?

"I was visiting my brother," Ann said. "I came back a day early to surprise the captain. Would you give me a ride?"

"Sure! I'm almost finished. Hop in!"

\*\*\*

The delivery van's tires crunched gravel as Mike drove up the circular drive to the front of Dr. Brainard's brick and white-trimmed cottage.

"Are you sure you don't want a ride into town?" The beer man put the vehicle in park, draping one arm across the top of the steering wheel to look at Ann in the passenger seat. "I'm heading past Siren's Cove."

"No, this is fine," Ann said. "Besides, I'd rather wait and

surprise the captain after the dinner service. I'm sure the doctor will be happy to drive me."

Mike grinned. "Suit yourself! Good luck surprising the captain. Between you and me, he could use a change of pace."

Ann forced a laugh and climbed down from the van. "I'll do my best!"

Ann thanked the beer man and waved goodbye as the delivery van turned back onto the main road. With the vehicle out of sight, she turned and dashed to the front stoop. Dr. Brainard opened the door after several seconds of Ann leaning on the bell.

"Ann? What are you doing here?"

"John's in trouble!"

His face crumpled into a worried frown. "Come in."

The doctor led Ann down the hall to the study, closing the door behind them.

"Mrs. Beaumont told me everything," Ann said, refusing a chair by the fireplace. "I know John used to be a freighter pirate, and how you and Mrs. Beaumont and the entire town tried to hide it from me."

Dr. Brainard flushed and averted his eyes. "It was with the best of intentions, although, I admit, it was ill-conceived and poorly executed."

"I also found the button from Bonnie's uniform in the sewing box. I know Bonnie was a time jumper and that's why John gave up being a freighter pirate," Ann said. "What John did in the past, or why he gave it up, doesn't matter. The freighter pirates are back, and John needs our help."

Dr. Brainard looked up from where he'd been staring into the fireplace ashes.

"I know. John told me Chohon-Lo was blackmailing him."

"You *knew*?" Ann looked at the doctor, incredulous. "Why didn't you—?"

"John knew he wouldn't be able to pay the pirates indefinitely," Dr. Brainard said, pulling a cloth from a vest pocket and cleaning his glasses. "He told me he had a plan to capture them."

Ann's thoughts raced ahead. John was in more danger than she imagined.

"Did he say how?"

"He didn't tell me the plan, but the captain will be all right." Dr. Brainard resettled his spectacles.

Ann's hands clenched. The fear she felt for John morphed into frustration.

"How can you say that?" Ann wanted to slap the doctor for his indifference. "He can't capture them!"

"The Captain is doing what he was trained to do." Dr. Brainard leveled his gaze. "Bonnie wasn't the time jumper. *John is.*"

Ann's breath caught in her chest. She sunk into the chair across from the doctor, unable to speak.

"John was never a freighter pirate," Dr. Brainard said. "His mission was to gather intelligence. Except for a handful of miscreants, special forces was able to kill or capture all the freighter pirates. But because of the few that got away, he had to stay undercover for his and Bonnie's protection. He was supposed to go to Andarria and officially close the mission file, but Bonnie's death delayed the meeting and John never went back. He's been living as a pseudo-fugitive ever since."

Ann shook her head in disbelief. "I showed John the button. Why didn't he just tell me the truth?"

"The simple answer is, he couldn't. John took an oath to play his part for as long as he's undercover."

Ann narrowed her eyes. "Then how is it that you know all this?"

"Bonnie told me the captain's secret before she died," Dr. Brainard said. "I'm the only one she told, and you're the first person I've told. Bonnie begged me to look after John to make sure he went back to Andarria. John threatened to kill me on the spot the first time I approached him about it. I've tried unsuccessfully for ten years to get him to listen." The doctor dropped his arms, defeated. "John's an experienced operative. He's been through tighter scrapes than this. Knowing the captain, I'm sure he has a plan and a damn good one at that."

Ann remembered the look of panic on John's face, and another dagger of fear pierced her heart.

"But John said the pirates are coming tonight," Ann said. "I don't think he's ready for them."

"Tonight?" The doctor's face pinched with worry. "I'm afraid there's nothing we can do. If we charge in there like an over-anxious bridegroom, we could put the captain in more danger."

Ann felt a flash of irritation and straightened in her chair. "You forget—I'm a time jumper, too."

"Yes, of course, but you've been on a long convalescence and are only now rediscovering your abilities. You have no idea what the captain has planned. You could be putting his life and yours at risk."

"There's got to be something we can do."

"If we knew how to reach John's handler, he might be able to do something," Dr. Brainard said. "But Bonnie never told me his name."

"What do you mean?"

"A fellow agent," the doctor said. "He was the captain's link to Andarria. John could contact him if he ever needed help or if he had vital information, but John has to be the one to initiate communication. It's all very cloak and dagger."

Ann bolted upright in her chair, gripping the armrests.

"A.K. Max!" She dug frantically in her cloak pocket. "When John was arrested at the shuttleport, he told me to contact him to help get him released. Max gave me this." Ann held out the white card so the doctor could see.

Dr. Brainard looked at the card, eyes widening. "That must be him. Max must have wanted you to be his eyes and ears as a backup."

The doctor activated the comm station on the desk. Ann entered the card's data link information and a message flashed on the screen: *No direct communication available at this time. Would you like to leave a video message?*

Ann swore under her breath. She activated the recorder and spoke into the comm.

"John Galeas needs your help again. He's meeting with the pirates tonight." Ann paused, remembering the code word. "Genie!"

Ann ended the recording and sent the message. She slumped back into her seat. Dr. Brainard rested a hand on her shoulder.

"I'm afraid that's all we can do."

"It's not enough," Ann said, shaking her head.

"It'll have to be. Do the captain and Mrs. Beaumont know you're here?"

"Mrs. Beaumont quit and went home early. She thinks John is working for the pirates again," Ann said. "John thinks I'm on my way to visit my brother."

"I see," the doctor said, his tone wary. "That explains your carpet bag. Do I dare ask how you found your way here?"

Ann cringed inwardly and tried to keep her expression neutral. "Mike gave me a ride. He won't tell anyone I'm here."

Dr. Brainard nodded and looked thoughtful as he leaned against the desk. "You're welcome to stay in the guest room tonight. You'll be safe here. We'll know more in the morning."

Ann closed her eyes and rested her head on the back of the chair. The keravnos implant gave a mournful whistle. She heard Dr. Brainard sigh.

"Please, Ann. I'm worried about John too, but it really is for the best."

Ann opened her eyes and looked up at the doctor. Weariness deepened the lines in the gentleman's face as if all the years of worrying for patients had caught up with him in a single instant.

Ann nodded. "Fine. I guess I don't have much choice."

"Everything will be all right," Dr. Brainard said, patting her shoulder. He gave Ann a reassuring smile that lifted his features and brought back some of his youth. "I'll ask the cook to set another place for dinner." He walked toward the study door. "I think we're having lamb tonight. Mrs. Kepler isn't Mrs. Beaumont when it comes to cooking, but she's not bad." The doctor paused with a hand on the doorknob, frowning.

"Don't tell Mrs. Kepler I said that. She knows where I keep the laxterium."

Dr. Brainard tossed Ann a lopsided grin and pulled the door shut behind him. Ann listened to the sound of retreating footsteps, relieved she hadn't told the doctor how she got off the shuttle. Ann went to work pulling open desk drawers, searching for the source of the familiar breathy notes she sensed while Dr. Brainard had been speaking.

Ann found the holster tucked deep inside the desk's bottom drawer. The grips of two ion pistols showed above the worn leather. Underneath the holster lay Dr. Brainard's night-driving goggles. Ann drew one of the pistols and frowned. *Gentlemen's pistols.* More suitable for dueling, the antique, brass weapons were only slightly better than throwing rocks, and, she noted, with the power cells at half-charge they wouldn't last long in a fight.

She gripped the pistol in her hand, testing the weight. The hum from the power cell traveled up her arm like an electrical fire. Steady. Ann took a deep breath to settle her nerves, remembering the incident with the ion rifle back at Siren's Cove. The prickling in her arm subsided until it danced across her fingertips.

Ann quickly holstered the pistols and grabbed the doctor's driving goggles before closing the desk drawer. She listened to the muffled voices of Dr. Brainard and the cook at the other end of the house. She picked up the carpet bag and hurried to the doctor's private washroom, locking the door behind her.

Ann stripped off her blouse and skirt. She opened the carpet bag and started to dress. The exercise pants and shirt were still dusty from the trip to the attic. Ann buckled the holster across her hips and crammed the quarterstaff into a pocket. She pressed an ear to the washroom door. Silence. Dr. Brainard hadn't returned to the study. Ann picked up the driving goggles and looped the strap over her head.

The washroom window overlooked a row of flowering shrubs at the side of the cottage. Ann sat on the window ledge and let her legs dangle over the side as far as she could before dropping into the bushes below. She landed in a flurry of petals and snapping branches. She stumbled backward out of the foliage taking a few scratches and blooms with her. Ann checked to make sure she hadn't lost anything in the fall then struck up a steady trot toward Siren's Cove.

# THIRTY

## *CHOHON-LO*

The footpath from Dr. Brainard's cottage led Ann down grassy slopes and across the fields toward the outskirts of Llewellyn. Below, the blue velvet of the harbor disappeared in the growing darkness. The twinkling lights of the town ringed the water's edge. The ocean breeze blew harder bringing with it the smell of salt and rain.

Ann stopped to catch her breath in the grove of trees behind the tavern. The dark shape of Siren's Cove loomed ahead. From what Dr. Brainard said, the best way to help John would be to stay out of his way and let him do his job. But that, Ann reasoned, didn't mean she couldn't keep watch and offer a helping hand if John ran into trouble. The trick would be to find a place where she could keep an eye on things without being seen or shot at if John heard Ann skulking around.

Except for a light coming from the master bedroom window, the house and winery were dark. Normally at this time of night, Siren's Cove would be in the peak of the dinner service. Ann adjusted Dr. Brainard's night-driving goggles and activated the switch. The goggles sang out a triad of notes, and the world around her brightened to a flat gray. With the specs in place, Ann could easily make out the courtyard and garden behind the tavern, right down to the individual cobblestones that formed the kitchen stoop.

Ann crouched and darted along the garden fence to the back of the winery. She pulled at the sliding doors. Locked. Ann looked around and saw a basement window partially obscured by weeds. She dropped to her knees and tried to lift the pane, but the window refused to budge. Ann jammed one end of the quarterstaff between the windowpane and the frame. She pulled hard until she heard the old wood crack. She carefully opened the window and slipped inside.

The machinery in the winery basement sang to Ann like a choir in a concert hall. Pipes and power conduits ran across the ceiling, connecting unseen generators and gauges to the equipment above. The keravnos implant chirped excitedly in Ann's ear. She covered the implant with her hand to quiet the sound. Stealth would be impossible, but without the implant Ann would lose an advantage she had grown to trust.

Ann hesitated then reluctantly removed the disc from her ear. Immediately, the sound of the choir faded, but the music did not disappear completely. She could still sense some of the individual notes even if she could no longer distinguish the tune. Ann blinked in surprise. She had not expected to be able to sense anything without the implant. She looked at the half-moon disc. Perhaps the device had given back some of her ability after all? Ann tucked the implant into a pocket and moved deeper into the basement.

The night goggles made navigating the dark basement as easy as serving tables. Ann ducked and weaved past machinery until she reached the wooden steps that led to the trap door behind the bar.

The door at the top of the steps opened with a squeal of metal hinges. Light poured into the basement momentarily blinding her. Ann jumped backward into the shadows and squeezed behind a stack of crates. She held her breath and listened to the sound of boots as they hurried down the wooden steps into the basement.

John walked to the workbench at the foot of the stairs. Ann shrunk deeper into the crevice behind the crates. Her heart pounded until Ann thought she could hear her own pulse echoing against the basement walls. John rummaged in the workbench, his back to Ann, opening drawers and cabinets. After a few seconds of searching, he grabbed a vice grip and clomped back up the steps.

The trap slammed shut and Ann let out a breath. She listened to John's footsteps above as he walked through the tavern into the winery. Ann slipped from behind the crates and crept back the way she came. She needed to get into the winery, but the trap door into the tavern was too risky. Ann worked her way through the passage until she stood under the winery again. Light from above now shone through a crack in the ceiling planks along the opposite wall. Ann stepped closer. A sliver of light fell on a set of steps directly below a service door. Ann climbed to the top step and listened. Hearing nothing, she rested her goggles on the top of her head and cautiously lifted the trap a few inches.

The service door opened underneath the bottling machine's conveyor belt. From her vantage point on the floor, Ann could look between the machinery's metal supports to the winery's control panel directly across from her. The wine tanks and stacks of crates blocked her view of the sliding doors, but to her right Ann could see the maintenance room door and the wooden steps leading to the tavern.

The maintenance room door opened. Ann ducked as John walked past to the control panel. One of the mini-bots flew after him. Ann could tell it was Port from the way the bot listed hard on its left side. John stood at the control panel, flipping switches and checking circuits, while Port settled on the wall a few feet away.

Ann watched as John worked. *What are you up to?* She couldn't see how he intended to capture the pirates. The winery looked as it always did; no weapons, no alterations of any kind. Each time John walked across the winery, Port trailed after him like a kite on a string, wings clicking and humming a senseless tune.

John glanced at the clock on the control panel and headed toward the winery's sliding doors. Port started to follow, but this time John spun and barked out an order.

"Port! Window!"

He pointed to the large glass block window above the control panel. Port changed course and sailed across the winery. The mini-bot attached itself to the window, flicked its copper wings, and sat motionless with its sensor dome dilated.

John disappeared behind the wine tanks. The sound of a metal bolt sliding back echoed through the winery. A second later, John reappeared and stepped to the control panel.

Minutes passed. Ann's neck and shoulders began to ache from holding open the trap door. She could feel John's tension as he paced. Ann blew out a silent breath to try and loosen the knot in her stomach.

The sliding doors rumbled. Boots scuffled on the wooden floor. John stopped pacing, hands clenched at his sides. Ann's pulse pounded as five pirates appeared from behind the wine tanks and spread out in the open area between the control panel and the bottling machine, pistols glinting in braces. Ann recognized the men as the same group from the tavern. The pirate who ordered John to bring a bottle to the table stood in the center, arms crossed over his leather pea coat. Ann wondered for an instant if this pirate was the group's leader, but then the men fell back as two more raiders stepped into view.

A man with long, white hair strode forward. With only a vest to cover his upper body, every movement showed the power in the pirate's muscular frame. Scrolls of tattoos moved like black flames across his skin. Gauging from the reaction of the other pirates, Ann reasoned this must be the man John called Chohon-Lo.

"Good evening, Captain Galeas. My apologies for our change in meeting times," Chohon-Lo said. Ann detected a modest accent in the roll of his speech. "Scrivani has found us another business opportunity." He gestured to the man standing next to him. "Our departure has come earlier than anticipated."

The pirate commander's appearance was so striking, Ann almost didn't notice the second man. His bald head glowed unnaturally pink in the bright light of the winery. His brown hair bristled from his scalp.

Scrivani smiled and stroked his bottom lip. "I trust the change in time was not inconvenient for you, Captain?" The other pirates chuckled.

That voice! A chill of recognition swept over Ann. The bald man was the off tourist who had attacked her in the tavern. Ann looked at John. She could see the muscles in his jaw working even from a distance.

"It was unexpected," John said, glaring at Scrivani.

"The details are unimportant...unless..." Chohon-Lo eyed Captain Galeas. "I am still in need of a navigator."

John met his gaze. "My business is here."

The pirate commander sneered and said something to his crew in a language Ann did not recognize. The freighter pirates broke into laughter, sounding more like a pack of dogs than men.

"So be it," Chohon-Lo said, turning back to John. "Perhaps you will be hungrier next month. Do you have our payment?"

John nodded, his mouth drawn tight. Ann watched as he turned and reached for a bag resting on the back of the control panel. John dropped his arm. His fist slammed on top of a row of buttons. Light flashed as electricity arced from the floor and zigzagged up the legs of the pirates.

Ann jerked backward as she felt the power surge prickle across her skin, but the current coming from the floor stopped short of her position in the trap door. Glowing strips of metal laid in the seams of the floor electrified the area between the control panel and the bottling machine.

The pirates convulsed and screamed. Two men standing farther back from the others watched horror-struck as their comrades collapsed and writhed on the floor.

The lights dimmed briefly, and a loud pop sounded, cutting

the current. John jerked his head toward the control panel, and for an instant, Ann saw fear in his eyes. He yelled to Port still roosting on the window.

"Port! Hand off!"

The mini bot swooped from his perch toward the captain's outstretched hand. A panel on Port's undercarriage slid open, and out dropped an ion pistol. John caught the weapon just as the mini-bot righted itself and blurred in a burst of speed toward the rafters.

John swung his arm toward the closest pirate and fired twice, hitting the raider in the chest. The man flew backward and landed splayed across the top of the bottling machine's conveyor belt.

Waves of bottles crashed to the floor. Ann ducked, pulling the trap door shut to shield herself from the hail of glass. When she opened the trap again, John was nowhere in sight. The second pirate drew a weapon and charged toward the back of the winery. Crates shattered. Bottles exploded into shards in the barrage of laser fire. Ann covered her head, trapped by the flying debris.

Chohon-Lo and the other pirates struggled to their feet.

"Vago!" The pirate commander pointed to the raider wearing the pea coat and shouted a command.

Vago stood and lurched in the direction of the wine tanks. Ann heard more laser fire and the sounds of a struggle. A second later, the two raiders emerged from the back of the winery, dragging John between them.

*No!* Ann caught her breath. The pirates hauled John forward, his arms locked in their grasp.

Anger burned on Chohon-Lo's face. "You've been shooting dice with the devil again, Captain Galeas!"

John struggled against his captors. He lifted his head and glared back, mouth bloody.

"Our partnership is at an end." The pirate commander pulled a curved knife from his belt. "Before you die, know I will give your woman to Scrivani as compensation for his injuries. Then...if there is anything left...I will kill her."

Chohon-Lo's lips slid back, exposing his teeth, eyes black with murder. "Your names will make a pretty addition to my gallery." The pirate raised his knife hand and took a step toward John.

Ann burst from the service door, firing both pistols. The bolts sliced the air, missing Chohon-Lo by inches, and struck the pirate standing next to him. The raider's face split open and he dropped to the floor, limbs twitching. The pirate commander and his crew spun toward the sound, drew their pistols, and locked eyes on Ann.

*Damn it!*

Adrenaline spiked Ann's blood from her head to her feet. She broke into a run, sprinting sideways along the wall and firing wildly with both pistols. The pirates scattered and returned fire. The bolts ripping into the wall behind Ann were so close she could feel the heat from the rounds through the back of her shirt.

Ann raced toward a stack of crates. As she dove for cover, she saw John break free of his captors and send a crushing blow with an elbow into Vago's face. When Ann peeked from behind the crates, she saw Vago on the floor, head in his hands. John yelled and charged toward the wine tanks.

"Port! Clean sweep!"

A shriek came from the rafters. A blur of copper dove toward the pirates. The raiders yelled in confusion and sought cover near the stairs. The men fired at Port as the mini-bot bore down on them. Ann crept farther behind the crates toward the wine tanks. A hand darted forward, grabbing the collar of her shirt, and slammed Ann against the wall.

"John, it's me!"

John looked at Ann with amazement and dropped his fist.

"That was you?"

Ann frowned and pushed the night goggles up farther on the top of her head. "Don't look so surprised."

John glanced around in a panic. "I need to get you out of here."

"I'm *fine*," Ann said, pushing John's hand away. "You're the one who's in trouble!"

A burst of laser fire strafed the wall above, showering them both with plaster. Ann ducked. John pulled her forward to take shelter on the floor between the wine tanks. He sat with his back against the metal tank. The expression on his face made Ann feel like she'd suddenly transformed into a four-eyed Osgath.

John's look of surprise collapsed into a scowl. "You were supposed to get on the shuttle!"

Ann returned his glare. "Technically, I *did* get on the shuttle. But, let's not argue about that now." Ann forced one of her pistols into John's hand.

He eyed the brass antique. "Where did you——?"

"I had to improvise. It's not like I had much of a choice."

Ann felt her patience slipping. John pressed his lips together. He looked around the edge of the tank, cocked the pistol, and squeezed off a few shots in the direction of the stairs.

Ann made a quick survey of their position between the tanks. "So, how are we getting out of here?"

"We'll sit tight for a minute and let Port wear them down," John said, turning toward Ann. "Did you bring anyone with you?"

"No."

More laser fire ricocheted through the winery, but this time the shots didn't reach the wine tanks. Ann leaned over and chanced a look. She saw the pirates clustered in the shelter of the stairs. Port had attached himself to the face of one of the raiders. She could hear the unlucky man's muffled screams as he threw himself about in a desperate attempt to shake the mini-bot loose. His hands gripped Port's sides, but he could not pull the bot off. His comrades tried to come to his aid but were at a loss as to whether they should shoot the mini-bot or try to help pry it off. Port detached himself from the pirate's face and flew at a high rate of speed straight for another raider, eliciting another round of laser fire and screams from the new victim. Ann ducked back down just as another yell echoed off the rafters, accompanied by the ping of laser bolts hitting the opposite side of the tank.

"Let's go," Ann said, tugging at John's arm. "We can get out through the sliding doors."

John shook his head. "No. There might be more of them outside. We'd walk right into an ambush." John fired a few more shots toward the pirates then looked at Ann. "Don't move."

John crouched and crossed over to the stack of crates along the wall. Ann watched as he lifted the lid of a wine crate and pulled out a black duffle bag. John looked up at the metal pipes connecting the two tanks directly above.

"We have to get away from the tanks," John said. "Port won't be able to keep the pirates busy much longer. Can you distract them?"

Ann looked down at the antique pistol in her hand. The power cell was almost depleted.

"You'll have to be quick."

John and Ann crept their way around to the front of the tanks. Port's diversionary tactics had been more than effective. Two pirates lay on the floor near the stairs, their faces charred like burnt milk. Port had retreated, but to where Ann could not see.

Chohon-Lo and Vago, his face covered in blood, opened fire from the doorway of the maintenance room. Ann darted across the winery, drawing their fire, and slid into the shelter of the control panel. She tucked herself into the small space, then let loose with a torrent of laser fire toward the maintenance room, sparking metal and splintering walls.

A laser bolt seared the back of Ann's hand, sending her pistol clattering across the floor. Ann jerked the injured hand to her chest, sucking air through her teeth. A wound from a laser bolt could burn for days, but Ann knew she was lucky the shot hadn't taken her hand off completely. From the corner of an eye, she could see John crouched at the end of the conveyor belt trading fire with Chohon-Lo and Vago. If John could keep them distracted long enough, she could retrieve the pistol.

"What an exquisite sight. A woman on her knees."

Ann stiffened. Scrivani's voice came from behind, toward the back of the winery. Ann dove for her pistol, rolled, and fired two shots. The bolts struck Scrivani in the chest. He continued to advance. He swung the board in his hands, knocking the pistol from Ann's grasp.

Ann looked up, dazed. *How?* She knew the small-caliber pistol didn't pack much of a punch, but it shouldn't have left Scrivani standing after hitting him twice at such close range.

The raider looked down at Ann and laughed. The pink skin pulled tighter across his cheekbones, stretching his mouth wide.

"I'm ready for you this time, kitchen girl. After our first meeting, did you really think I would have walked in here without some kind of protection?"

Ann's eyes darted to Scrivani's shirt. The laser bolts had burned two holes in the fabric the size of her fist. Underneath, Ann could see the dark gray ribs of a dielectric vest. She would have needed a weapon with ten times the power of the antique pistol to have any hope of cracking through the vest's electrical dampening field. Scrivani drew a weapon and pointed it at Ann's head.

A blaze of copper streaked from behind the wine tanks. Scrivani jerked his gun and fired as the mini-bot barreled toward him. The bolt exploded against Port, throwing him backward. Port struck the wine tank and fell to the floor, clattering like a saucepan.

Ann jumped to her feet. She pulled the quarterstaff from her pocket and activated the power source. The staff had been a curiosity, a plaything, but as Ann wheeled the staff over her head she could feel the thrum of power coming from the weapon's core. Ann slashed the staff downward and struck Scrivani's pistol, disarming him. She followed with a roundhouse kick to his chest. The raider grunted and fell backward into a stack of crates. Ann rushed forward and raised her staff, but Scrivani scrambled to his feet and grabbed a piece of metal pipe, deflecting the attack.

The quarterstaff flashed in Ann's hands, spinning so fast in front of her Scrivani's face took on a greenish hue. The bald man blocked every attack. The sound of Ann's staff striking the pipe rang out like chimes. Ann ducked, feeling the whoosh of air as the metal pipe missed her head by inches.

The muscles in Ann's arms and legs burned. Her breath came harder. Ann planted her feet and swung again. The end of the staff caught Scrivani across the bridge of his nose with a crack, drawing blood and driving him backward. He staggered. Ann dropped to a crouch to sweep the pirate's legs, but Scrivani recovered and swung the pipe downward.

Ann tried to deflect the blow with the staff, but the pipe slipped past her defenses and struck the goggles on the top of her head. The blow rocketed through Ann's skull and sent her crashing to the floor. Needles of glass from the shattered lenses penetrated her scalp. Stars sparkled and shot across Ann's vision like the tail of a comet.

Ann fought the blackness as it swarmed around her. Rough hands grabbed the front of her shirt. Ann was jerked to her feet, arms dangling useless at her sides. Her head lolled. Blood, wet and warm, oozed in Ann's hair.

"You surprise me, kitchen girl."

Ann lifted her head. Pain plucked her body like a string as she struggled to open her eyes. An enormous pink cloud floated in front of her. Ann blinked hard to clear her vision and Scrivani's face came into focus.

The raider gripped the front of Ann's shirt, forcing her to stand on tiptoe. The skin on his face stretched across gaunt features. Scrivani peered down at Ann with eyes like two black marbles sunk deep into the meat of his eye sockets.

"So many ways to break your neck," Scrivani said, moving his fingers to Ann's throat. His breath heaved from exertion. "The difficulty is in the choosing." He tightened his fingers, testing the curve of Ann's neck. "I could do it now." The raider's mouth stretched wide as if to devour her. "Or I could show you to Galeas first. He'll surrender, of course."

"No—"

Scrivani tightened his hold, choking off her words. Ann struggled to breathe, terrified by how quickly her lungs cried out in protest. Scrivani chuckled as he rubbed his thumbs downward across the hollow of Ann's throat, softening his grip. Ann sucked air to ease the ache in her chest.

"Oh, yes he will," Scrivani said. "You're why he refused Chohon-Lo's generous offer. You're the reason for all this unpleasantness in what should've been a straightforward business arrangement. We miscalculated your importance."

Ann's heart hammered in her chest. John and Dr. Brainard were right. She should've never come back. She'd failed, and worst of all, the pirates would use her against John just as he said they would.

Ann felt the fingers of her left hand brush against cold steel. Electricity danced across her fingertips. The fight with Scrivani had brought them back toward the winery's control panel. Ann shuddered and stretched out her hand.

"The moment after Galeas surrenders, I'll snap your neck. The look on his face..." Scrivani's lipless mouth curved into a smile. "Yes, I think that will be much more satisfying. What a pretty broken doll you will make." Scrivani lifted an index finger and ran it across Ann's cheek.

Ann struggled to keep focus. She pulled the power from the control panel toward her. The current coursed up her arm, growing heavier. She wound the current inside her even as it urged for release. Ann swallowed hard and peered at Scrivani through lidded eyes.

"He'll kill you," Ann whispered.

Scrivani chuckled. "Oh, no. It will destroy him." He leaned forward and kept one hand on Ann's neck while the other drifted down the front of her shirt until his palm rested on Ann's hip. Scrivani pulled her closer and pressed his mouth to Ann's ear. "You see, I know him. Better. Than. You."

Ann shot her right hand upward, slamming into Scrivani's exposed neck, and released the current. The power gathered inside her unraveled and exploded from her fingers clenched around Scrivani's throat. His hand tore away from her neck.

Ann felt the last of the current leave her body and she collapsed to the floor, white-hot light fading behind her eyelids. Every nerve ending in her body burned with the echo of the blast.

Ann opened her eyes. Scrivani lay on his back a few feet away with one arm extended to the ceiling. The hand that had held Ann's throat pointed upward like a five-pronged weathervane.

"Ann! It's time to go!"

John's voice came over the din of laser fire. Ann lurched unsteadily to her feet. Adrenaline made her vision sparkle. She retrieved and deactivated the quarterstaff, jamming it back into a pocket. She scooped up Scrivani's pistol from the floor and darted across the winery to John, firing towards the maintenance room as she ran.

Ann dove behind the conveyor belt and landed next to John as another volley of laser bolts struck the tank above her head. John grabbed Ann's arm and pulled her close, his face inches from her own.

"When I say go, fire toward the maintenance room and don't stop!"

Ann nodded. "What are you—?"

"Now!"

Ann stood and let loose with another frenzy of laser fire over the top of the conveyor belt. An explosion behind her was followed by a crack and the splintering of wood. Ann glanced over a shoulder. John held a rifle-barreled grappling gun. A cable, clipped to the harness strapped across his chest, ran to the gun in his hand. John looped an arm around Ann's waist and pulled her against his side.

"Port! Evacuate!"

Ann's stomach clenched. "Port was hit!"

John's eyes locked on to Ann's. Uncertainty rippled across his face.

"Hold on!"

Ann threw her free arm across John's shoulders. The cable jerked them upward and she tightened the grip on John's shirt.

Ann's feet left the floor and they flew—air rushing past—her stomach twisting with the speed of the ascent. She continued to fire downward on Chohon-Lo and Vago as the pirates charged from the maintenance room, weapons drawn.

Ann's heart leapt as she saw the familiar blur of copper streak toward the pirates, driving them back. Port turned at the last second, smashed through one of the winery's windows and flew out into the night.

The flight toward the roof of the winery stopped with a jerk. Ann's grip started to slip as the pair swung dangerously for an instant, but instead of air, her feet touched one of the solid crossbeams that ran the length of the winery.

"Easy," John said, helping Ann balance. "The beams are plenty wide as long as you don't lose your head."

Ann peered down at the conveyor belt where they stood only seconds before. Her senses rolled. Another eruption of laser fire ripped into the ceiling above. Ann ducked behind a support beam and checked her pistol's power cell. At best, she only had a few shots left.

"We can't stay up here."

John unclipped the cable from the harness and stowed the grappling gun in the pack on his back.

"This way."

He moved quickly along the beam, crossing over the pipes connecting the two wine tanks. Ann followed as best she could until they stood above the second tank. She could hear the pirates on the move, repositioning for another attack. She gripped the pistol and waited for targets to appear.

"Save your power cell."

Ann looked to John, perplexed. His pistol remained tucked in a belt. John reached into an outer pocket of his pack and pulled out a small black box with a single switch.

"You're not the only one who can improvise." John gave Ann a lopsided grin and activated the device.

A muffled bang came from below. The first wine tank began to sway. Metal groaned as the structure pulled away from its moorings. Pipes burst. Wine spouted, spraying droplets in all directions. The thunderous roar of the tank as it fell drowned out the screams of the pirates. The tank slammed into the floor, broke in two, and released a gush of wine, flooding the winery.

Ann readied her pistol, searching for any sign of movement. The only sound was the dripping of wine as it continued to spray from broken pipes. Ann looked to John and kept her pistol trained on the devastation below.

John held up a hand for silence. A frown tugged at the corners of his mouth. His eyes flicked toward the winery floor, searching. Ann held her breath and listened. Through the dripping of the wine a faint chirrup, slow and steady, drifted up from behind the fallen tank. The familiar sound made Ann's nerves prickle, and yet she couldn't place where she'd heard it before.

"What is it?"

John's face paled. His eyes grew round with fear.

"Flash grenade. One of the pirates must have dropped it by accident. It's on a timed delay."

Ann drew in a breath, suddenly aware of the vapors drifting up from the winery floor. She could taste the mist in the back of her throat. Beads of wine dripped from her face and had started to soak through her shirt. A shiver of fear ran through her. A single spark and the winery would go up in a ball of blue flame.

John grabbed a piece of twisted pipe and ripped it from the top of the second tank. Ann holstered the pistol and scanned the roof. Her feet poised to run as she listened to the chirrups and counted the seconds between.

"Can we get out through the roof?"

John shook his head. "No. We'll try a window."

Ann followed as John moved quickly along the cross beam to one of the windows overlooking the courtyard. He swung the pipe hard, punching a hole in the thick glass.

Ann continued the silent count and felt time compress with each new chirrup.

"Hurry!"

John finished clearing away the broken glass and tossed the pipe through the window. Sweat beaded his brow. He pulled the grappling gun from the pack, clipped the cable to his harness, and fired the clamp deep into the window frame.

Ann wrapped her arms around John's shoulders. The chirrups trilled faster, becoming a solid shriek of noise.

"Jump!"

John pushed back from the window ledge into the night air. His free arm tightened around her waist as they fell. Ann gulped giddy panic and gripped the back of John's shirt. The grappling line sizzled as it threaded out. A bang and a bright strobe of light burst from the shattered window above.

FOOOOM!

A roar of blue and orange flames shook the winery. Windows exploded, belching glass and flame across the courtyard. The wall of heat struck Ann, transforming the cool night into a furnace. She closed her eyes and buried her face in John's shoulder, away from the blast. John yelled, and the heat and the flames swirled around them through the rush of freefall.

Ann slammed into the ground. Her ankle wrenched, sending a bolt of pain up her leg. Her body crumpled and she landed on her stomach stunned, unable to move. Ann dug her hands into the grass as she fought to take a breath. Every one of her internal organs felt knocked out of place. Ann sucked air into her lungs. Soot and smoke burned the back of her throat. Heat scorched her clothes and skin.

She struggled to a sitting position and tried to rub the sting of the smoke from her eyes. Splinters of flaming wood floated through the haze like fireflies. John lay in the grass a few feet away.

"John!"

Ann's voice came out as a croak, no match for the roar of the flames consuming the winery. She crawled across the grass. John's face looked ghostly, even in the flickering light of the fire. The explosion had burned parts of his clothing. Cuts and gashes from flying debris covered his face and hands. Ann checked for a pulse and placed a hand on his chest. John's steady heart rate and breathing snapped Ann back into focus.

"John, we have to go! We have to get away from the winery!" Ann's eyes streamed from the smoke.

John groaned. His eyelids flickered. "I can't." His voice sounded as dry as ash. "I can't move." Siren's sounded in the distance.

Ann unhooked the cable from John's harness. She slung the strap of the grappling gun over a shoulder and struggled to stand. The pain in her ankle forced her back to her knees. Ann gritted her teeth. She would crawl if she had to. Ann grabbed the shoulder straps of John's harness. She pulled and crawled backwards on elbows and knees, dragging John across the courtyard away from the winery.

Ann flopped in the grass drenched in sweat and nauseated from the pain in her ankle. The heat from the fire beat down on them even from across the courtyard and under the safety of the shade trees. Ann watched the old building burn. Dry timbers crackled and groaned. The flames licked through the broken windows and the underside of the winery roof. Siren's Cove would go next. Ann clenched back the sob rising from her throat. She looked at the house she had called home.

Then the telltale green static of a fire shield flickered between the tavern house and the winery. Tears filled her eyes. John had thought of everything.

"It will hold."

Ann looked at John lying next to her in the grass. He gazed across the courtyard at Siren's Cove. His eyes reflected a peace Ann had never seen before.

"GAALEEEEEAAAAAS!"

The scream split the air, tearing every nerve from Ann's body and freezing the blood in her veins. A man stepped from the shadows of the house and staggered into the courtyard. One arm dangled from a shoulder socket. A collar bone glistened white as it jutted upward through the skin. A curved knife in the pirate commander's other hand reflected the light from the fire.

John sucked in a breath. "Run!"

Ann's heart quaked in her chest. She searched for their pistols. Gone. Most likely lost in the fall from the window. Without two good legs to stand on, her quarterstaff would be useless.

Ann's breath came in short bursts. "Our pistols!"

John struggled to form the words. His face twisted in pain. "The grappling gun."

Ann shook her head. "The cable snapped. The grapple's gone."

"No." John's eyes flicked to something just over Ann's shoulder. "Look!"

Ann's pulse rocketed. Her hands trembled as she slipped the strap from her shoulder and held the grappling gun. Her eyes widened. The steel point of the grapple's main prong winked from the tip of the rifle barrel.

Chohon-Lo's eyes swept the courtyard until he found his prey. His mouth broke into a snarl. He let loose a string of curses and charged across the courtyard, hair flying.

Ann raised the grappling gun and fired. The gun kicked hard against her shoulder and sent the grapple speeding toward Chohon-Lo. The prong head struck the pirate commander low in the belly, dropping him to his knees only a few feet from where Ann sat. The secondary prongs sprung on impact, piercing skin with steel fingers and tearing bloody tracks into flesh as they contracted. Blood splashed the cobblestones.

Chohon-Lo howled in agony and rage. His hands gripped the taunt cable now slick with blood. The pirate's eyes filled with hate as he cocked his knife hand.

A laser blast echoed through the trees. A bolt of white light flew past Ann's head from behind, blinding her for an instant. Ann felt the grappling cable jerk with a force that almost ripped the gun from her hands.

Chohon-Lo's knife fell from his hand, clattering to the cobblestones. The left side of the pirate's head, from the top of the scalp down to the cheekbone, had been scooped away as if by a spoon. Chohon-Lo's remaining eye, wide and staring, held

Ann in its horrible gaze.

Ann dropped the grappling gun. Without tension on the cable to hold him upright, Chohon-Lo slumped to the ground. Ann closed her eyes. She swallowed hard to calm the rolling of her stomach.

Boots tramped toward her through the undergrowth. Not one pair of boots, but many, spreading out in all directions. Instinct fought exhaustion and won. Ann reached for the quarterstaff in her pocket.

Squads of armed guards swarmed past. Some secured the courtyard and the house while others joined the fire brigade to fight the blaze. Ann looked through the trees where the guards had come from.

Running lights of a personnel shuttle glowed in the field beyond, and marching toward the courtyard flanked by four armed guards came A.K. Max. The gray field uniform of an Andarrian Intelligence officer replaced the pinstriped suit. The barrel of a high-powered sniper's rifle leaned against his shoulder, the stock cradled in the palm of one hand. The sculpted crest of A.K's hair defied the laws of aerodynamics in spite of the ocean breeze. Ann's fingers released the quarterstaff as the last of the tension fled her body.

The guards drew weapons as they approached and quickly surrounded them, the power cells of their rifles fully charged. A.K. looked down at John, face stern.

"Captain John Galeas, you are under arrest for treason and high crimes against the Andarrian Republic!"

The tension that had left Ann a moment before flooded back.

John sucked in a ragged breath and closed his eyes.

"End game."

A.K. dropped to one knee and gripped John's shoulder. His stony expression broke into a broad smile.

"Welcome back!"

John looked at A.K. and managed a dim smile before his eyes rolled back and he slipped into unconsciousness.

Ann slumped to the ground next to John and let the med

techs fuss, too exhausted to move. She watched as the techs loaded John onto a stretcher. John hadn't regained consciousness, and the medics wouldn't answer any of her questions about his injuries. Ann felt her stretcher lift and begin to move. She looked up and saw A.K. Max watching her as he walked next to the stretcher.

"Don't worry, Buttercup," the intelligence man said. "Captain Galeas is going to be fine. We'll treat him en route." Ann nodded. A.K. cocked his head and eyed her with interest. "I got your message."

Ann grinned. "I thought you might have."

A.K. turned his attention to stepping over a downed tree. "For the record, 'Genie' is the get-out-of-jail-free card." He looked over a shoulder and tossed Ann a confidential smile. "When you need reinforcements to keep from getting killed by a bunch of bloodthirsty freighter pirates, you need to say Big Foot."

# THIRTY-ONE

## *HERO'S WELCOME*

Light warmed John's face and limbs. Not the destructive light of heat and fire, but a glow that soaked into his skin like rain and wrapped him in soothing comfort. *Fire.* An uneasiness spread through his chest at the thought. John threw back the warm cloak of sleep and opened his eyes. A golden-honey light poured down from the ceiling panels in swirling hues tinged with pink. John blinked at the simulated sunrise and frowned. He recognized the light therapy panels used for pain management, but no hospital he knew of on the Colonies offered such sophisticated care.

Adrenaline hit him like a punch to the jaw. John tried to sit up, but his body wouldn't listen. He struggled and groaned with the effort. Hands gripped his shoulders and held him to the bed. A familiar gravel voice boomed in John's ears.

"Hold on. Just lie there and be still."

John relented, his strength gone. He settled back onto the hospital bed.

Colonel Wick stared down at John, the lines in his face gathered into a scowl under the black goatee. The colonel leaned back in his chair. Behind Wick stood A.K. Max. John's chest tightened as an aftershock of adrenaline coursed through his veins.

Wick looked at John. "Captain Galeas, do you understand why you're here?"

John's mind blurred. Chohon-Lo. *The fire in the winery.* He gulped air. There was only one explanation for why A.K. and Colonel Wick would be in the same room with him now. John's eyes shot to A.K for confirmation. A smile scrolled across the agent's face and he nodded.

John's heart lurched. He tried to slow his breathing. "Where's Ann?" His voice creaked like old machinery.

"She's fine," Wick said as he held a glass of water to John's lips. "She'll be in to visit when we're finished with you."

John sipped the water and felt his tongue and throat loosen. His pulse slowed to a steady trot.

Colonel Wick set the water glass on the stand next to John's bed. "First things first. You broke your back and shattered your leg. It'll be awhile before you can get out of here. Good news is, you're going to be fine."

John nodded. Now that he was awake, the light therapy panels no longer fully masked the pain that thrummed through his body. He looked to A.K. and braced for what he was sure would follow.

"Effective immediately, Operation Cryptid is closed." A.K. tapped the screen of a data pad and looked at John. "Chohon-Lo and his men are dead. Captain Galeas, you are no longer a mercenary, or an undercover operative. Your record is cleared. Your rank and all privileges are restored, and your official status is listed as inactive duty."

John closed his eyes and felt the invisible chain of the oath loosen and fall away. He expected A.K. would say as much, but not the crushing weight that accompanied the words. John turned his head to hide the raw emotion seeking release. He felt every shade he could name and a few he could not. John focused on joy along with her dark-eyed sibling, grief, and laid the rest aside for another day. He felt Colonel Wick's hand on his shoulder. John wiped his eyes with the back of a hand.

"Where you go from here is up to you," Wick said,

compassion pulling his gravel voice to an even deeper register. "Take your time. It's a lot to process." He narrowed his eyes. "You were always a hero..." John flinched. "...but this time everyone is going to know about it."

*Hero.*

John felt the color rise to his face. He wondered what the townsfolk of Llewelyn would think. He blew out a breath and looked to A.K. as a new thought crashed into his head.

"How did you know the meeting with Chohon-Lo had been moved up a day? I didn't have time to send you a message."

"General Rolland didn't want you getting cold feet again," A.K. said. "I flew to the Colonies a day early with orders to bring you back in restraints if you tried to back out on our deal. When I got Ann's message—"

John's eyes flew open in surprise. "Ann contacted you?"

The agent nodded, face grim. "I still almost didn't make it in time. I've made a career out of saving your ass. Thanks to her, I'll get another chance."

John frowned and fingered the pigtail at the back of his head. Ann would want answers. He'd kept secrets for so long, how would he be able to explain everything?

"She knows."

John looked up. A.K. met his gaze.

"I debriefed her," the agent said with a shrug. "All you have to do is fill in the details when you're ready."

John sunk back into the pillows. Somehow, it was easier knowing that Ann already knew. Colonel Wick headed to the door. The door slid open and he beckoned to someone in the hall.

John's heart cried out as Ann stepped into the room. She wore her time jumper's uniform. A blue brace wrapped her right ankle.

Ann's face brightened when her eyes found John. She went to the bedside and slipped a hand in his.

"One more item of business, Captain," Wick said, moving to the foot of the bed. "General Rolland has agreed to authorize reimbursement for the damage to your property. You should also expect a comm message regarding some back pay."

John stared at the colonel, mouth open. Ann smiled and squeezed his hand.

A.K. laughed. "Don't look so surprised. Did you think you were working for free all this time?"

John chuckled and shook his head. With all his worries, it never occurred to him to think about his paycheck.

"I do have one piece of bad news," Wick said. "While you're here and until I'm satisfied you're physically and emotionally fit for active duty, I'm your commanding officer." The Colonel's face split into a wide grin. "Welcome back!"

Colonel Wick and A.K. left, the door sliding shut behind them. John looked up at Ann. She sat on the edge of the bed, looking like a freshly minted cadet. Before John could speak, Ann kissed him. Her lips were soft and promised more. John pulled Ann as close as he dared and silently cursed his injuries and the excess of buttons on her jacket.

"Your ankle." John parted from Ann breathless and nursing a new ache to take his mind off his leg and back. "Are you all right?"

Ann smiled and nodded. She tossed her braid back over a shoulder.

"It was a clean break. Easy to mend." Ann glanced toward John's injured leg underneath the bed sheet, eyes full of sympathy. "I'm sorry about your leg. I heard the med techs talking."

John reached up to cup her cheek. "*We* should talk."

Ann combed the bangs from John's forehead with her fingers.

"A.K. already told me everything. You should rest. And don't worry about Sean, either. A.K. talked to him. He feels bad he misjudged you."

John cracked a smile. While good to know he didn't have to worry about being disemboweled by the Montressador's blade, it wasn't what he wanted to talk about.

"No. You need to hear the story from me." John said. "I just don't know how to begin."

Ann took something from a pocket and pressed it into John's hand. "I asked Mrs. Beaumont to send this. I thought maybe it would help."

John looked in his hand. The old button from his uniform glinted on his palm.

"I forgot Bonnie kept this," John said. Memories tugged at his heart. "We weren't supposed to keep anything that might blow my cover."

John looked up and saw Ann patiently watching him. He took a deep breath.

"My commanding officer called me to his quarters," John said, rolling the button between his fingers. "He needed a volunteer to go under deep cover. I was a young officer. I wanted to impress him, so I said yes. That's when I met A.K. He told me the first thing I had to do was get myself court martialed." John shrugged. "It's not easy being drunk and angry all the time, but A.K. said getting kicked out of the service would help me infiltrate Chohon-Lo's syndicate."

Ann nodded. "What did Bonnie think?"

John grimaced. "She didn't know...not right away. A.K. wasn't going to let me tell her, but I convinced him Bonnie could help." Ann looked at John, puzzled. He grinned. "Bonnie was a tech specialist. She could run the space-time beacon while I was gone. Bonnie took the news well. Better than I expected. We moved to the Colonies after I finished serving a six-month sentence after my court martial."

"That's when you opened Siren's Cove?"

"Yes, and it really was Bonnie's idea," John said. "She ran the tavern and used the space-time beacon to relay my coordinates to A.K. The beacon also made it impossible for anyone to track me coming or going to the Colonies. I came home every few weeks and sent information to A.K. whenever I had something useful to share. It was the perfect set up."

Ann tilted her head. "What happened to your ship?"

"Half of it is still sitting in the junk pile out by the shed,"

John said. "I sold the other half for scrap."

John rolled the button on his palm. "I remember when Bonnie showed me this button. We'd been on the Colonies about a year. I'd seen too much. I'd done things I wasn't proud of. It was late. I'd been drinking." John swallowed hard. "Bonnie didn't say a word. She just put the button on the table next to me and walked away." He closed his fingers around the bauble and held it tight. "It's easy to forget who you are when you're trying to be something you're not."

Ann took John's hand. "It sounds like Bonnie would've made a good time jumper."

John nodded and wiped his eyes. "I told her that once, but she said one time jumper in the family was enough."

Ann looked down, face drawn.

"What is it?"

"I haven't had a chance to tell you." Her eyes flicked to John's. "Colonel Wick offered to help get me reinstated, so I can be a time jumper again."

John's heart pinched. He'd known for a long time Ann wasn't a kitchen girl, but he wasn't sure if he was ready for this.

"I'll have to pass a few tests to see how much I remember, but the colonel says it should all be routine."

"That's great news." John forced a smile. Ann's face brightened. He took a deep breath. "I'm glad you brought it up. I've been thinking and there's something I wanted to ask you."

The door slid open, and a med tech entered pushing a medical cart. The sweet smell of maple syrup drifted through the room.

Ann pulled her hand from his grasp. Her eyes locked on the med tech's cart, her face pale and tight with fear. She stood and stepped away from the bed, back against the wall.

John frowned, perplexed. "What's wrong?"

The med tech lifted the bed sheet to expose John's injured leg and began slathering orange-red bio gel from a metal canister onto the bruised skin.

Ann shuddered. "I need to leave."

John looked blankly from Ann to the med tech and back again. He cocked an eyebrow in disbelief. "The bio gel?" John chuckled. "You can't be serious."

Ann cringed and nodded.

John smiled. "All right. We'll talk more later."

Ann gave a tight smile and darted for the door, almost bumping into a second med tech on her way out.

***

John slumped against the side of the master bed, legs splayed out underneath him like a newborn colt. The damn leg brace had caught his foot on a wrinkle in the throw rug as he crossed the master bedroom and sent him stumbling like a Founder's Day drunk. John struggled for a moment, unable to get his bad leg underneath him, then lay still and weighed the options. He could yell for help. Doubtful anyone would hear him, judging from the sounds coming from the tavern below. Or he could lie there until Ann came looking for him. John gritted his teeth and reached for the nearest bed poster.

Several minutes later, John stood panting and sweaty and gripping the bed poster with both hands. He swore as he yanked his uniform jacket from the bed and swung it over his head. The leg brace, a souvenir from John's two weeks in hospital, ran from the top of his thigh to the bottom of his foot. The device made walking manageable without crutches, but it gave John a stiff-legged gate and affected his balance. Ann's brother had taken to calling him Long John Silver. John didn't mind the teasing. It was the fact he didn't get the joke that bothered him. His relationship with the Montressador had warmed considerably, but John still didn't understand Sean's humor at times. Hopefully, he would only have to put up with the brace and the teasing for a few more weeks.

John finished buttoning the jacket and studied himself in the full-length mirror. His new uniform looked the same as the old one with the exception of the Distinguished Service Medal pinned to the left side of the jacket. The last time John had worn a uniform was at the court martial. John had acted under orders, but he still felt shame during the trial. Now the facts had been corrected and the praise felt undeserved. John sighed.

Colonel Wick's words came back to him from the debriefing sessions, "Stop thinking like a freighter pirate! Remember, you're one of the good guys." John smirked at his reflection and swept the bangs from his eyes. This hero business would take some time to get used to.

A knock at the door brought John's thoughts back to the present.

Ann stepped into the master bedroom. "Are you ready? Everyone's waiting."

John's stomach clenched. They'd only just arrived on the Colonies from Andarria late the night before. Mrs. Beaumont and Dr. Brainard had planned a welcome home party. All of Llewellyn waited downstairs in the tavern.

"Does this look all right to you?" John turned back to the mirror and tugged at the bottom of his jacket, hoping to free the butterflies in his stomach.

Ann looked at the reflection in the mirror and slipped an arm around him.

"Your hair isn't up to regulation, but I doubt anyone will mind," she said. A smile tweaked the corners of her mouth.

John chuckled and fingered his pigtail. Colonel Wick had called the stiff tail a healthy transitional device: *Cut it off or keep it – it doesn't matter.*

John looked at Ann. She wore a simple colony blouse and long skirt. Ann saw him eyeing her and cut him off before he could ask.

"It's your party. They've all seen me in my uniform. They're here to see you."

John snorted in irritation. "You're the reason I'm still here. It's your party too! If I have to wear this bloody thing, then so should—"

"Ahem."

Ann doused John's fire with a tranquil expression and pointed to the gold time jumper pin on her blouse.

He looked at the pin's miniature armillary sphere. Regret tugged at him, but only once. He'd made his decision.

John hitched a smile. "Fine. I suppose I can live with that."

John used Ann's shoulder for balance as he hobbled down the stairs. The pair rounded the newel post into the sitting room and stopped cold. Montressador Chapman and Agent Fionna Knox stood in the doorway to the kitchen, their mouths pressed together in a kiss that John thought could've boiled all the water out of Llewellyn's harbor.

Before they could retreat or give discreet warning, Fionna broke off the kiss. Eyes fluttered behind her yellow glasses. Fionna's eyes widened. Fury twisted her features. She raised a hand and delivered a slap across Sean's face that made John's own teeth ache. Agent Knox turned and stormed into the kitchen followed by the slam of the kitchen door.

Sean unscrewed his face from a pained expression and opened his eyes. He lifted a cautious hand to his cheek.

"Ow."

Ann sighed. "You forgot to tell her—"

"To take off the damn glasses again. I *know!*" Sean massaged the side of his face and looked at John and Ann quizzically for a moment. "I suppose I should try to talk to her?"

"She's a woman," John said with shrug. "She'll stay mad until you do."

Ann gave John a playful punch to the arm. "I should break your other leg for that." John chuckled. Ann looked at her brother. "What were you thinking before she slapped you?"

Sean frowned in thought and adjusted his sword belt. "I don't remem—" His eyes widened. "Oh, no." Panic flashed across Sean's face before he turned and clanked into the kitchen.

*"Fionna!"*

John cringed as the kitchen door slammed for a second time.

"I think your brother has his hands full," John said.

"Even without the glasses, he never stood a chance," Ann said with a smirk.

The crowd erupted into wild cheers when the couple

stepped into the tavern. John blinked in surprise and stared around at the smiling faces. Friends and neighbors filled the tavern to standing room only. Tables piled high with food and drink had been pushed to the walls. A Welcome Home banner hung along the far wall and music blared from somewhere outside.

Mrs. Beaumont rushed forward and swept Ann into a hug. Her eyes lit on John. He opened his mouth, but before John could say anything, the cook wrapped him in an embrace. She looked up at John, her face wet with tears.

"I knew it! I knew you were a good man!" Mrs. Beaumont burst into fresh tears and buried her face in John's chest.

John was at a loss for words as the cook hiccupped and sobbed on his jacket. He patted her back, hoping to stem the flow.

He looked to Ann, helpless. "I haven't had a chance to give her job back yet."

Ann chuckled. "I don't think it matters."

Duncan and Ross came to John's rescue. The men took Mrs. Beaumont by the arm and led her to a stool at the bar.

John called after them. "Get her a drink!"

Duncan looked back. "She's already had three!"

John turned to Dr. Brainard. "Thank you! You've been a better friend to me than I deserved."

The doctor rested a hand on John's shoulder. "Bonnie asked me to keep an eye on you. More than anything, she wanted you to be happy. I never regretted a minute of it."

John met the doctor's eye and tried to swallow the lump in his throat. He gripped Dr. Brainard's hand again and nodded, unable to trust his voice to say more.

Everyone congratulated the couple as they worked their way through the crowd. John saw that the party had spilled out of the tavern and into the street. Through the windows, he could see the source of the music. A band had drawn a crowd. Nearby, Captain Shaw and his crew of Shovelhead pilots stood in front of a row of kegs and helped Mike pass out pints of beer.

Dr. Brainard led John and Ann to a booth in the corner. Arnold looked up when the trio emerged from the crowd and broke into a wide grin. He pulled two bottles of wine from underneath his coat and gave a whistle. Port flicked his wings and dropped from his roost on the windowpane to the table. John's heart warmed to see the mini-bot. He had wondered what had happened to his little friend after the fight with the freighter pirates.

Arnold pushed back his cap and looked at John.

"Odd little bot you have here. Showed up on my doorstep the night of the fire and has followed me around ever since."

Port grabbed the neck of one of the wine bottles. He tugged on the cork with his pinchers until John heard a pop. The cork rolled onto the table.

John chuckled. "So you decided to teach him some new tricks?"

Port's sensor dome dilated at the sound of John's voice. He chirped and flicked his wings in greeting. John laughed and gave Port a friendly pat.

"It's nice to see you too!" He was an odd little bot.

"Now I know why Port could never fly straight," Ann said with a smirk. "You taught him to carry a pistol for you."

"Hadn't planned to," John said. "I found the hidden compartment when I refurbished Port and the other mini-bots. The weight of the pistol threw off his gyro and slowed him down." John grinned at his own cleverness and stroked Port's wings. "But it seemed a shame to waste a good hiding place."

"I saved the last few bottles from my shop," Arnold said, as he handed around glasses of wine. "People were offering me a hundred dories a bottle."

Ann looked at the wine in her glass. "Is this really the last of John's wine?"

"The last of what was fit to drink," Dr. Brainard said, taking a sip. Ann looked up, astonished. "We had to drink it! The wine was what attracted Chohon-Lo and his men."

"It's an old Colony superstition," John said, looking at Ann. "If an object brings you bad luck, you have to get rid of it, or put it to a different use. Remember how Mike made the bar stool from the barrel that fell on me?"

"We are dispelling evil spirits so to speak," Dr. Brainard said.

"It's a public service!" Arnold clinked his glass against Ann's.

She laughed and took a sip.

"Drink up, but enjoy it," Arnold said. "Even with this General Rolland footing the bill, it will be a while before the winery is up and running again." Arnold looked at John. "How long do you think it'll take? Two? Three months? I already have new orders coming in."

John took a sip, savoring the taste of summer berries. "With good weather, the winery should be operational in three months. And then I'm going to sell Siren's Cove."

Ann paused in mid sip, eyes wide. Dr. Brainard and Arnold stared at John in disbelief.

John nodded. "I've made up my mind." He looked at Arnold. "I'll give you first right of refusal on the winery if you want."

The doctor's face knotted in concern. "Are you sure about this?"

"You said yourself I was never meant to run a tavern," John said.

"But John . . . I never meant . . ."

"It's time. I should have done it a long time ago."

Dr. Brainard sighed. "Have you talked to Mrs. Beaumont?"

"Not yet." John looked at his glass. "I'm sure we can work something out. She practically runs the place now. I'll sign the papers over to her tonight if she's willing."

"I'll buy the winery if you really want to sell it," Arnold said.

John looked up, grateful for Arnold's support. The look on the businessman's face was like that of a child who didn't understand why he was being punished.

"But why sell it? You were never that superstitious," Arnold said.

"I'm not doing it because of an old wives' tale. Ann is a time jumper...or at least she will be once she's reinstated."

John felt Ann's hand on his arm. "John."

"Hear me out." John took her hand. "I'll be going back on active duty at some point, too. We can live in Palladium Beta. We'll see more of each other and your brother that way."

Ann shook her head. "But Siren's Cove is your home."

John blew out a sigh. "It wasn't supposed to be, at least not long-term. The tavern was part of my cover. I guess I forgot that when Bonnie died."

Ann put her glass on the table. "You can't sell Siren's Cove."

"Ann, it doesn't make any sense to stay here." John's frustration grew. He hadn't expected resistance. "I'm a time jumper! This isn't my life or our life anymore!"

"You said Siren's Cove would be my home for as long as I wanted," Ann said. "I still want it to be. Sean told me I can live on the Colonies and still be a time jumper, so why can't you?"

John raked a hand through his hair and tried to wrap his mind around the logistical nightmare of what Ann proposed.

"I just don't see how we can possibly—"

"John, if I may." Dr. Brainard caught his eye. "There's the military prep school in Idlewild. I don't know for sure, but there might be options you haven't considered."

"And if it's the tavern and the winery you're worried about, you know you can count on me," Arnold said. "The others will help too."

Ann nodded. "We don't have to decide anything right now. I'm sure we can find a way."

John looked at Ann. She couldn't be serious. Two time jumpers running a tavern? He couldn't think of anything more ridiculous. Ann looked back at John, her eyes steady. John's eyes misted. Finding Ann was like finding a golden coin at the bottom of a well.

"All right then," John said, his mouth breaking into a smile. "We'll find a way."

Ann smiled up at John, her eyes brighter than any galaxy

he'd ever seen. He looped an arm around her waist. His mouth pressed against hers. Wine bottles popped, glasses clinked, and John knew they had all the time in the world.

# ABOUT THE AUTHOR

Sara Judson Brown lives in the St. Cloud, Minnesota, area (yes, it's really as cold here as you think) with her husband, two children, and her dog. Sara worked as a freelance writer for several years slinging copy for magazines, blogs, corporate communications, and marketing clients, but it wasn't until 2009 when she decided to start writing her own stories.

When she's not writing about freighter pirates and time jumpers, Sara likes to spend time with her family or hang out at the St. Cloud Public Library. Sara is a graduate of Drake University in Des Moines, Iowa. SIREN'S COVE from her Perigalacticon Series is her debut novel. Sara is a member of the St. Cloud, MN, Granite City Writers Guild.

Connect Online:
www.facebook.com/SaraJudsonBrown
https://sarajudsonbrownauthor.wordpress.com

www.ingramcontent.com/pod-product-compliance
Lightning Source LLC
Chambersburg PA
CBHW070734180626
46818CB00007B/2833